Marius' Mules IX

Pax Gallica

by S. J. A. Turney

1st Edition

"Marius' Mules: nickname acquired by the legions after the general Marius made it standard practice for the soldier to carry all of his kit about his person."

For one of the best of all writers of Historical Fiction, a true friend, a lovely lady and a great talent, whose words flow like silk over alabaster skin: Prue Batten.

I would like to thank Jenny for her help in bringing Marius' Mules nine to completion and making it readable. One of my usual proofers and test readers, Lilian, passed away before I began this volume, and her aid has been sorely missed, as has she. Thanks also to my beautiful wife Tracey for her support, and my two children Marcus and Callie for keeping me smiling during my busiest times.

Thanks also to Garry and Dave for the cover work.

Cover photos by Hannah Haynes, courtesy of Paul and Garry of the Deva Victrix Legio XX. Visit http://www.romantoursuk.com/ to see their excellent work.

Cover design by Dave Slaney.

Many thanks to the above for their skill and generosity.

All internal maps are copyright the author of this work.

Also by S. J. A. Turney:

Continuing the Marius' Mules Series

Marius' Mules I: The Invasion of Gaul (2009)
Marius' Mules II: The Belgae (2010)
Marius' Mules III: Gallia Invicta (2011)
Marius' Mules IV: Conspiracy of Eagles (2012)
Marius' Mules V: Hades' Gate (2013)
Marius' Mules VI: Caesar's Vow (2014)
Marius' Mules: Prelude to War (2014)
Marius' Mules VII: The Great Revolt (2014)
Marius' Mules VIII: Sons of Taranis (2015)

The Praetorian Series

The Great Game (2015)
The Price of Treason (2015)

The Ottoman Cycle

The Thief's Tale (2013)
The Priest's Tale (2013)
The Assassin's Tale (2014)
The Pasha's Tale (2015)

Tales of the Empire

Interregnum (2009)
Ironroot (2010)
Dark Empress (2011)
Insurgency (2016)

Roman Adventures (Children's Roman fiction with Dave Slaney)

Crocodile Legion (2016)

Short story compilations & contributions:

Tales of Ancient Rome vol. 1 - S.J.A. Turney (2011)
Tortured Hearts vol 1 - Various (2012)
Tortured Hearts vol 2 - Various (2012)
Temporal Tales - Various (2013)
A Year of Ravens - Various (2015)
A Song of War – Various (Oct 2016)

For more information visit http://www.sjaturney.co.uk/
or http://www.facebook.com/SJATurney
or follow Simon on Twitter @SJATurney

Gallia est omnis divisa in partes tres, quarum unam incolunt Belgae, aliam Aquitani, tertiam qui ipsorum lingua Celtae, nostra Galli appellantur. (All Gaul is divided into three parts, one of which the Belgae inhabit, the Aquitani another, the third: those who in their own language are called Celts and in ours, Gauls.)

VENI...

Hi omnes lingua, institutis, legibus inter se differunt. Gallos ab Aquitanis Garumna flumen, a Belgis Matrona et Sequana dividit. (All these differ from each other in language, customs and laws. The river Garonne separates the Gauls from the Aquitani; the Marne and the Seine separate them from the Belgae.)

VIDI...

Aquitania a Garumna flumine ad Pyrenaeos montes et eam partem Oceani quae est ad Hispaniam pertinet; spectat inter occasum solis et septentriones. (Aquitania extends from the river Garonne to the Pyrenean mountains and to that part of the ocean which is near Spain: it looks between the setting of the sun, and the north star.)

...

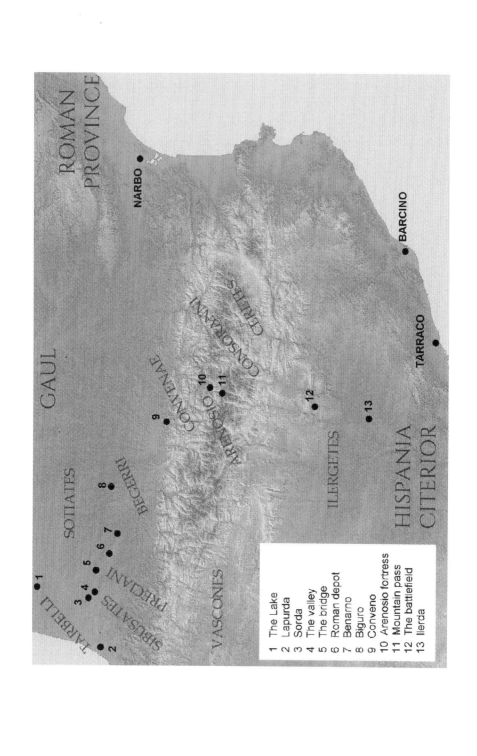

ROMAN PROVINCE

GAUL

NARBO

BARCINO

TARRACO

CERES

CONSORANI

CONVENAE

ARENOSIO

BECERRI

SOTIATES

PRECIANI

TARBELLI

SIBUSATES

VASCONES

ILERGETES

HISPANIA CITERIOR

1   The Lake
2   Lapurda
3   Sorda
4   The valley
5   The bridge
6   Roman depot
7   Benarno
8   Biguro
9   Conveno
10   Arenosio fortress
11   Mountain pass
12   The battlefield
13   Ilerda

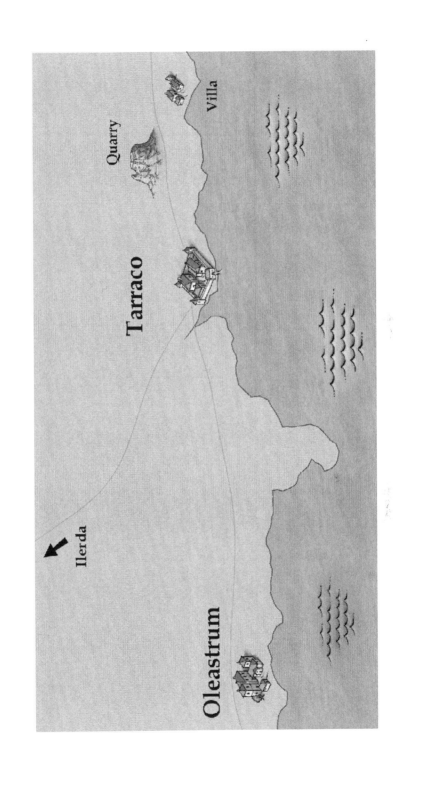

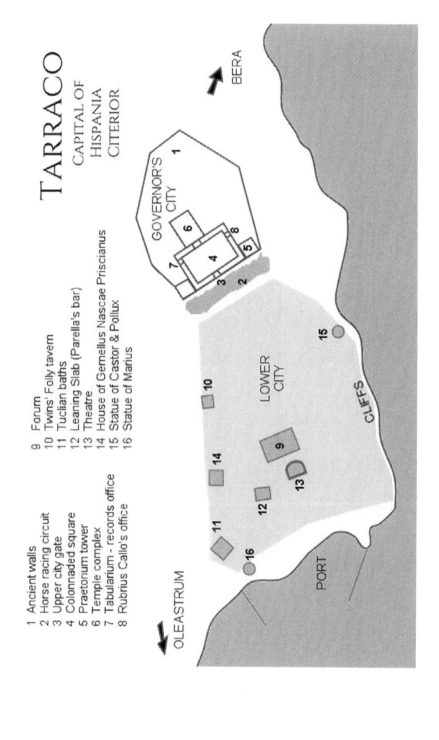

TARRACO

CAPITAL OF
HISPANIA
CITERIOR

1 Ancient walls
2 Horse racing circuit
3 Upper city gate
4 Colonnaded square
5 Praetorium tower
6 Temple complex
7 Tabularium - records office
8 Rubrius Callo's office

9 Forum
10 Twins' Folly tavern
11 Tuclian baths
12 Leaning Slab (Parella's bar)
13 Theatre
14 House of Gemellus Nascae Priscianus
15 Statue of Castor & Pollux
16 Statue of Marius

GOVERNOR'S CITY

LOWER CITY

CLIFFS

PORT

BERA

OLEASTRUM

Prologue

THE stone block was recent work, like all of them. So new that the chiselled lines were still clean and crisp with no discoloration or mossy growth. Half the height of a man and almost as wide, it was formed of a heavy, white stone that was not indigenous to the region. The block stood in a proud, haughty manner on a low bluff as though to suggest that it commanded all that it observed, from the high, snow-clogged peaks behind to the deep, shadowed valleys before.

It was Roman work. Obviously, but not purely because of the text. It was clearly Roman, because only a Roman would conceive of such a thing. Only Romans felt the need to quantify everything in their lives, to label and claim everything. To record everything. It was said that the Romans even wrote down everything that happened in their council meetings in case any curious individual felt the need to check the precise wording of an argument held years earlier.

Everyone knew the Romans were mad. But they also knew they were dangerous. Some said even unstoppable. The Belgae, who had spent a hundred generations terrifying even the tribes across the Rhenus, had succumbed to Rome like a dog rolling on its back. The Gauls, proud in their walled trading cities, held out to the last, falling late and hard to the invader. The Aquitanii? They were far from stupid. Unlike the belligerent Belgae or the proud Gauls, the Aquitanii watched the tide of steel and red sweeping across the world and simply nodded their head at Rome. Oh there had been pockets of resistance, when that animal Crassus had brought his legions to 'suppress' the region. And some of the tribes had answered the call of the Arverni king and hurried off to die in the drab flat lands of Gaul. But then, when the Belgae were a distant memory of a warlike people and the Gauls were more commonly found mouldering under the earth than standing upon it, the Aquitanii were still intact. Still strong.

They knew they could never hold out against Caesar and his armies, so they nodded at Rome and remained intact and strong. And that was why they were still here and still lords of the mountains and the valleys. And then, in autumn, the beak-nosed

1

general himself had toured the region, announcing his settlement and his peace and his belief in a unified province.

Caesar. Caesar had come. And everything had changed.

The altar on the bluff, formed of pale Roman stone, was suddenly cast into shadow, the two words delicately and neatly incised into the side thrown into darkness.

PAX GALLICA

The young man hit the altar hard, ribs cracking against the smooth stone. He was whimpering now. He'd stopped screaming half an hour ago, but the whimpering had gone on ever since. He was the son of a chief – a nobleman in his own right. He wore two armlets of silver and a torc that he had never earned in battle for his skin was smooth like that of an untouched girl. His hair was long and braided and hung down behind his ears in a manner that was almost as Gaulish as his moustaches, drooping in the Arvernian style. These lowland Aquitanii were hardly worthy of bearing that name, they were so like their Gaul neighbours. Not like the mountain tribes, who tended toward shaggy hair and thick beards, which granted an extra degree of warmth in the snows that clogged the passes for much of the year.

Not everyone wore such a beard, even in the mountains, of course, but those who didn't always had a good reason.

Two shaggy, muscular warriors stepped forward and grasped the panicked boy who was rolling around on the stone, trying to rise. With brutal roughness, one grasped his wrists and slammed them back against the smooth surface, while the other held his knees down, pushing him flat. The whimpering and sobbing began to rise once more in pitch and volume, terror and desperation driving the sound into a shriek.

A third warrior stepped to the altar and lifted his hands, spitting on them and rubbing them together. He then reached down and picked up the axe, which gleamed with a perfect smooth arc, barring the single small notch that a stray torc had caused. The boy's shrieking became deafening, and even the two muscular warriors were having difficulty holding him down now.

The axe rose.

The warrior wielding it turned to look at his master, waiting for the nod.

The nod came.

The axe fell.

The heavy blade slammed into the boy's midriff from the side, severing the spine a few vertebrae up from the pelvis. There was no need for a second blow to divide him. With the backbone gone, the pressure the other two men were exerting to hold him in place simply resulted in the tearing of flesh and the boy ripped unpleasantly in two, his torso coming away, leaving snaking trails of gut, while the other warrior staggered back, gripping a thrashing pair of legs that ended in a messy pelvis. The boy was still shrieking, alive even now he was but half a man.

The blood sluiced from the two severed halves and ran down the side of the altar, filling in the carved lettering first, so that the words Pax Gallica were picked out in dark crimson against the pale stone before the flood of red obscured the whole thing.

The man on the bluff, surrounded by howling warriors, lifted his eyes from the gruesome remains to the snaking valleys before him. He might have been smiling, and certainly his clean shaven face was open to view without the ubiquitous beard, but an old set of wounds that rose in a curved line from each end of his mouth, extending the bow up almost to his ears, made it hard to tell when he was smiling. It didn't happen often. And when it did, something nasty inevitably followed.

Pax Gallica.

Caesar had toured the region and returned to his own graveyard in the north, leaving behind his altars of peace. Soon he would return. Soon he would know how fragile his peace really was.

Chapter One

THE ship bounced gently against the jetty and the group gathered on the walkway near the steering oars lurched for a moment, trying to keep their feet. Once the vessel was entirely stationary, Balbus crossed to the rail and put a fatherly arm – the good, unwounded one – around Fronto, who was busy making sounds like an expiring hog as he continued to expel the air from his gut long after any real contents had gone. The weather on the sea to the west of Italia was often brutal in late autumn and winter. It was in these cliffs that Aeolus kept his four winds, and so the turbulence of the waters was quite understandable.

'How can you continue to retch for so long, Marcus? Are you trying to set some sort of record?'

Fronto turned slowly, heaving himself up from the rail and lifting his grey, waxy face to his father-in-law. 'You have no idea, Quintus. I swear at one point I was inside out. Exile or no exile, that is the last time I take a ship at this time of year.' With some difficulty, he straightened and staggered across to the rest of them. At least the wound in his side was healing well, and now no longer inconvenienced him.

It had been a matter of great concern to them all. They had tarried in Puteoli far longer than was safe. Every day they'd expected the senate's hounds at the door, arresting or ejecting Fronto and his family and impounding the villa. But they had clearly been tied up for some time impounding all holdings of the Falerii in Rome, and it would take time for their grasping hands to reach Puteoli. The family and friends had stayed until winter began to close in, for the medicus they consulted seriously advised against sea travel – or *any* travel for that matter – with so many nasty wounds among them still in the process of healing. And finally, when Fronto felt his side was comfortable once more, Balbus' head was no longer in danger, Aurelius' arm had been released from its sling and Biorix was unbandaged entirely, they had deemed it time to leave before the forces of the senate caught up with the exile.

Fronto had taken the unusual step of granting manumission to the villa's slaves before they left. There would be a full complement of household slaves where they were going, and if

4

these ones were still bound to the Puteoli villa, the senate would simply take them. So they were given their freedom and adequate funds to begin a small life. Throughout the trip, Fronto and his companions relied upon each other, the crew of the ship, and the slaves and servants wherever they put in for the night. It was little hardship, really.

And now here they were, putting to shore at last.

Balbus helped Fronto to the group, his own right arm still unfeeling and unmoving after the fight in the carcer. The others were gathered now, waiting for the ramp to be run out. The sailors shouted to one another in a westernised form of Greek. The group had taken a Grecian ship back to Massilia, for no Roman vessel could be trusted by an exile. Lucilia, her face proud despite the situation, held tight to the boys. Behind her Fronto's mother and sister, two Falerias each as powerful and shrewd as the other, stood with inscrutable expressions as they held tight to the hand of young Balbina. Galronus hovered close to the younger Faleria, as was usually the case these days. He looked every bit the Roman now, barring the lack of a toga. His mode of dress and his grooming were perfectly Roman, and only a faint trace of a Gallic accent would give him away in a crowd. But while he had adopted all things Roman, he was still a prince of the Remi, and not a citizen of Rome. The toga was not his by right. Fronto could see how the difference between him and the family he was almost a part of pained him. The women brushed it off, of course, as did Fronto, but Galronus was acutely conscious that he was still not truly one of them.

And then there were Aurelius, and Biorix, and Masgava and Arcadios. And Andala, too – the Belgic slave girl who seemed more at home with a sword in her hand than a comb, yet who Lucilia seemed to dote on. There was a sad hole left by the departure of Cavarinos the Arvernian, which had rather taken Fronto by surprise, but the man's path was his own, and he had made it perfectly clear that it lay in neither Rome nor Gaul.

Thirteen passengers then, altogether, who had left Puteoli and had finally arrived, worn and cold, at the safest of havens, a city beyond the reach of the senate, beyond the border of the Republic even.

Massilia.

5

They moved to the ramp and began to disembark. Further along the ship another ramp was run out and their horses and goods were brought forth and deposited on the jetty. As they alighted on the slimy, troublesome timbers, Balbus turned with a heaved breath.

'You arrange for everything to be taken up to the villas, Marcus, and follow on with the family. I'm going to visit a few people and find out what's been happening in this part of the world, then I'll meet up with you at your place. Best to keep abreast of events.'

Fronto nodded and clasped the old man's hand. Balbus had lived here for some time longer than Fronto, and his connections in the town were deeper and more varied. With a light farewell, the old man sauntered off toward the agora, and Fronto waited a while as their goods were brought ashore, trying not to look at the water or think about the food and drink that the others were discussing. In an effort to take his mind off his churning innards, he strolled over to the station of the carters and teamsters. With no slaves to escort them up to the villa, he hired a small group of men from the port to shift all the baggage up the hill to their destination, as well as a rickety carriage for the ladies.

Half an hour later, they were climbing the slope behind Massilia, making for the villa, and Fronto's stomach was finally beginning to settle with the comfort of solid ground underfoot. Briefly he considered making conversation, now that he wasn't suffering with the endless pre-vomit drooling any more, but the women were filling every foot of space with their own talk, leaving little room for others, so he remained silent and concentrated on the villa. It was odd coming back this time since, for the first time, this was to be the centre of their universe. It had been home for a while before, but the family had always had the townhouse in Rome, the villa in Puteoli and one or two other small estates. Now, this was to be their world.

The women were discussing what would need to be done and purchased as they crested the hill and made for the villa, but Fronto continued to march on in silence, listening to the creaking and groaning of the carts behind them. The house seemed to have been well-maintained in their absence, for the lawns were trimmed, the flower beds weeded and the stonework kept free of moss. The sun was beginning to sink slowly toward the waterline to the west, the walls of the villa positively glowing in the last rays. Even as the party approached, lights started to spring up in the windows.

Home…

* * *

The family and friends were lounging around the triclinium that night, barring the elder Faleria who had retired early and Aurelius, who was enjoying an extended soak in the bath suite, when Balbus finally put in an appearance. The doorman showed him into the room and then bowed and returned to his task, and Fronto's father-in-law stretched, reached for a glass, mixed himself a wine, and then sank onto one of the couches.

'It seems that the exile and disgrace of the Falerii is completely unknown in Massilia, as we anticipated.'

Fronto nodded. 'Massilia is safe from the senate. We can live here unmolested, and I can even continue to operate my business, so we won't run short of ready funds even if the senate take every sestertius in Rome.'

'Will it support the extended family?' Lucilia murmured. 'We need to look after your sister and mother, as well as your companions. That's many mouths, Marcus. You had little luck with wine last year.'

Fronto shrugged. 'Things had improved at the end, once I had Catháin. And he's still in Italia dealing with the Campanian wine makers. We will be fine, at least for a while. And I don't anticipate this being permanent anyway, or even particularly long-term. Caesar and Pompey have to come to some arrangement soon, lest they tear Rome apart. Caesar will throw some small olive branch Pompey's way and the knob-nosed fat fart will have to accept it, or he'll be put under pressure by the pro-Caesarians in the senate. Then all these issues that have arisen will be put right. Caesar owes me a few favours by now, so once he is back on good terms with Rome, he can see me right.'

'I think you're being naively over optimistic, Marcus,' the old man said, taking another sup from his glass.

'How so?'

'Caesar is procrastinating in Gaul, ostensibly Romanising the place, settling veterans, visiting tribes and drawing up treaties and the like, but there's no doubt in anyone I talked to that he's just really keeping himself busy. What he really has his eye on is the consulship. And there seems to be some dispute at the moment about when Caesar's command is up.'

'He has two years to run, yet,' Fronto said flatly. 'He took up a five year proconsulship when we first went into Gaul. Then back that year we crossed to Britannia it was extended by another five years. That's ten years and he's only been in Gaul for eight.'

Balbus nodded. 'Caesar sees it that way, too, apparently. But Pompey and his men in the senate have stated that the extension ran from the date it was given, three years into his command, and was not an extension of the original term. That makes it eight years and means his command will expire on the Kalends of Martius next year. A matter of months away.'

'That's insane.'

'It's a mess, certainly. Apparently there's a motion from the tribunes in Rome to let Caesar stand for office in absentia. Pompey and his men are doing their best to overturn that idea. Caesar might be in trouble shortly. If the date of his command's end is confirmed at next spring and the motion of standing in absentia is discarded, then Caesar will have to return to Rome a private citizen and face the very real probability of lengthy and dangerous court cases against him.'

'But if he can stand for consulship...'

'It's not going to happen, Marcus. Caesar's supporters in Rome are fewer and less powerful than Pompey's. If the rumours I hear are true, then Pompey already has the winners of the next elections picked out. He has the money and influence in Rome now to make that happen. And you know they'll be drawn from the anti-Caesarian camp.'

Fronto ground his teeth and picked irritably at the hem of his tunic. 'Then it's down to us. But I will continue to cleave to Caesar. Rome has turned its back on me, as it seems to be doing to the general. But I know Caesar as well as you do. Better, even. And he will endure. He'll come out of this on top, mark my words. Better to nail my vexillum to his standard than go it alone.'

8

'Would that we lived in better days, Marcus,' the old man sighed, 'when the senate was a co-operative and the consuls wielded the power. Before the rise of the oligarchs.'

Fronto simply nodded, though he could hardly lay claim to such nostalgic leanings. From his hazy memories of the old days, they were every bit as troublesome. Marius, Sulla and Sertorius. Rome had always been a snake-pit, in truth.

* * *

Winter came to Massilia suddenly, with icy blasts and heavy rain, and news from both Rome and the north was no better. Rome was gradually polarising against Caesar, while the general maintained that his command had years yet to run. In this tense world, in which Massilia sat nervously as a foreign city trapped between the two, the Falerii prepared to celebrate Saturnalia. Slaves and freedmen scurried around the villa putting up garlands and drapes and bringing the new amphorae from storage to settle in the house. The mood among the slaves was jovial, of course, for during the week-long festival, the gulf between slave and master closed, and even the most downtrodden wore their masters' clothes.

But the villa's owners and their friends were less cheerful, for the ever-present threat of trouble between Rome and its northern proconsul hung over Massilia like a thunder cloud.

Fronto was standing under the veranda, watching the rain battering the gardens, contemplating his choice of gifts for the others, when Galronus strode up beside him and leaned against the veranda.

'I am contemplating riding north in the new year, Marcus.'

Fronto spun a frown on his friend. 'What?'

'When Saturnalia is over. Back to the Remi. My people are now one of the most powerful in Gaul, favoured by Caesar and wealthy on spoils and trade. I have not seen my family for some years.'

Fronto's eyes narrowed suspiciously. 'You mean you're not coming back, don't you?'

Galronus looked uncomfortable, and Fronto stepped closer, his voice lowered. 'Faleria would be heartbroken. Don't be so stupid. Do you not love her? I'd convinced myself you did.'

The prince's eyes danced this way and that nervously. 'It's not that, Marcus. You know I love her. And she loves me.'

'I fail to see the problem, then.'

'The problem is that there are walls between us, Marcus, and I'm tired of scaling walls. I don't think we can do it.'

'What?'

'Marcus, I am not Roman.'

'Bollocks.'

'I'm not.'

'Alright, you're not a citizen. But you're more Roman than several patricians I've come across.'

'I'm not good enough for her. Faleria deserves to be with someone who can help rebuild her reputation after this disaster, not a foreigner who will further drag your name into the mud with the senate.'

'Piss on the senate,' Fronto snorted, but Galronus was shaking his head.

'It's not just that, Marcus, though I know that for the rest of her life all Romans would sneer at Faleria, because I know my father would sneer at me for marrying a Roman matron. We are worlds apart, Marcus. But there is another, higher, wall. Faleria's past haunts her. She has never, I think, let go of the ghost of her former suitor.'

'Listen to yourself, Galronus! *Former suitor*, indeed. You even *sound* like a Roman. And you're right. She's never got over Verginius. But I've never seen her closer to doing so than she is with you, and she never will without someone's help. And that someone can't be me.'

'Why not,' Galronus rumbled. 'What happened?'

'That's a long story, and for another time. A less happy time, I suspect. Suffice it to say that Gnaeus Verginius and I were close. Almost brothers. He was promised Faleria, but... events transpired that... Well, Verginius perished while we were away on joint command, and Faleria blamed me. She was probably right to do so. I blamed myself. Still do. And just like Faleria, I will never quite get over Verginius myself.'

He turned and stretched. 'I won't let you go, though, Galronus. You ride off and I will send an armed party to fetch you back. You need to face this and persevere. You both want each other, and even my mother, who has never been the easiest woman to please, approves of you both. Everyone wants it. And who gives a diseased dog's arsehole if it offends the Roman elite. We're exiles, after all. I am, right now, a citizen of a Greek city, so piss on the lot of them.'

Galronus chuckled and rested his elbows on the low wall, watching the torrential rain.

'I wasn't looking forward to riding in this weather anyway. You should be a politician, Marcus. You may not have their flouncy ways, but you could persuade a goat it was a horse if you put your mind to it.'

It was Fronto's turn to laugh, then, and he leaned on the wall next to his friend, gazing out over the gardens and the slope, across Massilia and the sea to the west.

Somewhere out there, past those many leagues of saltwater lay Hispania, the land of Fronto's first command along with Caesar. And somewhere in that warm, pleasant land lay a field of bones where Fronto's past lay unburied and raw. No, they all had to move on. Dwelling in yesterday did no one any good.

* * *

Saturnalia passed with muted humour and the rains abated soon after, giving way to howling winds filled with the ice of deep winter, whistling through cracks and making sea travel impossibly dangerous. Massilia all-but ground to a halt, the populace huddling indoors with burning fires and warm meals.

Fronto was seated in the triclinium, grateful for the underfloor heating and the blankets on the couch, when Balbus returned once more. The old man and his younger daughter had stayed with the family throughout most of the winter, their own villa holding the worst of memories and being too large and empty for just the two of them anyway. Early this Januarius morning, Balbus had wrapped up tight in an old soldier's cloak and headed into town once more to attend a meeting of the city's *boule* council and speak to his contacts and friends afterwards. His face was dark as he

11

stepped into the room, and Fronto peered expectantly at him as he shrugged off the cloak and shivered.

'What news?'

'Plenty, Marcus, and none of it good.'

The old man accepted a cup of warm mulsum from Faleria and sank to a couch.

'I spoke to a merchant who's just come from Rome. Marcellus and Rufus have laid down their consulships, it seems. But the new consuls, who are very much the ones Pompey paid handsomely to see secured in the role, are Marcellus Minor and Lepidus, and neither of them is a lover of Caesar. Once more the consuls are squarely in Pompey's camp. With his money and influence behind them, the pair are already engaged on a systematic campaign of destruction against Caesar. They're targeting any connections Caesar has in Rome, right down to his former officers. He's been denied the right to run for power in absentia, though that's moot anyway, since the senate considers his term up in two months and the next available consulship is a year away. It seems almost certain that Caesar will be an outlaw by March unless he lays down his command and returns to Rome.'

'Which he won't, because they will ruin him in the courts.' Fronto laughed. 'Mind you, if he *is* made an outlaw, he'll be an outlaw with *ten legions* at his fingertips, Balbus. An outlaw with an army that size can change the world.'

Balbus gave him a black look and thrust out a finger. 'Don't talk like that, Marcus. These are not the days of Sulla. Men should not be encouraged to march on Rome.'

Fronto shrugged. My lot is cast with Caesar, Quintus, and you know that. I am his man now, whether I like it or not. The senate has seen to that.'

'There is worse to come, Fronto. That's just the news from Rome. The boule of Massilia held session this morning too, and their discussions are worrying. They have voted to send ambassadors to Rome. They will make terms with the senate, for though Caesar has his legions within pilum throw of Massilia, the council believes that Rome offers them a solid future of trade and support, and they believe that Caesar will be ousted or dead within the year. They may be correct, of course. But that means they are preparing to turn against Caesar and they will close their gates to him. And that means that all his logistics personnel here will be turfed out and there will henceforth be no supplies or trade run through Massilia to the north. Where that leaves us, as Romans and former Caesarian officers, is not yet clear. I have friends in the boule, but you have never done yourself any favours politically with the city council.'

Fronto nodded, his face bleak as he felt the ground once more opening up beneath his feet. Massilia had been the one safe place he and the family could run from the senate. If Rome got its hooks into the council of the city, though, Fronto would be sold out and expelled or simply handed to the senate as part of any deal. Suddenly a peaceful life in Massilia looked increasingly unlikely.

'I have nowhere left to go, Balbus.'

'No.'

'The family will be safe here though? With you?'

'Yes.' Balbus looked uncomfortable, and rightly so. Fronto was the one the senate and their arrogant master in Rome would want to trouble. The rest of the family were unimportant. Balbus held no such stigma. And both villas were still in his name. The family would be safe here with the old man. But Fronto's continued presence endangered everyone.

'I will have to go.' He sighed. Somehow he'd known it would come to this sometime, but he hadn't expected it to be so soon.

'And take the soldiers with you. The ladies and I can stay as private citizens. I have the support of important men in the city and have long been known to be critical of Caesar, as you know. We will be safe. But any of you who are looked upon as Caesar's men will be in danger and will cause trouble for the rest of us.'

Fronto straightened. Galronus and Masgava were in the room, listening with tense expressions. Aurelius, Biorix and Arcadios were somewhere in the grounds, where the Greek was trying to teach the others the rudiments of archery. He had an odd suspicion, given her notable absence, that Andala was with them too.

'You wanted to ride north, Galronus.'

He ignored the surprised look on his sister's face as the Remi noble nodded his head slowly and seriously. 'But now not to see my family, yes? You will need support.'

'And he'll have it,' Masgava grunted, rising. 'Your singulares may be diminished, Marcus, but we are still by your side.'

Fronto smiled, his eyes flicking to the beautifully-hilted gladius hanging on the wall out of the children's reach. The sword he had taken from the treacherous tribune a few years ago. Would he have to raise it against a Roman again in the coming months? He hoped not, but the fact remained that whatever Caesar did, Fronto would support him. They were made bedfellows now by the snakes of the senate.

'Go find the others, Masgava. Tell them to start packing. We ride north in the morning. And if Andala's with them, tell her to stop it and attend her mistress.'

As Masgava nodded and left the room to inform the rest of the men, Fronto gave an apologetic smile to his wife where she sat beside his sister. As he crossed to her, Galronus came to his side.

'I'm sorry, Lucilia. I can't stay. Balbus is right. If the city sides with the senate, I will be worth a lot to them. I have to get out. You will be safe with Balbus, though. And Caesar will have some plan to resolve things, I'm sure. The old man's rarely wrong-footed. He'll sort everything out. And as soon as he does we'll come back to you and all will be peaceful again.'

Late Januarius

THE wagon roared like a wounded lion as the flames ate deep into the timbers, scorching the wood black, the glowing golden embers at its heart spitting and crackling. The smell of burned pork filled the air and even the hardiest of the warriors were moving about their business with their eyes screwed tight and their noses wrinkled from the smoke and the smell. The bodies of the slaves and workers hissed and spat in the midst of the conflagration. Two more such wagons of the dead stood nearby, their own infernos in earlier stages.

The screaming was as intrusive as the smoke and the stench, as the fat man hollered out his terror with every blow of the hammer. The crucifix was in the Roman style. A 'T' shape, with the man's arms over the cross beam and tied and nailed at the back, so that his shoulders would take all the weight. Now they were just nailing his bound feet in place so that he couldn't thrash around. Blood ran down the arms and feet, clashing rather badly with his purple tunic. He was a wealthy one, this Roman. His voice was cultured – *had been*, while he'd been pleading with his captors. Now, of course, he was just shrieking like they all did.

As the warriors gradually tipped the cross to the vertical, the weight pulled on the man's arms and he felt the nails ripping through his wrists, his shoulders slowly dislocating, and the agony of it all. His screaming reached a new pitch, particularly as the cross dropped into the hole that would hold it and the warriors packed the earth and stones in to stabilise it.

It was like some scene from the underworld.

A man nodded with satisfaction at the job done, and then turned and clambered up the scree slope to the raised rock mound. He was a warrior, and a strong one. His arms were adorned with silver rings. His mail shirt was of very fine quality, taken from a Roman officer a few years ago, and he wore a very expensive torc. His sword was long and strong and gripped in a powerful hand. His beard was dark and thick. His hair was wild and knotted like a bird's nest. A purple birth-mark covered one eye, giving him an odd, eerie look, as though he permanently wore an eyepatch. He bowed to the figure on the rock.

'Will this work?'

That cold grin turned from its contemplation of the burning wagons to regard the warrior. Even this well-built, battle-hardened man of the high valleys flinched at that face. There was something cold and otherworldly about it. It was not the face of a man, but of a demon sent by the gods to reap a bloody harvest. It was a face from nightmare. And the odd thing was that if you looked at it dispassionately, which took an awful lot of doing, you could almost see past those twin wounds that made that horrible smile, and see a handsome face beneath, Perhaps that was what made the face so utterly chilling. The iron grey hair did little to add compassion to the appearance, either.

'Caesar is arrogant,' the taller man said in his cold, hoarse voice, and the sound made the warrior baulk all over again.

'Of course, sire, but…'

'The Roman general is too arrogant to survive in the world of men. I have denied him the peace he claims to have won. And I will continue to ruin his *Pax Gallica* until he comes. He will not be able to countenance the continued failure of his efforts. And even if his own arrogance were not enough to bring him, his continued failure will make him look bad to the rest of Rome. He cannot afford that. No he will most definitely come, even if I have to burn every wagon and outpost for five hundred of their miles. If I have to crucify every fat Roman who strays close to the mountains, he will come.'

'And then?' prompted the warrior.

The cold, extended smile turned to look out across the rolling folds of land to the northeast.

'And then the general will march to his doom on an unknown battlefield as he deserves.'

The man on the cross sagged a little and his screaming reached a new pitch, and the warrior was sure that his master was now smiling deliberately.

16

Chapter Two

NEMETOCENNA had changed. It had, of course, been some years now since Fronto had been here. What had been a Belgic oppidum – quite a strong one too, with a Roman siege camp outside half a decade ago – had become something much different. The oppidum's walls were still there, and the gates, though even from a distance the travellers could see that the endless thatch within had in many places been replaced with legion-manufactured red tile roofs. And instead of a Roman camp sitting defiant some distance away, regarding the walls jealously, the Roman military presence was now contained within a massive walled extension to the town, enjoying a prime location between the oppidum and the river. Moreover, the natives had begun to build outside the walls, taking advantage of the Roman presence, living off their money and supplies in return for goods and services rendered. There were clearly even taverns and brothels springing up close to the walls.

'Gaul at peace, eh?' Fronto marvelled as they geed their horses once more and began the descent toward the town. 'Never thought I'd see it like this.'

'Almost makes seven years of bloodshed worthwhile,' said Aurelius, and the others looked at him with a frown, trying to decide whether this was off-colour humour or serious contemplation.

'I reckon there's three legions based here at the moment, from the size of the force,' Fronto mused. 'Can't see the flags, but that's my reckoning.'

'Let's get down there before it rains,' Masgava said, eyeing the leaden grey sky nervously. 'I don't fancy getting soaked again.'

They all murmured their agreement and put extra speed to their mounts as they closed on the principle camp of the Roman legions in Gaul – Caesar's court in the north. The journey north had taken them two weeks, through the worst season for Gallic weather. Few days had passed without at least some sign of rain once they had moved from Vienna and the Roman province into Gaul, and on rare occasions they had experienced sleet and hail. Now, on the ides of Februarius, they were finally at their destination.

As they approached the fortified annexe that played home to some fifteen thousand Romans, Fronto found himself both interested and nervous. It had been some time since he had served actively in the army, yet it felt oddly like a homecoming. His feet longed to drop from the horse and fall into the routine of camp life. This was no mean campaign fortification, though. Timber buildings had been raised for the soldiers and their officers. A bathhouse was visible toward the river, where a new extended channel had been run from the natural bend toward the Roman annexe. This was a semi-permanent installation. He would be willing to wager there were retired soldiers living in the oppidum now, married to buxom Belgic girls. Yet despite the inevitable excitement rushing through his blood, there was also a nervous tension. He was here to see the proconsul of Gaul, Gaius Julius Caesar, a man with whom he shared a close history of service stretching back to Fronto's first time in Hispania, yet someone with whom he had on occasion walked a rocky path. There was no guarantee of an easy reception, and he came as something of a supplicant, asking Caesar for a favour. Oh the general owed him for much in his time, but it was in the nature of arrogant men to forget favours owed but cling to debts unpaid.

What reception awaited them?

With his five companions close by, the former commander of the Tenth peered intently at the flags as they approached. There was the vexillum of the Ninth. And he could see the Eleventh represented. There were at least two others, but they were unreadable yet. As the half dozen weary travellers rode along the track to Nemetocenna, their three pack animals trailing along behind, innkeepers and whores called out from the new buildings to either side, offering their services. Fronto would love nothing more than to take up the offers of the former, and Aurelius' face said he was pretty keen for the latter, but nothing could be done until they had presented themselves at the headquarters.

The huge, heavy timber gate stood open, clear sign that peace had come to Gaul at last. Two rather bored looking legionaries stood at attention by the gate, and a couple more leaned atop the walkway parapet. As the party approached, one of the legionaries called inside and an optio emerged, tapping his long staff on the ground as he walked out to meet this odd group. Each of them

18

were wearing tunics of a military cut and colour, Fronto's being white with a stripe denoting his rank, and it would be quite clear even ignoring those garments and their military cloaks that they were military, if only from the blades worn at their hips.

'Good afternoon,' Fronto said to the optio as he reined in close by and inclined his head. The officer took in his tunic, age and bearing and swiftly surmised he was speaking to a retired officer. When he replied, his tone was direct but inflected with respect.

'Good day, sir. Might I enquire as to your business at Nemetocenna.'

'I'm here to see the governor,' Fronto smiled. 'I am Marcus Falerius Fronto, former Legatus of the Tenth Legion. The governor knows me well.'

'As do all, by reputation, sir,' smiled the optio. 'Welcome to Hades, sir. Just the lads' name for the place, because the weather can only have been planned by the underworld and the whores and innkeepers charge far too much.'

Fronto barked out a laugh. 'I've not been here since we first made camp. That was somewhere over there,' he added, waving across to a field of deep grass nearby. 'Could you show me to the headquarters?'

The optio nodded and gestured for them to enter. As the six rode through the gate behind him, two more legionaries appeared as if from nowhere and waited patiently.

'I will have your animals taken to the stables and fed and watered, sirs. If you would care to follow me on foot.'

Fronto nodded, sliding down from the back of Bucephalus, the shining black horse he had acquired after Longinus' death in their first year in Gaul, a lifetime ago. He was getting old now, though still strong and swift. Soon it would be time to put the old boy out to pasture – when this had all blown over, of course, and Fronto could call some grazing land his own once more. The others similarly dismounted, and together they strode off after the optio, leaving their mounts in the hands of the legionaries.

'Are you planning to stay, sir?' the optio asked.

'Sorry? Oh, I don't really know until I've been to the headquarters.'

'Then I'll have your kit taken to a spare barrack for now, sir.'

'Thank you.'

Fronto smiled as they passed through the camp toward the nerve centre of the place. The whole camp displayed all the hallmarks of an army on peaceful garrison duty. No racks of weapons ready for quick mobilisation, but strings of washing hanging between blocks, soldiers sitting on the verandas of their barracks playing dice, a stray mutt eating the remnants of some legionary's lunch. It was so familiar he almost wanted to join them. He was delighted as they closed on the centre to see flags of the Fifteenth Legion, but also of the Tenth, wavering in the distance. *His* legion. They were here. He wondered if there was anyone left in the Tenth he knew of old. Presumably Atenos…

Soon they approached the doorway of the headquarters, two more legionaries standing guard at the entrance. Fronto was intrigued to note the rather austere appearance of the building. It was the norm when Caesar made his gubernatorial court somewhere rather than just a simple military headquarters, to adorn it with the trappings of Rome and of command, especially when within sight of the natives, and this place was overlooked by the walls of the oppidum, though those native walls were, Fronto noted, also policed by legionaries.

Nothing changed inside. As they entered, the same Spartan appearance was evident throughout, and there was less busyness than Fronto usually encountered around the general, who slept little and often worked through much of the night, creating more work for those around him.

Finally, as they entered the cross hall, the optio saluted a tribune who was running down a list in a clerk's hands while he scratched his head in perplexity. The tribune, a young man from Rome, clearly only arrived this past season, looked up at the activity and frowned at Fronto as though trying to decide what he was.

'Yes?' he said sharply. He was overworked, Fronto thought. Pale and with black circles under his eyes, he needed sleep badly.

'This is former Legate Fronto of the Tenth to see the governor, sir.'

The tribune pondered for a moment, then turned to the clerk. 'We'll clear this up later.' As the man ran off, the optio bowed and retreated. The tribune gave them a tired smile.

'To be honest, anything that gets me out of that headache for a few moments is a welcome distraction. Well met, Legate Fronto. Your reputation precedes you. I am Gaius Rutilius Sura. If you'd care to follow me.'

Fronto inclined his head at the man and turned briefly to the others. 'The rest of you split up and source us food and drink and check with that optio where he's quartered us. Galronus, you stay with me. We'll meet the rest of you at the bath house as soon as we're finished.'

Leaving them to their tasks, Fronto and Galronus hurried after the tribune, who was now knocking on an office door at the end of the hall. A muffled voice called 'come,' and the tribune entered and announced the visitors. He stepped out once more and gestured for Fronto to enter.

The office was cluttered with scrolls, tablets and sheets of writing bark and vellum and it took a moment for Fronto to locate the occupant among the mess. Even as he blinked in surprise, the door was closed behind him, Galronus stepping beside him with an equally surprised expression.

'Titus?'

Titus Labienus, Caesar's long-time adjutant, looked up from the desk, pushing aside the list he was making. He looked no less tired than the clerk or the tribune.

'Marcus, what a damned surprise. Never thought I'd see your ugly mug this far north again.'

'Me neither. Titus, what's going on? I was expecting to see Caesar.'

Labienus let out something that was part laugh, part exasperated sigh. 'You asked to see the governor, didn't you?'

'What?'

'The proconsul has installed me as governor of this disorganised shit hole. After all, his term is coming to an end, and he's hoping that, if he can get back to Rome as a consul, he can formally recognise Gaul as a new province. I've got the sort of interim unofficial job of tying it all together while Caesar gallivants around the countryside drinking wine with allies and winning over the remaining populace of Gaul with his charm. The mess this land has been left in after eight years of war has to be seen to be believed, Fronto. And I don't mean *physical* mess,

21

though there's that too. But politically, economically, logistically, and in terms of population and resettlement, this place will take years to sort out. Maybe even decades.'

'He's pushing his remit a little setting you up like this,' Fronto said quietly.

'I told him the very same. I told him that the senate would spit feathers when they heard about it and that it would just give Pompey and his consuls fuel, but the general doesn't care anymore. He believes Rome can't be much more opposed to him. He might be right. We have ears in all the right places Fronto, and everything they hear is bad. Frankly, I'm worried about what the general is going to do. Soon he's going to be out of time and out of options, though he seems calm and collected and unconcerned as always.'

Fronto nodded. It was a thorny problem with no favourable outcome visible.

'Why *are* you here, Fronto?' but a dawning of realisation passed across Labienus' face even as he said it. 'Your exile. Of course. You're almost in the same situation as the proconsul, aren't you. He'd help you, Fronto, of course. We all know he'd move a mountain to help you. But I'm not sure he *can*. Still…' he mused, tapping his stilus on his lip, 'your arrival may have solved us a problem.'

'Oh? How?'

'The general is out of camp. He's at Samarobriva, in fact, some thirty odd miles from here. Been there for two days with the Twelfth and…. he's been… well, I'll let *him* explain that to you. He'll be back before dark and he'll want to see you. But let's say he has a job he wants doing and most of his good officers are tied up with things. He had Quadratus lined up for it but the poor fellow's come down with some dreadful illness in this horrible damp winter and he can't stop coughing his guts up and vomiting, so he wouldn't be much use.'

'Job?' asked Fronto, guardedly.

'How well do you know Aquitania, Fronto?'

* * *

'The general is waiting for you, sir.'

Fronto turned from Galronus, who paused in the midst of an explanation of Belgic decoration, to see a clerk standing behind him, so rigidly at attention he looked as though a stiff breeze might topple him. The two visitors had been standing under a canvas shelter close to the command building for half an hour, since word had reached them that Caesar had returned to camp. In fairness, given the noise made by the general's cavalry escort, it would have been obvious to most people that Caesar had returned without the need for confirmation. Fronto had hoped to catch up with Aulus Ingenuus, the general's bodyguard commander, but the horseman had not been one of the smaller unit that escorted him to the headquarters.

'Thank you, soldier.'

The clerk bowed and returned to his duties, and Fronto gestured to Galronus, who followed him across the road and into the headquarters. A quick question put to one of the legionary guards on duty directed them to an office at the opposite end of the hall to that of Labienus. The door stood open and no guards were in evidence there, but Fronto could hear the distinctive sound of Caesar's slightly nasal yet commanding tone from within. Intrigued, he paused.

'...that while he might owe Pompey, Marcellus is married to my great niece. Family should be above politics. Remind him of how unhappy I shall be if he continues to speak against me. And how... disappointed... Octavia will be.'

'And Lepidus, general?'

'I shall deal with Lepidus in due course. I have no immediate hold over him, but everyone has their weakness and I have friends looking into his. Now formulate that letter, Hirtius, and then bring it for me to peruse before you send it.'

'Yes, sir.'

Moments later, the gangly, greying form of Aulus Hirtius, Caesar's secretary, appeared from the doorway, bearing a stack of wax tablets and a pained expression. He paused, startled to find someone standing outside, nodded with a sour grimace to Fronto, and then stalked off like a crane with bad knees.

Fronto threw him a smile and almost jumped as the general's voice from inside called 'come in, Fronto. Don't dither.'

How did he know?

Fronto and Galronus strode into the office and stood before the desk. They did not come to military attention, though – after all, one was native royalty and the other a retired Roman noble. But neither of them could help slipping slightly into the at-ease stance.

'Be a good fellow and close the door will you, Galronus?' the general said, from where he was standing on the far side of the desk with his back to them, apparently studying a huge map of Gaul. Galronus pushed the door to with a click and returned to his stance beside Fronto.

'I shall not bother regaling you with my many woes,' Caesar said affably without turning. 'I am sure that the detail of my troubles is the talk of every tavern from here to Cremona, and I imagine you are already familiar with the matter.'

'I am acquainted with your issues, Caesar, yes.'

The general nodded as though the huge, impenetrable problems blockading his future were nothing but a small speck on a glass beaker. 'And you, I understand, have removed your exiled self to Massilia in order to evade the senate's reach. Sensible solution, to my mind.'

'Except that it seems Massilia are turning their back on you, general, and making overtures to the senate.'

The general nodded, displaying not even a modicum of surprise at the news. 'I can understand their decision. Much of the trade that maintains the city comes from Rome. However, I am rather disappointed in them. I may have to make my disappointment tangible at some point. And so, having been removed from Italian territory and finding Massilia rather unfriendly, you decided to call upon me and seek my patronage once more.'

Fronto felt faintly irked by the notion that a man whom he had financially supported in his initial rise and who owed a number of successes to him would think in such supercilious terms, but he *was* here as a supplicant in the end, and had to play this carefully.

'I believe that we share a common enemy, Caesar, in Pompey and his cronies. And I believe that we also share a time limit. As soon as your command is up – the senate's timing, that is, not yours – you have nowhere to go without falling into their hands. And the same is true for me, since your army is my last haven.'

'And you believe that we can be of service to one another? You may well be right, Fronto. And I like to help out old friends, anyway.' The general finally turned, and Fronto realised that the old man's sleep pattern – always too little and too late anyway – must have become almost non-existent from the dark circles under his eyes and his drawn features. His exhaustion was clear and his look made those clerks and tribunes Fronto had seen earlier appear healthy and full of vigour.

'And Galronus,' Prince of the Remi,' the general said with a tired smile. 'Are you simply passing through on your way home, or are you Fronto's man now?'

The Remi nobleman gave the general a strange, guarded smile, and folded his arms. 'I am accompanying Marcus here. I have... ties to the Falerii.'

Caesar's brow rose questioningly, and Fronto shrugged. 'My sister.'

'Ah, the redoubtable younger Faleria. You are formidable, master Galronus, for I had never thought that lady to be tamed once more.'

'Tamed is the wrong word, general.'

'Yes, you are correct. She is too powerful for that. *Contained* might be a better word. And I can see that her influence on you is no small thing, Galronus. I remember you some years ago as a cavalry commander, moustache and braids and arm rings and the whole Gallic look. And now I would not be able to pick you out of a crowd at the circus. By Jove, you have become more Roman than many of my friends!' The general let out a laugh, which seemed to ease some of the exhaustion in his face.

'Therein lies the second part of my reason for coming, General,' Fronto mused. 'Galronus is troubled by the social gulf between he and Faleria. While the senate is unlikely to be forthcoming with a solution, I felt that you might wish to reward the prince here for his years of faithful service in suppressing Gaul's rebellions?'

Galronus shot Fronto a look filled with embarrassment and shock, but the general just smiled. 'You are as impertinent, opinionated and correct as ever, Marcus. Very well, let me lay out my situation and my requirements and we shall see if we can come to a mutually beneficial arrangement.'

25

Here we go, thought Fronto. *Nothing for nothing with the general, as always.*

'What you need, Fronto, is security for yourself, your family and your friends, and assurances that your situation will improve as soon as the opportunity presents itself, am I correct?'

'That's the meat and bones of it, yes, General.'

'Then here is what I propose. I will have my agents in Rome and Italia secure whatever of your holdings and possessions have not yet been claimed by the senate. That gaggle of squabbling hypocrites work slowly, and the Falerii, if I remember correctly, have quite a collection of sprawling estates. You will have lost the house in Rome and the villa in Puteoli, sadly, but there will be other estates they have not yet touched. I will have them purchased by my factors under other names and held for you, along with any possessions, so that the senate cannot take them. Moreover I will take steps to secure the ongoing sector of your businesses in Italia. Essentially I will keep your interests safe until you can resume your former position. I will even see what I can do about acquiring the Puteoli villa, as I know that means a great deal to your mother. And I will vow here and now, on the altar to Venus if you wish, that the moment I achieve the consulship in Rome, I will renounce your exile, reinstate your family name and position and return all holdings I can secure to you.'

'That is quite acceptable, Caesar. We must just hope that the consulship does not elude you, then.'

'Worry not, Fronto. I will have my consulship one way or another. And I am content that I can do so without drawing Roman blood in the process. It is a matter of frightening the opposition – of being willing to go that step further if need be and making sure they know that. No, I will be consul next year and in Rome, be certain of that. And with it the Falerii will rise once more. Does that meet your requirements.'

And there was something about the matter-of-fact way the general made the statement that convinced Fronto of the truth of it. Caesar *would* be consul in Rome. He was sure. That it would happen without the drawing of blood was another matter.

'Perfectly, General.'

'And so to master Galronus. Your life would be easier if you were to share some level of equality with Faleria. It would not be within my power, even as a consul, to induct the Remi royal line into the patrician class. However, I can bring you close enough that the divide is crossable. Serve me one more time, and in return I will bestow upon you and upon your family Roman citizenship. After that unpleasant business with Comum's citizens last year no one will dare try to overturn a similar grant. They would open themselves to public derision, so you can be sure that *your* citizenship will be ratified in due course. Moreover I will, upon my return to Rome, grant you the *equus publicus*, making you one of the equestrian class. I will see to it that you have the right to sit in the senate. In order to qualify for the equites, you must meet the financial and property requirements and while I am certain that as a prince of the Remi you can meet the former, I will have estates passed to you so that you satisfy the latter. As one of the equestrian order you will be close enough socially to court the lady Faleria even in the most stuffy of circles. Especially as a senator.'

'And Caesar gets a grateful ally in the senate,' noted Fronto with a sly smile.

The general shrugged. 'A mutually beneficial situation. In fact it might be an idea to follow suit with a number of the more loyal Gallic and Belgic royalty. A man can never have too many allies, after all.'

'Now tell us the cost,' Fronto said, pursing his lips. 'Labienus was coy and evasive, but he did mention Aquitania.'

Caesar smiled. 'Yes. Aquitania. It seems interesting to me that we have spent eight years moving back and forth among the lands of the Gauls and the Belgae, but have had precious few dealings with the Aquitanii. Crassus claimed a victorious campaign there, though in truth he only really dealt with the low-lying tribes and found them to be very similar to their Gallic neighbours, as you will remember, Galronus, since you were with him. But last autumn I toured that region and I found that the true Aquitanii in the valleys and mountain passes of the Pyrenaei are somewhat different. They remind me more of the tribes of northern Hispania that we used to encounter in the old days, Marcus, though more hirsute.'

Fronto's expression became at once both wistful and dark. He had many happy memories of their time in Hispania, but recent dealings with Faleria and Galronus had stirred the ache of old wounds and now he could no longer quite manage nostalgia when he thought of the place. Hopefully that would fade with the union of his friend and his sister, laying ancient ghosts to rest.

'Anyway,' the general went on, stepping to one side to reveal the bottom left corner of the huge map on the wall, which covered Aquitania, the Pyrenaei mountains, and much of north-eastern Hispania. 'On my visit, I made assurances to a number of tribes and took their oaths of allegiance to Rome. I had altars set up at all the tribal centres to remind them constantly of their oath, but I also sent men to help build aqueducts, cisterns, roads and so on, to remind them of the benefits, as well as traders, many of whom went of their own accord. The Pax Gallica has been in place in Aquitania now for some time.'

'I foresee a "but" coming here, yes?'

Caesar nodded. 'The Aquitanii have not lived up to their end of the bargains we struck. Either taxes or payment in goods were agreed with each tribe, and while we saw minor, sporadic appearances of such for a while, nothing has been forthcoming for months. They have reneged on their promises as a region entire. Moreover, it seems that Roman merchants who have moved into the passes have disappeared. That, of course, is not unusual in barbaric places, but so too have small parties of legionary workers and engineers, and that I cannot overlook. The commander of the Lapurda garrison beseeches me for aid. Clearly the Aquitanii are flagrantly defying the peace to which they so recently agreed. I fear the tribes there need to be reminded of their commitment, their oath and, most importantly, the supremacy of the Roman military. Do you follow me?'

Fronto nodded. 'You want to send an army to stand on the toes of the mountain chiefs while you poke them in the eye. And I presume you wish me to take that army.'

'Indeed, Marcus. Succinctly put. I had marked down Quadratus for the task, but illness has rather laid him low. He is constantly in a sweat and his face is the colour of goat's cheese. And then, as if winged Fortuna herself had flown over the camp and dropped the answer in my lap, here you both are: one of my most successful and ingenious officers, who has a good working knowledge of both the Gallic and Hispanic tribes and with at least a passing familiarity of the region, and a Remi prince who was with Crassus when he crushed them the first time. All rather neat, wouldn't you say?'

Fronto nodded, his mind racing ahead. A largely unknown expanse of mountains, untamed tribes, a simple situation with an enemy facing you across a battlefield rather than enemies wrapped in togas who used pens and scrolls to fight you? Something deep in his blood stirred, and he realised he was grinning.

'Sounds perfect, in fact.'

'I knew you'd approve, Marcus. If I am to return to Rome in due course, I will need every morsel of support I can muster, and the favour of the public and the lower ranks of public office tend to be swayed by pomp and military victory. If I can say without fear of argument that Gaul is at peace, I will gain extra support.'

'What force were you planning?' Fronto mused. 'Just a single legion, I presume? Any more will become too cumbersome to move fast and efficiently in mountainous terrain. We discovered that two years ago crossing the Cevenna mountains against Vercingetorix.'

'My thoughts precisely.'

'And auxilia, General?' Galronus put in. 'Any cavalry or missile units?'

'I have had a mixed unit of slingers and archers three hundred strong prepared. Their commander is on their way from Vesontio as we speak. Cavalry-wise, I thought the standard ala attached to a legion would be adequate. Quadratus is a very able cavalry officer and was to lead the horse himself but in his absence, and given the fact that Fronto has fallen off more horses than he's stayed on, you Galronus would be the logical choice to command the cavalry.'

'Would regulars be willing to take commands from the Remi?' Galronus asked seriously. 'My experience with them suggests otherwise – they are a haughty and arrogant bunch.'

'You may be Remi,' Caesar smiled, 'but I will inform them that you are a member of the equestrian order in Rome. That should forestall any problems.'

Fronto nodded. 'What legion?'

The Tenth. Please let it be the Tenth…

'Therein lies the most interesting part, Marcus,' Caesar said with a knowing smile that made Fronto's nerves twang.

'What?'

'Part of the plan to settle the region is to put down any trouble. Another part is to garrison the area. I intended to settle veterans in colonies among their lands to keep the region stable and under control.'

'Veterans?'

'Indeed. I have had Labienus hard at work forming a single legion from all those men and officers who have reached the end of their term of service or are close to doing so. Every man in the legion prepared for the task is ready to retire. As you move through the region and work your wonders with its populace, you will leave small colonies of veterans behind you. I shall leave the specific details to you, of course, but you know the drill. And there will be a substantial train of pack animals to come with you bearing all the money and goods you need to settle the veterans, as well as the military diplomas for each man, which are currently being prepared. You will need a good clerk with you to confirm and detail each one in due course.'

As the general had detailed his plan, Fronto's eyes had widened and he was staring at Caesar in disbelief. When the general finally fell silent, Fronto coughed.

'You want me to march up into mountains controlled by rebel tribes with a legion of creaky old men and help them set up house along the way?'

'Oh you do have a way with words, Marcus. In essence you are correct, yes. Remember, though, that these "creaky old men" to whom you refer are well-trained and experienced combat veterans, and mostly, frankly, the same age as you or I.'

'And that should be adequate warning, Caesar, since I can't lift myself out of a chair these days without a bunch of creaks and groans.'

The general chuckled. 'The legion, which has no number, for it is in truth just a temporary vexillation formed from eleven different legions, is encamped a few hours' ride from here at Samarobriva. They are currently in training in the camp of the Twelfth, since they are formed from many units and need some time to begin working together as a single unit. And it will be a week or two before they are prepared to move, since we are waiting for all the goods, money and diplomas to be made ready and the unit of missile troops is still awaiting its commander and a half hundred men from Vesontio. Cretans under a prefect named Decius.'

A wide smile slowly blossomed on Fronto's face. Decius. The man he had fought alongside at Bibrax and who had crossed the Rhenus with him. Well that, at least, was a comfort.

'Decius is commanding the archers and slingers?'

'He is. Of course, you two know each other. This will be Decius' last season. I am not sure whether he intends to settle with the legions or return to Rome, but he has accepted a diploma this year. That is his choice. If you want all the details of the officers assigned to the legion, you can get the records from the camp prefect. In fact, I highly recommend you give him a visit. His office is across the hall.'

Fronto frowned. 'Very well. I think we have a deal, Caesar. I will see to your Aquitanian problem, and you see to my Roman one in due course. Galronus?'

The Remi turned a strange smile on him. 'A good exchange, I think.'

Fronto straightened with a contented sigh. Perhaps his specific command was not the one he would have chosen, but it felt good to be among the army once more and being pointed at an enemy and told to attack. The world became much simpler in these circumstances. And whoever else he might get saddled with, he would have overall authority, with Galronus and Decius as his seconds. It could be far worse.

'Very well, Caesar. I shall return once I have acquainted myself with the officers, and then we can discuss the intricate details. For now, I shall go see the camp prefect, then take a ride to have a look at this mobile cemetery I shall be commanding.'

Caesar snorted a laugh, and Fronto turned with Galronus and strode out of the room, closing the door behind them.

'What do you think?' Galronus muttered.

'It's a barking mad plan, full of holes and trouble, but like most of the general's plans I can see no distinctive reason it wouldn't work if we play everything right. A lot of our success will be down to the officers, I think, since they are such a disparate lot. I'm dying to meet them, as they'll make or break the campaign. I think it's too late in the day now to ride for Samarobriva. Let's go in the morning, and we'll take the others, since they'll have to be recognised as my adjutants by the legion's officers. I'll have to have someone polish my armour tonight, and you should wear a good mail shirt and a new tunic. Let's show them how impressively Roman and military we can be. But first let's get their names and details.'

Galronus nodded his agreement, and the pair crossed the hall to the camp prefect's office, rapping smartly on the door.

'Come,' called a muffled voice.

Fronto pushed open the door and stopped in the entrance, his jaw dropping in astonishment.

'*Carbo?*'

* * *

Fronto reached for the wine jug and poured himself a generous cupful, cutting it with two parts water.

'You were in this Uxellodunum the whole time? Ever since Gergovia?'

'Not quite. I spent some time with other prisoners in Gergovia itself. There were quite a few of us at the beginning, but the ranks thinned out over time, and we were few by the time we were moved to Uxellodunum. I was out of it for a while. I took a bad blow to the head when I fell at Gergovia, and it was a few weeks before I was near my old self. Then, of course, I started a decline. Atenos found me just in time, I think. I wouldn't have lasted much longer.'

'You were strong as a horse,' Atenos snorted from his cushion on the floor of the room.

'Liar. I was little more than a skeleton in rags. Still got poor muscles now, even half a year later. Caesar's expecting me to return to active service at some point, I think, but he's content to let me run the camp for now, and I'm rather enjoying the feeling of power over all these centurions and tribunes. There's something immensely satisfying about having senior officers come crawling deferentially because they want something.'

He laughed, and the others in the room echoed the sound.

'Though I sort of wish I was going with you, Fronto. I'd not be much use, of course, but it would be nice to be back in action with you and Galronus.'

'Same here,' grunted Atenos, 'but even if there was a place for me, I don't think our current commander, who's a bit of a knob if I'm honest, would let me go.'

Fronto leaned forward, sipping his wine, then peering intently at Carbo. 'So what can you tell me about my officers?'

'I've given you all the records.'

'Yes but what are they *like*. You must know some of them?'

'A few, mostly by reputation. Only three I know well, because they were drawn from the units stationed here. Your second most senior centurion is a man called Arruntius. Gaius Arruntius Piso. He's also one of your oldest at sixty three. He's been through three terms of service and is only stepping down this year because he says his fingers are starting to tighten and ache in cold weather, so he worries about holding a sword or vine staff.'

'Wonderful. The crumbly led by the decrepit.'

'Don't be fooled, Fronto. Arruntius would give any young soldier in the army a run for his money in the ring. He's a hard bastard. And a mad one. Has a habit of being the first one over a wall.'

'Fair enough.'

'And there's Terpulo. Lucius Terpulo. He's a character. A *proper* character. You'll either love him or hate him. Whichever it is, don't get into a conversation about bodily functions with the man. He can fart on command and it always reeks.'

'You're painting a great picture of my new command, Carbo.'

'Then you'll love Bassus. Gaius Acilius Bassus. He's a pretty bugger. Only got one ear, the most broken nose you've ever seen, one milky eye, missing two fingers, and a jaw that doesn't line up with his face. His men call him Pulcher, coz he's so beautiful. Good officer, though, for all he makes your eyes water to look at.'

'Can't wait to meet the rest of them. But Carbo, I'm going to tell Caesar I need you. Atenos, too. It's all well and good having a lot of experienced officers, but I've never met any of them. I want someone I can rely on. I want you as my camp prefect and Atenos as my primus pilus. Given Decius in charge of the auxilia, Galronus with the cavalry, and my singulares and my staff to rely on, I'm more confident about this. Besides, since we'll be settling even the centurions as we go, I need a core of officers who aren't going to set up home and leave me as we move.'

Carbo grinned. 'I'm yours if Caesar will let me go.'

'Same here,' Atenos chuckled. 'And I'd love to see my legate's face when he gets word from the general.'

'I don't like the idea of some prat leading my legion,' Fronto grumbled.

'The Tenth aren't yours now, Fronto. You have the Hundred-and-Tenth.'

'What?'

'Their average age,' snorted Atenos, and he and Carbo exploded with laughter.

* * *

The legion was forming on the parade ground of Samarobriva before Fronto and his group had even descended the hill toward the gate. Someone in command here was clearly horribly efficient. While that went some way toward allaying Fronto's fears, it also irked him, as he'd already pre-judged his new command to be troublesome and inefficient.

'They *look* good,' Aurelius noted as they rode toward the flattened area with the tribunal podium for the officers. And they did. They looked a proper legion. They *should do*, Fronto reminded himself nastily, with a combined experience of a hundred thousand years. He sighed. As the riders closed on them, the legion looked slightly less impressive. The helmets hid a lot from some distance, but closer up, they were largely old men. Oh, there were a few young 'uns among them, who had only served a five year term, or ten years, and who had accepted their discharge without wanting to go on in the hope of acquiring endless loot. But mostly they were of an age to call Fronto 'son'.

Yet they stood tall, and not one was out of position. It *was* a good sign. Finally, as the last men fell into place, the centurions stepped out beside their units, the most senior at the front of the legion. As they reached the parade ground and dismounted, Fronto handed his reins to a waiting equisio – yes, someone really *was* being efficient – and with his seven companions strode to the tribunal. A man in a senior officer's uniform was waiting there with a small command party bearing the standard of the Twelfth.

Fronto peered into the faces of his centurions as he passed, noting their steady gaze, their… *experienced*… features, and their clear efficiency. As he peered into one such face, he recoiled involuntarily, since some sort of grotesque seemed to have donned a helm with a transverse crest. It took him but a moment to realise that this was the Bassus of whom Carbo had told him – the one they called Pulcher. The hideous centurion gave him a smile of acknowledgement, and the grin actually made him uglier. Fronto tried to plaster an easy smile on his face in return as he passed, though he feared it probably looked more startled than warm.

Quickly, he bounded up the steps to the tribunal. Though the action made his knee ache, the comment about most of the retirees being his age seemed to have lodged somewhere in his subconscious and was making him try to act like a young man in defiance.

The legionary commander already there nodded professionally. He was a good decade or two younger than the visiting legate, and Fronto fought against disliking him on principle. He lost quickly.

'Gnaeus Favonius Flavinus, commanding Twelfth legion,' the man said by way of greeting.

'Marcus Falerius Fronto, commanding… er… *this* legion,' Fronto replied, slightly sheepishly.

'How long before you take them out, Legate?' Favonius asked, with an edge to his voice.

'A week or two. As soon as everything else is ready,' Fronto noted.

'Good. I'm looking forward to them being your problem.'

And with that simple comment, the legion became Fronto's, because he was damned if he would have his men, no matter how decrepit or strange they might be, spoken of in such a manner by an officer from a different unit.

'That they will,' he replied coldly. 'And fear not, for I'll keep them out of your hair in the meantime. I intend to take them on a march for a few days to give them a run-in.'

'Good,' Favonius said with feeling, and walked past Fronto without another word, down the steps and away from the tribunal. Fronto waited patiently for the man and his escort to leave the parade ground and return to the fort. 'Nice fellow,' Masgava said quietly. 'His face would look good with five knuckles stuck in it.'

'Then he'd look more like Pulcher,' Fronto said, with feeling.

'Men of the... er... the legion...' Fronto started in a loud, clear voice. It was odd. There were no standards and no flags. There was no eagle. This couldn't be a *proper* legion without an eagle.

'Sod it,' he said aloud, still addressing the legion directly. 'You *look* like a legion, and you're all obviously experienced, but you'll never *feel* like a legion until you have the standards of one. As soon as I get back to Nemetocenna, I'm going to have the fabrica there produce us an eagle and some standards and vexilla. And I can't just keep calling you 'the legion'. But you can't have a number, since you've not officially been raised as a new legion. So I'm going to call you the *Legio Evocati*. The legion of veterans. I'll have Caesar's bull put on the flags, too. You and I and my friends here are going to be together for a while, face some hairy bastards with bad attitudes and worse breath, and settle Gaul once and for all. Are you with me?'

He almost fell off the back of the podium with the roar that suddenly burst forth from the men. Well, they certainly didn't lack spirit.

'I am Marcus Falerius Fronto, formerly of the Tenth. Since all of you have served more than five years you'll probably know of me, and I suspect a number of you will have come from the Tenth, so you'll have served with me.' There was another roar, smaller but more enthusiastic. 'I probably know a few of you personally, in fact. In case you don't know me or my friends, I fought at the Sabis and the Axona. I defended Bibrax. I helped end the Helvetii and Ariovistus. I was at Gergovia and Alesia, and over in Britannia too. I was at Aduatuca and Avaricon. And I've yet to be at a battle where I didn't get blood on my blade. I'm no young fop with a commission from the senate and the desire to run home to papa so I can climb the ladder as soon as I can. I am a soldier, not a politician. And you lot might be on the cusp of taking it easy, but until you hold that diploma, you're still soldiers of Rome, so I expect the very best from each and every one of you. Is that clear?'

The affirmative shout almost knocked him off the tribunal again. He smiled. Alright, he'd been prejudging rather badly, it seemed. These were *his* kind of men.'

'And because this is not an official legion, we are not sent tribunes from Rome to run around and pour the drinks and get underfoot when important things are happening. So I've brought a few friends. This is Servius Fabricius Carbo, former primus pilus of the Tenth. He will serve as your camp prefect for the campaign.' Carbo raised a hand, and stepped forward for a moment. 'And this is Centurion Atenos, also a former primus pilus of the Tenth. He will be reprising that role for this force so my apologies if one of you were expecting that position.' As Atenos stepped forth and raised his hand, there was no angry call from the crowd. Either the assignment hadn't been given, or the deposed officer was content with the change.

'Galronus is both Roman equestrian and Remi prince, so he knows the ways of Rome and her armies as well as any of you, but also has that Gallic talent with the horse. He will be leading the ala of regular cavalry.' There was an uncomfortable silence, and Fronto noted the potential difficulty for later. It seemed that Galronus was not alone in seeing the difficulties over such a divide between peoples. 'Galronus is also one of very few people here with personal knowledge of what we'll be up against.' He huffed and moved on.

'Masgava here will take on the role of senior tribune, and I see no need for a gaggle of squawking juniors, so he will essentially be my deputy in all circumstances. In the first instance, if you cannot speak to me, and the primus pilus is absent, Masgava is your man.' The big Numidian stepped forth, then back. 'Arcadios here is a master archer. He will be assigned as second in command of the auxilia when they arrive, and Biorix is a senior engineer. He will be assigned the rank of centurion and placed in charge of all engineering projects.' The two men made themselves known. 'And finally, Aurelius here will be my aide and personal guard. Don't cross him. He's been with me through situations that'd make your hair turn white. And that, I think, takes care of the introductions from my side. As soon as the parade is over and before I return to Nemetocenna for the night, I want to meet each and every centurion, signifer, tesserarius and musician in person. I won't promise to remember all your names immediately, but I like to know who I'm going to be in battle with.'

Taking a deep breath, he exhaled loudly. 'Have any of you been told what we're to do?'

A centurion of roughly cuboid shape somewhere near the front shouted 'I heard we're bound for Hispania, sir. Just a rumour, but I'm hoping it's true. There's a lovely little whore house in Tarraco.'

Fronto stared at the man for a moment, then chortled. 'Not quite, centurion…?'

'Terpulo, sir.'

Oh yes. Terpulo. The one with the controlled emissions.

'I've been warned about you, Terpulo. Planning to gas a few whores were we?'

Laughter broke out among the men around Terpulo and he simply shrugged.

'No,' Fronto resumed. 'Sadly, Tarraco is not our destination, and your settlements and land grants will not be on that side of the mountains. We are bound for the Pyrenaei to put down some troublesome rebellious Aquitanii and remind them what hobnails taste like. We need to impose control over the whole region, and you will all be settled in groups as we go. Your diplomas and the gold will travel with us, so guard that pack train very well. It will contain your future.'

He let it all settle in for a moment, then began the last part of his address. 'We will be leaving for Aquitanii lands as soon as the supply train is ready and the auxilia arrive. I am hoping this will be within the week, but certainly not more than two. If we march south at reasonable pace, we should reach out destination in time for *Tubilustrum*, when the campaigning season officially starts. Once we reach the last proper Roman outpost down there I intend to gather some native scouts to help us, too. And that's the plan. I will discuss it in more detail with the officers as we travel south. In the meantime, however, I must return to Nemetocenna to arrange the standards and the eagle, and to confirm to the proconsul that all is proceeding according to plan. I will be back here with my men mid-morning tomorrow, and I expect you all to be packed up when I arrive, as we're going on a little march to see how you work together. I think three days with a little combat drill can tell us a lot. Alright, Atenos, dismiss the legion.'

* * *

The first day of the march had rather opened Fronto's eyes to his new command and deepened his respect for them. Not a single man dipped out of step, which was unheard of, even in the solid Tenth, over such a time and distance. Carbo had noted the variety of shield designs among the men, given the varied units they'd been drawn from, and had planned to have them all repaint their design, but Fronto had forestalled the plan and had instead had the units re-form so that all the men with one design were together, barring a few small units that were inevitably mixed. To his mind, not only would it make it easier to remember who was who in his new legion, but that also meant that men from one legion would be serving among former comrades, which would ease the transition to a single unit.

Even the oldest among the men, and Fronto had to estimate one particularly hoary fellow as over seventy, maintained their pace, even with a full pack hanging from their *furca* pole. And most of the men worked by instinct and experience now, having served so long. Rarely had a centurion to give one of the standard orders before it was already being obeyed. Give me a legion like this formed officially, Fronto mused, and I could conquer a province alone.

And as the sun sank behind the thick Gallic woodland just to the north, he'd been impressed at the speed with which the camp was dug and set. In truth, the ditches weren't quite as deep as he'd normally demand, and the rampart not quite as high, but he put this down to expediency and the inevitable knowledge that this was just an exercise rather than inability or laziness.

As the torches were lit in the gathering gloom he left his companions at the camp's centre, setting up the headquarters tent and their own accommodation, and began a tour of the ramparts. The sentries were all alert, he was pleased to find. He paused for a moment at a curious sight. A tall centurion was standing at one of the gates looking off into the distance, and some twenty paces away two soldiers were creeping toward him, slowly, on their toes.

One was an optio, judging by the crest and the staff in his hand. The other wore a standard bearer's helm, draped with a fox pelt. Fronto watched with interest as the pair closed on the centurion.

'Piss off, the lot of you,' barked the centurion without turning when the pair were still twenty paces away.

'How'd you know?' the optio said, straightening along with his friend.

'I might have a blind eye, but you make more noise than a ballista, Statilius, and Cavo over there smells like a bear shat on him. You'll have to do better than that.'

The two men laughed and turned, sauntering off. Fronto waited until they were some distance away, laughing, then crossed to the centurion, who turned and came to attention even as Fronto approached. Fronto recoiled automatically at the sight of Pulcher. Of course, *he* had a milky white eye.

'You put up with such foolishness with calm forbearance, centurion?'

The ugly officer shrugged. 'Gotta let the men blow off steam eh, sir. Besides, a soldier's only as serious as his commander, and they're Terpulo's underlings. In case you haven't noticed yet, sir, Terpulo's an idiot. A talented one, but an idiot, nonetheless.'

Fronto grinned. 'You'd have done well in the Tenth while I was in command, Bassus.'

'You might as well call me Pulcher, sir. Every other bastard does. Even my brother's picked up the habit in his letters, the prick. But then he's uglier than me, so we give him a bit of leeway.'

Fronto snorted his laughter. 'What's your opinion of the legion, Pulcher?'

'They'll do you proud, sir. Might even find a few of them decide not to retire after all and refuse their diplomas when the time comes. It always sounds nice, but then you suddenly face the moment of putting down the shield and it seems less appealing. You wonder what in Hades you'll do next. I've declined retirement three times now. I wasn't planning on retiring now, in fact, but I've a woman in the baggage train who insists. Wants to settle down and raise ugly children, she does.'

Fronto laughed. 'Women. Oddly, I know what you mean. I've retired twice, and here I am marching to Aquitania with a legion.'

'You'll do us proud too, then, sir. My one concern is that you'll have to settle colonies as we go, which will gradually diminish our numbers. What happens then if we run into real trouble with half the lads spread across the region planting crops and building houses?'

'I've been thinking about that,' Fronto replied, serious now. 'I'll set small units to start the colonies each time. No more than five hundred at most and probably a lot less, depending on circumstances. Then, when the job's done all the remaining men can be disbanded and sent to bolster the fledgling settlements. Seems the best compromise.'

'Very sensible, sir. Now *that*,' he added, pointing along the rampart, 'is less sensible.'

Fronto followed the man's gaze and spotted the blocky, almost cuboid, form of centurion Terpulo in deep conversation with his two men. 'Is he fit for the post, you think, Pulcher?'

'Terpulo, sir? Hades, yes. One of the best officers in the legion.'

'You called him an idiot?'

'But a bloody good one, sir. Go watch him at work. If nothing else it'll make you laugh.'

Fronto nodded and absented himself, striding over to the three officers, who were huddled conspiratorially.

'Evening,' he said by way of greeting. The three men turned and saluted, Terpulo replying for them. 'Good evening Legate. And a surprisingly fine one. We were about to engage on a game of Mister Rusty with the young feller on the next gate.'

'I thought we were playing Ghost,' complained the standard bearer.

'Not on young Beaky,' Terpulo replied. 'When we find someone not paying attention you can Ghost him. Care to join us, Legate?'

'I have not a clue what you're talking about, Terpulo.'

'Then you're in for a treat, sir. Come with us and look like you're deep in conversation with us.'

Fronto's brow furrowed, but he smiled and followed the three of them. Some short distance away another gate stood in the ramparts, facing a stream a few hundred paces down the slope. There were two legionaries on guard duty.

'See the bigger one, sir?'

'Yes.'

'Well the other one's Truculus, and he's an older legionary – a good man. But the big one? Don't know him. He's from the Eleventh according to his shield, and he's young. Can't have done more than a five year term. The young 'uns are always fair game. I walked past him earlier and noticed the state of his helmet.'

Still confused, Fronto strode with them toward the unsuspecting young soldier. As they approached, Terpulo struck up a conversation about logistical difficulties, and Fronto found himself having to ad-lib a little conversation. Naturally, the two legionaries snapped to attention as the officers closed on them. The four officers were passing the guards when Terpulo stopped suddenly and turned to the young man.

'What in the name of Minerva's hairy tits is that on your helmet, soldier?'

The legionary's face slid into an expression of utter panic as the centurion leaned closer to him, then swiftly untied the thong holding his cheek plates together, plucking the iron bowl from his head.

'Sir?' asked the confused legionary with a nervous tremor.

'That!' snapped Terpulo, pointing at the bowl of the helmet. As he spun it in the torchlight, Fronto caught sight of a blossom of rust perhaps two finger-widths across near the crest holder.

'Sir, I…'

'Close that mouth soldier, lest I push your helmet into it.'

The soldier fell silent. Fronto felt rather sorry for the lad, though he did deserve to be pulled up on the condition of his helmet. 'Dagger,' demanded Terpulo, holding out his hand. Close to panic, the legionary yanked his knife from its sheath and handed it shakily over. Passing the helmet to his optio and reaching into his belt pouch, the centurion withdrew a tiny, delicate glass bottle with a stopper and undid it. His tongue poking from the side of his mouth in concentration, he used the dagger to scrape the find red dust from the iron helm, teasing it down to the bottle, where he deftly tipped the rust inside. Fronto watched the skill involved and wondered how many times the centurion had done this. Finally, Terpulo stoppered the bottle once more and wiped the blade of the dagger on his tunic hem. He then gestured to the optio, who held out the helmet. The legionary took it, slammed it on and quickly fastened it. It was impressive just how much sweat was pouring from the lad's hairline now.

Once it was done, Terpulo slid the lad's blade back into its sheath and then held out the glass jar. 'What is your name and unit, soldier?'

'Gaius Sidonius, sir. Cohort two, century of Calpurnius Ferro.'

'Well, legionary Sidonius. In this bottle is Mister Rusty. Since you grew him, he can be your pet. Look after him well. I shall be checking in from time to time, and woe betide legionary Sidonius if I find him without Mister Rusty in good condition. And you'll need to sharpen and polish your blade before you buff out the marks on your helmet. And do you know what happens when you have Mister Rusty?'

'N- no, sir.'

'You can only have one Mister Rusty. So if I ever find you growing another one, I shall have you report to the medicus with instructions to insert that bottle somewhere only your lover might find it. Do I make myself clear?'

'Yes, sir,' replied the ashen-faced legionary.

Switching his attention away from the lad instantly, Terpulo gestured to Fronto. 'What were you saying about grain shipments, Legate?'

And so they strolled on, involved in small-talk until they were well out of earshot, when they stopped and the optio and standard bearer exploded into howls of laughter. Terpulo grinned lop-sidedly. 'That, sir, is Mister Rusty.'

'That poor lad almost shat himself,' Fronto chuckled. 'Maybe a little harsh?'

'I bet you'll never see another spot of rust on his kit, though, sir. You might be surprised to find out just how many men in my old legion are still carrying a Mister Rusty. But we had well-polished kit.'

'You might very well be insane, Terpulo.'

'A little insanity's healthy in a man expected to run at a wall of spears, Legate.'

'Can't argue with you there,' laughed Fronto. 'I'm off to gently soak my liver in Chian red. I shall see you bright and early.'

The three men, still chuckling, saluted, and Fronto wandered off toward his tent. As soon as everything was in place, they would march south. He was starting to feel quite confident in his men. Certainly life seemed unlikely to be dull in the coming months.

Martius

THE beardless 'smiling' man stretched and then folded his arms. Around them, the small outpost burned, dry timbers holding the heat as the flames crept along the beams and planks with searching fingers. The tiles on the roof of the main building were cracking and collapsing in the heat, and the thatch of the other structures roared liked a lion with its head back, calling defiance to the world.

At the heart of the small installation, beside the new well which now contained a dead goat just to be certain the place would be unusable, stood the Roman altar.

'Pax Gallica,' the man spat, his voice hoarse and whispering, difficult to hear over the conflagration.

As he stood and poured his scorn across the foreign obscenity, the six heads of the outpost's personnel were lined up on the altar, three to each side, staring outwards with wide, agonised eyes, the skin almost hidden by soot and blood, with just those horrified white orbs amid the mess.

'Some of the warriors are unhappy.'

The man with the smiling wounds looked around to see one of the older warriors standing close by, gore-coated axe still in hand from the beheadings. He was clearly a strong warrior, though perhaps his glory days had passed along with the last colour in his hair and the last of his lower teeth.

'What?'

The old man shrugged. 'They'll butcher Romans until the sky falls on them, but these are Aquitanii. Some of the lads don't like that we're killing Aquitanii.'

The hoarse voice began as a low, papery whisper and somehow the force in it cut through all the dreadful noise. 'These were *cattle*, bred by Rome to feed her legions. They were not men, let alone Aquitanii. If any man mutters dissent, send him to me.'

The old warrior faltered for a moment. Staring into that awful face stripped away the desire to argue any point, but the half dozen warriors below, who'd fired the last building, had been quite vocal in their unhappiness at the people they were now killing. Three other warriors had come close now and were hovering behind him. Their presence emboldened the old man.

'Why do this? We are greater than we have ever been. *You* are greater than you have ever been. Why provoke Rome and risk it all?'

The smiling man's arms unfolded in a fluid movement and the old warrior didn't even see the knife in them until it had ripped his throat from side to side in a single smooth rent. His neck opened and the blood gushed forth as he hissed and gurgled and toppled backwards.

'Why?' croaked the smiling man, his ruined face looking more menacing than ever. 'Because of vengeance. Because of an oath. Oaths must be kept. They are what separate us from base animals. Does anyone else wish to question my orders?'

The other three had melted away into the burning outpost before the old warrior's legs had even stopped thrashing. Alone once more, the man with the grinning wounds carefully wiped his blade on a rag from his belt and then sheathed it in its scabbard.

Chapter Three

FRONTO couldn't quite equate what he was seeing with his only memory of the place. It had been two years since he was last here, during that awful summer when Vercingetorix had almost driven Caesar to defeat.

Cenabum. Oppidum of the Carnutes on the Liger River.

The town had risen in revolt more than once, harboured some of the worst enemies of Rome, been a heartland for resistance and a flag for the Gauls to rally behind. For while the Arverni had been the tribe who had led that war under their glorious king, it had been the Carnutes with their druids and secretive ways who had begun the revolt and had been mostly behind it.

And yet Cenabum went on.

The place had been commandeered by Rome for a supply station. Given the regular trouble there, it had seemed expedient to have a local small garrison. But then the Gauls had driven their defiant standards into the ground here. Quartermaster Cita and his supply depot had been butchered and burned, all Roman presence razed. Cenabum had fallen back to the Carnutes as the first target of their great revolt.

And then the next summer Rome had come for revenge. Fronto had been there. Hiding in the boats down by the river, waiting for the noise across the bridge to draw out the Carnutes enough to open their gates. He had been one of the first through that portal and into Cenabum, where he had exacted a terrible price from the natives for what they had done to Cita and his depot. It was a rare occasion when Fronto let go of all control and surrendered to the beast that lurked inside every instinctive warrior. He hated it. He *hated* having no control, but sometimes he simply couldn't help it. He had rampaged through Cenabum taking life after life in violent, bloody vengeance.

He'd never thought he'd be back.

He'd have rather not, in fact. He would never again go to Alesia, or to Aduatuca, or to Gergovia, or a dozen other places. For such battlefields held the spectres of the dead who still sometimes came for him in his dreams. And he couldn't face thinking on the young lives he had taken in the name of Rome.

Yet somehow, this was different. It shouldn't be, but it was. Cenabum was among the worst of them. He should feel as sickened and hollow here as anywhere, and more so than most.

But he didn't.

Because Cenabum thrived. As the legion emerged from the treeline and the Carnute city lay before them beside the river, Fronto was struck suddenly by how lively the place was. Ships were coming and going from the dock in an almost constant procession, and their shapes even from this distance showed them to be both Roman and Gallic. Smoke rose in twisting columns from roofs of both thatch and tile. The north gate in the oppidum's wall stood open and inviting, and here and there farm carts could be seen on the road, heading for Cenabum to sell their wares. The city was full of life and the gentle distant hum of vibrancy hovered on the marginal breeze. Fronto could already almost hear the children playing, the fishermen hawking their goods, the priests calling their displeasure at all things worldly.

Not that he had expected to find a cemetery, of course, but from what he'd heard, Caesar and the army had come here again last summer in response to yet more Carnute trouble, and had found only a fledgling village amid the ruins of the old city they had destroyed. Even a year on, Fronto had expected at best a subdued and sparsely-populated place, not an energetic and busy place. With interest still quashing any dread and pushing back the distaste he'd expected to feel, Fronto moved to the front of the column and led his men down to Cenabum.

'Be careful here,' he said, knowing the officers would carry his instructions back down to the men. 'Cenabum was recently very much enemy territory and there could well be a great deal of resentment simmering here. The place has been free of our garrison for only two years, and our presence may not be popular.'

But whatever they found in Cenabum, Fronto was determined to spend a day there with the men. They had marched south from Nemetocenna for ten days, as soon as the column was gathered, and that was enough without a rest. It would take a total of around forty days to reach their destination, by Fronto's estimation, given the need to move at the speed of the supply train. The legion would march just over ten miles a day for ten days at a time, and then have a period of rest before moving on. He had planned stops at

Cenabum, then at Limonum, where apparently a small Roman garrison remained from the previous year's campaigning, then Burdigala, a town of the Bituriges, and then finally to Lapurda, where a Roman garrison awaited them at the end of the mountains.

'Atenos, we'll quarter the legion outside the north gate at a respectable distance. I don't want to push anything. Just the officers and myself and a small cavalry escort will go on. You and Carbo get the camp underway and we'll be back as soon as we've spoken to the locals.'

The column moved on along the dusty road and some thousand paces short of the gate, Atenos called for a halt and prepared to set up camp. Fronto, along with the senior officers and a dozen regular cavalry, rode on to the portal in the walls of Cenabum. His heart began to beat faster as they closed on it, remembering the blood and the screaming, the darkness and the dancing flames. But for all the trouble he'd expected, the gate remained open and the men on guard there nodded at him respectfully, issuing no challenge.

He motioned for the column to halt and reined in before the warriors. As he looked down, he was interested to note a new paved approach to the town had been formed with a very Roman style drainage ditch.

'Where might I find the leader or leaders of this town?' he asked in polite Latin.

One of the warriors frowned in incomprehension and looked at the other, who was working through the words slowly, as though translating them carefully, one at a time.

'Vergobrate. Druid. Hut of big. Water road fat. See?'

Fronto thought it through. 'A large house by the river, on a wide road. Thank you. Can we enter?'

Not that he had any intention of staying outside, of course, but he was also acutely aware of the fact that less than a year ago this place had been a burning heart of anti-Roman sentiment.

'You come. Good.' The warrior waved his hand to indicate their passage, and Fronto thanked him and rode on.

Inside, Cenabum showed more evidence of its recent troubles than had been clear from a distance. Wide swathes of the interior were empty lots with bare land or charred cobbles where houses had burned. But many buildings had clearly been constructed over the winter, and they showed distinct elements of Roman design, including verandas and tiled roofs. In fact, the second house they passed was roofed with red tiles that bore the distinctive bull and XI of the Eleventh Legion. As they clopped down the stone road toward the river and the gate where two years ago he had forced his way in, he pondered on the tiles' origin. Had they been in Cita's supply depot? Probably. Then reused by the locals in their rebuilding work. He felt he ought to be put out by such reuse, but found oddly that he wasn't. In fact, it was rather endearing to find the Carnutes of all people, in the ashes of failed rebellion, adopting and adapting those things their former enemy left behind.

All around Cenabum the scars remained, but the rebuilding was going on, and the repairs were working to remove the evidence of destruction. Fronto's initial fears about their reception began to fade and diminish. Sellers of bread and fruit shouted hopefully to them. Women did not whisk their children off the street at their approach, and the young lads poked each other with sticks, playing soldier. The calls of the fishermen down by the open river gate did not silence as mounted Romans approached.

The house was not hard to find, and Fronto nodded to the man standing by the door again.

'Is this where I will find the ordo or chief?' A look of incomprehension. 'Druid?' A nod. 'May we enter?' he pointed at the doorway and the warrior nodded. Fronto turned. 'Listen, we don't seem to be in any real danger, and I don't want to make their chief feel uncomfortable. Galronus and Decius come with me. The rest of you... maybe you could negotiate to have some vittles delivered to the camp? I'm sure the lads would like some fresh food and not to have to grind their own grain for a change. Fish might be nice?'

Leaving the others to it, Fronto, Galronus and Decius entered.

'It's a far cry from the east,' Decius noted.

'How so?'

'I've been in Vesontio a lot in recent years, and Vesontio has been undamaged throughout the war, Fronto. It's thrived on legion postings and become rich and content. Here, you can still see signs of the war. Scars.'

'*Healing* scars, though,' Fronto breathed. 'I hardly like to say it, 'coz we all know how capricious the Fates are, but it does actually feel like the war's over here.'

'And if the Carnutes of all people have accepted that, then it seems likely so have the others.'

'Indeed.'

There was no guard on the inner doorway and no actual door in it, and Fronto emerged into a large room formed of irregular stone block walls upon a timber framework. A mezzanine level with a railing reached by rickety stairs was partially hidden from sight, though there was movement up there. Below, in the centre of the room was a low, circular table of oak, with five chairs around it. Two were occupied.

Fronto peered at the druid in his long robes suspiciously, then moved on to the nobleman with his rich clothes and gold and bronze accoutrements. There was a good chance that he or Decius had fought against one or both of them in recent years, but neither seemed familiar, at least.

'Greetings,' the noble said, rising to his feet.

Fronto bowed his head. 'I am Marcus Falerius Fronto, commanding the... a legion of men freshly arrived from Nemetocenna. We are bound for Aquitania and seek your permission to make camp outside your walls and stay for two nights to rest the men. No soldiers will enter Cenabum without authorisation, and even then numbers will be limited. Do you have any objections?'

The nobleman glanced to the druid, who gave him an odd look. The nobleman chuckled.

'Ordetix here worries that parties of drunken legionaries in the town will cause trouble. They will not, will they, Legate Fronto?'

'I shall personally flog any man who starts trouble.'

'Then the council of Cenabum has no objection.'

'Thank you.' Fronto smiled. 'I am pleased to see that Cenabum begins to thrive and grow once more. I... I was here in less happy times.'

Blood running between the cobbles on the street outside this very house where he had forced the gate and rushed the Carnutes with a mind filled with blood and rage.

'War is over, Legate. My people were foolish and fell for the lies of the Arverni king. Now we have made our oath to Rome and peace is with us once more. Our tribe was almost wiped out, our farms were destroyed, our livestock taken and butchered and our houses burned. But we know this to be the fault of our hubris and the lies of Vercingetorix, not your people. For we made an oath to Rome and we broke it time and again, and the gods hate an oath-breaker. So now we will make children and begin again. Our farms begin slowly to yield, we import cattle and goats, and build our houses with the remnants of the old world. The Carnutes will live, Legate. It is what we do.'

'I am glad to hear it,' Fronto smiled. 'I have instructed my men to purchase appropriate food and drink for the legion. Hopefully we can contribute a little to your economic rebirth. I will have a small donation delivered to this council chamber in the morning in gratitude for your welcome, and perhaps, if it is of use, some of our engineers can help you with your work?'

'An interesting proposal. Let us talk.'

A quarter hour of pleasant small-talk ensued before deals had been struck, the two Carnute leaders ran out of things to say and finally Fronto, Decius and Galronus emerged from the house into the street.

'I never had you pegged as a diplomat,' Decius grinned. 'You seem like a different Fronto to the one I remember at Bibrax.'

'But put a sword in his hand and point him at an enemy and just watch,' snorted Galronus. 'He doesn't change.'

'Although it appears that the *world* does,' Fronto sighed with unexpected contentment. His gaze picked out half a dozen cavalrymen with Aurelius buying basket upon basket of fresh-caught fish, laughing as they negotiated. Across the way, more soldiers were finalising a deal with a baker. And further up the street, Masgava had the two boys with their stick swords facing each other, stomping through practise moves as though they were on a legionary parade ground.

'The world *does* change. And *that*, gentlemen,' he said, pointing out the scenes of international domesticity, 'is why we ride for Aquitania. Because Caesar's Pax Gallica is important. It does work. And what you can see here justifies more than anything what we've been through in recent years. No more fear and hatred between Roman and Gaul. After three and a half centuries of distrust living alongside one another, finally it can all end. We won a war, but not to destroy or conquer. To include and to adopt. Now Gaul can be another Narbonensis or Africa. Part of the republic, with its own identity. That is why we have to bring peace to Aquitania, even if it's by force.'

* * *

The Ides of Aprilis passed barely noticed somewhere en-route, the festival of Tubilustrum which marked the beginning of the campaigning season come and gone somewhere in the wilds on the march, too. And now as they stared the end of Aprilis in the eye four days south of Burdigala, a field hand who had stood blinking in surprise at the passing Roman column had confirmed they were in the lands of the Aquitanii. Specifically, in fact, the Sotiates, upon whom Crassus had planted his boot six years earlier.

Fronto watched as his men set up camp for the night on a long, low slope that rose toward the south, amid a huge pine forest that seemed to dominate the landscape. It had initially come as some surprise to find such a large swathe of clear land among the endless trees, but the reason had quickly become apparent to the scouts. At the top of the slope – at the far, southern, end – stood a deserted village. It had been empty for some time, with no sign of life, and the open expanse had been farmland, lovingly cut from the heart of the forest, but long since left to fallow.

'How long do you reckon the houses have been empty?' Fronto asked Galronus, who had ridden the perimeter with the scouts upon their arrival.

'It's hard to tell, they're so crude, but the roofs are largely intact and the timbers have not fallen apart on the doors, so my guess is no more than a year. Probably only half that.'

'So this is not the work of Crassus' campaign down here?'

'We never came quite this far west Fronto. We fought in the lands of the Sotiates, but further east. We took their fortress maybe fifty miles east of here, then turned south to take on the Vocates and the Tarusates. We never even got close to the mountains. Just the foothills. Anyway, there do not appear to be signs of struggle and deliberate destruction here. My guess would be that the population of this place picked up all their goods and their livestock and abandoned it sometime during last summer or autumn.'

'About the time Caesar toured the place.'

'At a guess. I only had the briefest of looks, though.'

Let's go have a look.' Fronto looked out over the steadily growing ramparts until he spotted Decius and Masgava deep in conversation. 'Decius? Grab your horse and come with me. Masgava, you and Carbo have the legion.'

The big Numidian, his lieutenant, nodded and went off to seek Carbo while Decius grasped the reins of his horse from the equisio who stood nearby and mounted, trotting over to where Fronto and Galronus waited.

'We're going to have a closer look at this deserted village while there's enough light. Come on.'

The three men – legate, cavalry commander and auxiliary prefect – rode off across the open grassland with Aurelius close behind, staying by the legate's shoulder as expected of a bodyguard.

The village was little more than a hamlet, really. Eleven houses and some sort of meeting hall, with various farm structures on the outskirts, including a granary on timber stilts and some sort of sty. There was something unearthly about the place in the dimming light of a spring evening, and Fronto couldn't suppress a shiver as they approached.

'I don't like this place,' murmured Aurelius to the rear. Fronto bit his tongue to prevent himself replying. The soldier was always prey to strong superstition, and it was the legate's wont to berate him for foolishness when he made unfounded credulous comments. But on this particular occasion Fronto could feel it too, and from the looks on their faces Galronus and Decius were of a similar mind.

'There is definitely something off here,' he muttered, slowing his horse at the first building and slipping from the saddle. As the others followed suit and tied their reins to a post, the four men began to pick their way around the village.

'Didn't they say that Caesar had an altar to peace raised in every Aquitani tribe's settlements?' Decius mused. 'I don't see one.'

'This place is too small and insignificant,' Galronus shrugged. 'Altars would only have been placed in the larger towns and the tribal meeting places.'

The auxiliary prefect nodded and leaned into the door of a hut. 'Smells musty and old. And there's holes in the roof. Are you sure it's been less than a year?'

Galronus passed through the doorway next to him and scouted around for a moment. Holding his hand over his mouth and nose against cloying dust, he picked something up and threw it to Decius, who caught it gingerly, as though half expecting it to bite.

'A cloak?'

'Part of one,' Galronus confirmed. 'Torn and so left behind, I presume. It's soggy and starting to unravel badly, but wool like that will be gone within a year if abandoned to the elements. Judging by the state of it, I'd say its owner left late autumn last year. It's been a wet winter, so the wool is in poor condition.'

Fronto nodded as he took the wool scrap from the prefect's hand and peered at it. 'So probably not long after the general made his visits around here. Wonder what he said that caused them to up and leave their village, livestock included.'

Aurelius peered into the gloom past them all. 'If they *did* leave of their own volition.'

'What do you mean?'

'Well it sounds to me like everyone's assuming that they just left. Let me check something.'

As the others ducked back to let him pass, the former legionary picked up a broken stick-broom from the wall near the doorway and began to move around the small hut, methodically prodding the floor. After some time, with the others watching in perplexed fascination, he finally stopped, slamming the staff into the floor in the same place several times. 'The moment of truth,' he said and dropped to a crouch, grabbing a piece of fallen timber and using it like a spade to clear away the dirt of the floor.

'What is he doing?' Decius asked quietly.

'I don't know,' Fronto replied quietly. 'I find with Aurelius it's best to wait until he's finished. His explanations can get a little... involved.'

Finally, Aurelius paused and heaved in a breath. 'That answers that question,' he said darkly, lifting something from the hole he had dug. A filthy bag lay in his hands and he quickly untied the thong and fished inside, producing a silver ring and half a dozen coins of varying origin.

'Explain?'

'Well you nobles, sir, have strong-rooms and factors who look after your money. Poor folk, be they Roman or Gaul, or apparently Aquitanii, bury their valuables to keep them safe. And this family's valuables are still here. So they didn't leave by choice, or if they did, they did so quickly, in a panic and a rush. They didn't stop to collect heirlooms.'

Decius blinked in surprise. 'Clever,' he muttered, nodding at Aurelius.

'Spread out,' Fronto said, tensely. 'Find whatever you can to help explain this.'

As the others started to scout through the huts and around their outside, peering intently into the gathering gloom, Fronto strolled to the centre of the small hamlet, where he could see the whole place. Standing still, he slowly turned full circle taking in the village. As he turned, his heel sank into soft ground and he stepped aside, frowning, and looked down at where he'd been standing. His heel had sunk into what had looked like hard-packed dirt. Not deep, mind, but half a hand width was more than he'd expect in this ground. The rest of the village was hard-packed light and dusty dirt.

Dropping to his knees, he brushed the dirt aside and gradually revealed a darker patch. The dry, poor, almost gravelly soil he had watched pass underfoot ever since Burdigala would not contain such a layer of darker, clay-like material. His studies of soil types for wine growing had taught him a few things, after all. So what was this?

'Galronus?'

The Remi noble came sauntering over and dropped to a crouch opposite him.

'What do you make of this?'

Galronus peered at it, picked up a little of the darker dust between his fingers and crumbled it, then sniffed it, and finally touched it to his tongue. 'I cannot say for certain, but I'd be willing to wager it was blood. Long enough ago that it's now just a stain in the soil. It was buried?'

Fronto nodded. 'That's what I thought. Someone was wounded or killed here and soil sprinkled over the blood. Not enough for a whole village, but maybe one or two people?'

Galronus nodded.

'Legate!'

They rose at the sound of Aurelius' voice and turned to see him standing by the pig-pen. Decius came jogging from a hut as they converged on the former legionary. 'Think we might have found evidence,' Aurelius muttered, poking the contents of the pen with his broken broom. Fronto peered into it. As the wooden staff shoved aside the old, congealed murk, bone became visible.

'So whatever happened here, someone was killed and then fed to the pigs. Not the whole village, mind. We've found signs of blood in the open square, but just of one or two people. An execution, I think, rather than a fight. And done to invoke fear and obedience. Otherwise why do it at the heart of the village in sight of everyone.' Fronto sighed and leaned back. 'Whatever happened here, it frightened the rest into leaving en-masse and quickly. Aurelius, I think your instincts were right. This place gives me the creeps too. Let's hope the rest of Aquitania's a little better. Regardless, I think we'll have a double guard tonight and move off at dawn. I want to get to Lapurda and speak to the garrison commander there.'

* * *

The column had changed imperceptibly over that night and the next few days. By the time the army was eight days out of Burdigala and less than two from their destination at Lapurda, the general pace had picked up, despite the increasing tiredness of the legion since the last day's rest. No longer were helmets carried hanging from the scarf as was common on long marches. Some indefinable change in the air had led to each and every man wearing his helmet. Moreover, shields had been unslung from backs and carried in hand despite the extra weight and encumbrance. On Fronto's order all marching poles and excess kit had been put in the wagons to be brought along behind. The legion was ready for a fight, and they could feel one coming in some inexplicable way.

Fronto rode at the front of the column alongside Masgava and Carbo. Galronus was out somewhere ahead with his scouts, Atenos with the first cohort and Decius was stomping alongside somewhere. The auxiliaries had been split into fifty man groups and surrounded the column.

Fronto peered ahead into the great flat distance, half expecting to see the Pyrenaei mountains that further southeast loomed like a tombstone above the lands of the Aquitanii, but it would be some distance south yet before the hazy blue sawblade of the mountains emerged on the horizon. Lowland slowly gave way to higher hills, then narrow valleys and finally high peaks The tribes lived in the lowlands all the way north almost to Burdigala, and west to the sea, east almost to Roman Narbonensis, and right the way up into the highest peaks. In fact, the Aquitanian tribes even inhabited the passes and the higher valleys on the far side of the mountains, where they looked down upon Hispanic tribes and the great city of Tarraco. Fronto was musing on how such a disparate topography could be said to give rise to one people when he heard a voice calling 'Legate.'

He turned and glanced to his left. There, a unit of Cretan archers strode alongside, nervously. They were hardly armoured at all compared to the legionaries, and yet had been assigned to the flank to add mobile protection. It took him a moment to recognise Arcadios among the others, so similar was he, apart from the officer's tunic he wore now. The former singulares archer was jogging out of the ranks toward him.

'What is it?'

'I cannot say for certain, sir,' the archer said, quietly, 'but I am fairly sure we're being watched.'

Fronto's attention once more shot to his surroundings as he scoured a circuit. To the right, down the gentlest of slopes, a sizeable dark lake brooded, mist rising from its waters and wreathing around the grasses and reeds protruding from the surface all around the edge. The front of the column had not yet reached the end of the lake. Both ahead and behind, scrubland stretched away to distant treelines and to the left the ground sloped up very gradually, with deep dry grasses and pine trees scattered across the landscape like the pox.

'How can you tell?' Fronto replied to the archer. 'Where?'

Arcadios shrugged. 'Across the lake. I have seen movement in the trees over there three times now. Too big to be creatures in the undergrowth, too small to be deer or bear.'

'Could a good archer take shots at us across the water with any real hope of success?'

'A *good* one, yes. They would have to be *very* good, but then I have heard they do have excellent hunters in these regions. It is possible that this is all innocent, of course, sir. Movement does not make them necessarily the enemy. Perhaps they're hunters?'

'Perhaps.' But something that was running along Fronto's spine like a frisson of energy said otherwise. 'Regardless, could you get the best archers and slingers on the right flank and have them as ready as they can be. And have a word with Atenos. I want the legionaries ready to shield them if need be'

'You expecting trouble, sir?'

'Always expect trouble, Arcadios, that way you're never taken unawares.'

Glancing around as the archer scurried off to carry out the orders, Fronto scanned the area until he spotted Galronus and a small unit of mounted scouts ambling back toward them, unconcerned. There were, of course, no Aquitanii among the native scouts, since he intended to pick up local help at Lapurda, but there were one or two southern Gauls from around the Burdigala area who had been part of both Crassus' and Caesar's expeditions, and were familiar with the region.

As he watched the scouts close on him, Fronto turned to see the senior centuries of the First Cohort tromping along behind him. He could just see Arruntius leading the Second Century immediately behind Atenos' First. Turning his horse, he dropped back along the column and fell into position alongside the ageing centurion.

'Arruntius?'

'Sir?'

'One of the men thinks he saw human movement among the trees across the lake. It's too tight woodland for horse, but I think we'll all feel a lot happier if we check it out. Pick two contubernia of your fittest, fastest men. Tell them to leave their pila and any extra weight here. Get them ready to run out and check over the woods. I'll have a couple of scouts go with them.'

Arruntius nodded and turned, selecting two squads of eight men and relaying the orders. Leaving the centurion to it, Fronto rode forward again to see Galronus. Fortunately one of the riders coming in with the Remi noble was one of those same Burdigalan natives he had been introduced to at Nemetocenna before they left.

'Might be trouble in the woods,' the legate murmured to Galronus, pointing out across the misty lake. I'm having two tent-parties of the best men run around and check it out but a couple of scouts, especially the more local ones, might be very helpful.'

Galronus nodded, and detailed two men to dismount and join the legionary party that was rapidly forming to the right. 'Do we wait?' the Remi asked quietly.

'No. Keep the column moving. Whatever happens I want to get to Lapurda fast. This place is feeling less friendly with every mile south we travel. In fact, I'm quite tempted to say screw the exhaustion and march through the night. If my calculations are right we could be there by dawn if we really push it. The men'll be ragged, mind.'

Galronus rolled his shoulders. 'Give the men a couple of days off when we arrive and you could march them over coals tonight.'

'Pass the word, then. We'll do that. No one in this column is going to be unhappy we're not camping in this shitty place, anyway.'

Fronto felt his nerves beginning to twang and the hairs stand proud on the back of his neck. He'd always had a talent for anticipating trouble, and could feel that odd sense beating at the fringes of his consciousness right now. Those men were no hunters, he was sure. But why were they watching the Roman column, and was it connected with that empty village in some way?

In the two days they had marched since that grisly discovery, they had passed through four settlements and each had felt less friendly than the dangerous and threatening dark alleyways of the

Subura in Rome. None of the villagers had been talkative beyond necessary answers and most had no command of Latin, claiming communication difficulties as an excuse not to talk to the Romans, despite the presence of able translators. None had been able – or more likely *willing* – to comment on their findings at the deserted village. There had been nothing specifically threatening about any of them, and nothing that Fronto could call them out on, but he had certainly felt unwelcome. And now there were hidden observers in the woodland? He was starting to regret having brought just the one legion after all. Perhaps Caesar could have spared the Tenth too. And he could have found a way to manage them all in the passes.

Shit.

He watched, his heart thumping, throat dry and forehead damp, as the small unit of legionaries and scouts pounded off through the undergrowth, rounding the end of the lake and making for the woodland on the far side. Now, even as he watched, Fronto could see the shape of a figure moving through the trees.

All seemed too quiet, and he was on the verge of having a musician blow the recall when the trouble began. As the eighteen men ran at the tree line a burst of arrows shushed forth from among the dark trunks. Fronto watched grimly as the shafts thudded into his men. Half a dozen legionaries fell, unable to get their shields up in time against the unexpected onslaught. He had no idea how many of the enemy there were, but there were enough to create a good cloud of arrows, certainly.

Recall or attack?

There was no choice, really. The very idea of leaving a threat unchallenged on their flank made him twitch.

'Atenos, have the advance sounded. We move at the double and each century forms testudo as they close on the treeline. I don't want to lose anyone we don't have to.'

As the legion fell into ranks and began to turn, breaking into a run through the undergrowth around the southern edge of the lake, Fronto kept his horse at pace with them. He could do no good on his own, and most of the cavalry were at the rear. Besides, among the trees they would be useless. He tutted to himself over his foolishness sending out such a small party when he'd already been convinced they would encounter trouble.

There was no sign of faltering among that unit, though. A dozen men were now moving on the trees, shields held high and tight, the native scouts sheltering behind them. Even as he watched, closing inexorably on the fight alongside the legion, a second arrow volley took out two more legionaries and one of the scouts. With a roar, the remaining eight soldiers charged into the woodlands, while the unarmoured scout dropped to the thick high grass out of sight. Clearly whichever legionary had seniority among the men had made the call that they were better charging an uncertain enemy than moving slowly and gradually being picked off with arrows. He may have been correct, but Fronto couldn't escape the conclusion that they would all be dead before help arrived. Perhaps the scout had had the better idea.

'At the run,' Fronto shouted. The men were tired. They had marched most of the day, and for the three preceding days, and yet the order was carried out without complaint, each and every man in the legion picking up his pace so that he was pounding headlong through the undergrowth, heedless of danger. One or two runners would probably fall foul of rabbit holes, but nine men were at risk now in the woods, probably already dying, and Fronto didn't want them to have died needlessly, allowing time for the enemy to prepare. The legion had to fall on the archers while they were still recovering from the first attack, lest it be wasted.

Regardless of the danger, as they closed on the trees, Fronto dropped from his horse, handing the reins to a surprised legionary. 'Take care of him,' he huffed as he ran. 'He's an old friend.'

The legionary ducked out of the column with Bucephalus as Fronto grappled his shield from him and took it in his fist, running full pelt to catch up and fall into place in the soldier's position. The others stared at him in disbelief as they ran but conversation was impossible, partially due to the heavy breaths of exhaustion and partially due to the sudden blaring of cornu and buccina and the throaty bellow of thousands of legionaries charging at the trees.

Moments later Fronto's world became one of sweat and pain, darkness and confusion as the men ran in among the trees. He had taken the position of a man from the First century and, though he couldn't see him, he could hear Atenos' voice calling out orders. Obedient to his junior officer, he joined his fellow soldiers, fanning out to the left, leaping fallen timbers, the bracken and undergrowth whipping at his bare shins, the combination of under-canopy gloom and heavy helmet restricting his vision and hearing.

He knew they were too late when he tripped and almost fell headlong over the twisted body of a legionary peppered with dark shafts. He staggered for a moment and pulled himself upright, sword out and lashing, expecting trouble, until another call from Atenos drew them all up short. Fronto found himself obeying instinctively and he peered around, trying to take in the confused situation. The bodies of legionaries were scattered across the dark undergrowth beneath the trees, each riddled with arrows. The enemy had not resorted to meeting them blade to blade, but had continued to fall back as the legionaries entered the trees, picking them off as they approached. It had been a massacre. One corpse had no less than twelve arrows jutting from him where he lay slumped against the bole of a tree.

Fronto broke ranks and jogged out front to join Atenos. The centurion seemed entirely unsurprised to see his commander suddenly in the fight, hefting a legionary shield.

'If you're going to join in, I'm going to have to issue you with a pilum, sir,' he noted drily. But both men were intent on the enemy, really, rather than conversation. There was clearly no chance of catching them, which was why Atenos had called the halt, to preserve their energy from a hopeless chase. The archers were already some distance away through the woods and rapidly disappearing from sight. They clearly had no intention of sticking around to face off against a legion.

'Shit,' Fronto grunted, wiping his mouth with his wrist. 'We're going to have to move very carefully from now on. It appears that we are finally in enemy territory proper.'

He became aware of laboured breathing by his side and turned to see Arcadios, heaving in deep breaths, Galronus close behind, with his long Gallic blade out at the ready.

'Where did you...'

'Hush now,' interrupted Arcadios as though speaking to a noisy child, and Fronto frowned himself into silence. Even as he formulated an indignant reply, the archer whipped his bow from his shoulder, drew an arrow with a single swift motion, nocked it and released with barely a pause.

63

Fronto watched the arrow fly. At the rear of the departing ambushers one man seemed to be struggling with his leg, though his anguish at being left behind was quickly snuffed as the Cretan's arrow plunged deep into the back of his neck and he fell.

'Find him,' Arcadios barked at two gawping legionaries. 'Bring him back.'

Fronto turned to the archer, who was slinging his bow across his shoulders once more. 'Damn good shot.'

As the legionaries began the grisly business of making sure their comrades were dead and snapping off the arrows so that they could be moved comfortably, Fronto, Atenos and Arcadios stood watching the fallen enemy being located, collected and carried back through the woodland.

'What do we do with the dead, sir?' a legionary asked Atenos, who in turn glanced the question to Fronto.

'Put them in the wagons. We haven't got time to stick around and bury them, and I don't want any cremations that'd send a column of smoke up to the sky telling everyone exactly where we are. If we march hard we'll be in Lapurda before dawn and the dead can be honoured and laid to rest there.'

Atenos nodded and issued the appropriate orders. Most of the cohort was now moving back out of the woodland to join the rest of the legion, who were returning to the column and to the Tenth Cohort who had remained to guard the valuable baggage train.

The native scout who had dived into the grass a few dozen paces from the trees had arrived now and was standing near Arcadios, brushing himself down, his face angry and bleak. He watched, hawk-eyed, as the legionaries brought the body of the ambusher across and laid him on a fallen tree-trunk. The man was clearly dead. His leg displayed a deep cut, which had clearly been the reason for his slowness and tardiness, the only blow the small force of legionaries seemed to have managed to land. But Arcadios' arrow had plunged through the neck, transfixing the man as it burst out through his vein, bleeding him dry in moments.

'I'd have liked to question him,' Fronto grumbled.

'You were damn lucky I hit him at all, sir,' Arcadios snapped. 'This dampness is playing merry Hades with my bow string.'

Fronto smiled sheepishly at the archer. 'Of course. And it was, as I said, a most excellent shot.' He called the native scout across and pointed at the body. 'Can you tell us anything of use?'

The scout was a native of the Bituriges Vivisci from just south of Burdigala, not a native Aquitanian, but his knowledge would still be unparalleled in the column, after two campaigns in the region.

'He is not a local,' the scout said in a flat, matter-of-fact tone.

'How so?'

'We're in the lands of the Tarbelli, spitting-distance from the Sibusates, Legate. What have you seen of the Aquitanii we've encountered between Burdigala and here?'

Fronto frowned. 'Nothing special. They look like all Gauls, I suppose.' Galronus nodded his agreement, as he sheathed his blade and stepped forward. 'Looks like all the ones I fought under Crassus: the Sotiates, Vocates and Tarusates.'

'Precisely. But remember, they're Aquitanii, not Gauls.' He glanced at Galronus. 'The lowlanders are influenced by the border tribes, including my own Bituriges. All the ones you fought were lowlanders. They wear moustaches and braid their hair back. They wear tunics and light trousers with leather shoes. Look at the body, sir.'

Fronto did so, and his brow creased further. The dead archer was clad in furs and his legs were tightly bound with wraps. He wore a beard like a Greek philosopher, though shaggier and dirtier, and his hair was long and wild, like a dandelion gone to seed. 'So who is he then?'

'One of the mountain men, sir. The southern tribes. If I had to guess, I would say Begerri or Consoranni.'

'And they're not local, then.'

'Maybe sixty or so miles southeast, in the foothills and mountains of the Pyrenaei, sir.'

'Then what in Hades' icy arse cheeks are they doing all the way down here loosing arrows at a Roman column. Something odd is happening in this region. There's more to it than meets the eye. This isn't just scattered flames of revolt – not if tribes are far outside their own territory. Reminds me more of the months before Vercingetorix's revolt. This is not good. Not good at all. Get the men ready to move immediately. We march double time through the night. I want to be behind the walls of Lapurda as soon as possible.'

Who are you? He asked the body silently as his men scurried back to work. *What are you doing here?*

* * *

Lapurda was not a sight, even in the early dawn light, to cause sighs of relief to the anxious column. The region had only been even sparsely explored by Rome over the past half-decade, and direct control and influence were less than a year old. The Lapurda fort had been constructed following Caesar's visit and, though it was clearly destined to become a permanent fixture, at this point it resembled a temporary camp more than a lasting fortification, with timber parapets above turf ramparts and wooden buildings within with no stone footings. The fort stood on a small hill to the south and west of a confluence of rivers, with a ferry in place across the more major one to the north and a new bridge across the smaller one to the east.

The fort was occupied, which at least was a relief, for there were figures moving around on the walls and smoke rising from one or two buildings. No civilian vicus had yet grown up around the place on the slopes, but a sizeable native village lay a little to the west on the river bank. Fronto wasn't sure what he'd been expecting – a small island of civilisation in a wild and dangerous region, perhaps – but the small, meagre fort failed to live up to whatever expectations they were.

Moreover, the chances of the legion fitting inside the walls were non-existent. The fort was just big enough for a small garrison of perhaps five hundred men. Five thousand was simply impossible. The walled safety they had all looked forward to evaporated instantly, and Fronto could almost feel the column sag with the realisation that they would still have to camp in tents outside the place, still setting guards and living 'campaign-style'. Moreover, the bath house below the fort visible from across the river could hardly hold more than ten or twenty people, and five thousand tired, dirty soldiers had just hoved into view, each hoping for a bath. Even in shifts they would still be cycling round by dusk.

Fronto straightened. He had worked with worse, and perhaps the place would look more inviting when the sun was fully up and not just a golden glow on the eastern hillsides.

'Carbo? You need to organise everything here with the legion. I can't see us getting more than twenty men at a time across that ferry, so it's going to take most of the day. And you'll need to start setting up camp on the far side as close to the fort as you can manage. We'll be staying for a few days, so make it good. I'm going to take a few of the others on the first crossing and visit the commander.'

The camp prefect nodded his understanding and began to give orders to the various centurions and signallers. Fronto gestured to his companions. 'Atenos? I want you there, and Masgava, Galronus, Decius and Aurelius. Also centurions Terpulo and Arruntius. Come on.'

As the seven named men pulled out forward, Fronto slid from Bucephalus and handed the reins over to a legionary. The eight of them then strode down to the ferry on the bank. The Aturrus River was wide – two hundred paces at an estimate – fast flowing, and clearly deep. Not a river to play around with. Snaking a further four miles through the countryside, it carried vast quantities of mountain water and emptied it into the ocean to the west. There were no personnel on the jetty, but a huge pewter gong hung on twin ropes, dents and dips across its surface mute testimony to its regular use. A long stick hung beside it with a lead ball at the end, and Fronto picked up the ringer, took a deep breath and banged the gong three times. The sound was deep and ear-splitting, and the echoes and reverberations carried up and down the river, ringing along valleys and through trees.

Two figures at the far bank emerged from a small hut and peered across the river before hastily unfastening the ferry from the bank and pushing it out into the current. As one punted them away from the bank, the other slid his oars into their fittings and began to row. Moments later the other man followed suit and the craft slid quickly across the water, both men angling upstream to counter the current. They knew their jobs and the river well, for in short order they were pulling in to the jetty exactly on target, where they tied up and saluted the Roman officers waiting.

'Sirs. Welcome to Lapurda.'

Fronto nodded. 'Thank you. I need myself and the officers taking across, then slowly the legion will need to cross. Unless you have unlimited reserves of muscle, you might want to pass the job over to my men to take turns.'

The men shook their head. 'Not a good idea, sir. The Aturrus is a fetid bitch of a river, pardon my Greek. Unless you know what you're doing, the boat will end up a mile downriver or floating out into the ocean.'

'Then you've a tiring day ahead of you, soldier. But I take your point and thank you. I will make sure you are appropriately rewarded at the end of the day.'

Moments later they were aboard and the ferry was pushing out into the current once more. Aurelius made warding signs against ill luck and tipped a little wine from his skin into the water as an offering, desperately trying to guess the name of the god of this river. Fronto smiled at his superstitious bodyguard, then watched the high mound with its timber fort sliding slowly toward them.

'You seen the bridge, sir?' Centurion Terpulo muttered as they crossed. Fronto peered off toward the bridge that spanned the narrower channel at the confluence.

'What about it?'

'It's got a gate. And a guard unit. Like it's been fortified. Not a good sign. I think the garrison of Lapurda is nervous.'

'Great.' Just what he wanted. The people he was about to look to for support were seemingly as worried as those who were just arriving. His sense of unease grew as they neared the far bank. Closer examination exhibited more warning signs. There was no civilian vicus on the slope, though huge square shapes in the grass made it clear that one had *been* there, but had been removed mere days or weeks ago. Two watch towers had been constructed, rising from the northeast and southeast corners of the fort, adding visual coverage of the surrounding land. And Terpulo was right. The near side of the bridge had seen a hastily constructed palisade with a wooden gate, and half a dozen men seemed to be stationed there. With a gentle bump, they touched the jetty at the far side, and Fronto stepped onto the timbers, thanking the ferrymen for their smooth ride and once more promising them something later in gratitude. As the boat pushed out into the river once more, Fronto and his companions looked up the slope at the fort. The gates were firmly shut and there were more men atop the walls than Fronto would normally expect.

'Come on. Let's find out what's making them so nervous.'

The eight men walked quickly up the hill. As they approached the gate, Fronto was impressed to note that, although a defensive ditch seemed to have been begun and abandoned due to the difficulty of the terrain, sharpened stakes, lilia pits and obstacles *had* been placed, forming a triple defensive ring outside the walls, and small bolt throwers were in place on each low tower top, all of which trained on the new arrivals as they moved. The legate and his officers stopped twenty paces from the gate.

'Who goes there?' called a voice from above.

'Marcus Falerius Fronto and the officers of the Tenth Legion,' he called back brazenly. It was a lie in essence, for sure, but not being able to identify his legion would hardly settle these men's fear. And besides, several of these men *had* served as officers in the Tenth, so it was, strictly speaking, the truth.

He heard a voice from somewhere inside shout 'The relief is here,' and moments later the gate swung open. A centurion with a drawn face and hunted eyes stalked out to meet them, bowing as he came and then thrusting out a hand. 'Well met, sir. The Tenth. Glorious. The boss will be mighty pleased to hear that.'

Fronto shook the clammy hand, then surreptitiously wiped his own on his tunic. 'Well, let's not get ahead of ourselves. Can you show me to your commander. I need to see him immediately.'

The centurion nodded, his eyes flickering from man to man as he took in the motley bunch of new arrivals. Then he turned and marched inside once more, waving his vine cane.

'We were drawn from the Fourteenth during the general's visit for a one year duty here. We've done our best to make it liveable, but as you can see it's hardly palatial.'

'After four weeks on the march, you'd be surprised at what feels palatial,' Fronto smiled, trying to hide his visual disappointment at what their destination had turned out to be.

'And I'm looking forward to slipping into someone more comfortable,' grinned Terpulo. The local centurion turned an odd look on his counterpart. 'Then you're out of luck. The brothels and bars have been torn down and ejected. You might be able to find services in the local village, but you're putting both your life and your dick in their hands if you do.'

Fronto began to fidget as they walked. 'Looks like you're prepared for trouble, centurion.'

'Just playing it safe, sir. The boss will answer your questions.'

The headquarters building was a low timber affair with a single vexillum of the Fourteenth hanging above the door bearing Caesar's bull emblem. Even with the lamplight from within it did not look particularly inviting. The eight of them followed the centurion in and to the commander's office, where the local stepped inside, announced them, and then retreated again to make room. Fronto walked in with the others at his heels.

The man behind the desk looked tired and dispirited. His face was pale and his hair wild and uncombed. He was perhaps thirty years old, going on sixty. He wore an officer's tunic and belt, but no armour. He rose wearily as Fronto entered.

'Legate Fronto. Your reputation precedes you, as does that of the Tenth. I am Prefect Publius Didius Barba, commanding Lapurda outpost.'

Fronto inclined his head. 'I must apologise for a tiny misunderstanding. The Tenth are not with me. I have officers of the Tenth, but my legion is in effect a giant vexillation taken from all Caesar's active units, and without a designation of its own. We have an eagle and flags, but no number.'

'How peculiar,' Barba said, sitting once more. 'Do I then assume you are not the relief for whom we've been hoping?'

'Not exactly. Your centurion said you were here on a year's service. Surely you are not expecting relief yet?'

Barba waved to a chair, but Fronto shook his head and remained standing. 'Well,' the prefect explained, 'I've written more than ten missives now to the general asking for relief or aid. You see we're a little cut off down here, Legate Fronto. We control important routes for imports from Hispania into Gaul, and we are the only full-strength and permanent Roman installation in Aquitania. We effectively have the job of maintaining tax on imports and exports along the coast and ensuring the peace of the region.'

'And there comes my next question,' Fronto said quietly, but Barba held up a hand and went on.

70

'We are aware of trouble throughout the region. We contacted the general months ago and frankly we were beginning to think he'd forgotten about us, or didn't care. We used to have a nice comfortable supply situation here, what with goods coming in by sea and river and with ample trade with the natives. But then the native merchants stopped coming. And the Roman merchants stopped returning. And the locals refused to sell us their goods. Well, it was made clear by Caesar when Lapurda was established that we were here to maintain peace and cordial relations, so I thought it prudent not to force the issue. But I started sending patrols inland to try and find the missing merchants, to secure supplies and to investigate the vague reports we were getting of trouble. And the patrols never came back.'

'So what did you do?' Arruntius put in, stepping forward.

'Do? I sent half a century with a cavalry escort to find out what happened to my men. Can you guess what happened?'

'They never came back,' Fronto said quietly.

'Correct. I fretted about it for a while, then I bit the blade and sent a full two-century party with twenty cavalry. Might as well have tipped them into a deep hole. Never heard from them again. So rather than continue to throw good men away, I started to seal up Lapurda tighter than a Massilian's purse, to rely on seaborne supplies and to send repeated letters to Caesar asking for help. It had occurred to me that my couriers might well have met the same fate as the patrols and merchants, but it appears that at least one got through, because *you're* here.'

'The region does seem to be overwhelmingly hostile,' Terpulo noted. 'We ran into trouble two days north of here, and we've seen signs of older trouble too – killings and evacuated villages.'

The prefect nodded. 'We get weekly reports from those few locals who still speak to us, telling us of violence and burnings out there, but I've left them to it. I started the winter with four hundred men. I've a little over two hundred now, and only ten cavalry. My plan was to hold out until we got help or, if I heard nothing from Caesar, to wait 'til late summer and just abandon Lapurda and march north along the coast until we saw a friendly face.'

Fronto straightened. 'Alright, Didius Barba. I need to know everything you can tell me. We have been sent here to bring peace to the region. I am to put down insurrection and to settle veterans in strategic positions around Aquitanii territory.'

'Good, Legate. It will be nice to have allies in the area, even if they're retirees. The evocati are always a force to be reckoned with. I've hated being alone here. But I hope you know what you're up against. This lot aren't like the Gauls we fought a few years ago. They're harder and more bloody-minded. Less organised and less civilised, but more brutal. You have to kill them two or three times before they realise it and lie down.'

Atenos chuckled, and Fronto leaned on the desk. 'Tell me about the tribes, then.'

'Well the locals are the Tarbelli, with the Sibusates just beyond them. On the whole they seem to be calm. The Tarbelli are the ones who still get news to us, but even many of those are gone now. Most of the lowland tribes have deserted their settlements and moved up toward the foothills of the mountains. Don't ask me why. We tried to look into it, but when we look closely we get killed, so I stopped that. All the tribes had a Pax Gallica altar put in place during Caesar's visit. The Tarbelli still respect theirs, holding festivals around it and so on, but I've heard tales of the most appalling desecrations of our peace altars.'

The prefect poured himself a wine, didn't even look at the water jug, and took a swig. 'Then there are various other tribes. As I said, the lowlanders have more or less gone, moved up to the mountains and the foothills. That's the Sotiates, Elusates, Ausci, Vasates, Lactorates and Aturenses.'

'What of the Vocates and the Tarusates?' Galronus put in, noting the absence of those tribes from the list. 'I fought them under Crassus six years ago and they were not a force to be ignored.'

Barba gave the Remi noble an appraising look and nodded clearly impressed. 'The Tarusates are a negligible group. Your army crushed them so utterly those years ago that they'd have trouble raising enough warriors for a bar brawl, let alone an insurrection. And I think what remains of the Vocates consider themselves more part of Gaul than this lot, so they're still up by the Garonna River trying to be good. The Sibusates are the first proper tribe of the mountains heading east, and we've heard nothing from them. Word is their settlements are deserted, but we can't confirm that. Beyond them are the Begerri and they're nothing but trouble. They were even trouble when we were all theoretically at peace. Then there's the Aspiates up in the snowy valleys. They're worse. Skin their own mother over a bad stew, they would. And as for the Consoranni...? Well you're getting the picture. Then there are dozens of smaller tribes in the mountains, some of whom we know very little about. Some, like the Monesii and the Camponi, we don't even know the location of. It's complete *terra incognita* up in those mountains.'

'So,' Fronto huffed, 'if we're looking for the source of the trouble, it seems we want to head east into the mountains.'

'That sounds like the answer to me.'

'Good. Then that is what we shall do.' He turned to Galronus. 'Any knowledge of the mountain areas from your time down here?'

'Not much,' the Remi shrugged. 'We reached the foothills. We might be on the periphery of familiar regions. Some of the men of the Seventh went up into the passes after the campaign was over to crucify prisoners as a statement to the Aquitanii, but most of us stayed in the hills. Mountains are not good territory for cavalry, after all.'

The legate smiled at his friend and turned back to Prefect Barba. 'Now, my legion has travelled for four weeks on poor supplies. I do hope your ships bring in acceptable wine?'

'They do, Legate Fronto. We have shipments of Hispanic wines from Hispania Citerior. The same wines the nobiles drink in Tarraco. One of the few things we get plenty of.'

'Good. My men will need a few days' rest, then we'll be moving east. In the meantime, I want to learn every tiny morsel of information I can get about the region, and I want to drink some of that wine. Oh, and I promised a reward for the ferrymen who are busy making about seven hundred trips across the river with my men.'

Late Aprilis

IT was a lovely image. Caesar on his knees, his old bones and muscles creaking, that little scar below his eye twitching as his eyelid flickered with the tension. Would he beg for his life? Naturally, one would say no, for who could picture even in their imagination the great hero of Rome begging? And yet in the king's experience, everyone had their breaking point, no matter how proud and noble they might think they were. And with time he would find Caesar's. He would find that one tiny twist or jab that would make the general cry out and beg for his life.

It would be glorious.

It was one of two dreams that had kept that bitter smiling face content during the long, cold nights. The other... well, it was complicated, and while it made him grind his teeth and wish for blood and black vengeance and the end of everything, bringing the whole of mankind down into a boiling, cleansing pit of death and hate, it also left him crying when he awoke. A slave had caught him sobbing into his pallet once and had had to be killed, despite everything.

A cleared throat made the king open his eyes.

The hot spring was one of several in the high, snowy passes, and had been covered with a timber building that held in the heat, leaving the bathing king sweating in his water. None of the other warriors used it. They held that dirt was the gods' extra armour against cold and disease. Let them live with their superstitions. It made them easier to manipulate. He liked his warm water.

He blinked, remembering the clearing of a throat that had announced he was not alone. Shuffling back, he put his arms over the age-smoothed stone at the edge of the pool and took a deep, stifled, warm breath.

'Ah, good.'

The four men were roped together at the ankle, limiting them to three feet distance from one another, and their wrists were bound so tight that they bled. Their decoration and bearing, even in captivity, announced them to be chiefs and kings in their own right, even if they insisted on the ubiquitous wild beard and shaggy hair. Only four men had brought them in, but those four were good men, and well-armed, while the prisoners were bound and unarmed. With swift strikes behind the knees, accompanied by sharp yelps, the four chiefs were made to kneel.

Well, they weren't Caesar, but every dream had to start somewhere.

The smiling king took a deep breath, launching into powerful words in the jagged harsh tongue of the Aquitanii.

'Your tribes are small. Only small tribes remain. You cannot hold out on your own. When Rome comes for you, you will lose everything it is to be Aquitanii. Your name will vanish from the tongues of men and you will be merely lesser Romans like the Gauls and the Belgae. I offer you something more. Not a *lot* more, just to be sure. But a little. You will follow me and work toward my goals, or you will die. It is a remarkably simple choice. Speak.'

There was a long silence. The king examined his new prisoners. One he could see was going to be trouble. A younger man with haughtiness in his eyes. He had never experienced defeat. How naïve would he be? The answer came a moment later as the young chief opened his mouth.

'What assurances do we get? What do our people stand to gain?'

The king frowned at the young man for a moment, then gestured to a warrior behind them.

'My luck is clearly waning. I need more. Cut off his cock and have it dipped in lead.'

The young man's eyes bulged and he started to scream and struggle as two burly warriors freed him from his bonds, holding him tight, then stretched him out while a third drew a long, serrated knife. The young man was shrieking through floods of tears now, but the king turned his attention from the noise as it reached a crescendo. When the boy was dropped to the floor to bleed to death, the king smiled – some might say he had no choice about that, but *this* smile was genuine, and genuinely *nasty* – and pointed to something that glinted in the light of the lamps. The remaining three chieftains looked up at the king's standard where it leaned against the wall, eight lead penises hanging from the lower bar, occasionally clanking into one another.

'Even the Romans know the phallus brings luck. Now, let us continue. It is a simple choice: join me, or die…'

Chapter Four

'YOU would do well to leave a few men here,' Terpulo said, lifting one buttock from the wooden bench to let rip a fart that would have men in the nearby tents scrabbling around, holding everything down and waiting for the tremors.

Fronto, long since used now to the highly efficient yet highly peculiar centurion, swiftly took a huge swig of his wine then pulled up his scarf and wrapped it tightly around his nose and mouth. He would swear on the altar of Apollo himself that the air actually changed colour when Terpulo broke wind. Around the tent the others rushed to pull up their scarves, barring Aurelius, who had left his with his kit and, eyes wide in panic, excused himself quickly and ran outside ahead of the miasma.

'Will there be enough men who want to stay in to make a difference,' Fronto burbled through the muffling linen.

Terpulo blew out his cheeks and took a deep breath that should by rights kill him.

'Maybe settle a hundred or so lads here. Grant them land here and then they can be called on in trouble. I'm sure the prefect would be extremely grateful.'

'I'm sure he would,' Fronto agreed, 'but I might have need of those men myself when we ride out tomorrow. It might be months before we get back here.'

'A prefect's gratitude is never to be sniffed at,' Terpulo smiled. 'Especially a prefect who has control of the wine imports.'

'Gods but you'd laugh if you knew what I was doing this time last year,' Fronto snorted, wondering how Catháin was managing the business in his absence.

'We're still going to be within fast courier reach of Lapurda for a week or two yet,' Pulcher said through his muffling scarf. If we need supplies or to get information anywhere we might be relying on the goodwill of the prefect.'

Fronto nodded. He couldn't deny their logic.

'Alright. And I'll give them a little extra encouragement if they'll play courier for us too.'

There was a tentative knock at the door of the barrack block Fronto and his officers had taken for their own.

'Come.'

The door swung open and a legionary entered. Fronto watched with amusement as the air quality insisted itself on the soldier and his eyes started to water almost immediately. Not safe to remove the scarf yet then.

'What is it?'

The soldier stared helplessly at him, his face taking on a green tint.

Fronto frowned. 'Speak up, lad. Ignoring an officer can be a very unhealthy habit.'

Terpulo snorted. 'He can't answer you, Legate. He's a ghost.'

'What?'

'Caught him paying less attention to the landscape than to his own pimply arse. I ghosted him.'

Fronto's frown merely deepened, and Arruntius coughed. 'Terpulo declared the lad dead through his own incompetence. He's not allowed to speak, touch anything, eat, drink, or lie down until the first watch of the morning. He's a ghost, you see.'

Fronto chuckled. 'You're an inventive bugger, Terpulo. Hang on, isn't that…'

'Yes indeed,' Terpulo said with an edge of menace. 'Come on, soldier. Show me Mister Rusty.'

Fronto watched the poor lad he remembered from their first exercise, clearly the chosen butt of the centurion's humour, as he helplessly stood before the officer. The young man looked torn and panicky, unable to comply with his orders to produce the bottle of rust because he was now officially dead and not allowed to touch anything. He'd risked everything just to open the door, after all. Added to that, the miasma in the room was clearly beginning to make the lad feel light headed. Fronto worried for a moment whether the lad might faint.

Terpulo leaned forward and plucked the glass vial from the lad's belt pouch, examining it. He then did a quick circuit of the soldier.

'Rust free armour. Good. Just Mister Rusty in his bottle, and it looks to me like you've even polished the bottle.'

The young man looked hopeful for a moment.

'Shame you went and cocked it all up by failing to pay attention while on guard. You've been caught out twice, now. Only an idiot doesn't learn from his mistakes. Are you an idiot, Legionary Sidonius?'

The lad almost answered, then realised at the last moment, and shook his head.

'Good. Because where we're going we'll be fighting, and fighting hard, and I won't have time to coddle idiots. Back outside, lad. Still a ghost until first watch, though. Then you can get a bite to eat. And don't let me catch you a third time, else you'll lose your retirement benefits and I'll find a new hiding place for Mister Rusty.'

Dejected yet silent, the lad left, bowing to the officers as he closed the door.

Fronto removed the scarf, tested the air for a moment, then stuffed it back into place.

'You think the men will hold up well on campaign? Some of them are a little... advanced, let's say.'

Arruntius gave him a look that would wither steel, and Fronto had to concede he wouldn't want to question the veteran centurion's quality. One harsh look from him could cut a hole in a man.

'Fair enough,' he said quietly.

'I remember this mad old bastard at Sucro,' Pulcher snorted, gesturing at Arruntius. 'I'd just been promoted to the centurionate, and was desperate to make a name for myself. Saw myself as primus pilus of a legion within a year. Then I had my first lesson in humility. Arruntius here was already second most senior in the legion. Were you at Sucro, Legate?'

Fronto shook his head. The battle, fought around the Carthago Nova and Saguntum area during the Sertorian war, had taken place a dozen years before Fronto had even set foot in Hispania. That these men had been centurions two and a half decades ago was impressive.

'Well the whole thing was a mess. Sertortius was a good general. Pardon my saying so, as I know he's not a popular figure to revere in Rome these days, but if you were serving in his army there was nothing you wouldn't do for him.'

'You fought for Sertorius?'

That meant that for a short time at least, these men had been classified as enemies of Rome. With an odd jolt of kinship, he suddenly realised that he had more in common with them right now than they knew.

'We did. Sertorius met Pompey's army by the river bank and we all fought like crazed bastards. The battle was going nowhere. Both sides were just as good as each other – we were all legionaries, after all – and both were doing a good job of turning each other's flank, so we were starting to rotate like a giant bloody wheel. Then Sertorius rides down from the tribunal where he's been commanding, and tells the men he's damned if he's going to lose to Pompey. He starts kicking his horse forward and joining in. Well you can imagine the effect it had on the lads. Everyone started pushing that bit harder, and even though the general then retreats to his command post, the job's done. And the primus pilus shouts out that he'll give his own silver torc to the first man to break the enemy line. Well I went at it like a bull in a cowshed. I reaped the shit out of Pompey's forces that day, and I've still half a dozen scars to show for it. And I was way ahead of most.'

He grinned and sat back. 'I burst through the enemy's ranks into their reserves, leaving them a complete shambles, and I thought "This is it. I've done it. I'll be rich and famous."'

'And?' Fronto prompted.

'And there was Arruntius. He was already way ahead of me, surrounded by enemies, entirely on his own, and he almost killed Pompey. Got in a damn good cut. Saw it with my own eyes. Then it was chaos. All around us, our lads were breaking through and Pompey's lot were starting to run. And I just stood there like a stricken idiot, watching Arruntius grumbling because Pompey managed to ride off without dying.'

'Now I know you're pulling my leg,' Fronto laughed.

'Oh?'

The legate pursed his lips and leaned forward. 'You're telling me that Arruntius was the one who gave Pompey his scar? I've seen it. It was a hair's breadth from a killing blow!'

Pulcher reached up and pulled down his scarf, taking a tentative breath, then relaxed. 'Course, if we'd had Terpulo there we could have taken down a whole cohort at a time with a single gust. Juno, man but you need to put a plug in that thing.'

Terpulo chuckled. 'Careful, Pulcher. I could take umbrage at that, and I know where you sleep.'

Fronto laughed and removed his own gag, taking a strong pull of wine. Along with his own veterans he was grateful to have the support of men such as these. In the morning they would march into Sibusate territory and, while that tribe might still be loyal, they might equally be either absent or belligerent. Who knew what the unknown lands of Aquitania held? One thing of which Fronto was absolutely certain: there would be a hard fight involved somewhere.

* * *

The journey through Tarbelli lands and into those of the slightly more distant Sibusates took two days. Well rested, the column had made good time, following the Aturrus River inland for some forty miles. And over the past five or six, the native scouts, augmented with a small group of loyal Aquitanii from Lapurda, had confirmed that they were in the territory of the Sibusates.

There was one notable difference between the two tribes' lands. Life.

The Tarbelli they had passed had been quiet and withdrawn, clearly uncertain and unhappy about the Roman army among them and the situation among their neighbours, holding to their oath and causing no trouble, selling goods as requested. The less cultivated, more forested lands of the Sibusates had yet, in those five or six miles, to yield a single human being, just as Prefect Barba had indicated. Two villages they'd passed had been completely bare, just like the one they found on the slope south of Burdigala. The similarities had everyone looking to the trees for archers.

Moreover, Fronto was starting to become convinced that even the animals were shunning this place, for birds were scarce and rustling in the undergrowth seemingly absent. His fears were in no way laid to rest by the presence of Aurelius, who was currently strung tighter than a ballista, and when the man snapped, Fronto didn't want to be around.

Finally, though, the scouts reported that the first major settlement of the Sibusates, a place called Sorda, was close. Shortly thereafter, the river forked, the more major channel running almost due east, while a lesser channel branched off southeast toward the distant mountains. There was a brief discussion as to chosen route, but with this Sorda lying less than two miles along the southern branch, that was the clear choice and the army picked up the pace automatically, sensing the end of the march approaching. Fronto gestured to Carbo, who was riding close by, and the bald, pink-faced officer trotted ahead to join him.

'Sir?'

'When we get to Sorda, the first thing will be to confirm whether or not they are holding to their oath. On the assumption they are remaining loyal, or at least professing to do so, we will set up camp somewhere close by, send in a diplomatic party and try to trade with them. Let's set up talks, make sure we're all good friends, and then ply them for information. The Tarbelli seemed to know nothing about what was going on, but this lot are closer to the trouble, and they should know more. The scouts say the town is on the north bank of the river, but the river is quite narrow here and there should be a bridge.'

Carbo chewed his lip reflectively.

'And if they *haven't* held to their oath?'

'Then I daresay we'll find that out pretty quickly. Besides, there's still a chance the place will be empty like all the other places we've found. Pass the word to Atenos and the others. As we approach the river I want everyone ready. Be prepared for anything. For archers, in particular.'

'Sir.'

Carbo dropped back with the instructions and Fronto waited tensely for a few moments as Bucephalus' steady gait carried him along the greensward between the wooded flanks. The scouts had already checked out the forest, so there was supposedly no chance of another surprise attack like the one back at the lake, but Fronto had not lived to his good age by presuming safety.

What had happened to these tribes? Like the Tarbelli, this Sibusates lot had been hungry consumers of Roman goods, including wine. They had sold their goods to the local traders and garrison, and then, as if plucked from the land by the hands of the gods, the whole bunch of them seemed to have vanished.

Fronto remembered times in northern Hispania when he'd seen similar things. In Caesar's time as governor of Hispania Ulterior, he had led an army into the northern tribes of that peninsula, sending Fronto via Tarraco and the east to become the second pincer along the southern line of the Pyrenaei. Several times he had encountered empty tribal lands, just like these, though the reason for that had been the advance of a belligerent Roman force. The same could not be said in Aquitania. The peoples here had left long before the Romans arrived.

'It's not like Hispania,' he muttered, willing the trees to move aside so he could see this town of Sorda.

'In what way?'

He looked around to see that Galronus had fallen in alongside him.

'I found deserted lands when I led the Ninth across northern Hispania, but they were fleeing from us, which is not what's happening now.'

'How did you end up in northern Hispania,' the Remi officer asked with a quizzical look. 'I understand Caesar was governor in the south.'

Fronto nodded. 'It's complicated. We were there twice. Oh, I think it was sixteen or seventeen years ago when Caesar went to Gades as a quaestor and I went with him as a junior tribune. He'd pulled strings, you see, to have friends moved into the province with him. I took up a place with the Ninth, who were still a pretty new legion. I got to know Hispania quite well that year, and when Caesar returned to Rome I stayed on for another year and went to serve as an attaché to the governor of Citerior up in Tarraco, a lunatic by the name of Popillius Aquila. Got to know the north as well as I had the south. When I went back to Rome, my family tried to force me up the Cursus Honorum with not a great deal of success, and basically I kicked my heels for a while. I fell in with Caesar and when my father died and I inherited the estates, I helped fund the general quite a bit. So when he went back to Hispania Ulterior as governor four years later, I naturally went with him, as did Verginius.'

'Back to the south, though.'

'Yes. But he had a plan this time. Hispania was mostly untouched lands and unknown tribes, and they had gold. A lot of it. Caesar looked at the tribes to the north and saw a way to pay off the huge debts he'd run up in Rome securing his positions. He led two legions up from Italica into the untouched lands fighting a war not of conquest but of loot. And because he was a little worried about what his counterpart the governor of Tarraco might say, he sent me and Verginius there with the Ninth. Well it turned out that the new governor, Vedius Caepio, was a much more accommodating man than the last one I'd met. For a promise of a share in the spoils, he lent me an extra legion and I took the Seventh and the Ninth across the southern edge of the mountains and crushed the tribes against Caesar's force. The armies joined up and... well there was a bit of a mix up and Verginius paid the price.'

'And Caesar went back to Rome rich,' Galronus noted with an odd sour tone. Fronto sighed. Sometimes it was easy to forget that his friend had been born to a tribe who had similarly watched Rome's boundaries roll across their lands. But perhaps talk of Faleria's former betrothed had helped change the mood too.

'He did. And once again I stayed for a year and sorted everything out with Caepio in Tarraco. To be honest, I didn't really need to stay, and Caesar was urging me to return with him. But after Verginius, I just wanted to wallow in drink and misery on my own for a while. And I couldn't face returning to Faleria. I almost turned into my father that year. I drank Hispania dry. Only the arrival of the new governor stopped me. He was a miserable bastard, Figulus. He told me to go. Wouldn't have a drunk on his staff, and sent me packing back to Rome. I didn't care anyway. The Ninth had shipped out for Cisalpine Gaul, so most of my mates had already gone. I went back to Rome, hoping Caesar would still find me a place with the Ninth. Instead I spent another year in the city being glared at by Faleria before Caesar secured me the Tenth.'

He sat back and stretched. 'The rest you know. Half a year later we were marching north against the Helvetii. I do sometimes miss Hispania, though. I spent one miserable drunken year there, but three happy ones. It gets under your skin, does Hispania. It's warmer than Gaul, and more temperate. I'll take you to Tarraco some day. Feels like a second home even now.'

Galronus said nothing, his face still brooding, and Fronto sought to change the subject. 'Look,' he said, pointing ahead. 'That must be Sorda.'

The trees had pulled away from the left of the field, giving them a clear view of the river. The land was relatively flat, and the torrent that rushed through it narrowed for a while. Where it did so, with old beech and chestnut trees dotted along the near bank, a township sat on the northern shore. It was the most sizeable place they had passed through since Lapurda, with perhaps two dozen houses and two or three farms around the edge, a large open square at the centre and a sturdy timber bridge across the river.

And it was empty. That much was clear already. No noise, no movement, no sign of smoke rising from chimneys.

'The Sibusates have abandoned their centres and moved into the hills, also,' Galronus noted.

'It certainly appears that way.' Fronto gestured at Atenos, who was stumping along behind them in conversation with Carbo. 'Looks like the place is empty. Sun will be going down in the next few hours, so have camp set up on the grass opposite the town. I'm taking a few cavalry and checking the place out.'

Atenos saluted and Fronto continued to walk Bucephalus slowly forward while Galronus gathered a turma of horse. Once they were assembled, Fronto gave the signal and the small force rode off ahead of the column. Already two scouts were sitting at the bridge waiting for them, and Fronto couldn't help but note the grim expressions on their faces as they sat patiently.

'Problems?'

'The scout simply pointed across the river, and Fronto's gaze passed over the bridge and the gurgling waters beneath to the square at the centre of Sorda. High-sided wagons stood in the middle, forming a crescent with its back to them. Roman wagons.

'That can't be good,' Fronto muttered, and urged Bucephalus on with his knees. Despite the clear emptiness of the place, Fronto found he had drawn his sword and was riding with it readied. 'Come on.'

With the cavalry and the scouts falling in behind, Fronto and Galronus trotted onto the bridge, their hooves clunking on the heavy timbers as they crossed the torrent and entered the town – a small affair without walls. Fronto suddenly found himself fixing on that point and a notion began to form.

'I've not seen any walled places yet apart from Lapurda's Roman garrison. They don't seem to have oppida down here like that Gauls. Is it possible that they've pulled out of places that aren't defensible? If that's the case, then we really might have a big fight coming.'

Galronus shrugged. 'The Aquitanii are a different people. As different to ours as are the tribes across the Rhenus. More so, perhaps. I can tell you that we fought walled settlements a few years back, but they were to the north and east, in the lowlands, closer to the borders of the Nitiobriges, the Cadurci and the Volcae. But they were not mountain people. Who can say what goes on this far south?'

It was with a mounting sense of dread that Fronto led his men from the bridge and into the town, circling slowly around the edge, his eyes darting to the windows and doors of the surrounding structures and to the rear sides of the high vehicles. He found that, as he approached the end of the wagon line, he was chewing nervously on the inside of his cheek. It was no ambush that awaited him, and he felt safe enough. The birds were still chirping overhead, so he felt sure they were in no danger, but his nostrils had started to catch just the faintest whiff of carrion, and that sickly-sweet smell of decay never boded well for anyone.

Sure enough, the dead awaited them within the curve of the wagons.

Fronto found himself instinctively averting his eyes as he came into view of the unpleasant tableau, lifting his scarf with his free hand and covering his face in the same manner he did when in a confined space with Terpulo.

The whole Roman caravan was here, in Sorda. They were dead, but they were here. The wagons were empty, looted and broken, and their masters and operators had been cruelly murdered. The slaves, guards and hirelings lay in neat rows on their backs, arms by their sides and legs straight, and each one's head rested on the pit of his stomach. Each one seemed to be glaring accusingly at Fronto, and he found it difficult to pull his eyes from them, though the rest of the scene was, if anything, worse.

Three men had been crucified. One – the centre one – though he was already in an advanced state of decomposition and weathering, had clearly been a fat and fulsome man. The faded and pecked tunic he wore was a rich and very carefully-tailored one, and Fronto would be willing to bet it had come from Rome itself.

A filthy blue cloak lay tangled on the ground beneath him, the no doubt expensive brooch that had fastened it taken by his killers.

On one side of him was a man in a similar tunic, though of less high quality. He was likely some sort of factor or overseer, judging by his appearance, but his lesser status had not saved him from the same fate as his master. On the far side, the other figure was clearly a heavy – the leader of the caravan's guards, presumably. He had the build of a former soldier or fighter, and wore a tunic that, though year-worn and stained and now scratched at by carrion feeders, may well have once been the russet red of a legionary.

Crucified.

All three with a 'T' shaped structure to which they had been bound and then nailed in place. The heavy had been the only one to attempt escape, for his hands and feet were mangled where he had torn them clear of the nails. The other two had died hopelessly and slow, surrounded by the headless bodies of their servants, pecked at by crows.

But even this was not what truly drew Fronto's gaze.

In the centre of the clearing was an altar bearing the words PAX GALLICA. And the whole damn thing was a dark brown with old blood, crusted and stained and with lumps of unspeakable stuff clagged to it.

'I know you keep saying the Aquitanii are not like the Gauls,' Fronto murmured through the blessed cover of his scarf, 'but is crucifixion one of their things? I've never heard of it in Gaul or among the Belgae or Germanic peoples, so I'm surprised to see it here. And the nails and timbers they've used were taken from the wagons.' Fronto's lip curled with distaste. 'Do you think this was the Sibusates before they left, or has someone done this afterwards?'

'Hard to tell,' Galronus murmured, peering at the bodies. 'What I do remember is that Crassus had the captives of the Vocates and the Tarusates crucified up in the mountains as a warning to the locals not to pick up the revolt and not to involve the tribes from the other side of the mountains.'

'Bit long to harbour a grudge, though. Surely they'd have done that the next season, as soon as Crassus pulled out. One thing that's certain,' Fronto said quietly, 'is that this is a statement. This was left to be found. It's no ritual thing. And using Roman nails and Roman timbers to perform a Roman execution? This was left to be found by *us*. Someone around here hates Rome enough to not only break his oath, but to take the whole damn region with him. Come on, let's get back and tell the others, and send a detail to clean this up and bury the dead.'

* * *

Morning had broken with sullen discomfort. The legions had lost that energy with which new campaigns often began, forced out by the sour recollection of what was going on in the region. The small, low mound that covered the unnamed Roman dead across the river had drawn almost all eyes until they were out of sight of Sorda.

The army was full of veterans. No one had served less than five years, and most had served at least four times that number, and yet they were soldiers who had spent much of the previous decade fighting the ongoing wars in Gaul and few of them had had the misfortune to see civilian casualties. Or if they had they had usually been enemy ones and therefore easily dismissed, of course. A few, Fronto presumed, had seen the aftermath of the revolt at Cenabum. But for most of them the sight of murdered, abused and dishonoured Roman civilians was a new and appalling thing.

It had sucked some of the spirit from the campaign, but Fronto was not worried about that, because in its place during the last hour or so had formed a hardened diamond of determination to revenge themselves upon the bastards who were committing such atrocities.

The average soldier was a base thing. He thought of money, and of whores and food and wine. As he got a little older, he started to think of wives and children and of retirement. But Rome bred a certain type of warrior, and Fronto had seen it time and again. Where other nations relied on their citizens taking up arms when required – as Rome once had – Fronto's people had developed a whole warrior class who took the call to the legions for half a decade or more and made it their life. And yet despite this reliance on war as a way, they still looked to Rome as an ideal that they were bringing to the enemy. To many they were a force of civilisation, pushing back the ridiculous boundaries of the outdated barbarian world. And when they saw things that did not conform with their ideal of a civilised world, it was surprising how even the lowest, meanest legionary began to see himself as an advocate of culture.

Now, civilisation was coming to Aquitania. And it was wearing hob-nailed boots and brandishing a sword to make it's point felt.

Fronto was just contemplating the nature of his strange veteran legion, who marched in silence with the determination of a disciplinarian, when the column hit trouble.

Fronto had dropped back to ride alongside Carbo, hoping in some way that the usually-cheerful prefect would initiate light conversation and lift his dour spirits. The two men had, however, ridden along side by side in silence, for Carbo's expression was unusually dark. Ahead, the infantry column was led by the First century of the First cohort as usual, with a turma of cavalry at the fore to react swiftly to anything they found, and scouts ranging up to a mile ahead, checking out woodlands and dips for potential trouble. They had missed it, apparently.

The scream was the first thing that attracted Fronto's attention and warned him. It was an unearthly, shrill noise, and it was followed two heartbeats later by another.

Exchanging concerned glances with Carbo, Fronto nodded and slapped the reins on Bucephalus. Even as Carbo halted the column and gave the order for each century to fall in with their shields out and swords drawn, Fronto was riding forward to the cavalry, whence the scream had come.

The horse had pulled up short and even danced backwards a little, and Fronto took in the scene with dismay. One of the lead horses had accidentally found a hole in the turf. His leg had dropped into the dip and had broken as the beast's momentum had carried it forward.

Such a thing was regrettable, but happened from time to time. So many of nature's creatures burrowed holes in the grass that it was a constant fear for riders. And yet a second horse had done the same some fifteen feet away, and that was too much to be a coincidence. As the distraught cavalrymen went about the regrettable business of cutting their mounts' throats to save them from worse pain to come, Fronto frowned and dropped from

Bucephalus to the turf. The grass here was deep – at least a hand width. And yet, despite the funny looks he was getting from the others, he crouched in it and looked out across the land a mere foot from the turf.

The grass dipped repeatedly. It was hard to tell looking down on it, but from a more level position he could see that the meadow was honey-combed with holes like the ones that had claimed two horses so far. Even as he stood to call out another horse at the far side of the column, who had strayed a little too far from the group, fell into another.

'Don't move!' Fronto bellowed, and ran forward, brushing at a dip in the grass. The hole within went down two feet and was almost a foot in diameter. Just right to break a horse's leg. Or to maim a legionary for that matter. It was disturbingly close to the lilia pits Roman forces dug around their fortifications, filled with spiked timbers.

He dropped again and scanned the ground. The dips were everywhere. The turf sloped down to the river on the right, and the holes went right the way to the bank. And they covered the rise in the other direction to where it met woodland.

'What is it?' Galronus asked, riding up and reining in a safe distance back.

'Lilia pits. Someone has dug pits for hundreds of paces along the grass, from the river to the woods. Someone wanted to cripple cavalry. It's my bet that whoever set this up meant to draw an army to it and them cripple them and come in for the kill. Perhaps we've somehow messed up their plans and found it first. Either way we've lost three horses, but if we'd hit this field charging, half our cavalry would be gone.'

'So someone expected us to come this way.'

'I guess so. Whoever made that statement at Sorda is presuming we'd follow the river toward the mountains. You know, I'm very much inclined to double back a few miles and cross the hill to the other branch of the river, then follow that east.'

'Unless whoever did this was expecting it to turn you back and send you that way?'

Fronto looked up sharply at Galronus. 'Gods, I hope they're not clever enough to think like that, or we're in the deepest of shit.'

Early Maius

THE four scouts sat astride their horses on the slope of the hill beneath the shade of a small stand of pines. The morning was already warming for a hot day. The riders' beasts snorted and pawed the turf impatiently, having remained in place for almost half an hour. Indeed, the scouts themselves were beginning to get twitchy.

Below, the Roman column had turned back from the traps, leaving the pitiful bodies of a few horses still and forlorn among the pits. There had been a brief discussion between their commanders, and then with surprising efficiency the entire column had coiled back on itself like some kind of snake and slithered away over the low hill toward the north. There were a lot of them, but not as many as any of the scouts had expected.

The senior of the four turned to an old grey-beard with gleaming eyes and leathery skin.

'Adiatuanus, ride for the Preciani. Tell that slow-witted fool Borios that he has underestimated the Romans. They have already found the traps and changed their route. The Preciani chieftain has lost his chance. If he wishes to pull any kind of success out of this failure, he will have to meet the Romans at Ortus, for they are now on the other river. Tell him to kill as many as he can, even if he has to send his own children to their deaths, but make sure that their general lives. *His* neck is for the king alone.'

The old scout inclined his head slightly and rode off along the edge of the trees, where he would attract the least attention. There were a dozen different ways to reach the Preciani from here without coming too close to that armoured serpent with the red banners, and Adiatuanus knew them all. As he disappeared into the distance to chastise the slow chieftain for his failure, the lead scout turned to the others.

'Opinions?'

'They are so few. I expected so many.'

'Rome's legions are far more dangerous than the same number of men from any other tribe,' the leader warned in a dark tone. 'Do not underestimate them. Borios made the mistake of thinking they would be slower and because of his failure a trap has been sprung too early.'

'I thought the general would travel with more pomp. They have these things called lictors, they say. Some kind of creature with sticks and axes who follow them and protect them like a tamed bear.'

The leader nodded thoughtfully. 'They say the general sometimes fights alongside his men. Perhaps such splendour is saved for Rome? But I did believe Caesar would bring more legions. He has eleven with him among the Gauls, or so they say, so why bring just one? Unless he is even more arrogant than we have been led to believe.'

He sighed. 'Ride for the Begerri and the other Convenae. Tell them to begin preparations. Caesar is on the way, and I do not expect the Preciani to do much more than delay him a little.'

The other riders nodded and turned, riding off eastwards, leaving the lead scout peering down at the departing Romans. The general was visible even now, talking to a man on a horse with some kind of banner. He did not look like the sort of demigod that rumour made out. A child of the Roman love goddess? Pah! Only the Romans would send a descendant of a love goddess to lead a war.

Yet the scout felt an odd frisson of uneasy energy as that figure on the horse turned and seemed to be looking straight at him. Unnerved by the whole thing, the scout retreated deeper into the shade of the trees and then turned and rode off to report to his king.

Chapter Five

'I am absolutely twitching to move faster,' Fronto grumbled as he once more slowed Bucephalus so as not to outpace the column. The legionaries looked no happier, for though the pace was easy for them, it meant longer days of marching and a longer campaign overall. But the pace of the column was no longer dictated by the slow grinding of the wagon axles at the rear.

'Better slow than dead,' Decius said rather flatly.

It was true. With the knowledge that traps could now be set for them as well as ambushes, the pace had been slowed and the scouts trebled, leaving none in reserve. Every man available was now ranging out ahead and to the flanks watching for hidden archers, pitfalls, or anything else that could hinder or damage the legion on its march.

It had taken a whole day to move the army back toward Sorda and then over the hillside to the northern branch of the river, and Fronto had been half expecting an ambush at every given moment. But peace seemed to reign as they turned alongside the new waterway and followed its southern bank. This river was generally wider than the other branch, but here and there it narrowed as it cut its way through rocky terrain, with jagged, hard white banks. Apparently, they were moving into Preciani territory though, as always with these things, there was no visual clue to the change. Fronto had quizzed Galronus, but once again his friend had come up with nothing useful. Crassus' campaign had simply been too far east and north to have encountered these people.

'Fronto,' Galronus called from his position a few paces ahead, gesturing out across the grass. Here, the river looped slightly to the left, hidden behind a small patch of woodland, though the scouts had said it curved back south, so the army could cut the corner. As Fronto peered out, he could see two riders hurtling back toward him across the grass ahead. A prickle of anticipation ran through him and he had to fight to resist the urge to ride out and meet them. Decius and Galronus pulled in close to him, as well as Masgava and the ever-present Aurelius, and the five men waited for the riders to rein in close by.

The two men threw out salutes after a fashion, neither being Roman nor regular army, and Fronto acknowledged them with a similarly half-hearted effort.

One of the two scouts turned to Galronus and began to rattle off his report. Fronto listened intently, though with little hope of picking out anything. Even after eight years in these lands, his command of their tongue was limited to a few words, such as wine, fight and tavern. And even then dialect differences between regions had quickly taught him that the words he had learned were Aedui and from the region around them, and that the northern Belgae, and the western and southern tribes had their own variants. As for the Aquitanii? Well, what the scouts seemed to speak didn't even sound remotely similar to Gallic. It was more like a man gargling a live frog.

'What's he saying?' he nudged impatiently, earning himself an irritated look from Galronus as the Remi nobleman continued to listen to the report. Once the man had finished and fallen silent, Galronus turned and passed on the details.

'His accent is a little difficult, but it seems that ahead is a crossing of the river. There is a town on the far side, but set back perhaps half a mile, not close to the river or the bridge. The town seems to be occupied as smoke rises from chimneys. The crossing, he thinks, is Roman and recent. There are three men on the bridge waiting. They seem to be noblemen and the scouts are certain they are Preciani. They appear to be waiting for us.'

Fronto chewed his lip in thought, reaching up and swatting away a fly that had taken a particular interest in his sweaty hairline. 'Just the three?'

'So the scouts say. There are woods on the far bank, but they are a little set back, not close to the bridge, and only low scrub nearby.'

'Sounds like a difficult place for an ambush, then. Sounds like they want to talk. I would be extremely interested to hear what they have to say. Galronus, you'd better come with me. I'll need a translator, but this could be delicate. I don't want to go in heavy handed and push away the one chance we've found so far to actually communicate with these people.' He turned to Masgava behind. 'You have command. Have the column halt on this side

93

just short of bow-shot from the other bank. I'll just go with Galronus and Aurelius and speak with these three.'

'Take a guard unit with you,' Carbo said firmly.

'I told you I don't want to push these people into turning against us.'

'And I don't trust them as far as I can piss. Take a guard unit with you.'

Fronto frowned, but Aurelius was nodding vehemently, and looks of agreement were plastered across the faces of his friends. Shaking his head in defeat, he chuckled. 'Alright. One contubernium. Just eight men, but not legionaries. Regular cavalry. I want to be fast and mobile. Galronus?'

Hardly had he finished speaking the Remi's name before the man was gone to pull in eight cavalrymen. In a dozen heartbeats he was back with the riders close behind. 'Come on then, Fronto.'

The legate felt that same sense of tense anticipation building as they passed the end of the woodland and approached the gentle incline that sloped away down to the river and the heavy bridge. The three men on the crossing were standing tall and easy and as the Romans approached, Fronto took the opportunity to size them up. They were something different to the other lowlanders they'd seen. Perhaps the Preciani were not quite mountain people, but these were also not closely related to the Gauls. They had long, shaggy hair and beards, though their manner of dress and decoration seemed to be similar to the other more northern peoples. They wore mail shirts of good quality, though very different to the Roman manufacture, more like a single long tunic than the shorter shirt with doubled shoulder protection. The one in the centre could be a chief. If not, he was clearly some sort of noble. None of them seemed to be druidic, which was a relief. He hated talking to druids. They always had that same superior *'I know something you don't'* manner that seemed to afflict Roman priests and augurs. The three men straightened slightly as Fronto approached, pulling out slightly ahead, with Galronus beside him. Aurelius came forward and drew level with Fronto, his hand on his sword hilt and his shield ready.

'Greetings, I am...' Fronto began.

In a flash, the world changed. The three nobles threw themselves backwards and to the timbers of the bridge. There was a series of thuds from Aurelius' shield as he hefted it, and Galronus cried out as something smashed into him, throwing him backwards, only the tight, four-horned saddle keeping him astride his mount. His horse, though, was also crying in pain.

Fronto had only a moment to realise that slingers had risen from among the cracks and dips in the rocky banks, loosing their heavy stones at the Roman party.

'Shit,' was all he could manage before Aurelius was there, covering him with his shield, and grabbing Fronto's reins with his free hand, pulling back hard so that the bit jerked deep into the horse's mouth. Quick as he could, the bodyguard forced Bucephalus to walk backwards. 'Sit deep and pull,' Aurelius shouted and then cried out and let go as a sling stone caught him on his left leg with an unpleasant meaty thud. Fronto took over, obeying without question, walking his horse backwards as fast as he was able. Aurelius, his shield still rattling and thudding its protection, was keeping pace, pulling his own beast backwards.

Galronus was having less luck. His horse had been struck in the head with a heavy stone and was rearing now. The Remi was still winded from the first stone that had struck him in the chest. The mail shirt had spread much of the impact and though there would be an enormous bruise across Galronus' chest, at least nothing had broken. However, even as Fronto and Aurelius moved back to the end of the bridge, Galronus' horse shied in pain and panic and the cavalry commander suddenly found himself at such an angle that the horned saddle no longer held him tight. With a dazed squawk, Galronus slid from the horse and fell to the bridge's timbers with a thud. Stones rattled off the wooden struts at the side and one hit the Remi in his mail-armoured shoulder, knocking him heavily and painfully to one side.

Even as Fronto and his bodyguard managed to pull back off the bridge, Fronto knew the dreadful danger his friend was in and was shouting Galronus' name in warning. The man's big white horse was being pounded with numerous heavy stones, breaking bones and drawing blood, and then it fell. Somehow, miraculously, Galronus, even dazed, had managed to pull his legs up so that the falling beast did not crush them as it landed in thrashing agony. He could do nothing more though than lie there in stunned pain as the horse tossed and kicked, and stones clattered across the timbers, occasionally catching the dying horse or clipping Galronus' limbs or mail. The Remi wore no helmet, and the first blow that caught him on the head would likely kill him.

The slingers were good. Even though the Romans had pulled back to the near bank, the stones were hitting men. Aurelius, his leg bleeding profusely and hanging limp, grabbed at Fronto and yelled 'back! Further back. Get out of range.'

Another stone thudded into Aurelius' shield and then one clanged off the very crown of his helmet, knocking his head painfully to the side. Already two of their cavalry escort were down, screaming as their horses kicked and shrieked, stones clanging off iron and bronze.

'Galronus!' Fronto shouted in desperation as Aurelius guided him further and further from danger.

The situation was going from bad to worse as Fronto's professional command eye took in everything. The three nobles who had lured them onto the bridge had crawled back across the timber and out of the storm of flying stones, where they had risen and begun to shout orders. Perhaps twenty or thirty slingers were still standing among the rocks, their repeated shots easily crossing the narrow river and playing havoc with the Roman honour guard. Barely a man had escaped injury already, and even as he looked, another horseman fell to the ground with a cry, his head stoved in. Galronus lay on the bridge beside his horse, which was kicking its last, though whether the Remi was alive or dead, it was now impossible to tell. Worst of all, in response to the nobles' shouted commands, the Preciani were pouring from the treeline all around the far side of the river, rushing toward the bridge, the front-runners pulling bows from their shoulders. What was already a disastrous situation was about to get much worse.

'Get out of the way of the fucking stones!' bellowed Aurelius, pushing Fronto hard.

'Galronus!'

'I'll get him,' snapped the bodyguard.

'Don't be stupid,' Fronto snapped, though already Aurelius was dropping from his horse, battered and dented shield held ready. Fronto watched helplessly as the former legionary tested his wounded leg and almost fell as it gave way. With a grunt, he pressed on regardless, limping badly, but forcing himself on into the cloud of deadly missiles. In a moment, two of the cavalry guard were with him, their hexagonal shields held high protectively, forming the world's smallest shieldwall as they closed on the bridge. Two other riders joined Fronto as he finally reached a safe distance. One of them was badly wounded and the other had lost his shield, his arm running with blood and hanging limp. Four riders lay dead along with their horses.

Fronto realised with an odd start that neither Bucephalus nor he had taken a single strike. Either Fortuna was being unusually helpful or something else was going on. He watched helplessly as the three men, crouched behind their shields and at the centre of a storm of stone that clunked, clattered and clanged, moved to the end of the bridge.

A series of buccina calls, centurions' whistles and urgent shouts drew his attention back over his shoulder and he glanced up the slope to see that the legion was now in close sight – the lead elements at least – and that Decius had clearly noted what was going on. The auxiliary prefect was hurtling down the slope, his own Balearic slingers and Cretan archers at his heels. Fronto's gaze went back to Galronus. The Remi's horse was now still, its only movement an occasional quiver as a stone thudded into the carcass. Galronus had also not twitched.

'Stay put, sir,' Decius yelled as he ran past, alongside his men. Moments later, the northern branch of the Aturrus River became a small slice of Hades as archers from both armies settled into position and arrows and slingshots began to fly from both banks. Into this endless multidirectional hail of steel, wood and stone the three soldiers pushed, countless missiles of both types pounding at them.

Fronto wanted to shout, to call Aurelius and the others back. A good commander should. It was terrible tactical sense to send three men into a deadly storm in a hopeless attempt to save one man, especially when that man might already be dead. But this was Galronus. Fronto had known him for seven years, and for most of those the Remi prince had been almost a brother. He could no more let Galronus pass from the world on that bridge willingly than he could throw away his own life. If nothing else, what would he tell Faleria? That he had led the two men she had loved into battle only to leave both dead on foreign soil. It would kill her.

His will hardened with that realisation. He would rather die himself than leave Galronus and go home. Just how happy was Fortuna feeling?

Aurelius and the other two were at the end of the bridge, but had pushed no further. The archers and slingers in Decius' auxiliary unit were assiduously avoiding the trio, but the enemy were making no such attempt and all three had stopped and were huddled behind their shields, each of which resembled a hedgehog, with all the arrow shafts jutting from it.

Why was I not hit? Fronto mused. Even with Fortuna's cloak about his shoulders the chances of him having braved that storm without even a scratch were minimal. Unbelievable, really.

Narrowing his eyes, he slipped from Bucephalus and handed the horse's reins to one of the two cavalrymen. The soldiers stared at him in surprise.

'I am considering the very real possibility that I am indestructible,' he said with a grin that, if he'd been able to see it, he'd have been the first to note was made four parts in five of madness.

Turning, he marched toward the bridge.

'Sir?' the cavalryman lunged after him desperately.

'No. Absolutely not. You stay here out of danger and you keep my horse safe. I inherited him from the best cavalry commander you'd ever meet and he's worth more than a turma of riders to me.'

'But sir…'

Yet Fronto was gone, marching with purpose back to the bridge. Archers paused in their onslaught to stare as he walked past into the shower of missiles. Decius was suddenly next to him, tugging at his arm.

'Get down here you mad bastard.'

'Leave… me… alone,' Fronto replied, pulling himself free of the prefect's grip and stomping onwards into the hail, toward the three men hunkered down at the bridge end. Even as he approached, one of the two cavalrymen accompanying Aurelius took an arrow in the calf, just around the edge of the shield. The man cried out in pain, but each and every soldier in this army was a veteran, and there were no cowards or idiots. The man gritted his teeth, left the arrow in place, and pulled his leg back further behind the shield, remaining in position.

Fronto strode on toward them like Jupiter himself pushing aside the clouds as he brandished his thunderbolt. His theory was correct, and he almost laughed aloud. In fact, he probably did a little. For in the very midst of a storm of missiles, he walked unharmed. Yet this was no trick of Fortuna's. The enemy were deliberately not targeting him. In fact, as he moved, he could see the men on the other bank shifting their aim.

Oh, sooner or later he would take a hit purely by accident, but it would not be a deliberate attempt to kill him. He'd had the nagging feeling that that was the case since they'd pulled back from the bridge and of all those eleven men present, only he and one other had not sustained a wound. And that other man had been at the back. Fronto had been at the very fore. A *blind* man should have been able to hit him.

With a crazed laugh, he walked onto the timbers, straight up to the three men huddled behind their shields. He was impressed at how many arrows had hit those painted boards, and the seemingly unwounded one was in fact no such thing. An arrow had punched through his shield and his arm in one, pinning the two together, its barbed point jutting out inside. Pointing down at the wounded troopers, he addressed Aurelius. 'Get them to a capsarius as quick as you can.'

Aurelius stared up at his commander and seemed to realise suddenly that the hail of missiles had dropped away to almost nothing with the legate beside him.

'Sir?'

'Go.'

Aurelius, catching the look in Fronto's eye, nodded and, between them, the three men began to slowly retreat from the bridge, keeping their shields to the fore at all times. Fronto watched them go, and an arrow whipped past him, close enough to score a thin red line across his arm. Hurrying now, aware that it was only a matter of time before he took a serious hit even by accident, he closed on Galronus. The man was lying still, blood blossoming through mail and tunic on both arms and torso.

'Galronus?' He closed and knelt, his heart lurching coldly. Gods, no. Not now.

'Come on,' he said, reaching down to the man's neck to feel for a pulse.

'How in the name of Taranis are you not covered with arrows?' grunted the Remi, one eye snapping suspiciously open. Fronto almost burst out laughing.

'I thought you were dead.'

'*I* can't understand how you *aren't!*' the Remi noble retorted, but let Fronto help him up.

'Can you walk?'

'Walk? Here? No, but I can bloody run.'

And with that he was moving. Fronto, still laughing, fell in close to him, but made sure to keep behind his friend, shielding him from any stray missile. The enemy might not want to hit Fronto for some reason, but they would happily kill Galronus, he was sure. A few dozen heartbeats and they were back off the bridge. The army was arriving in force now, and most of the senior officers were closing on the scene. Several centuries of veteran legionaries were hurtling forward, holding up their large curved shields, and as Fronto and Galronus passed the auxiliary archers and slingers, they found themselves protected by a large force of burly veterans. Aurelius was suddenly with them again, then Decius, then Atenos and Arruntius.

'I honestly thought you were dead,' Fronto said between gasps of breath. 'You weren't moving.'

'First rule you need to learn facing archers, Fronto. If they think you're down and you're no longer a threat, don't disabuse them of the notion. I stayed down and played dead and they felt no great urge to fill me with arrows. My poor horse saved me from most of the barrage after that.'

With the threat to any personnel diminished, the archers and slingers were now pulling back out of enemy range, and within mere moments the barrage had stopped altogether. The bridge sat like an invitation to suicide between the two forces. Whoever moved onto the timbers now would put themselves in danger from enemy archers, and so a stalemate was forming.

'How do we get to them?' Fronto murmured.

'Cross the river as well?' Atenos replied.

'No. It's not wide, but it's deep and fast and with high, rocky banks.'

'Extend the bridge,' Biorix said, appearing as if from nowhere. 'Cut huge timbers and make ramps. Ferry them down and use them to bridge the waters.

'Possible,' Fronto conceded, 'but we'd still lose a lot of men to their missile troops.'

'I have an idea,' Galronus said quietly, 'but I'm having trouble thinking and breathing in this mail. Someone help me.'

Atenos quickly helped the Remi peel off the mail shirt, as delicately as he could manage. The gathered officers drew in excrucied breaths as the tunic rode up with the mail to display a huge black, red and purple welt that stretched from side to side and from collar bone to diaphragm.

'Crap, that must hurt.'

'A little,' Galronus shrugged it off, but the hissing and wincing as he moved to smooth out his tunic told a different story.

'Your idea?' Fronto nudged.

'I'm going to draw the cavalry off a way and try something, but I don't want the enemy to see.' He turned to Carbo. 'How slow and noisy and messy can you make the job of setting up camp?'

'How noisy do you want it?'

'Enough to cover the departure of the entire cavalry. Make camp and wait.'

'What for? How will I know what to do?'

'You'll work it out. Doesn't matter how long I take, just wait and watch,' grinned Galronus, and then hissed with pain and began to wander back toward his riders, who were gathering up the slope.

'There goes a complete madman,' Fronto said quietly.

'This from a man who walked into an arrow storm with nothing to protect him but a mad grin.'

* * *

Fronto was up early and out in the fresh, cool air, despite the damp mizzle that filled the world from horizon to horizon under steely grey skies. He knew something was building. Like the crackle of static in the air before a thunderstorm, and the slow building of pressure that causes headaches, he'd been awake in the middle of the night, feeling expectant and tense. He had done a couple of circuits of the camp ramparts in the damp air before even the first strains of light began to filter in through the darkness to the east.

All was perfectly normal, which was in itself odd, given the strange tension. The men on guard stood quiet and pensive, watching the enemy across the river, camped in their own ground, roughly equal in numbers to the legion though with only a few sentries and no other thought to defence. Over the last hour and more of darkness, Fronto had contemplated more than once sending a foray across the river. The bridge would constrict any attack, but perhaps – just perhaps – a swift enough and unexpected attack could secure them the bridge and put enough men on the far bank to deal with that enemy force.

In the end he had clenched his knuckles in frustration and held back the order behind barred teeth, for there was the strong possibility that this was not the main enemy of his campaign that he faced, but a smaller force on the periphery. He could not afford to commit to such a potentially dangerous action when he might yet need every available man further on in the campaign.

And so he had stood and watched as the sky began to lighten above the layer of solid cloud, the sun a pale orb barely visible. The enemy seemed as content to stay encamped as they. The legions were now answering the calls of their officers and the bleating of the horns dragging them from their cots. They scurried from tents with their tunics loose and unbelted, hanging down to their shins, hurrying over to the water butts and dipping their heads in, blowing snot from nostrils, squeezing the water from their hair and rubbing weary eyes. Some were faster than others and were already beginning to belt their tunics or slip into their leather subarmalis, the protective vest that kept the rings of the mail from pinching flesh or ruining linen. Here and there chosen men were already kneading bread dough or cooking up salted pork or eggs, preparing the morning meal for their tent party. It was, all in all, a scene of domestic camp life he had seen a thousand times in a thousand places.

And across the river, the locals – the Preciani, it seemed – were beginning to stir and dress, eat and prepare. Would there be a battle today? It seemed likely, given the building of expectation that infected the air, and yet neither side could easily cross that bridge in the face of enemy aggression without risking total destruction.

Standing at the northern gate of the camp, Fronto glanced across at a carefree, tuneful whistle to see Terpulo swaggering toward him.

'Morning.'

'Good morning, sir. Taking the air?'

'Couldn't sleep,' Fronto replied quietly. 'Feels like something's building.'

'Felt it myself, sir. Pressure. Like I'd pinched my nose and closed my mouth and blown. I swear my ears popped just now, and we're not that high up yet.'

Fronto nodded. If Terpulo felt the same, then probably so did the others in the camp. There was definitely a certain expectancy about the men, who were getting themselves ready but without the normal morning laughs and banter.

'The Dis-damned horns are giving me a headache,' Terpulo complained. 'It's the fact that each one echoes half a dozen times around the countryside, so there's a constant ringing.'

Again the legate nodded. His own head felt tight and strained, though he put it down more to the pre-action tension than to the sounds of the buccinae, cornua and tubas being blown around the camp.

Something there was wrong. Fronto's head tilted to one side as he listened and thought it through. What was wrong with that sound. Something unexpected.

'Did you hear that?' Terpulo asked, his hand straying unconsciously to the pommel of the decorative sword hilt at his side.

'What? Sort of...'

'The tuba.'

Fronto blinked. The tuba.

But the cavalry weren't in camp, and the tuba was a horse signal.

'Sound the alert,' Fronto barked. 'Quickly. Fall the men in.'

As Terpulo ran off, shouting to the signifers and musicians, Fronto turned back to peer across the bridge, his own hand gripping his sword hilt as he watched the battle begin. The Preciani suddenly began to scramble around, grabbing weapons and jamming helmets on heads in a desperate panic, hurrying this way and that in a disorganised rabble as their nobles and leaders shouted conflicting orders and then began to argue with one another.

And in the midst of this chaos, the tuba calls were no longer muted as Galronus' horsemen burst from the treeline on the far bank like a flood of equine muscle, pouring onto the grassy slope and ploughing into the first few of the Preciani who had managed to assemble themselves in small groups. Two men had managed to get long spears braced in the ground and impaled a charging horse, the rider being hurled from his saddle to the ground with an almost certainly fatal crunch. But that victory was a small lone thing in a world of pain for the unprepared natives. The cavalry raced through the panicked defenders, swords sweeping wide and low, spears thrusting and stabbing.

The Preciani fell in their dozens just in the initial strike, leaving open a path into the enemy camp, which had no form of physical defence.

Behind Fronto, he could hear the centuries falling into position, the centurions' whistles shrilly blowing in the wet morning air, the jingling of four score mail shirts, bronze apron straps and sword fittings ringing out across the camp. He turned. Two of the centuries were already formed, others still falling in.

'Engage as soon as you're formed,' he bellowed. 'We need to support the cavalry!'

It came as no surprise to see that one of the two units that had formed so swiftly and efficiently was the First under Atenos. He had been the training officer for the Tenth for years and their primus pilus since then, after all. The other was that of the ageing centurion Arruntius and, if anything – and Fronto was ill prepared to admit it – they had formed slightly faster than the men under Atenos, *and* they looked sharper.

The two centurions blew the three shrill blasts on their whistles, the standards dipped forward for a moment, and the units moved out, even as a third was beginning to form. Fronto drew his blade and was unsurprised to see, as he scrambled down the earth bank to the gate, Masgava and Aurelius closing on him. The latter was limping badly and in serious danger of falling in a heap, but somehow seemed to be keeping pace with the huge Numidian.

Fronto was determined to be part of the attack. Arruntius was old enough to have drunk with Fronto's own father to his birth, and the very idea of standing at the back while the old man led an army from the front was unthinkable. Fortunately, Fronto had been at the gate, and so was well ahead of the two centuries. He burst out into the open past two startled legionaries, and Masgava and Aurelius were suddenly with him.

'Stay here!' he bellowed.

'No.'

'No, sir.'

'Masgava,' Fronto shouted as he started to jog toward the bridge, 'you're my adjutant. You should be commanding back there. And Aurelius? Your leg will go any moment.'

In answer both men simply looked at him defiantly, and Aurelius actually started to run faster, the limp giving him a strange loping motion that put Fronto in mind of those African deer they occasionally showed off in bestiaries in Rome. Disobedience should be dealt with, Fronto knew. In his years as a legate, he had only suffered this kind of attitude from those he respected utterly. The problem was that very thing applied to both these men. Aurelius was his bodyguard and took the job very seriously, and Masgava had fulfilled that same role for years, even bringing Fronto back from the edge once or twice. Both men had been with him through some of the worst episodes of his life, and he could no more discipline them for their care than he could his own family.

Without conscious decision, all three men slowed very slightly as they approached the bridge to allow the two centuries of men that had flooded from the gate to catch up. Across the river, one of the Preciani leaders had cut through the chaos with his shouted orders and had sent a small force to hold the bridge while they attempted to deal with the cavalry who had fallen on them so unexpectedly and with deadly consequences. Surprise had made a great deal of difference, but the fact remained that the cavalry numbered less than three hundred against several thousand Aquitanian warriors, and even now the Preciani were beginning to pull themselves together, ordering their ranks against the mounted enemy. Galronus' impressive manoeuvre would be utterly wasted unless the infantry used the time to cross the river and get stuck in.

Fronto figured the enemy closing on the bridge to number perhaps two hundred, with one or two archers and slingers in the ranks. Nothing ordered or planned like the previous day. This was pure desperate reaction and nothing more.

'Cuneus,' bellowed centurion Arruntius from somewhere just to Fronto's left. 'Five man wedge on me!'

Suddenly he was next to Fronto, and the legate was astonished at the speed with which the old, blue veined legs pumped.

'Scuse me, sir,' the ageing centurion said with no hint of a smile as he pulled past Fronto with the lead elements of his century, moving at a fast run. At his order the wedge formed, and Fronto found himself among the centurion's men suddenly. With the mad grin of the hopelessly combative, Fronto held his sword upright so as not to inadvertently injure his comrades and slid into position in the wedge, directly behind Arruntius, forming the heart of the wedge. Masgava and Aurelius were still with him at his shoulders and the century poured onto the timbers of the bridge at full pelt, hurtling toward the assembling force.

The wood creaked and thundered beneath hundreds of booted feet as over a hundred legionaries and officers poured across the bridge toward the wide-eyed Preciani. A few arrows and stones were loosed, but the missile troops were not in strong positions, and had simply fallen in among the warriors, sending out a shot when they suddenly saw an opening. It would be far from enough to deter the advancing century. A few stones and shafts rattled off the shields at the front of the wedge and something sliced through the plume of Fronto's helmet sending a flurry of red horsehair strands wafting through the air.

The wedge of men hit the Preciani at the far end of the bridge like a runaway cart racing downhill. No two hundred men born into the world would have been able to hold back the momentum of Arruntius' century, and Fronto could hear the frustrated roars of Atenos somewhere behind him, complaining and demanding that his fellow centurion leave someone for him to kill.

Fronto's world became a small thing in the confines of the fight: the bodies of his comrades all around and the desperate snarling and slashing of those enemies ahead, the stink of sweat and fear, of blood and mud and urine. As the enemy were forced back and apart by the wedge, so the fight opened up. Arruntius, killing with an almost mechanical accuracy that astounded even Fronto, carved his way through the Preciani into the open, where he turned and began to flank them The century had cut the enemy force in two, and now they wheeled, free of the confines of the bridge, both left and right and began to butcher without mercy. Fronto found himself facing a burly bearded warrior with an old notched iron sword and panicked eyes, his sword raised above the press and ready to slam downwards. With a deft flick of his blade, Fronto stabbed out into the space under the raised arm and felt the tip of the gladius slide through the soft flesh of the armpit. The man was big enough that Fronto had to stretch on his toes to find the angle to drive the blade deeper where it didn't simply scrape on bone, but suddenly the gladius sank deep and carved through the man's innards, robbing him of life in moments.

Barely had he managed to pull the blade back out of the falling warrior at such a difficult angle when another man was there. Fronto stabbed out and felt his sword cut through mail and leather, smashing into the side of the shirt the man wore and scattering tiny iron links. He had to lean to one side in the press of men to avoid being carved by the man's retort, and felt a flash of irritation when Aurelius' blade calmly lanced out and slammed into the warrior's neck. As the man fell away, Fronto flashed an angry glance toward his friend, just in time to see Aurelius' leg give way at a crucial moment. The former legionary started to collapse and a Preciani warrior, filled with glee, spotted his chance, chopping downwards with an axe at the falling Roman.

Fronto leapt forward, throwing his sword out and all his weight into it. The falling axe caught his beautiful gladius and clanked along the blade until it hit the hilt, where it left a deep dent across the face of one of the gods embossed in the orichalcum. The parry had not been enough to stop the momentum of the falling axe, but it had deflected it and as the heavy weapon slid past Fronto's sword, it slammed into the turf a hair's breadth from Aurelius' elbow, where the man was already struggling to push himself back upright.

Snarling at the damage to his favourite sword, Fronto swiftly stabbed out into the axeman's face, ignoring the resistance of bone and the horrifying noises as the man screamed, then yanking it back out. Spinning, Fronto looked for another target, but they had beaten the defence force at the bridge, and already the other centuries of the legion were pouring across the bridge and running at the chaotic, panicked Preciani. The enemy were dithering, unsure of which force to fight, many breaking ranks and fleeing for the town or the treeline. Fronto almost laughed when he saw Arruntius storming after a fleeing warrior, bellowing for the man to stand still, the centurion's arms and legs sheeted with blood.

The legate's arm was throbbing where he had taken the jarring axe blow, and he reached out with his other hand to help Aurelius to his feet. Masgava appeared from nearby, oddly free of gore apart from around the mouth. Fronto opened his mouth to enquire about that, but quickly thought better of it and nodded at the man instead. When Masgava grinned, the white teeth in his midnight face swam in a lake of blood. Whoever the Numidian's victim had been, Fronto pitied him.

The thought suddenly struck Fronto that the invincibility he had felt yesterday when they were deliberately trying not to kill him seemed to be absent today. But then today was different. He'd been in the press of men, and most of his distinctive red plume had been sheared off on the approach. Likely they had not realised it was him.

As Aurelius straightened on his trembling leg, the three men watched the legion at work. While there was still fighting going on, the battle was clearly already over. What Preciani were still standing were being scythed down with professional skill by the veterans, and those who were fleeing the scene were being chased by the less restrained legionaries and a number of Galronus' cavalry.

'Legate?'

He turned to see the gore-caked figure of Arruntius stomping toward him, wiping the blade of his sword on a rag. Atenos appeared from the press and made to join the small group too.

'Centurion,' Fronto smiled., 'that was very impressive.'

'Legate,' Arruntius said with a face of fury, 'if you truly want to get your privates hacked off with the grunts, resign your command, pick up a legionary shield and dig the shitters with the rest of them, and I'll happily let you in my wedge. Until then you are an officer and your place is directing us, not supporting us.'

'Always in the thick of it, the legate,' Atenos laughed as he joined them.

Arruntius' face went through several expressions, including grudging admiration, but settled on irritated with a shade of concern.

'Sir, the centurionate has a near sixty percent casualty rate in any campaign, because we lead from the front and by example. And we get paid well to do it. But when a centurion falls, there are fifty nine more in the legion who can step into his job, and sixty optios waiting for promotion. Yet there is only *one* man in the whole damned legion who knows the campaign and its goals and with the experience of planning expeditions and battles. Who's going to step into your posh boots when you get yourself gutted by a random warrior just because you like to play soldier.'

Fronto stared at the centurion in the face of the outburst. Like the disobedience of Aurelius and Masgava, he was well within his rights to discipline Arruntius for speaking to him like that, but the centurion was correct. The Tenth might be used to their idiosyncratic commander after years of experience, but these men were not. Narrowing his eyes, he nodded and reached down to his own belt for his rag to clean his blade.

'I appreciate your position and your candour, Arruntius. And in many ways you are correct. But I am no senate-appointed politician. I am a veteran like you. I've drawn blood on every battlefield from Britannia to Hispania, and when battle calls I answer. Simple as that. I shall make sure not to confuse your own formations during battle, but never expect to see me standing on the tribunal at the rear and watching the fight.'

Arruntius watched him for some time, his eyes appraising, and finally he stuck out his hand. Fronto shook it tersely and the pair nodded at each other. Once the elderly centurion had turned and gone to shout at his men, Fronto heard a stifled guffaw and turned to see Aurelius grinning.

'What's so funny?'

'I just realised that Arruntius is basically you in twenty years' time.'

Masgava chuckled and the pair wandered off, leaving Fronto watching the white-haired centurion. Somehow that thought was not particularly comforting.

* * *

'What's the butcher's bill?' Fronto asked as Carbo strolled out of his centurions' briefing.

'We lost twenty two cavalry, and four more lost their horses. Six more of them are wounded. Low figures really, considering the shit they were in before the legion arrived to help. Sixty one dead or critically injured infantry. Including five centurions and three optios,' he added meaningfully. Clearly Arruntius had been casting around his opinions again. 'And eighty or so in the hospital tent for patching up. Not bad at all considering what we were up against.'

'Quite. What of the enemy?'

'We've not counted the dead yet. They're still being gathered into piles for disposal. Estimates are of maybe three or four hundred escaping the field. We have forty seven captives, including two who seem to be nobles.'

'Good. Let me speak to them.'

As they strode toward the enemy prisoners, who were roped together under the watchful eye of a number of legionaries, Carbo shouted for one of the native scouts to act as interpreter. Fronto came to a halt and peered down at the dejected captives.

'Why have you attacked the forces of Rome?'

Silence.

'Tell me about the pit traps that caught our horses.'

Silence.

'The Preciani have no reason to war against Rome, have they?' It was a slightly foolish question, as Fronto knew too well. Rome had all-but annexed Aquitania, and though they'd not faced war like the Gauls, they were every bit as much a conquered people. Yet he hoped that the push and his offended inflection would goad someone into an answer. It worked. As he scanned the eyes of those dejected warriors looking up at him, he could see the younger of the two nobles having trouble keeping his words in, his lips thin and tight. The other noble seemed to have noticed too, for he was giving his peer a hard, disapproving look. Fronto recognised the older one as the man from the bridge ambush yesterday.

110

'For the mere greed of the Preciani leaders you have all paid the highest price imaginable,' he baited them further.

The young warrior stood, his hands gripped into fists, though he only rose to a stoop, for the restraining ropes prevented anything further.

'The king in the mountains did this to us!' the young man snapped in surprisingly good Latin.

The older noble suddenly leapt on the younger, other prisoners being jerked and dragged about by their mutual restraints. Even as Fronto shouted orders to restrain the man, the noble from the bridge had grabbed the younger one and pushed him to the ground. As legionaries stepped forward, their pila levelled menacingly, the older noble ignored them and grabbed the younger man's head by the hair, dashing his face against the hard ground twice, three, four, five times. By the time legionaries reached him and pulled him off, the young man was prone, face down. His legs thrashed and twitched for a while until he lay still, dead, his brains and the remains of his face smeared across the ground.

'I want that one interrogated by torturers,' Fronto snarled, pointing at the older man.

As legionaries unroped the prisoner and took him away, Carbo huffed. 'You know he'll tell us nothing. He'll die first. I know his sort.'

'Then at least he'll die badly for that little display,' Fronto said nastily. 'Come on.'

The two turned, and Fronto spotted Galronus staggering across the battlefield, carrying his saddle.

'Horse alright?'

'Yes,' the Remi said, hissing at the pain in his bruised torso as he moved. 'Some Preciani managed to slit one of the straps that holds it in place. By the end of the fight I was sliding around on the poor beast's back like I was on ice.'

'The prisoners are too defiant – or maybe too frightened of something – to tell me what's going on, but one of them blamed a "king in the mountains",' Fronto said quietly. 'What d'you think?'

Galronus shrugged. 'Who knows. Could be any king or chief of any of the tribes up there. The big tribes are the Begerri, the Consoranni, the Ceretes, and I suppose the Sordones, though they're within the Roman province at the far end of the mountains.

But apart from those large tribes, there are a dozen or more smaller ones, and it's a sad tendency even among our tribes for smaller groups to take ever grander titles to make up for their lack of true numbers and strength. I cannot imagine the Aquitanii are immune to such vanity. Without more information, we're as in the dark as we were before.'

'Except for two things,' Fronto said as the three men walked side by side. 'Firstly, we know now for sure that the answer lies in the mountains, and secondly we know it is down to one man and he calls himself a king.'

'Which at least gives us a specific target to aim for,' Carbo said.

'But it worries me. This whole thing is faintly reminiscent of Vercingetorix, if you think about it. A king rousing the tribes against Rome. There are a lot fewer Aquitanii than Gauls and Belgae, but that doesn't improve our immediate situation, for there are a lot fewer of us than there are of Caesar's full army, too.'

Carbo nodded his agreement. 'So what are your orders?'

'We'll stay here two nights. I want the army rested up and time for the minimally wounded to recover and for the cavalry's horses to rest up. The army can continue to inhabit the current camp. But while that happens I want this battle site cleared and the village thoroughly searched. I want it perfectly clear and fresh by the time we leave. And I want you to find five hundred volunteers from among the centuries to remain here and begin to establish a colony. The critically wounded can stay with them. Those that don't recover can be buried with the fallen and those that do can join the colony. Each man can have his appropriate honesta missio payment, and we'll leave them the forty six captives as slaves to help set things up.'

'They've a good town to start out with,' Carbo noted, nodding at the empty settlement up the bank.

'Exactly. And this bridge will be a vital crossing, so I'd rather have it manned. Plus this place is clearly important to the Preciani. The scouts found a *Pax Gallica* altar in the square. So having a veteran colony settled here will help maintain control in their tribe's land. This can't be anywhere near all of them, and I don't want to repeatedly find the Preciani rising up. To that effect, I'd like to make sure that there are good, cool, diplomatic heads among the settlers.'

Carbo nodded again. 'We should send a rider or two back to Lapurda to inform them of the colony, so they know about it and can begin to send appropriate supplies. And we'll have to leave a cart of stuff for them.

'How far away is Lapurda?'

'Perhaps forty miles, I think,' Carbo replied.

'Maybe we should have settled another place somewhere in between?'

The prefect shook his head. 'We can't afford to shed too much manpower as we move. You're leaving a cohort here as it is. That's almost a tenth of our whole force, and we're not even in the foothills and valleys yet.'

As Galronus and Carbo went off to variously arrange settlers and repair saddles, Fronto stopped at the bridge where they'd so recently fought so hard and peered off into the distance. Still, those great mountains that rose like a barrier between the lands of Gaul and Hispania were not visible. Somewhere beyond the rolling green slopes and forests there were high grey peaks clogged with snow for much of the year. He had seen them from the far side many times, never thinking he might be on this side looking back one day. Never thinking that he might lead an army up into them, which it seemed increasingly likely he was about to do.

The king in the mountains.

'Who *are* you?' he asked quietly, peering off into the distance and looking at something that wasn't quite visible.

Mid Maius

THE young man was barely old enough to be considered a chieftain. He had muscle enough to swing a sword, and a budding beard, though still soft and downy, but he was yet to take a scar or achieve that flatness of the eye which spoke of a man who had taken lives. Yet he wore two bronze arm rings and his tunic was of high quality, as was the mail shirt he wore over the top. His belt was of leather and bronze and the decoration labelled it an import from the Hispanic tribes across the mountains. His sword was shorter than was common, but broad and strong, with a hilt decorated with leaping stags.

The lad looked rather nervous as he carefully pulled apart the ornate bulbs at the terminals of the grand golden torc, enough to fit it around his slim neck. Once it was round the throat, he pushed the soft gold ornament closed once more and straightened.

He was a chief now, for all his youth.

The king was speaking again, and the young man swallowed nervously, hoping the torc would hide his throat apple bouncing anxiously up and down. The king's strange hoarse voice filled the room and there was no escaping its sibilant power.

'Your father made poor decisions.'

The young man glanced around the room, aware that it felt more like a prison than a chieftain's house. Especially with that creepy, ever-smiling face sitting so relaxed in the chair upon the dais. The room displayed the shields and standards and other trophies of a dozen tribes the Begerri had defeated in the endless internecine wars that had afflicted the Aquitanii for centuries. No longer. Now there was peace, *of a sort*. Peace enforced by something infinitely more dangerous and terrifying than any of the armies that had carried these trophies into battle. Peace enforced by the will of the man in that chair. Even the druids had left, and that should have been a warning to everyone.

He wondered if he could flee into a life of quiet obscurity? Perhaps he could be a farmer? Perhaps he could make it to the Roman province and seek a new life there? Perhaps he could get across the mountains with a purse of gold and settle among the Vascones? No. The mountains were the very haunt of the smiling bastard. He should be running *away* from the mountains, not toward them, even if that meant running into Caesar's seemingly unbeatable legion.

'I hope your loyalty is more dependable than your father's?'

The young chieftain nodded his head. He knew he'd kept his back straight and that he'd not trembled, though inside he was shaking like a corpse in a noose, a metaphor he'd applied to himself more than once this morning.

'When Caesar comes,' the king went on, 'you will have the opportunity to add an eagle to the decoration in this hall. I care not about the baubles they carry, nor the gold in their wagons. Your Begerri can have it all – be richer and more famed than ever – just deliver me the general, and you will find yourself the most favoured chief in the whole region.'

The lad nodded again, his eyes flicking to the standards and shields around the walls again, then looking through them, and through the timber and stone walls to which they were fastened, through the great fortified mound of Biguro with its houses and shops, its kilns and granaries, its walls and gates. Its sacred grove, empty and untended since the druids took umbrage at the king's arrival and abandoned the people.

He shuddered and hoped it was not noticeable from the throne.

Of course it was. The king saw everything. Was he actually smiling now? It was always so hard to tell, and even when he did it was rarely a good sign.

His gaze swept around once more and this time caught sight of the body that he'd been trying so hard not to look at. His father, the former chieftain of the Begerri, decapitated and lying face down in a lake of his own blood. And not just *head*less…

Despite his desperate desire not to, his eyes strayed across to the king's banner, where a tenth lead phallus clanked and clonked against the others. Some said that the king would only be invincible while he carried that banner. Nescato, new chief of the Begerri, somehow doubted that. Some men were larger than life, favoured by gods either good or wicked. The king was one such and it would take a god or a gods-born spirit to stop him. In the silence and privacy of his own heart, Nescato wished Caesar luck, praying that the Roman gods-born general carved the king a new smile, this time in his neck.

115

Chapter Six

THE outpost was clearly long since deserted. Nestled against the north bank of the river, it had the hallmarks of any Roman military enclosure across the republic. A timber and wattle fence stood atop a turf mound, all surrounded by a good ditch, though the small size of the place had meant it required only one entrance.

The fence had gone in three or four places some months ago, and the gate had been turned to little more than kindling. Brush and earth had been used to fill parts of the ditch, making it possible to cross without the attack being slowed too much.

Barely forty paces across, the place had held one or two contubernia of legionaries. Fronto had seen such places before. Not a permanent installation, but expected to remain for some months while its occupants worked on some project or other. Two timber buildings stood inside the depot, leaving little room for anything else. Washing and bathing would have taken place in the river close by.

'Come on,' Fronto called across to Galronus, and the two, accompanied by Aurelius, trotted forward to the small outpost.

'What happens if it's not deserted?' Aurelius asked archly, ever concerned with his job as Fronto's bodyguard.

'It is,' replied Fronto with conviction. 'And we're out of Preciani land now?'

Galronus nodded. 'According to the scouts, we passed into Begerri lands over an hour ago.'

'Then this lot, it seems, are no friendlier than the Preciani.'

'You could say that,' Aurelius noted, pointing at the ground as they passed. A Roman helmet lay half buried in the churned mud of the track, missing a cheek piece and with a dent the size of an apple in the crown.

Behind them, the army continued its approach perhaps a quarter of a mile back, but the scouts had spotted the outpost and come to report. Fronto had immediately ridden forward despite the disapproval of others, taking his two friends with him. He had forbidden the scouts from entering any settlement they found without checking in first, partially to prevent them from disturbing the scene before he'd had a look, but also to reduce the potential for greedy fingers to make off with anything valuable unnoticed.

116

Consequently, the scouts had skirted around the outpost and then reported back to Fronto.

There were no bodies in evidence around the fort, and the occasional fragments of broken armour and weapons were partially covered by the mud, clearly placing the fight that had taken place here some months earlier.

With a sense of quiet distaste, the three men rode in through the ruined gate, and Galronus tied the horses to a hitching post inside that had taken some damage but remained intact enough to serve its purpose. The place was small, but the signs of extreme violence around the ruined walls told the tale of a bitter and heroic defence by its meagre force.

'Spread out?' Aurelius suggested, but Fronto shook his head. 'No point, there's nothing going to jump out on us.' Still, he found that he'd drawn his gladius just in case, and Galronus and Aurelius followed suit. With the other two at his shoulders, Fronto wandered over to the left hand of the two structures. Both buildings had a window in each of three walls, and a door in the fourth. Aurelius hurried ahead along the side of the building and craned to peer in through the window. He stepped back and shrugged, shaking his head. As he re-joined the other two, they moved to the door. The wooden portal was intact, so clearly no one had been forced to fight their way in.

The interior was dim. The windows were largely obscured by shelving, as was the centre of the room. A storehouse. The near end of the building was open-plan with a hefty work table. Half an adzed log lay on the bench, along with the tools that had been in use. A large tool box sat in the corner, open, and a small stack of similar untouched timbers lay to one side.

'Wonder what they were here to do?' Aurelius said quietly.

'Looking at the timbers and the tools and what's on the shelves, I'd say they were starting on a bridge.'

Striding out of the warehouse and workshop, Fronto beckoned and led them up onto the surrounding turf rampart, the wall-walk of which had been paved with rough timbers. Engineers! They could never do anything by halves. Around the ramparts they trod until they reached the south wall, where they peered down the short slope. Sure enough, there were the bare bones of a new bridge. Amid a small copse of trees, six of which had been felled some time ago, four heavy timber pylons rose from the water, still awaiting the superstructure, even though they only marched out across a third of the water.

'They were only here to build a damn bridge,' Fronto snapped, glaring down at the water. He'd somehow come to terms with the Gauls and the Belgae. Half a decade of fighting with and against them had given him something of an insight into their world, and he'd begun to appreciate what these people, who Rome had sought to suppress and conquer, were. But this? The Aquitanii seemed to have risen under some king against a non-existent threat. There had been no occupying army here. No governor. No oppression. Hardly anything in the way of tax and tribute, if Caesar was to be believed. Just one fort at the western end of the mountains controlling trade. And these people the maniacs were killing? Many of them were clearly other Aquitanii. And even the Romans had been merchants, here to buy the locally-mined lead and quarried marble and limestone and in return to sell luxury goods from other lands and heady Hispanic wines. And then there were soldiers, like the ones who'd been stationed here. Oppressing, fighting and causing trouble? No. They were building a damn bridge. And because they wore the russet tunics of Rome while they did it, they had been attacked.

Angrily, Fronto turned.

'Come on. Let's go see what nightmare awaits us this time.'

Back down the rampart and across the depot, they peered into the side window of the other building, but again there was nothing to be seen. Round to the front, they peered at the door. It had been smashed to pieces and hung from one hinge with the locking bolt still extended where it had burst from its socket under the pressure of Aquitani hammers and axes.

Gingerly, he pushed the door aside and stepped in. The smell of old rot hit him immediately, like a musty, dusty grave. The interior was dark, and he moved across to one of the windows, reaching up for the black-out blind that had been fashioned from a military cloak. Even as he unhooked it, Aurelius did the same at the window opposite and cold, grey unforgiving light flooded in to illuminate the room.

The barracks had four double bunk beds, a stove, a table and four chairs. The armour and weapons, like all the useful loot from the stores next door, had gone, and in their place had been left a scene from Fronto's night-terrors.

Four legionaries knelt beside a heavy log – one of the ones that was being used for bridge piles, by the size and shape. Their ankles and wrists had been bound, and they had been draped over the log. Their necks had been pinned to the timber with iron pitons driven through the back, hammered in until they stuck deep into the log. Each neck had broken and lolled and stretched unpleasantly, but all remained at least partially attached. *Four* men. Where were the other four?

'Spread out and find the other four.'

As Galronus and Aurelius left the building and did a quick sweep of the depot before checking the ditch outside, Fronto jogged off toward the approaching column of men. Masgava and Carbo were at the front, and he gestured to them. The pair rode across and reined in close by.

'What's it like?'

'Messy,' Fronto replied. 'I don't want news of this spreading round the legion. It's bad finding Roman merchants butchered, but tortured legionaries will have a strong effect.' The others nodded. Such a thing could go one of two ways. Either it would enrage the legion and make them hunger for a fight, or it would unnerve them, and then the officers would be starting to look at trouble among their men.

'What do you want us to do?'

Fronto chewed his lip for a moment. 'Take the column on, slightly further away from the river and past the outpost. Set up camp a mile or so upriver. And can you send me half a dozen of the natives with shovels. We've bodies to bury and they're less invested in it than the soldiers would be.'

Masgava nodded and as he rode back to give the legion the commands to veer to the north a little, Carbo sought out the native scouts and sent them to the wagons for shovels. Fronto left them to it and wandered back toward the small fortlet. As he approached, he could see Aurelius waving at him from the copse toward the river. Picking up pace into a jog, Fronto ran past the broken ramparts and the infilled ditch. Masgava and Aurelius were standing close to the waterline on a timber platform the engineers had constructed as part of their project.

119

'Found the men,' Aurelius said darkly, and pointed.

Fronto's gaze slid down to the water, where the scalps of four men were visible as hairy domes jutting out of the water. Each man had been bound to one of the bridge supports.

'How did they drown? Surely it's not tidal this far inland? Was there a flood?'

Masgava shook his head. 'Same principle as crucifixion. You're not too bad until you start to lose the strength in your legs, then they give way, you can't support your weight and the inevitable happens. With crucifixion, that's the shoulders separating. In this case it meant that once they lost their strength, they simply sank beneath the surface and drowned.'

'Vicious bastards,' Fronto said, glaring down at the four poor souls under the river's glassy surface. 'They're goading us, you know,' he added, remembering how he'd provoked the Preciani noble into giving away something he shouldn't. 'They're deliberately goading us. Maybe even drawing us in, which is a bit of a worry.'

'Do you think we should inform Caesar and maybe send for another legion or two?'

'Shit, no,' Fronto snapped. 'I want the bastards responsible for this and I want them now. I want to know why this king is so angry at Rome that he tortures the living and dishonours the dead just to rile us. Get them cut loose and bring them up to the fort. We're going to burn the whole damn place to the ground, bodies included. Let's make it a funeral pyre they can see from the mountain tops.'

* * *

'This is one of their main settlements?'

Galronus relayed the question to the native scout, who rattled off a long answer that had the Remi noble frowning as he tried to penetrate the thick, unfamiliar accent. Finally he nodded to the man and turned back to Fronto.

'There are maybe five or six major towns of the Begerri. The main one – the king's capital – is a fortress called Biguro a little more than twenty miles further east, though if we're following the river up to the mountains we'll not go near there. Then there are a

120

few lowland places and some higher up toward the peaks. The Begerri cover a large area. Much larger than the other tribes we've passed through. And they have proper oppida.'

'I can see that,' Fronto said, sourly, peering across the flat ground to where the settlement, which had been labelled as Benarno by the scouts, rose on high ramparts. It did not display those strong walls Fronto remembered from the north and the Belgae lands. These were not ramparts built in what the engineers liked to call *murus gallicus* style, with a framework of timber infilled with rubble and faced with good solid stone. These were more like walls cobbled together from rubble with periodic timber – simple stone faces with occasional upright beams amid the face. Less solid, Fronto surmised, than the heavier defences of the north.

Whether the fact that the gate lay open relieved him or not, Fronto couldn't decide.

'I think the army can stay down here on the plain. The sun's already on the descent, but I'm not sure whether this place is a good one for a camp yet. The terrain's good, and the scouts have checked the surroundings for a mile or two, but these dead towns give me the creeps.'

Galronus nodded his understanding and his agreement.

'So do we check the town?'

'This is a big place. Not like that little depot. It'd take hours for the three of us to search it.' Fronto turned to Masgava. 'Have the legion stop on the plain between Benarno and the river. Tell them to fall out, eat, drink a little posca and wait, but keep everyone alert. Anything could happen at short notice.'

He then turned back to Galronus. 'Have all the scouts that have reported back move into the town and begin to search it. You and I will go to the nemeton first – see if we can find anything informative.'

Galronus waved the scout back over and issued the orders, and Fronto peered once more at Benarno. At perhaps three hundred paces long by two hundred wide, the town sat atop a natural ridge around a mile from the river. It held an estimated sixty or seventy buildings, which made it little more than a village by comparison with some of the oppida in the north and east, but one of the larger, more populous settlements they had found in the south-west. And maybe three hundred paces from the oppidum, atop a small mound of its own, the outriders had reported finding a small grove and temple.

Finally, the scouts were gathered and moving off into the town, and Fronto and Galronus veered off as the legion began to arrive and rest, making for the smaller wooded mound close to the town. There were no defences around the nemeton, but a hedge of cunningly-tended living bushes was interwoven as impenetrably as any wicker fencing. The two riders completed a circuit of the place before finding the entrance, which faced north. There was no gate, but the misshapen, lumpy-faced figure of some god or other stood to one side with an expression of constipated disapproval and a face full of lichen. The path was well-tended, though weeds had begun to grow through, suggesting that it had been empty for only a matter of weeks. That was much more recent than other places they had found so far, and Fronto felt the hope of discovery rise a little within.

The trees along the path that led to the low summit were again well-trimmed and tended, and emerging into the heart of the druid's domain, Fronto felt that familiar thrill of nervous energy he always experienced when entering a place of power. Once upon a time it had been an interesting thing, but that grove with the girl flautist and the gory recreation of Epona he had encountered a few years ago had changed everything, and now he felt tense and twitchy entering such a place.

It seemed, from Fronto's experience, that every nemeton was different, even within a tribe or region – as different as the druids themselves. He had found stunning constructions, rural temples, simple shrines, woodland glades and more in his time in Gaul. This one was something of a composite.

The centre of the small wooded hill held a circular glade of lush green grass. At the centre, a tree of unbelievable antiquity rose toward the heavens, its branches imploring the gods, each reaching up like an arm in supplication. The trunk was oddly bare of branches for the first ten feet, and naturally so, showing no sign of interference by man. In front of the tree sat a small deep pool, lined with smooth flat stones and surrounded by a ring of white gravel. Then came a circle of painted logs and a low wall. Beyond that the grass was deep green and pleasant, still kept cropped short by the two sheep that ambled around the periphery, seemingly uninterested in wandering off through the gateway to freedom. Around the circle, the well looked after trees again presented bare trunks up to around ten feet, and each had some sort of stylised creature etched into the bark. At the far side to the entrance stood a small building that could only contain one room, stone-built with a roof of thatch.

'This is a particularly careful druid,' Galronus noted as he dismounted and tied his horse to a purpose-made rail near the entrance. 'This place is beautiful and well-kept.'

'I was thinking the same,' Fronto replied, following suit. 'Come on.'

As they entered the circle, rather than skirting around the turf, the Remi noble led them across the various concentric lines toward the tree and the well. Reaching the pool, Galronus muttered something in his native tongue and slipped a ring from his finger, tossing it into the water. Fronto's brow arched at the sight. He remembered his friend paying a small fortune for that gold ring outside the Circus Maximus, because its representation of the Capitoline triad of Jupiter, Juno and Minerva reminded him of some three faced god worshipped by the Remi. What had just dropped into that pool represented several months' wages for a legionary.

Still, every bit of help might be important in this uncertain campaign.

Fronto paused at the pool and patted down his tunic. He had coins in his pouch, but gods liked something personal over mere monetary value. His glorious sword was going too far, of course, even with the new dent across one face. He still wore his simple, perfect torc, but that had been a gift years ago from Galronus, and he was not about to discard it. That left either one of the twin goddesses that hung on thongs around his neck, or one of the two rings he wore.

Fortuna? No. He would almost certainly need all the luck he could get this next few months. Nemesis? Only a truly short-sighted idiot slighted a vengeance goddess. The family signet? To throw that ring was essentially to admit the end of the Roman line of the Falerii, as the senate seemed to be aiming for. No. It was one small link to what had been lost and needed to be recaptured.

With a sigh, he pulled the other ring from his middle finger and peered at it for a moment, with its rather stylised image of Mars standing with spear and shield. That also felt like a betrayal and an ending, for it had been a gift from Verginius all those years ago. Still, of all the valuables he had about his person, it was the one with the fewest links to the current world. The ring disappeared with a plop into the deep sacred well and he saw Galronus giving him an odd look. Unwilling to be drawn, he straightened, cast a quick prayer for protection and the successful conclusion of their mission, then started to stride on toward the small building. Galronus was by his side again a moment later as they approached the door.

A low keening sound suddenly arose from within, and Fronto's hand went to the hilt of his sword before the noise changed pitch and began to warble into a melody. His fingers stayed at the weapon, though, even as the pair moved into the doorway.

'Hello?' Fronto said as lightly and airily as he could manage, though a lead-heavy sense of presence was beginning to weigh on him in this sacred place.

The song stopped instantly, and the voice from the shadows said 'Latin?'

'I am a Roman officer,' Fronto said quietly, feeling it best to lay out the situation clearly straight away

'Yet you cast offerings to Leherenno, who knows not your people except as an invader.'

Fronto smiled. 'Foreigner or local, only a fool angers a god.'

There was a hoarse laugh, and a figure rose from the floor in the shadow. emerging into the light from the door. Fronto almost recoiled. The druid was hideous. His eyes had been put out, and two ruined, raw sockets stared at him, their eyelids gone too. His cheeks, from eyes to chin, were lacerated with many vertical cuts that were only a few days old and were still crusted with blood. His ragged grey hair was dirty and caked with gore, and the concentration of dark red at the sides led Fronto to suspect that both ears had been cut off. His left arm was so heavily slashed with knife wounds that it looked as though he wore a striped sleeve, and his right arm had gone at the shoulder. Other injuries there probably were, but it was impossible to tell as the man's once-

124

white robe was now a dark red and black, stained beyond redemption.

'Belenos!' snarled Galronus, with a rare invocation of his native gods, and he and Fronto rushed over, the legate's hand leaving his sword and reaching instead for the ravaged druid.

'Curious that the people of the mountains would turn on their own and it takes a Roman to show sympathy,' the druid said, and smiled. Fronto shivered as that smile opened up the cheek wounds again.

'Who would do this to you?' the legate said in a breathy tone. 'I thought your people venerated you above almost all things?'

'My people?' Again the man laughed. 'I am no longer sure who my people are. We *were* the Begerri, but it seems the Begerri are to be no more, for the smiling demon in the mountains has proclaimed a change.'

'Smiling demon?'

The man seemed to ignore the prompt. 'The Begerri are now part of the Convenae. The Consoranni, too. And others. Our great heritage is to be purged and a new heritage of mindless subservience created as the Convenae. My king is dead, butchered for refusing to serve another, and his son is a king in name only, for he serves the smiling demon like some lackey.'

'Smiling demon?' prompted Fronto again.

'And now the Begerri are gone. You have been to the town?'

Fronto nodded, and Galronus tried to indicate to him that the druid couldn't see.

'Yes. Well, my scouts are looking around it now. It's empty?'

'It is. The women and children, the old and the lame, they are among the Convenae now in the mountains. Not I, for I refused to go, and this is my punishment. But, Roman, be prepared, for whoever they serve, the Begerri are warriors born and warriors bred. A thousand seasons of battle have prepared them for any war to come, and they wait for you.'

Fronto stepped back. 'The Begerri wait for us?'

'Their stinking master uses them as a rampart to hold you and thin your ranks. They wait for you at Biguro. They have left signs in blood and misery to direct you there.'

'We found one of them.'

'You respect the gods and have a good heart for a Roman. I would save you all the pain I can. In the best world, you would turn around and march away from the mountains. You will find only pain and destruction there.' Fronto opened his mouth, but the druid smiled and went on. 'I know you will not. Romans are the only ones I have met who are more bloody-minded than us. But still, I counsel that you leave. Remember when this is over that I told you not to go on. But if you do, you can march south from here to the mountains, where you will find your true enemy. You need not meet the foolish warriors of my tribe. You need not take Biguro.'

'Tell me about this smiling demon.'

'I cannot. I am bound by gossamer chains and oaths of iron and stone. I know that everything I counsel you will ignore, but it is my place to counsel it anyway. And when you do ignore it I pray that Leherenno protects you and that your pain is bearable.'

With that the druid retreated into the shadows away from the door.

'We can help you. I have a medicus with me, and several field-physicians.'

'The shade and the breeze sooth my wounds and I take comfort in knowing that my revenge will be enacted, even if I counsel against it. Leave me.'

Fronto opened his mouth to argue, but Galronus gestured to the door. With a frustrated sigh, the legate followed his friend back out into the fresh air. A curious sheep looked up from nearby and, apparently consigning Fronto to the category 'uninteresting', went back to cropping the grass.

'Abusing a druid?' he said as they strode away from the hut back toward the horses. 'This bastard has some guts.'

'He advised you not to go to Biguro. We don't need to fight them.'

'But he also knew I'd go. From a personal viewpoint, I want to stamp on this. Their warriors need to be shown a lesson in not following madmen and breaking their oath. From a military stance, only a poor general leads his legion on into enemy territory while leaving a slavering enemy force intact behind him. That's an excellent way to get trapped and obliterated. No, we have to take on the Begerri. We have to take Biguro. But we have been relieved of one burden, at least.'

'Oh?' Galronus mused. 'What is that?

'He said that their civilians were up in the mountains. Only the warriors are at Biguro. That means we don't need to pull our punches. I don't like mad violent assaults if there's a chance of killing an innocent populace, and it sounds a lot to me like the Begerri are victims here as much as they are dupes. We can throw everything we have at Biguro and know that only enemy warriors will be struck by it.'

Galronus nodded his agreement. 'It's not much of a relief, but it's something at least. You might have been right before. You know, when you compared this to Vercingetorix. There are clear parallels.'

'No,' Fronto said as they reached the horses and he climbed into the saddle. 'No, this is different. The Arvernian rebel modelled his revolt on the Greek world. As they had leagues made up of city states, he had a grand force formed from individual tribes, and though they all fought for him, they maintained their autonomy. Their leaders still led them. This is different. This is more like Rome.'

'Like Rome?'

Fronto nodded as the pair kicked their horses' flanks and urged them back through the entrance and away from the sacred grove. 'Once upon a time, Rome was just a small settlement on a hill. Then they started to take over their troublesome neighbours and expand. Soon we were enveloping tribes all over Italia. There were Etruscans and Oscans and Samnites and so on, but they're all Romans. They might still think of themselves as Oscan while they teach their kids, but they still go to a forum to register with clerks and they still obey the laws that come out of Rome and they still cheer the consuls. And having lost their own leaders and institutions, gradually they've lost their identity. Now, they're all Romans. That's what this man is doing – this king in the mountains, this smiling demon. I've never met him, but already I hate him. I hate what he's doing to these people, and that makes me rather uncomfortable, given that this is exactly what my own ancestors did to our local tribes.'

'Whatever is going on down here, and whoever this king is,' Galronus said quietly, but with malice in his voice, 'Caesar was right to send us. This needs to stop.'

The pair rode in silence for a while, each wrapped in their own thoughts. The scouts were visible here and there on the ramparts of Benarno, but it was clear from conversation with the druid that they would find nothing there. The warriors were all at Biguro, luring Fronto's legion to battle, and the civilians were up in the mountains as part of this new tribe, and would have taken with them anything worth taking. This new 'Convenae' answered a few questions. Not least: where were all the people going from these abandoned places all over Aquitania.

The legion was now falling out across the plain, relaxing as best they could in their brief rest. As the two riders closed on the army, Fronto spotted Carbo, Arruntius, Atenos and Masgava in discussion and veered toward them.

'Gentlemen.'

The officers broke off their conversation and turned to Fronto, saluting.

'It seems the Begerri are waiting for us at their capital of Biguro, twenty miles or so east of here. There is a badly wounded druid at the nemeton, who has refused any assistance, but who counselled us to simply avoid Biguro and head south. I am not accustomed to leaving enemies behind me, so we will move on Biguro and remove the warriors there first. And whatever he said, that druid needs medical attention. I want the medicus and a pair of orderlies, along with a couple of the more local native scouts, to visit the nemeton and render him assistance, calmly and carefully, but firmly.'

He slipped from Bucephalus. 'Moreover, we're moving on slowly. We'll spend the night here and move eight miles the next three days. That should ensure the men are as rested as possible when we arrive at Biguro and in the best position to utterly crush the Begerri. There are no civilians there, just warriors, so unless they surrender when we arrive, we will give no quarter.'

'And although we're moving into ever more dangerous territory and about to march into a probably fierce fight, I want the next five hundred men chosen from the lists. We will be leaving a garrison here to found a new colony. Riders can be sent back to the one at Sorda linking everything up and sending word to Lapurda. And while they're at it they can see if a wine shipment can be sent back along the line at speed. The men are going to want to celebrate or commiserate in the coming days.'

'Doesn't look like there's anything in the town, sir,' Carbo noted. 'The scouts haven't shouted or reported in.'

'I doubt they'll find anything interesting at all. The populace is all either in Biguro or up in the mountains, and that is something I think we need to discuss. Give the command to set up camp for the night and as soon as everything's moving, meet me up in the chief's house in town, and bring all the officers and senior centurions. There have been interesting developments I think you all need to hear.'

* * *

Biguro was a difficult proposition, clearly, and Fronto's erstwhile imaginings of simply sweeping up the hill with his legion and swamping an unprepared enemy shattered. The oppidum rose from the wide swathes of forested land like the top of a domed skull, bare and forbidding. There were a number of small farms surrounding the place, their acreage of fields carved out of the woodlands, but the place itself was surrounded by only a few hundred paces of open land until the forest took over. The legion had marched slowly along a well-used trade road through the woodland, wide enough for four men comfortably, or a cart. But there was little or no space to form up an army to attack the place. If the legion attempted to form in one of the farm lands, they would then have to break formation again to move through the trees to the target. And if they attempted to form ranks in that narrow verge below the fortress, they would be doing it within range of enemy archers. As for siege engines? Well there was precious little chance of getting any through all this.

'Shit.'

'Quite,' Terpulo said with a nod. 'They've chosen their place well. Maybe with a couple of days we can clear enough woodland to give us room to work?'

Fronto shook his head with a grunt. 'No. They've been waiting for us. They know the land better than us and they've had time to prepare. There's nowhere nearby we can encamp the whole legion for days. We'd have to camp in individual cohorts in the farms or some distance away. I don't see us making it through the first night without a few really nasty surprises.'

'Then what do we do?'

'There was ample camping space where we crossed those two streams a couple of miles back. Most of the legion won't have got there yet. Have the lead elements return to that spot and pitch camp for the night. With any luck no one will have noticed us yet and they won't know where we are.'

Terpulo saluted.

'And as soon as you've delivered the orders to Carbo, have all the seniors report here. We need a tactical discussion.'

Another salute and, as Terpulo rushed off, Fronto sat beneath the gently swaying branches of the old beech tree and looked up the slope to where the solid defences of Biguro lay. It would be a tough fight, and the legion was already down to eighty percent manpower, having left a thousand men behind now to found new colonies. Perhaps the druid had been right and they shouldn't have come. But then he could just picture the legion marching off into the foothills of the mountains, finding some crazed army of this smiling demon king and engaging them, only to be hit from behind by several thousand slavering Begerri. No. Military sense – even *common* sense – required that he remove any threat lurking behind them first, before moving on.

His gaze took in the oppidum around which Terpulo and he had ridden over the past half hour, while the disapproving Aurelius and the advance scouts sat back beyond the trees out of sight. The army was moving up slowly around a mile back. But the two men had eased their horses along game trails and hunters' tracks through the woodland, finding good positions periodically to observe Biguro. Nowhere had they smiled and decided that they had found their spot. The place was well protected.

The whole oppidum sat on a natural north-south ridge, the plateaued hilltop sloping slightly down toward the east. The southern and eastern flanks of the hill were solidly bolstered with walls that were stronger than those of Benarno, if still not up to the strength of Belgic defences. Moreover, they were surrounded by a good ditch that had long since filled with brackish water, creating a swampy moat that would make access extremely difficult. The western side of the place was steep naturally and, when the rampart was added it would prove tough enough even without the addition of the ditch. And the north was hell. Steep slope with rocky protuberances below the rampart, a soggy area at the treeline below, and then nowhere to marshal an attack. Nature herself protected the north of Biguro.

Fronto sat and stared, occasionally catching a glimpse of a figure or the flash of sunlight off bronze as warriors moved about the ramparts. In his mind he ran through everything they had with them. Bolt throwers. Given the angle of the slope and the ramparts at the top, they'd loose a thousand bolts to injure a single man. Hardly a worthwhile exercise. Siege tower? Not a chance up that slope. Undermining and vineae? No, and besides, apart from artillery, they had nothing with them. It would all have to be constructed on site. Oh they would not be short of timber, but it would take a while, and if they wanted to construct anything close to where it would be used, they would be in danger from above while building. After all, there were almost certainly at least as many enemy warriors in Biguro as there were legionaries approaching, and probably more even than that.

No. Best to dismiss all thoughts of traditional sieges. Ramps and tunnels and engines and so on. All pretty much useless in this situation. And he wanted to take Biguro down quickly and move south while the going was good. Every day gave this madman in the mountains more time to prepare.

He was still fuming over the impossibilities and impracticability of the whole thing when the officers began to arrive half an hour later with Terpulo leading them. As they closed along the narrow trail, he pulled back from the edge of the woods and joined them in the little clearing forty paces or so into the trees where the scouts and Aurelius waited.

'I'm trying not to let them know we're here yet, though they're bound to find out soon enough. In the meantime, though, I'll tell you what Terpulo and I have seen of the place, then I want you one by one to head to the treeline and have a look. Then, when you've acquainted yourself with Biguro, we'll talk tactics.'

For the next quarter hour, Fronto went over everything they had seen, with interjections periodically from Terpulo and occasional input from the native scouts that were standing nearby. Then another half hour passed as the various officers and the eight remaining senior centurions stalked through the undergrowth to take a look at Biguro. Finally, as the last man returned, scratching his chin, Fronto took a breath.

'Here's how I see it. We cannot afford to tarry here more than a couple of days, if we want to keep our momentum up and move into the mountains. I don't want to still be here in three days, for certain. And that means we cannot consider clearing out stretches of the woodland, constructing heavy siege engines or suchlike. Our artillery will barely make it over those ramparts, and the archers will be little better off, because of the distance and gradient. The only places to marshal enough men for a proper push are far enough back that all formation would be nullified by having to move through more forest, or so close that they would be forming under enemy barrages. I am more or less stumped. In previous years, I might add, when I have witnessed the best and most successful sieges in the history of Gaul, most of them have been the brainchildren either of Caesar or of his engineer Mamurra. Both of them are such ingenious lateral thinkers that they can overcome this kind of issue. So I'm hoping there's someone here has that same kind of mind as them. Find me a way into Biguro, gentlemen.'

There was a short silence, and eventually one of the centurions cleared his throat. 'Undermine the ramparts, sir? Then we don't need to form up the men anywhere special. We would have a breach to go for, and could push men in by the century.'

Fronto shook his head. 'Tunnelling up that gradient into rocky ground is unfeasible. I've already ruled out ramps and tunnels and the like.'

'Subterfuge?' Carbo murmured. 'We have natives – or as near as damn it – with the army. Maybe we can get men inside and open it from within?'

'They'll be too watchful. They've drawn us here, remember, so they know what's going on. As soon as they know we're here they'll be on to it like dogs down a rabbit hole.'

'We can form the men into contubernia in the trees,' said another voice, 'then they can each join ranks quickly in the open and move up.'

Fronto smiled at Pulcher. 'Best suggestion so far. Unfortunately, I don't think there'd be room to marshal more than a cohort that way. I think we'd be feeding troops at the walls too slowly to make an effective assault.'

Arruntius coughed meaningfully, and Fronto turned. 'Thoughts, centurion?'

'You don't think a cohort could make an effective assault, sir?'

'I think it would be dangerously irresponsible to try. There's an extremely high probability that it would just be a case of throwing away men. With less than four thousand to take against the mountains, I can't afford to risk too many men here, and with defenders and ramparts like this, anything short of a full-scale assault is too risky.'

'Begging to differ in my opinion, Legate, but I think that's crap.'

Fronto raised his brow. 'Oh?'

'You know those chests you're carrying in the carts? The ones with Caesar's bull on them and enough locks to keep out Alexander himself?'

'The coin chests, yes.'

'Would you be willing to devote one of those to opening up Biguro?'

Fronto's brow sank into a furrow. 'I doubt they're open to bribes.'

'Are you willing, sir?'

'Well, yes. For certain. What have you in mind?'

Arruntius turned to Terpulo. 'You've got the authority. Can you ride to the baggage train and secure one of those chests for me?' Terpulo grinned, touched his fingers to his forehead, mounted and rode off back toward the column. As the others followed on, Fronto gestured at the elderly centurion.

'What do you have in mind?'

'Incentive, sir. Incentive.'

* * *

Fronto followed Arruntius and the cornicen from the centurion's unit as they approached the cart standing in the open space around the standards, surrounded by a sea of legionaries taking the rare opportunity for an unscheduled rest, mid-build. The half-completed ramparts surrounded them, and no tents had yet been raised. Arruntius was all purpose and energy, which was nothing new. Despite the centurion's advanced years, Fronto had never seen him anything less than entirely active. Arruntius vaulted up onto the cart with an agility rare in a man half his age and, trying not to feel irritated by it, Fronto clambered up behind him, praying his knee would not give way in the process. Arruntius stepped to the front of the cart and gestured down to his cornicen by the rear board, who took a deep breath and blew a short staccato burst of notes. Every face across that green field turned to face the sound.

Fronto watched the faces of the men around them, men drawn from eleven legions working remarkably well as one independent unit. There was interest on display, and respect, and relief.

'Sit down, all of you,' the centurion shouted, his voice carrying easily over the wide, flat ground, and the legion gratefully sank to the turf. 'There may yet be some of you who are unaware of our current destination. We are bound for an oppidum by the name of Biguro to put boot to backside in that special way that only we know. The Begerri, who are waiting for us, are the ones who have butchered Roman merchants in the area, as well as engineering parties. They have given over their service to an enemy of Rome, and sent their civilians away. Biguro is a tough place and every man in it is a warrior with our names etched on his blade.'

There was a murmur of acknowledgement. Though there had been as yet no official briefing about what was to come, word spread throughout a legion like a forest fire, and this was news to no one.

'There is a small problem, however, in that we cannot bring siege works or engines against the place, and there is precious little room to marshal a force to storm the ramparts for these endless bloody trees. The legate here is dubious about committing a single cohort, as he doesn't believe a cohort can take the place and he doesn't want to throw away your lives.' Fronto glared at the centurion. He didn't like the way this speech was going.

'All very laudable,' Arruntius continued, 'but I think I know you mad, hard bastards well enough. I think a cohort of you lot could take Biguro, even if you went in naked and blindfolded.'

He fell silent and the atmosphere was one of tense but positive energy. There were nods of heads around the field. Fronto clasped his hands behind his back so the men couldn't see him fidgeting. It was starting to look like this entire legion was as barking mad as the old centurion. Arruntius bent and flung open the chest on the cart, pulling out a small handful of silver coins. Straightening, he held it up so that the spring sunlight glinted on the money.

'This is what you fight for. Oh, I know we fight for Rome and for the general and for the eagle and for the gods and so on, but this is the cold, hard remuneration that sees you all through. You're each due four thousand sesterces with your honesta missio, some of you a little more. This chest contains somewhere in the region of five hundred thousand sesterces at a guess, and the generous legate is offering to add it to the retirement fund of a single cohort if they'll help me take Biguro. That's an extra thousand sesterces a man. I want six full centuries, including officers, so that's four hundred and eighty legionary volunteers. I shall also want five more centurions, six men to serve as optios, and one cornicen. Stand now if you're with me.'

There was an odd pause, and then men started to rise. Arruntius lowered his hand and cast the fistful of silver coins into the crowd, where laughing legionaries caught them and examined them. More men rose, and Arruntius leaned down from the cart to a soldier in just his tunic with a tablet and stilus. 'Headcount, please, Silvanus.'

The clerk waited until each man was standing and then climbed up onto the cart to see over the heads of the men, where he began to count and mark off on his tablet. After some time, he clicked his tongue and ran down the tallies.

'Three hundred and twenty five men, sir, including four optios and eight centurions from the crests.'

Arruntius nodded and cleared his throat, addressing the crowd once more. 'Too many centurions. Caetronius, Menenius, Hirrius, Vivianus and Tullius, you're in. The other three will have to keep their swords sheathed and play with themselves until we find the next tribe. Are any of you lot cornicen?'

Two men raised their hands.

'Alright, I'll take you both. Everyone move off to the side and be ready to give your name and unit to Silvanus here.' As the men filtered out of the crowd, the centurion smiled. 'I want another hundred and fifty five legionaries and two optios. How about the legate sweetens the pot. I'm sure he won't mind you keeping all the loot from Biguro and any slaves we take, without the usual apportionment.' He turned a meaningful look on Fronto who, irritated at being put on the spot, was left with no option but an easy nod.

'There you go. The choice pickings from Biguro, too. Anyone else with me?'

Slowly another fifty or so men rose from the seated legionaries. Arruntius grunted his irritation. 'You're disappointing me and embarrassing me in front of the legate.' Another twenty or thirty men rose, and finally the centurion pulled at his ear. 'Very well. I make that four hundred and ten or so men altogether. That'll be enough. We'll rip the bastards out of Biguro for you, Legate. Keep your eye out for a standard up on the ramparts – we'll filter through the woods during the last watch of the night and launch the assault at first light.'

Fronto grinned. 'You might well be insane Arruntius, but you truly are mad if you think I'm not coming with you.'

'We've had this talk before, sir,' the centurion said seriously. 'I won't have you endangering yourself and ruining my unit cohesion.'

'You won't *have* unit cohesion,' Fronto retorted. These men are from all over different units.'

'Respectfully, Legate, so is the whole legion and we're doing just fine so far.'

'I'm still coming. Get used to the idea.'

Arruntius held Fronto's fierce gaze for some time, and finally gave a tiny, curt nod. 'Very well, but this is *my* assault. You command the army, but once the cohort breaks cover on that hill I am in charge, and if you want to come on my assault, you do as I say.'

Fronto narrowed his eyes in the face of that eye-watering gaze, but finally relented and nodded. 'Alright. What do you want me to do.'

'We're down one optio. You can take optio role in the sixth century. That means you will be the rearmost man. You can use that vine staff I see you carry sometimes like you're a centurion to smack the arse of any dawdlers. But you *stay* at the back where I put you, and if I've misjudged this and everything goes completely tits-up, you run back down that hill like your arse is on fire and get back to the legion.'

Fronto briefly considered arguing the point, but the look in Arruntius' eye suggested that he would get no further, so he nodded, wondering what plan the old centurion had in mind to take so few men against so many and yet achieve victory.

Tomorrow morning would tell, anyway. For now, he needed food and wine and then a good night. Even right at the back, Biguro would probably be a hard fight and he would need to be as well rested as he could.

Mid Maius

THE king concentrated hard, frowning at the scarred face staring back out of the bronze mirror. He paused, aware that he'd not always looked like this. Long ago he'd been hailed a handsome man. He regarded the grainy, dark stubble still covering the left side of his face. He knew the rest of his men – even those he considered close and trustworthy – disapproved of his shaved face, but he wouldn't grow a beard, even if he realistically could.

With a grunt of self-loathing, he picked up the heavy, razor-edged dagger once more, dipped it in the bronze bowl of water, and began to scrape away the stubble from his neck, slowly working up to the jawline. There, he felt it move with the undulations of his flesh from the wound that no one ever noticed. His face, he knew, was so striking that few ever looked beyond it. But there, beneath the jaw, were the marks still left by the rope garrotte. A regular pattern around his entire neck. Carefully, he worked around the damage, then took a breath, rinsed off the blade, and began on his cheek just below the eye, dragging the steel across the hairs.

He hissed in pain as the blade caught the 'smile' scar and drew blood. It happened with almost every shave, so deep and pronounced were the scars. Lowering the knife, he stared again at that familiar/unfamiliar face in the bronze as a thin trickle of red began to run down the gulley in his cheek to his lips, where they spread and began to drip to his chin.

'Who are you?' he whispered.

The face stared back out at him defiant. Wicked. Deformed. Hollow…. Vengeful.

The clang as the dagger hit the beautiful bronze mirror rang out across the room. The shining, imperfect surface rocked back and forth, the huge dent that ruined the mirror distorting his face into even more a thing of nightmares. With an angry bark, he cast the dagger away and swept the blood from his face with his thumb, staring at the crimson running down his digit.

Chest heaving, pulse thudding, the king stood in the dim room as the door slammed open and Ategnio barrelled in, sword in hand. The warrior, his right hand man, looked this way and that and calmed almost instantly.

'I thought there was trouble.'

'Just *old* trouble,' the king replied quietly. 'Close the door.'

Ategnio did so, though remained on the inside of it. 'I still don't know why you bother shaving.'

'As I've told you a thousand times, I want to see my scars. And I want others to see them too. They have become who I am. *I* have become my scars. I wear them like a banner. They are every bit as much my livery as my standard or the wolf banners. They remind me of who I was, and of who I now am.'

The burly warrior stooped and scooped up the fallen blade, turning it over and over and examining it distastefully.

'And I cannot fathom why you would want this thing.'

Wandering across to the king, the warrior proffered the knife, and his master took it and laid it beside the water bowl.

'Because, Ategnio, as much as my scars, it is a reminder of things long gone.'

The warrior huffed his disapproval, then folded his arms. 'Once you are ready, we will move, my king. We should be at Tredos by sunset.

The king simply nodded, and his warrior huffed again and wrenched the door open, exiting and thumping it shut behind him, leaving a solitary figure once more in the dim interior, watching a ruined face swinging back and forth on a hook. Reaching out, he steadied the mirror and reached for a towel, dipping it in the water and wiping the blood from his face. Satisfied that he was almost ready, he reached for the well looked after pugio dagger lying by the bowl, turning it over and over as he examined the blade. Perhaps he would use this very Roman dagger to cut out Caesar's heart when he came.

Chapter Seven

FRONTO rolled his shoulders and picked up the heavy rectangular shield with the slight curve – standard legionary fare. For all Arruntius' words, there was no way Fronto was wielding a stick and prodding legionaries in a fight. Besides, if these soldiers were half as insane as they seemed to be – and even a quarter as insane as the centurion himself – then they would need no chivvying on. More likely they would need to be restrained. So Fronto had taken sword and shield. He had kept his plumed helmet, though. At Sorda he had walked through an arrow storm unharmed because the enemy seemed to be unwilling to target him. So while it was usually dangerous to mark oneself as an officer, as it drew enemy attacks, there was the tantalising possibility that in his case it might actually save rather than damn him.

The rest of the force was already moving out of the clearing and into the trees, and Fronto's century – the Sixth – was last to move off, his place at the rear of the very last contubernium of men making him the very last human into the woods. The animal trails had been widened and well trampled down by the other groups of seven men (not the usual eight, for the number of volunteers had not made up a full cohort) who had moved through the woods into position. The organisation made sense. The cohort would move in seven man groups into position, and each century had been allotted an area of woods marked out by their officers. The First century had peeled off to the left into their position, the Second to the right, the Third to the left, and so on, gradually closing the gap until the Sixth filled the centre at the last. As they broke from the undergrowth, each ten groups would re-form into a century and move on the defences.

Fronto was still boggling at the centurion's apparent folly as he picked his way through the trees to his position. The legate had been unable to determine any strategy that would see them into the oppidum and so had thrown open the floor to all the senior officers. None of them had been able to come up with a usable plan, but Arruntius had been so sure he could take the place that Fronto had simply accepted such, assuming that the old centurion had some cunning manoeuvre in mind.

His opinion that the man was clearly one mushroom short of a basket was confirmed when he'd enquired as to the plan while they moved through the forest in the pre-dawn light.

'Plan?' Arruntius had said with a frown.

'Yes, your strategy for scaling the walls.'

'Run at the bastards screaming, and stick a sword in as many as I can,' the old man had replied, calmly and in a matter-of-fact tone. Fronto had been so taken aback by the basic irrationality of the 'plan' that he'd remained silent for the rest of the walk. The same could not be said for the legionaries of Arruntius' volunteer force, though. Each and every man was upbeat, chatting amiably, many comparing how they had tweaked the standard manoeuvers the centurions had trained them in long ago to achieve swifter or more defensive strikes. Pulled from eleven different legions, most of these men had very different and conflicting ideas as to what worked well in a fight, though they all knew the main basic manoeuvres, and the weeks they had spent at Samarobriva had allowed them to grow used to a new set of calls and melodies so that they could work well as a unit for all their differences. In fact, the legionaries were so jolly and enthusiastic the entire endeavour felt more like a summer picnic in the woods than a march into a brutal siege. Arruntius and his officers had to silence the men as they closed on Biguro for fear of alerting the enemy, and for the rest of the journey, the legionaries whispered to one another and chuckled under their breath.

And so Fronto travelled with them in silent disbelief. Four hundred men were about to charge perhaps four or five thousand enemy who were comfortably packed behind defences up a steep slope, and they seemed to be *excited* at the prospect. And what was their officer's grand plan? Run at the enemy, screaming. Brilliant.

It was hard to deny the distinct possibility that Fronto was about to throw away a tenth of his entire army on the most ridiculously futile attack. And yet while it was his right – perhaps even his duty – to call it off, he found that he couldn't, because something about Arruntius was infectious, as though his reckless madness was a virulent disease. Certainly the legionaries had caught it. When you listened to him talk, the part of your mind that wrestled with doubt seemed to be totally subdued. And after all, had Arruntius not been the man who had broken through Pompey's army alone at the Sucro? If anyone could do this, then surely it was Arruntius.

Fronto reached into the neck of his tunic, wrestling with the scarf until he produced the small figurine of Fortuna hanging from the thong, and gave it a kiss for luck before tucking it back inside, almost tripping over a tree root as he fought with his bulky shield on the narrow trail. At least it was nice and dry under the canopy of the woods. Perhaps an hour before dawn, as they'd set off from camp, there had begun one of those mists that could burn off with the morning sun, but could just as easily develop into a soul-destroying drizzle or even full blown rain. The world had been dark, but the lack of twinkling stars had confirmed that a blanket of cloud covered the sky. Maius was always an unpredictable month for weather, no matter where you were, but among the foothills of a mountain range, that uncertainty was compounded.

As they pushed through the trail, the legionary two in front of the legate said something in a throaty whisper, and the next man in line chuckled quietly.

'Can't wait to get stuck into the buggers,' the legionary replied to his friend lightly and in a sibilant whisper. Again the other soldier said something that made his friend laugh.

'And I hope you get a Gallic spear up that stinking behind of yours Vedetius.'

Fronto had been about to silence both men, but the light-hearted manner of such a dark comment concerned him, and instead he cleared his throat and whispered to the man in front 'If you two don't like each other, maybe you should be separated.'

'Don't like him?' the man whispered in reply, turning with a grin. 'Best mate is Vedetius, Legate. Come up through the Eighth together, we did.'

'Then you might be better not wishing him a brutal death,' Fronto hissed disapprovingly.

'But we're *going* to lose men, Legate, and don't forget that every man who drops increases the share of the gold pot for the rest of us, eh? Vedetius gets himself pinned and I get richer. Sometimes the gods have funny ways, don't they, sir?'

Fronto stared in horror at the man, who grinned. 'Don't worry sir. I won't wish anything nasty on you. You're not in the pot anyway, see?'

With a guffaw he turned back and moved on again, leaving Fronto staring after them all. They were clearly as mad as Arruntius, each and every one of them.

A quarter of an hour later, as the first strains of light were beginning to filter through the leafy canopy and the moist morning had begun to penetrate the branches to drip forlornly beneath, the legionaries fell into position, and Fronto found himself standing at the back of a line of six other men, staring up the steep grassy bank to the forbidding ramparts above. He was, oddly, in almost exactly the position from which he and the officers had observed the place the previous day.

Above the oppidum, the grey fleecy sky told a tale of coming rain and possibly even storms. So much for the sun burning off the mist, then. It struck him that he should be thanking Jupiter for the weather, really. Any enemy archer who had his bow out would find it more or less useless now, the string soggy and stretched, and those who'd kept them sensibly in a cover or indoors, out of the wet, would hardly have time to fetch or unpack them and bring them to bear on any swift attack. There would likely still be slingers up there, but at least arrows would be a diminished threat.

Somewhere distant there was a rumble of thunder.

Of course, the general dampness in the atmosphere would make running up a grassy slope treacherous to say the least – especially if seventy odd men had gone up in front, churning the turf to mud. Still, Fronto knew that this assault was a make or break thing, rather than just part of an ongoing siege situation, and so rather than facing a week of being bogged down here, one way or another it would be over within the hour. If they succeeded, then Biguro was theirs. If they failed there would be little choice but to move on south with the rest of the legion and deal with being flanked by the Begerri when the time came. And so, either way, Fronto prayed that the storm would hold off an hour or so until it was over. It didn't look likely.

Fronto heard a muttering ahead, which seemed to be repeated all across the treeline, and the instructions were gradually passed back and forth across the men. Finally, the legionary ahead of Fronto turned and whispered.

'One owl hoot and we move out. First whistle and form into contubernia. Second into centuries. Third we run.'

143

'It's a cunning plan, there's no denying it,' Fronto replied in exasperation, at which the legionary simply grinned. For the first time, Fronto began to wonder why he'd been so adamant he wanted to be part of this. It had nothing to do with glory or the need to rush an enemy headlong. In fact, it had mostly been inquisitiveness – the desire to watch this impressive veteran in his natural environment. Suddenly Arruntius' natural environment was looking ridiculously dangerous and foolish.

It was odd to stand in such a position. Fronto had fought for his life alongside the legions many times, but he had always been either in the thick of it from the start or had been in a commanding position. Never had he endured such a wait among the rear rankers, and he hadn't realised how tense it made a man. Not that his companions seemed to be suffering so. If anything, they seemed to be enjoying themselves. Weird.

He missed the hoot. The first he knew of the attack was when the man in front of him began to push forward through the undergrowth. Fronto shoved forth in his wake, branches scratching the painted design from his shield, and barely had he emerged from the trees before the centurions' first whistle went.

The rain had begun while they were beneath the trees, though at this point it was little more than the odd spot, but the air had a curiously washed-out appearance between them and the oppidum above. The contubernium of seven men fell into line in the order they'd emerged from the woods just six paces from the next group, and Fronto was still busy lining himself up with the man in front when the second whistle blew. The head of his contubernium held up his hand to keep them in place as the contubernia to either side hurried across with a jingle of metal and the clonk of wood, forming up to either side. Suddenly Fronto was at the rear of a century of seventy or so men, and he could just see the transverse crest of the centurion as he fell into position at the front

Amazingly, the entire manoeuvre had taken perhaps twenty heartbeats – from lurking in the woods to waiting expectantly in century formation on the grass. It had taken the Begerri by surprise, for sure, and the alarm was beginning to go up in surprised shouts from the ramparts only as the centuries formed.

Then the whistle went again, echoing across the forest edge from each centurion, and the unit surged forward. Fronto had burst

144

into a run to keep up with his unit – the many long-serving old legs in the unit seemed to be young and agile enough right now. Praying his knee would hold up, especially in the damp weather, the legate pounded on. He found himself suddenly wondering what to do. He had commanded and fought in many battles, and he knew that centurions commanded at a unit and melee level. He knew that optios supported the centurion and chivvied the soldiers along from the back, whacking dawdlers on the legs with a stick. He'd seen them doing it many, many times, and yet now, thrust into the role of one, he couldn't decide what to do. None of the men were dawdling – if anything it was him lagging at the back. He couldn't decide on any words of encouragement, for the soldiers were now raising a cacophony that was probably audible as far as Egypt. He was essentially redundant, and so he ran on.

As the slope began to tell and footing became more difficult, the centurions bellowed the order to unsheathe swords. 'Til this point each man had kept their blade sheathed due to difficulty among the branches and undergrowth and the potential for accidents among the close press of bodies. Now, at the command, each soldier drew his blade as he ran. No pila here – the gradient made them a largely pointless weapon in such situations.

The centuries were beginning to fragment a little as they moved onto the slope of the hill. The rain was increasing steadily, though as yet it counted for little more than a light patter, but the ground underfoot was slippery and dangerous, and Fronto had to fight to maintain his footing with every pounding step, paying attention to his balance and keeping one eye on the terrain as much as possible. Even the wildlife of Aquitania were proving troublesome to Rome, for here and there Fronto could hear a squawk and clatter as a man fell foul of some animal's burrow or den, and it was a testament to the quality and collective experience of all those present that they managed so successfully to skirt the fallen and continue on their way as they ran.

'Broken leg,' someone up ahead shouted gleefully. 'The shares just went up, lads!'

There was a cheer at the news that Fronto felt was just a little too cold for his liking, though as he passed the man of whom they'd spoken who was floundering by a rabbit hole with a turned leg, he was surprised to find the man not screaming with pain, but

145

angrily bellowing at his friends to 'leave my damn share alone yer vultures!'

Mad, the lot of them.

Fronto could now hear the Begerri, who sounded a lot more nervous and desperate than the tiny force charging at them up the hill, and he clucked in irritation as raindrops dinged off the bronze of his helmet. Then one clang almost sent him flying flat on his back and he staggered for a moment, recovering his footing carefully to avoid sliding back down the slope. As he steadied himself and ran on to catch up, more raindrops dinged, their pace increasing, but another sling stone like the one that had almost sent him flying glanced off the doubled mail at his shoulder, sending a thrill of pain coursing along his arm.

A few dozen Begerri had taken to the rampart top with slings and were using them with deadly accuracy. Fronto's view was rather restricted by a full century of men in front, but he could just see the shapes of the defenders, swinging their slings with that expert single circle release that seemed to be the mark of the true professional. Here and there, soldiers were falling to the smooth stones and their companions would whoop and jeer and bellow threats to claim their shares of the prize. Fronto shook his head in disbelief as they closed on the defences at the top of the hill. Miraculously, due to the speed and surprise of their assault and the wet weather that had largely nullified the use of bows in the oppidum, remarkably few legionaries had fallen during the ascent, perhaps a score of soldiers scattered across the grassy rise, and most of them sporting relatively minor injuries or trying to pull stone-dented helmets from dazed heads. Once more there was considerably more angry cursing and whoops of delight across the slope than there were screams of pain or anguish. It was altogether the oddest assault Fronto had ever experienced.

As the ground began to level out once more close to a stone rampart the height of two men, Fronto was finally able to stop paying close attention to the terrain and fixed his eyes on their destination. The lead elements were already reaching the defences and as the legate's gaze played across the line of the rampart he was not remotely surprised to see the lithe but hoary shape of Arruntius, shieldless and bellowing the many epithets of Mars as he pulled himself up the rampart toward dozens of lancing spears and jabbing swords. No wonder the men were mad, when you looked at who led them…

There were shouts of fury and warning from the leading ranks of Fronto's century as they hit the rampart. Like the other oppida Fronto had seen thus far in the region, the defences were formed from an earth bank with the outer face cut away and revetted in stone. They might *look* more solid than the murus gallicus of the north, but it was merely a façade of strength, comparatively.

The century hit the stone face and began to surge up it using a number of different methods, depending on their original unit's preferences. Some simply dropped their shields now that they would become an encumbrance and climbed with one hand and both feet, using the cracks and gaps between stones for foot and hand holds, jabbing upwards with swords to keep the defenders at bay. Others were giving their mates boosts, the ones below with forethought wearing leather gloves to protect them from the nailed boots of their companions. Still others were using their shields as a set of steps for their mates to jump up, gradually ascending to the wall top, the height of two men above them. It was chaos, but it was proving to be equally chaotic for the defenders, who had no idea how to defend against such a varied and inconsistent attack. Consequently there was no concerted defence with orders from commanders and the whole thing came down to the will and wit of the individual. The Begerri fought back, but the Romans were roaring and surging ever upwards. Even as a dozen Romans fell from the walls, spears sticking out of them, heads mashed by sling shot or horrific sword wounds to their arms and torsos, so the first man reached the wall top – a legionary bellowing something about Juno's rather impressive chest as he swung and stabbed, lanced and chopped with his blade, using it in a dozen ways for which a drill master would punish him, and yet to stunning effect.

The man was finally struck a dreadful blow from a Gallic blade, his chest opened in a spray of broken chain links and blood, and he fell on the bodies of his five glassy-eyed victims, but by that time three more legionaries were in his place, clambering over the wall top and shouting their cries of victory. The rain suddenly picked up its own assault battering down heavily on both forces.

'Going up, sir?' grinned one of Fronto's men, gesturing to a line of three men who had formed a ramp up to the wall top with their shields held overhead. It looked rather treacherous, but Fronto found that he was grinning and nodding, and ran. With a spring in his step, he jumped onto the lower shield and almost fell disastrously to one side. The rain was coming down in earnest now, and it was making the shield surfaces extraordinarily slippery. Scrabbling and trying not to topple to either side, he stepped to the second shield, then finally to the third. A spear came lancing down at him and he knocked it aside with his shield, glad he'd not cast it aside, though wondering how he was going to climb the last five feet with the great board on his arm. Then suddenly the man sweeping down with the spear, trying to skewer him, suddenly shrieked and toppled past Fronto to the churned ground below, a huge rent in his neck-shoulder area spraying torrents of blood. An excited, leering legionary face appeared over the parapet, yelled something rather crude, and then disappeared again.

Fronto unclasped his hand from the shield grip, dropped it to his feet, then took hold of the rim. With an effort that he felt might unseat his shoulder joint, he heaved the shield up and tipped it over the wall parapet above him, then set about climbing the last few feet with that aching arm. Below him, the shield upon which he stood wobbled for a moment as another man stepped onto it and shouted for him to 'get a bloody move on, sir.'

Grinning, feeling like a young man once again, Fronto hauled himself over the parapet and grasped his fallen shield just in time to deflect an axe blow that carved the bronze edging from most of the shield's top. Dropping to a knee and jabbing out with the gladius, the exhilarated, grinning legate delivered a perfectly accurate killing blow to the Begerri warrior's unarmoured groin. As the man screamed and fell away, his life blood gushing out from below his chain shirt, Fronto stood, watching the mess around him as Roman and Aquitanian struggled all along the wall. Oddly, there was a gap in front of him for some reason, and as he peered into it, the smile slid from his face.

There was a wide space given over to small vegetable plots at this end of the oppidum's interior and it was *filled* with enemy warriors. He had expected there to be more of them than of the legion, but not by this kind of margin. For all the amazing success of Arruntius' straightforward tactics, there was no hope of so few men subduing that lot. The attack was over before it had truly begun.

* * *

'Stop!'

The command rang out across the oppidum like the toll of a great bronze bell in a public square and, like such a ring, it had the effect of silencing the attack. Even as the noise descended, that same voice called out something in a native tongue. The effect was the damnedest thing Fronto had ever seen. The entire attack stuttered to a halt, men of both forces poised with swords raised for a killing blow. A few stragglers were still fighting at the periphery, unable to hear the shouts for the battering rain, but after a brief pause, realising that the fight had halted, they too stopped.

Fronto turned in surprise to see the tall, imposing figure of Arruntius standing on the gatehouse, already coated with blood and boosted by the bodies of half a dozen warriors beneath his feet. The whole oppidum – somewhere in the region of three hundred legionaries and six thousand Begerri – stood watching in fascination and surprise.

'You signed the Pax Gallica,' Arruntius bellowed, then to Fronto's surprise, repeated the words in some Gallic dialect. 'You made an oath to Rome and Rome made one to you.' Again he repeated himself in their own tongue – or at least in some more northern Gallic tongue that they seemed to understand.

'Where I come from, oaths are binding and those that break them the worst sort of criminal,' he said with the tone of a scolding teacher. Fronto was astounded to see a few of the Begerri lower their weapons to their side and their eyes to the floor as though embarrassed as the man repeated this reprimand in a Gallic language.

'However, I know that you are being oppressed by a new king in the mountains.' A pause, then a repeat in the Gallic tongue. 'And I know that the Begerri reneged on their oath for fear of this king's power.'

There was more than one exchange of sheepish looks among the locals, and Fronto almost laughed.

'But here, now, you have a chance to hold to your oath and to put things right. Any man who fights for Rome on this hill or lays down his arms and walks away will be given amnesty.'

Another pause. Another repeat. Fronto watched the uncertainty form over Biguro in a cloud thicker than the ones above that dropped torrents of rain upon them.

'I offer you a chance to return to your homes, resettle your town and trade for good Hispanic wine as you chose to in the past, and fear not about this smiling king in the mountains, for my commander will pull his heart out through his arse before summer is done.'

This last, when repeated in the native tongue, saw a hundred weapons lowered.

A voice from further back, toward the centre of the town, called out in the native tongue, a harsh language, all throat and sharp edges and, though Fronto could not follow what was said, the indignant, defiant, and furious tone was unmistakable. The warriors were wavering in the face of Arruntius' seemingly-generous offer, and one of their leaders had arrived to command them back into the fray.

It started again with a single clang. One of the Begerri on the wall had snarled and lurched forward, chopping down with his heavy sword, the startled legionary just managing to get his gladius in the way in time. And with that, battle recommenced, surging across the ramparts of Biguro. A sling shot hit Arruntius, but seemed to do little more than irritate the centurion, who bellowed a cry to Minerva and jumped from the gate top into a mass of warriors below.

Fronto had a moment before that odd gap in front of him closed once more, and through it he saw the strange and not unwelcome effects of Arruntius' speech. Most of the warriors in the centre were still surging forward, their weapons brandished, but a number had turned and were fighting their own people. Moreover, some cunning Begerri bastards had used the confusion to push their way out toward the back of the enemy host and now they were turning, laying swords, axes and spears into the backs of their own tribesmen. The enemy forces had split, some clearly seeing their future as either Roman or dead, others clinging to the original plan of defying the invader. In theory there were too few

150

who had changed sides to make a great deal of difference in the great scheme of things, but as Fronto watched the utter chaos and carnage ensue he smiled, realising what Arruntius had done. The centurion had not *expected* his offer to end the fight or to change things so thoroughly. But he knew warriors and he knew what went through men's minds when facing a furious, concerted Roman attack. His calculated words had been designed to sow dissent and nothing more. Where a few moments ago each man within Biguro had waited impatiently for their chance to hack and stab at the Romans, now at most half of them were doing so. Others were busy fighting their own men and, Fronto was fairly certain, a number of rebels were busy killing other rebels in the mistaken belief that they had turned back to Rome. It was utter carnage as Begerri fought Begerri regardless of what they each stood for, and the cohort simply started to whittle away at the edges, leaving those below to fight one another and concentrating on removing the defences of the rampart.

Fronto laughed then, realising how easy it was to become a follower of this mad old centurion. A warrior appeared close by and Fronto turned, raising his shield, blocking the stab of the sword, then using the defensive board as a weapon – its secondary function of design. Smashing out with the shield, he jabbed the iron boss into the warrior's face, smashing bones and teeth and then pushing him back from the rampart where he tumbled down the turf bank into Biguro, clutching his ruined head. The legate paused to use the back of his hand to wipe away the rain from the portion of his face visible through the helmet. A deep crack of thunder made him jump slightly, and a ripple of uncertainty ran through the entire Begerri force. The storm was almost here.

A legionary to the left of Fronto whooped and jumped from the wall-walk, plunging down the slope into the press of Begerri, howling like some blood-hungry animal as he shield-barged the press of the enemy. With a grin, Fronto barrelled down after him. Against all the odds, they had secured the rampart and most of the cohort were now in the oppidum, the stragglers already crossing the parapet to join them.

The crowd below was in total disarray. Some were stabbing one another in the press, others trying to flee the slaughter. Whatever their intentions, almost the entire Begerri force was now in one huge mass, pushing back and forth, chopping one another to pieces.

Gradually, as Fronto and the legionaries nearby took out occasional Begerri warriors who broke from the mass and charged them, grabbing the opportunity for a breather before the next heavy push, things started to change. A sense of order was beginning to instil itself among the tribe as various enemy nobles called out to their people and the mass stopped killing one another blindly.

Still, Fronto had to acknowledge that the centurion's calls had done their work. The enemy had thinned out by almost a quarter in the chaos, and had paid such little attention to the Roman forces that even some of the wounded had crossed the wall and moved into the oppidum, unwilling to let leg or arm wounds rob them of a cut of the treasure. When the legionaries had burst from the trees they had faced a hard fight to attain the walls, and even then odds of fourteen to one. Now, the cohort were facing perhaps ten to one, and they were inside the oppidum. It was still odds that would have a book-maker at the circus sweating, but they had improved so drastically in so few moments that it already felt like a victory. What was more, even though most of the chaos had ended, there were still clearly those among the Begerri who clung to the centurion's words and were fiercely fighting their own people.

This time, Fronto saw the white blaze of lightning sheet across the sky above the clouds, and started to count. He'd only reached three before the boom of Vulcan's hammer cracked the sky in two. The storm was here.

'By century, on your commander,' Arruntius bellowed somewhere off to the left as the rain lashed down with sudden ferocity, 'Testudo!'

The reaction was instant. Each man had practised the manoeuver at least every other day for anywhere between five and forty years. Despite not having marked men to work from, due to the rather haphazard, random nature of the cohort, each man was experienced enough to see where he was needed and shuffled into place to plug any gaps left by the fallen, and each used their centurion as a left marker, forming on him. There was a moment of dithering, and the century began to swarm to Fronto's side.

The legate had been in a few testudos in his time, including horribly complicated manoeuvers such as testudos that had to march backwards up a slope. It was nothing new to him, nor was carrying it out at a moment's notice in mid-fight. But this was the first time he had been the marker one formed on and as the men fell in with him, shields clonking together around and above, he realised with a start that there was no centurion in the unit. Whoever the man with the crest had been, he had fallen somewhere in the assault and now command was falling to Fronto. He found to his surprise that he felt an odd pride at that. He had commanded legions in battle, and sometimes multiple-legion forces, yet he had never had proper command of a century of men. And he knew damn well that no matter how clever or successful a senior officer might be, to the ordinary legionaries he was still just the commander, while a centurion was a figure of legend, as untouchable as a demigod. It was an odd feeling to suddenly achieve that position, and with a thrill he found he understood what drove the backbone of the Roman army to be what they were.

The centurion's whistle blew somewhere off to the left and Fronto realised he had no whistle to echo the call, but it seemed there was no need to spread the word to advance, for the testudo began to lurch forward suddenly. Fronto kept his shield out steadily, forming the rear left wall of the tortoise formation, and made sure to hold it locked in position. What was the plan? With no centurion here and unable to hear the calls of other units' commanders within the sweaty, echoing confines of the testudo, Fronto could only guess. They were in a formation designed to provide the maximum protection and marching forward into a massive enemy force.

It was all about damage and confusion, he surmised. The enemy were still so numerous compared to the cohort and were beginning to regain their order through their commanders' shouts. Arruntius was evening the odds. It was like sending one of those African horned beasts – the ones they sometimes had at games – into a crowd. Do as much damage as possible and instil utter chaos.

'Swords,' he shouted. 'Kill 'em. Kill 'em all.'

The men in the testudo pushed the tips of their blades through the various tiny gaps in the shield wall of the tortoise, and began to stab out. There was no chance they might miss. As the century stomped into the thick press of Begerri warriors, the sheer numbers meant that the enemy simply could not get out of the way in time. Half the warriors around them attempted to flee and were lacerated by the fifty blades jabbing repeatedly out of the shield-box. Others tried in vain to destroy the Roman war machine in their midst, desperately hammering at the shields with their own weapons. But the press was just too tight for them to be able to do much more than flail and then fall foul of the jabbing blades. The Roman formation moved slowly, inexorably through the throng, mincing the Begerri with their blades and leaving a trail of blood-slick and twitching bodies. The rain hammered down like a wet club, drumming on the wood of the shield roof and soaking the Begerri outside to the bone. Fronto almost laughed as another flash, barely visible inside the formation, clearly shook the spirits of the enemy, and the crack of thunder that followed saw several of them pull back in fear. The Gauls were a superstitious race, almost on a par with Aurelius, who would be fuming back in camp at the order not to join him. The possibility that their gods were angry at oath-breaking was occurring to many now that Toutatis was hammering in the sky.

As was inevitable, after a few moments, a lucky enemy strike caught one of the legionaries and he fell, crying in pain, out of the formation where he was butchered by howling warriors. Fronto shouted to fill the gap but the men were already on it, one of those who had formed part of the roof lowering his shield and stepping to the side to plug the gap left by the dead man. The torrential rain poured through the hole he'd left in the roof, making the interior of the testudo that little bit less pleasant.

'Watch your pace,' he said loudly in the close world of the shield-shell, for the footsteps of the men had become rather disconnected during the press.

'Ju-no, Ju-no, Ju-no,' chanted two of the men at the front in time with their footsteps and in a matter of heartbeats their companions had all fallen into step with the chant.

'Cae-sar, Cae-sar, Cae-sar,' started someone else, and the chant morphed from Juno to Caesar as the thud of boots rhythmically ground the open spaces of Biguro into dust.

Fronto grinned. There was simply no feeling in the world like being in the midst of some great fight on the fate of which everything hung. He snorted as he realised that the chant had changed again and had now become 'Cae-sar's Bas-tards, Cae-sar's Bas-tards.'

A man at the front of the testudo suddenly took a violently lucky strike that managed to press through the gap between the shields, slamming into his throat. As he gurgled and dropped, the formation fell apart, for another legionary tripped over the fallen man, knocking the side walls as he went down. A moment later the testudo had dissolved into a rough oval of men forming a desperate shieldwall around the tangle of fallen legionaries. Fronto felt a thrill of panic, but it quickly transpired that they had broken through the mass of the enemy and left a wide swathe of destruction behind them. Fronto grinned to see two more testudos fall apart, one due to heavy losses, but the other to a cry of 'Melee!' from its centurion. Good call.

'Melee!' Fronto bellowed. They would never be in a better position. The formation now broke up, the men marking their targets in the confusion and stabbing out swiftly, putting the nearby Begerri down. It was like a sweep of a scythe taking out an arc of wheat. And before the enemy could recover, he shouted again 'Pull back and form shieldwall on me.'

The men, accustomed to blind obedience, did just that, disengaging from their individual fights and backing toward Fronto who was now in a clear area, just a public square and a number of houses behind him. The shieldwall formed in moments and Fronto managed a quick headcount. Twenty eight. His heart fluttered at the realisation that he had lost in excess of half of his unit since breaking cover of the trees. Still, who could ever have conceived that they'd last this long against sixteen to one odds. The cohort had pushed through the enemy host and out the other side. Now, the six shattered centuries were in the heart of Biguro, and the remains of the Begerri were between them and the rampart across which they had so recently surged.

Another call in the native tongue drew Fronto's attention as he was about to begin marching the century forward again, back into the fray, and the Begerri pulled back from the legionaries, reforming in the open. The legate peered across the crowd, trying to pick out Arruntius, as his century stabbed and lashed out at any Begerri who came close enough to strike. Similar scenes were playing out across the open space as the two sides separated.

155

Two of the centuries moved to follow, but Arruntius' voice rang out with the command 'Hold your ground.'

Slowly, the remaining Begerri pulled back, retreating like a tide back into the open space of Biguro's trampled and ruined vegetable gardens, the furrows now sown with the dead. Various small knots of the enemy remained in position but, as the legionaries shouted jeers, those remaining men bellowed 'Pax Gallica' to confirm their allegiance and hurried to fall in with the Romans. Fronto watched as the enemy retreated and the space opened up between the two sides. Now would be the perfect time to bring up reinforcements and pincer-grip the tribe, but there were none to bring, the rest of the legion remaining in camp two miles away. He estimated the enemy numbers to have dropped to somewhere between two and three thousand, and while the cohort's numbers had roughly halved, they had picked up allies among the enemy which actually made the attacking force more numerous than it had been at the start. Now they would number somewhere between five and six hundred by Fronto's reckoning, and while any general with half a brain would think twice about five to one odds, to have brought it down to that from sixteen to one was a feat worthy of legend.

'The enemy are massing under their leaders,' Arruntius shouted across the rag-tag remains of his force. 'Remember that these people were not always our enemy. They are the brothers and sons and fathers and friends of our allies in this place, and they fight us because they are driven to do so. We must charge them again, brothers, but this time we will break them for good, because we are going to ignore the Begerri warriors and make for their leaders. We will kill their chiefs and nobles and remove the yoke from their necks. Break into contubernia of eight men and each form in line to make a solid front eight men deep. We're going to march into them, and then each contubernia will pick a noble and go for the throat. Got it?'

There was a roar of agreement.

'And everyone knows the name of their thunder god, I expect. Make him your chant, for they're frightened and close to breaking.' To add divine approval, the gods sent an almost simultaneous flash of white and boom of thunder, and Fronto shuddered at the sight of the blood-caked centurion holding his sword aloft in the storm as though daring Jupiter to just try it.

'How much are your shares worth now?' Arruntius grinned, and then took a breath. 'Form contubernia!'

* * *

The cohort surged forward at Arruntius' whistle. Few of the centuries numbered more than half their original complement, yet they attacked with a ferocity and sureness of which Fronto felt proud to be a part. The Begerri were losing heart with every passing moment, and Fronto noted with satisfaction how, even in the face of their nobles' haranguing, the enemy were pressing back as the legionaries approached, as if trying to push through their own force to safety. Their weapons were brandished almost defensively, a ridiculous thing given that they still outnumbered the Romans by five men to one.

Yet superstition was doing its work. The Romans seemed unaffected by the storm, the rain simply making their armour that little bit shinier, their russet tunics turning the colour of blood with the wet, the gore spattered across them running down in fearsome rivulets. Fronto could imagine how terrifying they looked even in small numbers, especially given that the fewer there were, the more fierce and warlike they seemed to become. By comparison, relatively few of the enemy wore helmets, and not more than one in ten sported a mail shirt. Thus, the enemy were becoming bedraggled and waterlogged and thoroughly despondent, certain that their gods were furious with them for their hubris. Their hair and beards were running with water, plastered uncomfortably to their skin, and their wool tunics and trousers clung to them as they moved.

The units of eight men had formed remarkably quickly and efficiently, given that not a single contubernium had survived above half strength from the start, though here and there units of six, seven or nine were telling that these were not regular units but hastily cobbled together in the thick of battle.

Fronto's contubernium, pressed between others formed as randomly, hit the enemy like an enraged beast – like the bull that adorned the flags of all Caesar's units. The legate, at the rear of his unit, peered across the press as they struck the crowd, looking for tell-tale signs. Here and there he spotted a wolf or boar standard held aloft, or a carnyx or some other flag or emblem. None were close enough to their unit, and other contubernia would fix on them. Then, as he was clucking with irritation, he caught a red plume not unlike his own through the crowd. Rising, he craned his neck to peer above the press, where the front two rows of men were busy carving their way into the enemy. Sure enough, though he lost it for a moment, he once more spotted that plume. It was a Roman plume – an officer's helmet, and certainly there would be no Romans among that mob so the nature of the red horsehair on display before him was clear. Some bastard had taken the helmet as a prize from a butchered Roman officer.

Fronto had his target, and it suddenly mattered not whether the bastard beneath the crest was a noble, a warrior or just a suborned farmhand, Fronto would see the man suffer for what he'd clearly done.

'Directly ahead – a man with a red plume. He's mine.'

There was a surge of acknowledgement, and the men pressed forward with a little more vigour.

'Not *ours*,' Fronto clarified. 'You can kill who you want, but that prick's mine!'

And with that Fronto heaved. Another flash illuminated the scene and the corresponding crash of thunder rang out across Biguro as the Roman force burrowed into the mass of men before them.

Begerri were fleeing. Fronto couldn't see much more than the sweaty, soaked ranks of legionaries in front of him and the surging, ebbing, groaning mob of the enemy beyond, but he didn't need to see to know that they were fleeing. At the periphery, he knew, men would be breaking for the open and running for cover of the houses. Others would be climbing the slope of the rampart and dropping over the far side, away from the butchering blades of Rome. And the rest were divided. Some pressed back, trying to get away from what was coming, pushing through their own ranks where, inevitably, their leaders had them killed for fleeing. Others desperately fought off the serried ranks, largely in vain.

Men were dying on both sides, but the numbers were drastically tipped in Rome's favour. Fronto watched the man at the front of his column fall, then a second, and eventually a third, and the same was happening all across the front of the Roman force. But for every Roman that fell, three or four Begerri were dropping to the sodden earth, chopped, flayed, minced and broken.

The fourth legionary fell, and Fronto suddenly caught sight of the red plume again. Other soldiers and officers along the line were now closing on their targets and the Roman formation broke up here and there, moving from a single line into individual arrow heads that cut through the meat of Biguro, aiming for the hearts and souls of the tribe – their leaders.

Fronto felt that old familiar battle-mist falling upon him, and fought against the simplicity of Mars' hand on his heart. It made a man a killing god but robbed him of all sense in the process, and sense was what was needed right now more than mindless violence. As his remaining three men began to spread out into a wedge with the legate behind the lead man, Fronto locked his mind on that red plume, ignoring all else.

Another push and a stagger two steps forward and the man in front of him cried out in agony, a Begerri sword ripped back and raised high in bloody triumph. The legionary fell, gurgling, clutching his neck, and Fronto was left with no option but to simply trample over the mortally wounded man. Battle was a harsh mistress and left little room for pity or respect. The howling warrior instantly regretted raising his sword in victory as Fronto's blade slammed into his armpit, twisted and withdrawn in the fluid move of a practised killer. A torrent of blood followed the extracted blade, and the man fell. Fronto snarled as he saw that red plume again, just behind the next man. His shield came up a foot or so and he braced, slamming out forward and throwing every bit of his weight into it.

An entire section of the enemy mob reeled under the sudden push, men falling under their comrades' feet, and the warrior he'd battered squawked and fell to one side where Fronto's companion stabbed at him.

The man in the red plume had almost fallen with the shield-barge, staggering and trying to right himself. He was a man roughly Fronto's age, with grey moustaches and beard hanging from a lined, experienced face with an oddly sad expression. The man wore silver arm rings and a simple torc of copper. His mail shirt was of Roman manufacture – though missing the shoulder doubling through damage, Fronto could see the bronze hook arrangement where it should be fastened. The sword the man bore was long and Gallic in style, and he had no shield.

And he was a dead man.

One thing Fronto knew from his years of experience was that a long sword in a tight space was less use than a fist. As he pulled back his own shorter stabbing blade, the veteran Begerri warrior before him struggled, trying to pull up his blade in the press. The tip hit Fronto's shield and bounced away again, unable to rise to a useful height. There was only one thing the man could do, and Fronto knew it, for he had done much the same in his time.

As the warrior dropped to a crouch to use his long blade among the legs where it was trapped, Fronto snarled 'Oh no you don't,' and slammed his shield down, angled slightly forward. The bronze edging of the heavy board smashed into the toes of the warrior's boots, mangling their contents through the thick leather. As the warrior screamed, his face tipping upwards to look at Fronto, the legate's sword stabbed down, entering the open mouth and scything through it and into the neck and chest below.

Fronto had no time to celebrate his triumph, as 'red plume' disappeared beneath the feet of the press and the legion pushed on. Of Fronto's two remaining men, the one on the left gave a sudden cry and fell away, leaving the legate open to the enemy. This was it. For all their heroics, they were about to lose, in the end simply outnumbered. Aurelius would curse him even at his tomb-side for his foolishness.

A figure was suddenly at his shoulder, and Fronto glanced left to see a hairy native with a fur cloak roaring, his black hair plastered across half of his face as his axe rose and fell, lopping the raised arm from one of the enemy.

'Pax Gallica!' the man bellowed, grinning madly at Fronto as he cleaved his way into the crowd. All along the line, Begerri were now among the legionaries, pushing at their own.

Fronto grinned and, faced with few options, surrendered to the war beast inside.

* * *

160

Fronto leaned on a stone trough, watching with fascination as the tiny drops of crimson plipped from his nose, chin and various other places into the water, only to be lost in the endless spots and ripples of the rain as it battered the surface. His latest – his last – victim lay by the trough clutching his throat even in death, his hands crimson, the last feeble pulse pumping out between blue-grey fingers.

Fronto's fury had run its course, but it seemed that his ire had outlived the Begerri's will to fight. Even as that warrior had slid down the side of the trough, gurgling and clawing, Arruntius' shrill three whistles had shrieked out through the downpour, signalling the legion to disengage.

Drip.

Red among the clear falling water and the green-ish contents of the trough.

Drip.

The blood of the Begerri spilled unnecessarily because of some mad king in the peaks.

Drip.

A man who seemed to follow a very Roman dream of conquest and assimilation.

Drip.

Was what Fronto was feeling something that had coursed through the Samnites as their world came to an end in the face of Roman iron?

Drip.

'Legate Fronto?'

He turned his weary face without rising. Arruntius stood close by, a thing from nightmare. Barely a hand's-breadth of the man's entire body was free of gore, and Fronto could see half a dozen small flesh wounds as yet untended. The centurion looked angry.

'I know. I was to stay at the back. I have no business fighting in your unit. I should know better. What would happen if... et cetera, et cetera. Can we just pretend you've ranted at me for half an hour and I've valiantly defended my desire to serve Rome? I'm too tired to do it now.'

A number of odd expressions crossed the elderly centurion's face and, most unexpectedly, it settled on a grin.

'I don't believe we set the terms of the bet.'

'Bet?'

Arruntius put on an expression of hurt innocence. 'You didn't believe a cohort could take Biguro. I thought otherwise. I'm sure I'm due at least a skin of wine.'

Fronto, exhausted though he was, chuckled. 'I have a large jar of Alban in the baggage carts I was saving for a big occasion piss-up. I could maybe spare half of that? Or perhaps, given what we've achieved today, you'd like to help me share it with a few choice officers and men in the comfort of my tent later?'

Arruntius snorted. 'That'll do. You alright, sir?'

'Miraculously unwounded, apart from a cut on the brow and a few bruises,' Fronto said, though as he rose, his knee gave way and he staggered for a moment. The centurion peered down in concern, but Fronto shrugged. 'Old wound. Still bad when it's damp, and it's rarely as damp as this.'

'We owe our success to that damp,' Arruntius muttered, reaching out to help Fronto steady himself. The legate bit down on a defiant urge to refuse help from an older man. Arruntius was not your ordinary old man. 'No bows among the enemy,' he noted.

'And Vulcan's hammer broke their spirits. On a nice day we'd still be fighting to the death now. But their warriors thought they were in the wrong. Thought the gods were angry, and by Juno, they were right. We killed more than two thousand by best estimates today, and we lost just over three hundred men. Leonidas of Sparta would be nodding at us.'

Fronto smiled. He could hear the cheerful shouts and even singing of the legionaries. Their shares would be rather large. Each man who settled here would be a wealthy man.

'It's a good job their spirit *is* broken, though,' Arruntius said, quietly. 'If they got it into their heads that this wasn't over we could still be massacred. There are over two thousand of them left, disarmed but simmering. On the bright side we have more than a thousand of theirs who turned to join us and helped us win the day.' Arruntius pointed and Fronto followed the man's gaze. In the town's square not far away, a few natives were scrubbing the gore and stains from the Pax Gallica altar that stood there. 'And there are eighty nine intact legionaries with just scars and bruises like you. And around fifty walking wounded. The rest won't make it or are already being moved into the dead piles.'

'What are your plans with the place and the settlers.'

Arruntius frowned in incomprehension.

'Well you're the ranking officer among the settlers,' Fronto replied 'so I'll leave it to you to plan what happens now.'

The centurion barked out a laugh. 'I'm not settling here, Legate.'

'But you led the group of settlers. You organised the money. You'll be even wealthier now.'

'Bollocks, sir. I led the fight because I wanted to prove it was possible, not because I was ready to stop.'

Fronto shook his head. 'I don't want to be indelicate, Arruntius, but with your age as it is, you know Caesar will just pension you out anyway if you return to the army. Might as well make the most of it here with the added bonuses.'

'Oh I'll settle. If nothing else, I cannot be bothered to walk back across the breadth of Gaul to the general's camp. But I'll settle when it's over. When this smiling king is hanging from a cross. *Then* I'll open a little tavern or something. Until then, I'm with you.'

'And I'll be glad of your company,' Fronto smiled.

A commotion caught their attention, and both officers turned to see half a dozen legionaries and a couple of the Begerri leading three men on knotted ropes. Prisoners with all the accoutrements and garb of nobles.

'Who are they?' he asked as they approached.

'Sir, these friends of ours say they are mountain men, sent by the Convenae to control the Begerri.'

'Popular now then, I'll bet.' Fronto turned to the warriors accompanying the legionaries. 'Can you translate for me?'

The soldier who'd spoken smiled weakly. 'It's a bit complicated, sir. I've a passing command of a Gallic tongue from around the Bituriges, and this warrior can speak both that and the tongue of the mountain people. Talk to me and we'll do what we can.'

'Alright,' Fronto said, straightening as the rain gradually washed the remaining blood from his skin and armour. 'Tell these three that one of them is going to be granted a very quick, clean death, and he's the lucky one.'

163

The legionary relayed the words to the warrior, who translated them into the jagged tongue of the southerners. The three men threw sour expressions of defiance at Fronto.

'Tell them that the one who gives me useful information can die clean. The others I'll give to the loyal Begerri, and I think we can all picture how that's going to end, since they owe all this death to these three men and their smiling king.'

Again the words were translated. Fronto was gratified to note a slight uncertainty – even fear – cross their faces before they became steadfast and defiant once more. Good. Three men left him a spare.

'Go and find a dozen angry looking Begerri, give them each a knife and direct them to the Pax Gallica altar,' the legate smiled unpleasantly. Two legionaries hurried off, and Fronto, Arruntius and the others dragged the three prisoners over to the open square. 'Tell these lot that there's no point in cleaning it any more. It's about to get messy again. Tell these three that they have about twenty heartbeats to talk to me.'

The words were relayed, but still defiance greeted him in their eyes. A few moments later, the two legionaries returned with twelve sour-faced Begerri, armed with sharp knives. Despite their ongoing recalcitrance, Fronto could now feel the fear emanating from the three Convenae leaders.

'You,' Fronto pointed at the strongest looking one. He turned to the twelve Begerri. 'He's yours.'

The legionaries cut the rope anchoring the noble to the other two, and his eyes went wide as they pushed him into the waiting arms of the Begerri. Fronto intensely disliked torture. It was not a noble thing and often failed to achieve its goals. But once in a while there was call for it, and he forced himself to watch what the angry Begerri did to their captive. The legion's torturers could learn a thing or two from watching the twelve men work, he thought, his gorge rising into his throat with each laceration or each peeling. The captive noble continued to shriek for half a thousand heartbeats, even after his tongue was taken, the screaming then accompanied by a horrible gurgling.

The other men forced the two remaining captives to watch the whole thing, and Fronto noted, glancing at them, that both men had gone deathly pale. When finally, after what seemed like a week, the Begerri's victim finally died with a sigh of relief and a final twitch of the leg, Fronto stared down in disgust at the small pile of parts the torturers had cut off.

'One of you is going the same way,' he said in a flat voice, waiting as the translation was carried out. 'It's up to you two which one.'

Quarter of an hour later, Fronto and Arruntius stalked off, leaving the grisly scene of the Begerri's revenge and the single grateful Convenae noble lying with his throat cut.

'Not much really,' Fronto said. 'Perhaps we could have pressed for more.'

'I doubt it,' Arruntius replied. 'They were terrified. They'd have sold out their mother by now. The simple fact is they didn't know much. They were lesser nobles, sent here for a purpose. The man running this whole thing is cunning. Clever enough not to put important men or nobles with too much to say in danger of capture.'

'And they were given specific instructions to save Caesar for their king? Do they think I'm Caesar? That's how it sounded to me.'

'To me too. Perhaps that is what this whole thing is about. They've been luring us in all this time, but they think Caesar is with us. They think it's his army and that you're him. I suppose to these people any man with a plume and a cloak could be Caesar. They probably don't know the difference between a general, a legate and even a tribune. They're trying to lure Caesar, and they've hooked you instead.'

'This king is going to live to regret that,' Fronto said emphatically. 'So the Convenae are a growing group of tribes all across the mountains, based at this place they call Conveno. Clearly that should be our next stop. Did you catch where they said that was?'

'About forty miles southeast of here, up one of the deepest valleys.'

'And they said the king was among the Arenosio?'

'They did.'

'Well that makes sense in one way but not in another. The direction you're describing must be roughly between us and

Arenosio territory from what I know. But the Arenosio are a tiny tribe. Small and not remotely influential – or at least they were a couple of decades ago. We had them working alongside us back in the day, when Caesar was up in northern Hispania. Scouts from the Arenosio were with my army. I cannot fathom how they could be important enough these days to lord it over the other Aquitanii. Still, at least we now have a name and a direction. I'd best get back down to the camp and speak to the others. I'll send another cohort of men up to help sort things out here, but could you stay and oversee the clearing of it all? We'll tarry for two days and help the settlers set up here, then we move for Conveno.'

Mid Maius

SNOW remained upon the peaks and in the deep saddles of the passes, glowering over the fortress nestled on a dome of rock at the end of a narrow spur at the heart of the wide valley. The sky was a clear, almost pristine, blue which turned the snowy heights into an absolutely dazzling sea of white. There was nothing soft, though, nothing colourful about the fortress. This was no civilian town or fortified oppidum of the lowlands. This was little more than a garrisoned castle, with stout grey walls rising from equally colourless rocks, heavy dark timber buildings inside matching the gate that stood like a monster's maw facing down the valley. A forbidding and cruel looking place, constructed for defence and to both impress and oppress those who saw it.

And the maw was opening, for half a dozen riders had approached along the road up the valley, climbing the last stretch to those steadfast ashen walls. They were mountain men – scouts equipped for fast riding and reconnaissance, and they were tired and travel-worn, one with a spare horse, a figure draped across it like a human saddle. A guard met them at the gate, and the riders entered, the drumming of their hooves on the rock in the gateway causing reverberations that brought fresh sprinkles of snow from the arch above.

The riders slid from their horses, stamping their feet to bring life back into cold limbs, and then the leader, a man with more years of battle behind him than most men had years of life, handed his reins to another and directed the men off to one side. He himself shrugged off the cloak over his shoulders, gave it to the guard, and marched toward the fortress' central structure. All around the walls warriors watched the passes and the valley, and many more moved among the interior buildings, going about their daily business.

The king's hall was an impressive thing. Built of the same hard grey stone as the rest of the fortress, the walls were iron-coloured to the height of a man, then formed of stout, adzed timbers above, the whole surmounted by a roof of huge trunks that formed a triangular lid, their bases driven into the ground, their tips meeting at the apex. Smoke billowed up through a hole in the roof, the fire that warmed the building roaring away inside and keeping at bay the cold that howled through the passes even into late spring. Then there would come a sudden change with the arrival of summer, and the temperature would rise, clearing the valleys, while the white would cling to the peaks and highest places. But for now, what was spring here could easily have been winter to the lowlanders.

The scout reached the door and nodded to the next guard, who gestured inside without moving to stop him. The door creaked open under his chapped hand and swung inwards, allowing a blast of welcome warmth to sweep across him. The rider paused for a moment to relish the experience, and then stepped inside, allowing the door to close behind him.

The king's hall was a single room, large enough to accommodate a feast or a council of war, a fire roaring in a stone-lined pit at the centre, a stripped carcass slowly rotating over the flames by the hand of a young boy, sending greasy, porcine smoke roiling up through the room to that hole in the roof. The windows were unshuttered, despite the cold, allowing light to penetrate the gloomy interior. The mezzanine level was reached by a ladder, and was pitch black, for the king sat upon his throne in the main room, with his closest advisors by his side. There was no movement above. The king had no family, and took no girls to his bed. In the early days men had joked about that. They had soon learned not to.

'What news, Korisos?'

The scout approached the fire, the smell of the cooking pork bringing a rumble to his hungry belly. He bowed from the waist, then straightened.

'Caesar's army overran Biguro, my king. It was the most astounding thing I have ever watched. From boyhood my father always told me the Romans were like women, only able to fight because of their numbers and their armour. The men that took Biguro were warriors that would make Belenos proud. He took few casualties and destroyed the Begerri, even taking some back into his arms.'

'That was to be expected. I never imagined that the Begerri would do more than inconvenience Caesar – whittle down his army a little. The general is simply that good, and I have told you many times not to underestimate the legions. They are no feeble warriors. They train to kill every day, whatever the weather. But what of his numbers. Have more legions joined him? I had presumed that reinforcements would arrive by the time they reached Biguro.'

The scout shook his head. 'If anything, his force diminishes with each passing mile. He has little more than half his legion left, now. He keeps leaving men to found settlements along the way.'

Again the king nodded. 'Roman policy, and sensible too. He increases the Roman presence in the lowlands, preventing any further risings and solidifying their control on Aquitania. But if he is settling men, then they are veterans. Are his whole legion such old men, I wonder? If so, the general has more self-belief than even I credited him with.'

'They are all ancient grey-hairs, my king. They are little more than fleshy skeletons circling their own tombs, but they fight like maniacs. I bring the young chieftain, whose failure is now complete. My men have him in the yard, though he cannot tell you how tough the old Romans are, for he fled like a coward once his people were in danger.'

The king clucked his tongue noisily for a moment. 'Even with half a legion, Caesar will be a tough proposition. But we must punish the surviving Begerri for their menfolk's failure and easy capitulation. Have half the women and children executed and send the rest back to Biguro carrying the heads of the dead. That will send a clear message of my disapproval to those cowards who went back to the Romans, and will help unsettle the veterans who have remained there. Hand the Begerri boy over to Ategnio. He will make an example of him. And then everyone needs to begin preparations. Caesar will move on Conveno next, and then from there, he will come up into the passes to our very gate.'

The scout nodded and, understanding the instructions to carry an innate dismissal, turned and left the room. The fire crackled and the pig hissed and spat, filling the strange silence that followed, until the old man sitting two seats to the left of the king leaned forward.

'We have the most defensive walls across all the mountains, my king, but I worry about the Romans. If they can take Biguro so easily, perhaps this fortress is not as safe as we assumed? How do we ensure that we keep Caesar out?'

The king's head snapped round, his brow arched, which created a strange facial architecture along with his vicious smile.

'Keep him out? Caesar will not be kept out, no matter how hard you try. Gods, man, if the general's army cannot overcome our walls, I will swing open the gate for him myself. Do you not understand yet? You are the fortunate few, for you ride with me on my great journey, but no others matter. The Begerri were a slingshot to cast at Rome, and nothing more. Similarly the Convenae – all of them. They are but tools to an end. And this place? This is not a home, but a tower from which to spit at Caesar. You think I care about this place? About the Arenosio? I would leave them, each and every one, to be pecked at by crows if it took me further along my path. I have no care for any man, and mercy is not in my soul. By the summer months I will have Caesar at my feet, begging for a mercy that I cannot grant. Then he will learn the hardest of lessons – that the world is cold and cruel and the Fates are as merciless as I.'

The silence returned, and each man in the room with the king once more thanked his personal gods that he was one of the king's chosen few.

Chapter Eight

CONVENO proved to be nothing like Fronto's expectations. *Physically* it matched what he'd heard and extrapolated from such information.

The centre of the grand new federation called the Convenae rose on a low hill some two hundred feet above the wide flat valley that snaked between spurs which jutted from the mountains. Behind the hill, separated from it by a narrow vale, rose a horseshoe of wooded slopes another two hundred feet higher, and beyond that the great peaks and troughs of the Pyrenaei rose, hazy and blue in the distance.

Conveno was not a new installation. Fronto had somehow assumed that this place had been purposefully constructed by the order of this shadowy king to accommodate the new super-tribe he had created. He had expected new walls and a fresh, ordered city.

What he now saw was clearly an old settlement, presumably once belonging to one of those tribes that had now gone, wholly subsumed by the new federation. Conveno consisted of a ramshackle collection of old houses and farms surrounded by a rampart and a wooden fence. And while the settlement itself was nothing that Fronto had anticipated, neither was the situation, for he had expected this, the heart of the Convenae, to be bristling with warriors and full of the tribe's civilian population, huddling defensively against the Roman threat approaching from the lowlands.

Conveno was empty. That was plain even from a distance, just as the scouts had reported. The gate stood open and there was no smoke, no sound and no movement. Clearly the Convenae had vacated their town and moved into the peaks, possibly upon receiving news of the Roman victory at Biguro. Had they run for the hills to save themselves, hiding in the lofty valleys of the mountains? It would not stop Fronto. Once they had confirmed what seemed to be the case – that Conveno was a city of ghosts and nothing more – the legion would move on up into the mountains, into the lands of the Arenosio, who they now knew to be at the heart of this strange localised rebellion.

The scouts had, once more, circled the place and examined it as closely as they could, checked out the surroundings, and then

171

reported back to the army's commanders. Consequently, Fronto had taken his companions forward to examine the place. He had left Masgava and Carbo to run the legion, taking Galronus and Decius, as well as the omnipresent Aurelius and a small cadre of guards. After Fronto's fight at Biguro, Aurelius had treated him to a half hour diatribe on the necessity of taking a body guard with him even when he was not expecting danger, on how important he was to the legion, how little point there was in having a bodyguard if he was to be consigned to the wagons whenever Fronto fancied a punch up, et cetera, et cetera. Fronto had caught sight of old Arruntius, busy washing the gore from his arms and face, grinning at the same rebuke that he had so recently himself given. Since then, throughout the ensuring five day journey, Aurelius had left Fronto's side only when he was lying in his bed or crouched over the latrines, clinging to him like a limpet every other moment. Worse still, between them, Aurelius and Galronus had selected six cavalry to serve as a guard unit, and Fronto could now not even ride alongside the army without being watched and surrounded by men.

Still, now, as he rode up the slope toward Conveno, and the oppressive feel of an empty, haunted place settled upon him with a shudder, he felt rather grateful for the nine soldiers with him and the two scouts that accompanied them all.

The eleven horsemen entered Conveno by the south gate which stood inviting and wide, and along a wide thoroughfare lined with empty, sad-looking buildings. The road curved up to an open square at the centre of the town, and as they reached the edge of that wide space, Aurelius gestured and the six cavalrymen spread out and circled around the periphery, leaving Fronto and his three officers to stare in dismay at what awaited them in the square.

It no longer caused horror. The things that had been done across Aquitania in the name of this king in the mountains had been so damned unpleasant and unbelievable that Fronto had become inured, almost numb to the endless display of cruelty. And yet every time they encountered this series of grisly scenes the followers of this smiling king had seemed to be able to add a new aspect of terror to what they had done.

172

Crucifixion was not new on this campaign, nor was the death of Romans.

Six bodies hung upon crosses that stood in an arc in the square, surrounding a heavy, unusual blueish stone stained with telling dark rivulets and standing amid a dried pool of that same dark liquid. As the Romans closed on the dead men, Fronto peered up at them. They were Romans, and more clearly so than the other victims they had seen so far across the region. They were not traders, nor unfortunate engineers. The four officers dismounted, tying their reins to a post near the main road that led to the gate, and strode across to the dead men. Flies in their thousands buzzed around the centre of the square and Fronto tried pointlessly to swat away clouds of the things as they approached the crucifixes. All six victims were well-born Romans of quality. Their clothing was of high standard, and each wore the torn and bloodied remains of togas, strands of the shredded garments dangling down toward the ground. Though they had clearly been dead for some time, Fronto spent every heartbeat on edge, half expecting one of them to move suddenly, and he was grateful when the cavalrymen finished their circuit and crossed to join them.

'Their sort shouldn't have been in Aquitania, surely?' Fronto said, pulling his scarf up to cover his mouth and nose against the smell of aged death and the ever-present insects.

'Not from what I understand,' Decius replied, peering at them. 'There were merchants out here, and soldiers, but the only nobleman would be the prefect at Lapurda. Togate figures? Where did they come from?'

'I don't know,' Fronto said through layers of muffling linen, 'but it's yet another goad for us. They're not messages. I think we've got the message loud and clear by now. These are purely made to draw us on, as if we needed the incentive now. But if *Caesar* had seen this? Well these men represent the very basis of Roman rule. And they have to have come from the Narbonensis province or Hispania Citerior, which means this king has a long reach.'

'Shit!'

Fronto turned and frowned at the outburst from one of the cavalrymen – something he'd not expected from a veteran in the presence of his officers, but something about the trooper's face cut off his angry retort. The man had gone rather pale and was leaning forward in his saddle, peering at the nearest of the six bodies.

'What is it?' Fronto asked.

'I think I know him, sir. It's kind of hard to tell, but I reckon you will too, Legate.'

'What?'

The trooper handed his reins to his friend and slid from the horse, approaching the hanging body. Fronto closed with him, and the pair ended side by side before the grisly remains.

'How could you recognise him,' Fronto queried. 'The birds have had his eyes and most of his face.'

'But sir, you were with the Ninth, back in the old days. I was with you when we went against the Cantabri – when we met up with Caesar's army in the north. You remember Valerius, sir?'

'The Ninth? Valerius?'

'Limpy, sir.'

Fronto's frown deepened and then his eyes widened in recollection. 'Valerius. Cavalry decurion. I remember him. Had one leg a bit shorter than the other. Good man in the saddle, but leaned to one side when he walked.' As he spoke, so his eyes dropped to the feet of the man on the cross. Unlike the other five, who had had a nail driven through their feet to keep them in place, this man had had to have both feet nailed separately, as they were not at the same height. 'Surely not.'

The cavalryman approached the body, wafting away the flies and reached up, grasping the edge of the body's tunic sleeve. 'See, sir? A tribune's tunic, I reckon. And look.' As he lifted the stained material, Fronto could see revealed on the upper arm a tattoo of a horse's rear end. 'Result of a failed bet with another of the horse officers. I remember him getting it done in Tarraco after the campaign. Got infected. Left him a mess for weeks. This is Valerius.'

Fronto nodded, hardly believing his eyes and ears. Ghosts were rising to assail him from all sides this spring. 'So what happened to him to end up here with five, what, city councillors I reckon?'

'He suffered a fall, I remember, sir, about a year after the campaign. Probably about the time you left for Rome. But his family are prominent, so instead of the usual sick dismissal, he got promoted to tribune and shuffled into some desk job in supply for the governor in Tarraco. That would be, what, nine years ago, maybe, sir? Looks like his career stagnated there.'

Fronto nodded. 'So we assume that Valerius never left Hispania Citerior and stayed a tribune to the end. That means that he and these five others came from across the mountains in Hispania. Where from? I mean, how far into our lands has this bastard been? Are they from Osca? Ilerda? Gerunda? Are they from Tarraco itself? The more I see of this bastard's handiwork, the more I want to beat every little secret out of him.'

'There's something else about this, too,' Galronus muttered.

'What?'

'Caesar is the connection in all this. They think you're him. They think they're luring Caesar into a trap or a fight. And now a man turns up dishonoured and murdered, and he happens to have been an officer in an army Caesar led on campaign? That cannot be a coincidence, surely? Whoever this man is, he has a grudge against Caesar strong enough to destroy nations to satisfy it.'

Fronto nodded. Ghosts. Too many ghosts.

* * *

The Pyrenaei were impressive. Fronto had seen them from the eastern reach as they dropped to the sea not far from Narbo, and he had skirted their southern fringes as he rode with the army across Hispania to join Caesar all those years ago, but he had never had cause to push into the valleys that led up to those giant snow-capped peaks.

The valley that led into Arenosio territory from Conveno was one of the most pronounced in the entire range. From that empty town it snaked up into the heights, curving this way and that, narrowing into defiles and widening out into green valleys, and all the time rising ever higher into the mountains. And throughout the journey no other towns seemed to crop up. Fronto figured they must exist, and the scouts presumed them to occupy side-branches of the main valley, but they could ill-afford to divert the army up each branch just to find other towns, for there was every chance that any settlement they found would be empty anyway. So they marched on up the valley, encountering only abandoned farmsteads in the more fertile areas and tiny empty hamlets near the treeline.

Six days the legion slogged up the winding valley, the supply train rumbling along slowly at the rear, struggling every foot of the way. It was becoming ever more troublesome with each passing mile. Horses were becoming an issue now. Lameness of cavalry steeds and of pack beasts had drained the spares, and now every mount was needed every day, and numerous cavalry steeds had been commandeered to aid the supply train, leaving cavalrymen walking alongside the legionaries. The only bright spot was that the scouts had informed them this morning that they had passed into Arenosio territory, and so the end was now close. Fronto just prayed they would have the strength and the manpower to achieve victory at that end.

The legate's gaze wandered ahead, from where he rode at the front of the column, with Aurelius so close they were almost sharing a saddle. The valley once more curved here, veering off to the left. He was now rather turned about due to their winding path and only during a few hours early and late in the day could he judge the direction from the sun. By his best estimate, the valley was turning east again. A huge spur of land reached out from the mountains like a giant's hand grasping at the earth, his fingers green and welded to the ground, and Fronto peered once again at the small tower atop it. The scouts had confirmed the watchtower was empty half an hour ago, but Fronto could only assume that it had only just now emptied. Why have a watchtower if you have no watchers in it? Clearly the men there had seen the lead elements of the army and abandoned it before the scouts arrived. Fronto was certain they'd been being watched now for at least two days, and that all meant that the enemy knew they were here. There would be no hope of surprise as at Biguro. No, the enemy would be fully prepared this time. And they would not be led by wavering idiots like the Begerri. The Arenosio were supposedly led directly by this very smiling king in the mountains, and would be of steely resolve.

'Sir?'

His thoughts reeled back as the scout that had been riding toward him reined in and walked his horse alongside the legate.

'Yes?'

'We've found another execution, sir. Thought you ought to see it.'

Fronto nodded and urged his horse forward in the wake of the scout, Aurelius and the six cavalrymen staying close behind as they rode on. Some mile ahead of the army, the scout reined in at the top of a steep slope and pointed down it. Fronto peered into the river valley. The torrent that flowed all the way down the valley and became the Garona as it flowed wide and powerful through Tolosa and finally Burdigala into the great western sea was here perhaps twenty paces wide, chest deep and as cold as a senator's heart. It was also extremely fast flowing and had cut a deep defile along the centre of the wider valley, and more than one man and horse had fallen foul of the slope and the current in the past few days, such that the army now steered clear of the river except in places where the banks lowered.

Here, almost at the spur where the valley turned, the rocky heights came down close enough to the river that the legion would be forced to cross the river or suffer the difficulty of moving the supply wagons along the side of a steep slope, which would be difficult and likely to result in at least one wreck and lost vehicle. Appropriately, the scouts had picked out the best route, which led down a track to this point, where an old stone bridge just about wide enough for a cart crossed the torrent, high above. The banks had been washed away in places by some recent flood and the army would have to be slow and careful on the approach to the bridge.

But it was not the terrain they were here to see. Fronto peered at the body on the bridge and, handing his reins to the scout, dismounted. Aurelius followed suit, and the pair of them slowly and carefully descended the bank to the riverside path. Skidding on grass, they ran the last few paces of the slope and out onto the bridge. The sound of the Garona here was deafening. The torrent thundered down its rocky path beneath the stone bridge with a sound like a cavalry charge. A gibbet had been hastily erected on the side wall of the bridge – just a single huge, curved branch dropped into a socket made in the stone. The rope had been tied to a protruding woody knot at the top and from it, in the noose, hung the body of a rich native. He was young, only just out of boyhood, but he wore the clothes and bronze and silver adornments of a

177

noble, as well as a chieftain's torc around his neck. Though he still wore his clothes, he was devoid of weapons, headgear or boots. His hands and feet were a black-purple colour, his face a blue-grey and lined with little blood-marks, while his eyes bulged and his tongue protruded. The legs were caked and stained with urine and faecal matter, and an awful lot of dried blood, the mix also visible as a mark on the stones beneath.

'A chieftain,' Fronto noted.

'Recent, too,' Aurelius added with a sniff and a sour face.

'One of the Begerri perhaps? A punishment for their failure?'

The bodyguard nodded. 'Makes sense. What caused the blood, I wonder? You don't see a lot of blood with hangings.'

Fronto nodded and drew his sword, using the tip to lift the hem of the tunic. The trousers beneath were saturated through with old clotted blood at the groin. 'Whatever happened to him before he was hanged, it was nasty and it happened to his manhood. Don't think I'm fascinated enough to look any closer, but I can only hope for the poor bastard's sake that the blood loss had knocked him out before they strung him up.'

'No such luck,' Aurelius said with an air of authority. 'The colour of the extremities and the voiding is all stuff that happens when you hang a live, conscious man. And look at his fingernails. He's ruined them clawing at the rope around his neck.'

Fronto shot an unpleasant glance at Aurelius. 'I shan't ask how you're such an expert. How recent do you think, since you're the authority?'

Aurelius shrugged. 'The blood's separated. See how it's hardened into a solid clot and left a yellowing stain?'

'I'm not looking that close. Just give me a time.'

'I don't know, sir. I'm not that much of an expert. But more than an hour I'd say. Certainly less than a day, too.'

'So he was put on display for us a few hours ago. That suggests to me that we're close to our destination. A few hours would mean anywhere within maybe twenty miles at a guess. I think we'll find our king and his Arenosio army in the next couple of days. Give me a hand. I want to tip this poor sod over and drag him away into the bushes. Then some of your men can clean the bridge down. Stuff like this unnerves people.'

Aurelius nodded emphatically and made a warding sign against bad spirits before he reached up to the body.

* * *

'It's not going to be easy,' Decius muttered, his horse dancing slightly, impatient to move in the barren, cold terrain. Fronto grunted his agreement as he peered down at the fortress in the wide valley bottom.

The scouts had found the place, an unrecorded site whose name was unknown, a few hours ago and had hung around just long enough to confirm that it was most definitely occupied and by a visible force before pulling back in case they were seen by the enemy. Fronto had shrugged at that. He was sure that the enemy were already well aware of the location and size of the Roman force. So he had once more left Masgava commanding the diminished legion of less than three thousand men, bringing them slowly up the valley at the painstaking speed of the supply train, while he and a small command party had ridden ahead to check out the fortress.

This outpost of the Arenosio sat on a pronounced hillock to one side of the valley, the river Garona flowing past a few hundred yards away, fed by another stream that looped below the fortress. Due to the approach and elevation, the only way they could achieve a good overview of the place was from higher up the valley side. And so Fronto and his friends had very carefully and slowly climbed the northern slopes almost a mile down the valley, which at this point stretched east to west, as evidenced by the blinding sun early that morning before the clouds began to set in, rolling over the world like a fleecy blanket. The way had been treacherous up to the heights, almost a thousand feet above the valley, and the landscape at the top was forbidding and bleak, all scree and scrub grass, with scattered sick-looking trees, in stark contrast to the slopes directly above the fortress on either side, which were thickly wooded. Here, though, for all its bleak appearance, the view of the enemy position was unparalleled, and Fronto could even see inside the compound.

The place had been fortified by nature and improved by man. Sitting at a point where a lesser valley ran off to the northeast, it guarded a crucial meeting place of routes through the mountains. The ramparts, which had been formed of what appeared from a distance to be dry-stone-walling, were twice the height of a man, and just as thick, backed by turf slopes. The whole place was roughly 'L' shaped, with the short side facing the lesser northern valley and the long point jutting out into the main vale. Two gates stood in the walls, one at the long end, facing the valley bottom and the other in the short side, facing the northeast. A small river ran down from that lesser valley and contrived to form a loop around the place to the east, south and west, effectively cutting it off from the wide valley with a deep gulley. That defile was crossed by means of a narrow stone bridge that carried the approach to one gate. The north-western reaches were not protected by the cold torrent, but there was no flat approach, for the rise upon which the fortress sat dipped only to meet the great slope of the wooded valley side.

'That, Fronto, is a shitty place to contemplate,' Carbo said, echoing Decius' sentiments.

'It's mostly the problem of terrain,' the legate murmured. 'The walls are no better than Biguro's, and probably worse. For all their appearance, they're just packed stones, which can be pulled apart or climbed without too much difficulty. But getting men to the walls is going to be troublesome.'

He turned and peered at the silver serpent that was the legion moving up the valley toward them. There had been an appreciable increase in pace among the men, for their destination was almost in sight, and no matter how hard the battle at the end of it might be, each man in that column would be grateful simply to stop marching up the same seemingly-endless valley. In half an hour the lead elements would be in place, mapping out the terrain for the camp. He returned his gaze to the fortress.

'What's your opinion, everyone? Biorix?'

The engineer scratched his chin. 'Getting a battering ram up to a gate would be the work of Hades himself. Both gates are at the top of slopes, and the men would be fighting the gradient with all their strength, leaving little for actual attacks. No siege engine will fit across that narrow stone bridge, even if we had one. Crossing the gulley en-masse would require some quick-built temporary bridges. The engineers could knock you up some wooden trestles to span the gap in half a day, but you'd still have to get down the steep slope, across them and back up the equally steep slope at the far side. The northern approach is the obvious one, but between the slope and the woods there's no way to encamp a legion up there, so any attack we make will have to completely skirt the place from the valley bottom before we try for the walls. Either way, siege-wise your best weapon is probably going to be siege ladders. Essentially, as soon as the defences are constructed, I'll get the lads cutting timbers on the far side of the valley and bringing the timber into camp. We'll start on siege ladders and then bridges. If we work hard we could have the ladders all ready for maybe noon tomorrow, and temporary bridges by sundown.'

Fronto nodded unhappily. 'If that's all we can reasonably use, then that's the way we'll go. Get your men on it, and take as many legionaries as you need to speed up the process. I want to be able to launch a full-scale attack by tomorrow afternoon.' He turned. 'Decius?'

'Hmm. Sling shot range for my lads is maximum about two hundred paces, but at that range it's only good against targets the size of a barn. About seventy to a hundred paces is our usual battle range, and anything less than fifty paces and they could take out an eye. Archery's not much different. My Cretan lads can hit a human sized target one time in three at about a hundred and fifty paces. Less than a hundred paces and they're more or less spot on.' He frowned, breathing slowly. 'Of course, the angle of attack makes a difference too. I reckon that river gulley is just under two hundred paces from crest to walls. So if I got my men to the top of the gulley we'd stand a reasonable chance of doing damage across the walls. It's too far for careful targeting, but we'll take a few out and keep the heads down. Of course, we don't know whether they have archers and if so how good they are. It's plausible that they can do the same back to us, and we won't have the benefit of walls. Only way to learn that is to test it, which makes me nervous. From the northeast, up the lesser valley, we'd be too low. Arrows and stones wouldn't make it over the walls. And from the northwest, by the time we get far enough up the slope to negate the elevation problem, we'd be in thick woods and at the limit of range. Essentially, missiles are only feasible from south and west, across the gulley.'

Fronto sighed. 'Anyone got anything positive to say? Carbo? Atenos? Arruntius? Galronus?'

'Seems to me,' Carbo said, rubbing his bald, pink head, 'that the only truly feasible solution is to cross the gulley, for all the trouble that would bring. With Biorix's help, we can bridge the gap on both sides of the stone crossing. That would give us enough width to send a sizeable force across. Decius can hopefully give us cover from the far side as we charge, and that approach faces the narrow long end of the 'L' so we're facing the minimum width of defences. With luck we can swamp that section of the walls and hold them against the rest of the defenders while Decius comes over to join us and the reserves come up. Of course this all falls apart if we discover they've set traps, obtained artillery, or they have archers as good as ours.'

'How many are we facing, you reckon?' the legate asked.

'From the number of buildings and the size of the place,' Atenos said, drumming his fingers on the bicep of his folded arms, 'I doubt it could hold more than two thousand and probably less than that. That's our good news. At worst we should be at one to one odds. Of course, those odds are somewhat tilted by the addition of the defences we'll have to overcome.'

'You're all filling me with confidence,' Fronto muttered. 'But I agree. It seems that's the only realistic approach. We'll set up camp in the valley bottom across from the fortress and I want a deep ditch and a high bank. These bastards seem to be pretty cunning and fearless and I don't want to wake up in the middle of the night with this smiling king standing next to my bed.'

* * *

In fact, it was not the king that appeared next to Fronto's cot in the middle of the night, but regardless, his hand reached for the sword by his bed as his blurred eyes adjusted and took in the shadowy shape in the gloom of the tent.

'Galronus?'

The Remi nobleman leaned down closer. 'Gods, but you're hard to wake, Marcus. I actually checked your breathing to make sure you were still with us. I've been shaking you for ages.'

'I was having a dream, about the earth trembling. That was you, I guess.'

'Fronto, get up.'

The legate frowned. 'What is it?'

'Trouble, now get up.'

Worried by his friend's manner, Fronto was up in a flash, slipping his feet into his boots without the comfort of socks, wrapping his sword-belt around his rumpled, sleep-sweated tunic and rolling his shoulders. Galronus all-but dragged him from his tent and stopped outside. 'Look.'

Fronto peered myopically into the night air, which was chilly but dry. The lack of moon and stars, all hidden by that same blanket of grey that had set in yesterday afternoon, provided precious little by way of illumination, but it took the legate only moments to pick out what the Remi noble was indicating. High on the eastern peak, towering above the fortress, a golden blaze rose into the darkness.

'Signal fire?'

'What else?' Galronus replied. 'But for who?'

The two men squinted into the black.

'I think…' Fronto said uncertainly, 'is that another flame? There, over the tops a couple of miles away?'

Even as they both peered into the distance trying to decide whether the tiny wink of light was another beacon, it roared into life, bright enough that even two miles away it was clearly visible. Both men turned slowly, taking in their surroundings. No further fires suddenly burst into life around the tops, which was small consolation at best.

'Signals to the east. I think we need a meeting. I'm going to get properly dressed. Call the usual reprobates into the headquarters. I'll be there shortly. Oh, and send for one of the scouts. Get them up to a high place to give us a better idea of what's happening.'

Leaving Galronus to organise it all, Fronto returned to his tent and removed the crumpled tunic, slipping into his spare white and red one, then his leather subarmalis with its embossed medusa head and decorative pteruges. Quickly he slipped on two thick wool socks against the cold of the mountains and then returned to his boots, lacing them swiftly. He fastened his belt around his midriff and threw on his cloak, forgoing armour, sword and helmet. This was a briefing, not a fight – he hoped.

A few moments later, having dipped his head in the bowl of ice-cold water and smoothed down his hair, contemplated shaving the grey bristles from his chin, and stuffed down a mouthful of bread and cheese and a cup of well-watered wine, Fronto emerged into the cold night air again and scurried across to the command tent forty paces from his own. As he arrived, Carbo and Decius were entering, and both nodded their greetings to him.

Inside, the officers stood in a crescent around the table on which sat a large sheet of vellum bearing a hastily drawn map of the valley and half a dozen tablets detailing the strengths of the various units in the Roman force. It had made for tense, unhappy bedtime reading for Fronto. Taking a deep breath, he skirted the gathered officers and stood opposite them, behind the table.

'Signal fires,' he said simply.

'Drawing enemy reinforcements is the best guess,' Decius shrugged.

'But who?'

'The Convenae,' Galronus said. 'Has to be. We know that most of the local tribes were forced to join them and they serve the Arenosio king. There was no one at Conveno, so they had to all be further up in the hills. The king is signalling for his Convenae allies.'

'But why now?' Fronto asked in a concerned voice. 'I'm absolutely certain that they knew we were coming. In fact, given that they've been setting traps and leaving executions for us to find since not long after we left Lapurda, I find it hard to believe they haven't been watching us all along.'

'We took them by surprise at Biguro,' Pulcher noted.

'We took the *Begerri* by surprise at Biguro, not the king or his Arenosio. In fact, if they were watching the Begerri surrender and retake their oath on the Pax Gallica, that would explain the brutal execution of what seemed to be a Begerri chief just down the valley. No, they have known where we were all along. I'm in no doubt about that. We've been drawn here by design.'

'How do we know that this isn't just another Biguro and that this king isn't further on yet?' Terpulo asked.

Fronto rolled up the map of the locale. Beneath it was the rather sparse and basic chart of the entire region. He tapped their location with a finger and then brushed it in an arc to the south. 'This is the last of the good land. In another five miles or so you're approaching the snowline and the treacherous passes across to Hispania that even the locals only use in high summer. It's harsh, awful land. I heard horror stories about the tops when I served in Hispania, from the tribes who lived up here, including the Arenosio. Past here there's really nowhere liveable. This has to be it. If this king's not here, then whatever he intends to do will be done here. But I think the king *is*. I think he has a personal problem with Caesar and he thinks I'm the general, so he's drawn me here. And if he wants to obliterate Caesar and his army here, I ask again: why now light the signal fires? If he's been expecting us, why not already have the Convenae here?'

There was a chorus of nods around the tent. Fronto spoke sense and they all knew it.

'Well,' the legate went on, trying another angle, 'given the lighting of the beacons and what that means – the approach of a probably massive Convenae army – what are our options?'

'Fight now or retreat,' Arruntius said flatly. 'We cannot afford to get caught here by a second force. They would grind us against those walls until we're a paste. We have to either take the place before the reinforcements arrive, or give up and retreat down the valley to somewhere defensible.'

'And we can't do that, as we all know,' Fronto replied. 'We're too few to hold anywhere unless it already has strong defences. To stand a chance against a large force, the first truly defensible place is Conveno, right down in the foothills, a week's march away. If we do that, we might as well abandon the whole campaign. And if that's clear to us, then it's clear to the king inside those walls. We have to fight, and we have to fight as soon as we can.'

'Then for some reason,' Masgava said quietly, 'the Arenosio king is forcing us to attack him. Whatever his design, he wants us to assault his fortress now, with the odds we have currently. He's playing a giant game, forcing us along his path all the way. He's drawn us into the mountains and now he wants us to attack.'

'But not just to destroy us,' Biorix put in. 'If he just wanted to annihilate our army, he would have brought the Convenae in. So what is his game? I hate having my steps guided but, without knowing his end goal, we can't hope to outmanoeuvre him.'

Fronto nodded. 'The upshot, then, is that we have to attack. None of us like it, largely because it's exactly what the enemy want, but they leave us no other choice. If we run, we lose our chance, and if we delay, we get swamped by another enemy. Alright. We attack tomorrow. Whatever he wants, we can't even try until we have the ladders and bridges. How are they coming?'

Biorix shrugged. 'We've got nothing completed yet, but we cut all the timber we needed last night, and a lot of it's already prepared. I've got the lads working in shifts through the night debarking, cutting and adzing. And not just the engineers, either. I can have two dozen ladders and sufficient crossings ready by noon at a push.'

Fronto clucked his tongued nervously and peered down at the map again, mentally placing the beacons he'd seen. His finger searched the mountains and found three small dots marking known tribal sites. 'If we assume that the settlements we were already aware of are the largest ones in the mountains, and they constitute the most likely location of the Convenae, then that places the reserve force somewhere between fifteen and twenty miles away. Depending on how fast they can gather and be ready – and I suspect they were already assembled and waiting for the signal – they could get here in what, a day? Two?'

'So what that means,' Terpulo muttered, 'is that we have tomorrow to take the fortress, or there's a good chance that we'll suddenly be surrounded by angry tribes. No pressure.'

'Well, then,' Fronto sighed, straightening, 'that's our plan. The army prepares in the morning and moves into position. Biorix brings the ladders and bridges up to join us. Decius moves his men into position on the ridge and starts to skewer the enemy as best he can. Then we run out the extra bridges and flood across the gulley with siege ladders and try to take the wall. Tomorrow's going to be a busy day. I suggest you distribute the orders and then get as much shut-eye as you can.'

* * *

Fronto stood on a slight rise and watched. The noon sun was finally beginning to burn off the cloud and the promise of a blue, clear afternoon would have brightened his mood, had this scene not been playing out in front of him. The legion had moved into position half an hour ago, close to the gulley and split into six cohorts. He had to give credit to the adaptability of his veterans. Given the need to constantly re-form the units as men were settled or lost, few people had stayed in the same century for more than a week, and some men had changed unit half a dozen times since they'd left Lapurda. And yet, they'd managed swiftly and efficiently at every stage, and he'd had no complaints or issues beyond the expected occasional grumble. He was even starting to wish this was a permanent command, and not a legion of men on their way to retirement before autumn.

The cohorts stood ready, impassive, waiting for the call. The siege ladders had already been passed down – one for every century except the sixth cohort, which stood at the rear, ready to move up as a reserve.

The engineers were now ferrying the temporary bridges across to the site of the battle. Putting them in place would be a risky business, and half the success of the attack at least would ride on them being positioned swiftly and correctly. Even as he watched, he could see Decius' archers and slingers approaching the gulley's outer ridge, where they would position themselves. They stopped just short and awaited the signal. All was more or less in place. The only part of the army that would not be committed was the cavalry, and Galronus was already twitching at the impotence of his horsemen, but there was simply no place for them in this siege. The terrain made the horse unfeasible. Instead, the riders ranged across the valleys and the lower slopes for some five miles in all directions, adding their numbers to the scouts as they watched for advance signs of the Convenae reinforcements putting in an appearance.

Aurelius, standing a few paces away and holding the reins of both his own horse and Bucephalus, cleared his throat. 'Try and look more posh and constipated.'

Fronto turned to look at him. 'I'd love to hear you say that to Caesar.'

'The general's a proconsul and full of self-importance. You're supposed to be him. Stop slouching.'

Fronto grunted, but did as his bodyguard said, anyway. It had been Aurelius' idea as Fronto had stepped from the tent in the morning. The enemy seemed to think they were facing Caesar, and so if they truly wanted to learn what the enemy wanted, they should not disabuse them of the notion that the general was here. Fronto had been in two minds about that. It was equally possible that if the enemy realised that Caesar wasn't here after all, their plans could fall apart and the Romans might gain an edge. It was a coin-toss, since nobody could predict the truth of it. In the end, rather than listen to Aurelius banging on about it, Fronto had gone along with the idea. His red plume and white tunic, combined with his dress cuirass that he rarely wore, would make him passable as Caesar. He'd taken out his red dress cloak and donned it, since that was known to be an affectation of Caesar on the battlefield. And finally, he had grudgingly agreed to swap horses with Aurelius, lending the bodyguard Bucephalus with his sleek black coat and borrowing his bodyguard's placid white mare, Europa. Caesar rode a white horse, after all. Most irritatingly, Caesar rarely involved himself in the fight. He was always on the battlefield, in view of his men where he could boost morale, but only in dire circumstances would he join the fighting. That meant that Fronto would spend the afternoon standing on a hummock, plainly visible to all, with the standards and banners and a bodyguard of cavalry, looking impressive but getting steadily more bored and leg-achy as the day wore on.

'They're in position,' Galronus called from his place off to the left.

'Give Decius his signal.'

This was it. They were committed. The buccina off to the right gave a short blast of five rising notes, and Fronto watched the archers and slingers rush forward, already reaching for their ammunition as they ran. Not for the first time that day, Fronto threw up thanks to Jupiter Pluvius for holding back rain which would render the bows useless. Yes, it would do the same to any defending archers, but the defenders could still throw down stones and the like on any attacker, and the rain wouldn't stop them. At least this way Decius' men stood a chance of influencing the outcome of the fight.

The missile troops reached the ridge almost in perfect unison, a tribute to the efficiency with which Decius had commanded and trained his unit. Before even the last man fell into position, the first arrows and slingshots arced up across the wide gulley at the walls on the far side. Fronto watched, biting his lip so hard he felt the tang of blood drawn. The first few volleys were ranging shots and many fell into the abyss of the narrow gulley, plunging into undergrowth or water, or struck the slope at the far side or the rampart above, ricocheting back into the stream at the bottom.

Fronto was starting to worry whether the auxiliary prefect had wildly overestimated his men's range when the first sling stone skittered across the stone parapet and into the fortress. There were perhaps a score of enemy warriors standing atop the ramparts on the narrow end of the L-shaped wall, and two of them lurched out of the way of the whizzing slingshot, only for one of them to step directly into the path of the first arrow that crossed the parapet. The shaft struck him in the shoulder and the man reeled. Clearly the arrow had been at long enough range that it no longer had the power to punch through the man's armour, but it had clearly hurt from the way the man had lurched backwards. Good. If they could hurt the enemy they could keep them busy.

Another signal needed giving, but not until the last moment. The legate watched the missile troops a few moments more and the longer he watched, the more of their arrows and shots were reaching the wall top, until every third one was striking home. He was about to give the signal when there was activity on the ramparts and enemy archers and slingers took position, sending their own missiles back across the gulley. To Fronto's relief, even after a number of ranging shots, very few of the enemy missiles reached the ridge where Decius' auxiliaries were positioned. Even as he prepared himself for the next stage, he smiled to see the Roman archers and slingers shift target slightly to pick off the opposite numbers specifically.

'Give Biorix his call.'

A second buccina call went up – three notes rising and falling – and in two heartbeats' time the engineers were moving. Each of the eight sections of makeshift timber bridge was six feet wide and as long as the small stone bridge that crossed the river at the bottom. Each was manned by two contubernia of men, one at the front and one the back. Fronto watched the manoeuvers, fascinated. The work of engineers was always of interest, especially when they had been given a brief and left to their own devices.

Each of the sections of bridge was constructed of rough logs formed into a surface with tightly-tied ropes. The first two approached the stone bridge, slipping quickly down the slope, and almost sending the men at the front sliding and careening into the river below. By some miracle of balance they remained upright as they neared the bridge. The enemy archers and slingers urgently shifted their aim, trying to take down the soldiers near the bridge, but relieving their barrage of Decius' men proved disastrous, and many Arenosio warriors fell even as they tried to adjust their ranges. Endangered by a scattering of enemy shots, the engineers reached the bridge and ran across it, leaving the wooden structures on the near bank and unfurling coils of rope as they ran.

As they neared the far side, a legionary took a stray slingshot to the head and with a yelp vanished over the bridge's low parapet, plunging into the shallow, rocky torrent some twenty feet below. The rest rushed on to the far bank and the slope that ran up to the narrowest expanse of the fortress walls, peeling off to either side as they did so, away from the path that led up to the gate. Another man from that same unit took an arrow in the leg a moment later and fell, sliding down the turf and grasping desperately at undergrowth to prevent tumbling down the gulley and into the stream where the body of his companion lay broken on the rocks, his blood turning the white frothy torrent pink. Another man, from the other unit, slid on the grass and barely regained his footing. The enemy concentrated their shots on the men at the bridge now, heedless of the damage they were taking from Decius' men. Another legionary fell, then another. But despite the losses the engineers found their marked position and began to haul on their ropes. The log bridges began to move out across the gulley on the cables, and Fronto marvelled at the strength of the dozen or so remaining men on both teams as the log bridges slowly began to cross the gap and move into position.

Another man fell on the left unit as a slingshot struck him on the elbow and shattered the joint, sending him screaming to the floor. Having now lost three of their eight man team, the strength of the pull began to wane and the logs' advance halted. Biorix, though, was already adjusting to the circumstances, and so was Decius. As the archers on the ridge began to specifically target the defenders near the bridge in an effort to lighten the cloud of missiles, Biorix sent another four of the men from the near side of each bridge across to join their fellows on the far bank. After all, those on this side only had to hold the bridge steady and then peg it into position at the end. Those on the far side had to haul it across and pull it into place while being struck by enemy missiles.

Fronto watched, tense, as the new additions reached their fellows on the far bank, and the added muscle hauled the bridges across and into place. Another two men fell to lucky blows from the walls as the two units painstakingly drove stakes into the turf and roped the bridge to them, tying off the knots. Even as another legionary fell, they were making their way back across the stone bridge and out of immediate danger. Their task completed, the teams on the near bank pulled the bridge taut and secured it to deep-driven stakes in the same manner. In two hundred heartbeats the slung timber bridges were in place, and access across the gulley had widened from two men to six at a time.

Fronto watched the next bridges begin to slide down the hill. Now was the immediate test. Engineers always sounded sure about their business, but you could never be quite certain it wasn't all bravado until the results were tested. Biorix had already changed the format of the second run, sending twelve men ahead and leaving four to maintain the near side.

The legate held his breath as the engineers reached the new bridges and ran across them, one team to each. Their feet pounded the temporary structures, which were being tested to the limit immediately, carrying the weight of twelve men each. He let out the breath explosively as they reached the far side with only one loss due to a stray arrow. In twenty heartbeats the third and fourth bridges were being hauled into place alongside the previous two. With a total loss of three men the teams tied off their bridges and returned, heaving in breaths as they arrived back with their fellows. The near side was secured and a six man approach became ten.

Even as he felt his burden lighten with the latest success, Fronto's eyes drifted up to the walls on a hunch, feeling that odd, unsettling, hair-raising shiver that a person gets when they know they're being watched. His gaze drifted along the walls, where he could not make out the individual details of the defenders due to distance, but could identify whether they were an archer, a slinger or armed with sword or spear to defend the walls. And there, as his gaze slid along the defences, they alighted upon a single figure who stood tall and, though there was no way of confirming it for certain, Fronto knew the man was looking at him. The figure stood so confident and tall despite the constant barrage of Decius' men, and Fronto was hardly surprised when Decius suddenly concentrated his men's barrage on the figure. Two more warriors appeared to either side of the watcher and threw up huge heavy shields, protecting the figure from missiles. He was still watching Fronto.

Watching to see what he would do. The man was expecting Caesar to do something. To join in the attack? Somehow Fronto knew in a trice that he was being measured as a man, even though mistaken for Caesar. And in a heartbeat the enemy decided what would happen. He disappeared from the walls, gesturing to someone inside the fortress.

'I've got a bad feeling about this,' Fronto muttered to Masgava and Galronus.

'Everything's going according to plan,' Masgava said.

'For now. But something's not right.'

He watched with a growing sense of trepidation. There was no logic to his feeling of apprehension. In fact, it was what Priscus used to rib him about, and how, he realised, he now did exactly the same to Aurelius. But it was impossible to shake the feeling that he'd cast the dice and they'd come up wanting.

'Cornicen, I want that mouthpiece next to your lips from now on, and ready to blow the recall any moment. Something is horribly, horribly wrong.'

To his surprise, Aurelius was next to him, nodding. 'I feel it too.'

The fifth temporary bridge fell to disaster. Two lucky shots from the wall took out men holding the rear of the bridge on the near side and the weight was too much for the two remaining engineers. Their grip slipped and the whole artifice slid and rolled down the hill, taking half the lead party with it into the gulley and the stream. The survivors ran for safety.

'There you go,' Masgava said. 'There's the bad luck you were feeling.'

'No,' Fronto peered down as the last two bridges were run out. 'That wasn't it.'

A desperate last attempt by the defenders took out too many of the advance unit and the last bridge slid down into the gulley before it could be anchored. Only four of the twelve engineers made it back.

'That's all the bridges,' Carbo said from off to the left. 'We lost two, but it's still widened from a two man crossing to a fourteen-man one.'

Fronto answered with a noncommittal grunt.

'Fronto, we're ready,' Carbo urged him. Still the legate stood in silence as the bridges swayed slightly, clear of all legionaries, the only sound of battle that of Decius' men exchanging missiles with those on the wall.

'Marcus, give the call,' Galronus said breathily.

Silence. The legate was peering at those walls as though expecting them to open up, revealing row upon row of teeth, and begin to eat the army by the century.

'Marcus…'

Fronto dropped a hand and the cornicen gave two loud, sharp, high blasts, then two low. The cohorts began the descent to the gulley, moving first at a slow march then, at a whistle from their centurions, the lead century doubled their speed. Another whistle and that lead century broke into run, the second into a fast march, the rest at a steady tread. By the ordered change of pace, the centuries moved into position to cross the bridges.

'We should recall them.'

'What?' Carbo said incredulously.

'This is wrong.'

'Look at them,' Carbo said. 'They're almost at the walls, with ladders ready. There's less than fifty men on that stretch of the defences. The cohorts will be over in twenty heartbeats.'

'They'll be dead in ten,' said Fronto, darkly.

They watched, tense, as the legionaries reached the base of the dry-stone walls and began to raise the ladders. They had suffered maybe a score of casualties to missiles as they crossed the bridges and climbed the slope. It was negligible in the grand scheme of things. And yet...

Fronto closed his eyes. It was changing now, he could feel it. When he opened them, only one small adjustment had been made. The enemy missile troops were no longer aiming at the Romans below them at the walls. Instead, they were loosing like mad at Decius' unit. Suppressing shots. He realised with a frown that the warriors on the walls had changed subtly while he'd been watching the progress of the cohorts. No one up there bore a sword or spear any more. The wall had bulked out with archers and slingers, and the sudden increase in numbers was putting Decius under pressure. He was starting to suffer proper casualties. The enemy were keeping Decius busy, and there was no one on the walls prepared to take on an attacker.

'Sound the recall,' Fronto barked.

There was silence. Carbo was staring at him, as was Galronus, though Aurelius simply nodded vehemently. The cornicen had his horn to his lips, but remained silent, clearly thinking he'd misheard or that something had gone wrong.

'Sound the fucking recall,' Fronto snarled.

The cornicen blew into the mouthpiece as though his life depended on it, his eyes wide in perplexed panic. But it was too late. Fronto watched the new defenders reach the parapet, lifting their heavy burdens. Decius' men could do nothing about it, as they were being pounded mercilessly by Arenosio archers and slingers.

'Run, you idiots,' Fronto said under his breath, watching the attack.

A full cohort was spread out across the wall now, almost five hundred men, raising their six ladders, unaware of the mortal danger appearing above them.

'Hades, no,' Carbo breathed.

'Shit,' was Galronus' succinct response.

Fronto watched with sick fear as the new arrivals on the wall top tipped their cauldrons of heated sand over the parapet onto the five hundred men below. The screams began instantly, but what was being done to them was no swift death, and they went on for a long time as the soldiers of Rome melted below the walls, their skin blackening and sloughing away under the onslaught of white hot material that clung to them even as they fell and rolled. Even those who made it to the water, heedless of the hard rocks beneath the surface, were too late. Their burns were too bad for them to live.

The second cohort, who'd just begun to reach the far side of the bridges, reacted in chaos to the carnage ahead of them and the recall signal behind. Many fell to the missile troops on the wall, as they switched targets once more. Decius' men had been forced back, and now arrows and stones smacked into fleeing legionaries, leaving the slopes of grass strewn with bodies.

'I should have...' Carbo said, his voice wavering. 'You said...'

'There was no reason for it. I just knew. No blame on you, Carbo. And we couldn't have expected anything like heated sand. The Gallic peoples don't use tactics like that. This is all the work of that smiling bastard of an Arenosio king. He watched me. And as soon as he knew I wasn't coming, he changed it all. He'd been all-but inviting me in, and when I stayed here, he took it out on the men. When this is over I am going to have a few very hard words with that animal.'

'The other cohorts are pulling back in good order,' Galronus said quietly, 'and Decius has most of his unit out of enemy range.'

'What do we do now?' Aurelius asked, his face pale.

'We retreat. We think. We plan. Then we come back and we tear this bastard a new smile.'

* * *

'What's the damage?' Fronto said quietly, his opening words for the command meeting in the central tent of the camp.

'Eight hundred and fifteen dead, sir,' Carbo said bleakly. 'Oddly only thirty or so wounded. Few who got injured made it out alive.'

'Over a quarter of our men. Nearly a third, in fact. And all in about quarter of an hour. And it's my fault.'

'*Your* fault?' Carbo said in surprise.

'That bastard wanted me to attack. Caesar, I mean. He wanted *Caesar* to attack. If I'd gone in, that wouldn't have happened.'

'Or you'd also be lying on the grass with a melted face, sir,' Terpulo argued.

'No. I don't think so. This is too personal. All of it. That was me being punished for not committing myself. We did very little damage to the enemy today and took horrendous casualties in the process. I presume you heard about the beacons?'

There were nods. 'Two more beacons lit,' Arruntius, one of the few miraculous survivors of the assault, said. His left arm was scalded, and wrapped in cold, damp bandages, but otherwise he'd managed to run from the danger just in time.

'And lit further off, too. They're answers. And that puts the Convenae less than a day away. At the very latest, they'll put in an appearance by tomorrow afternoon. My only hope is that this insane king is so avid that he wants me to attack him that he'll hold off with the Convenae long enough for that to happen, but we cannot rely on that. He may be methodical and clever, but he's also clearly madder than a bag of toads, and madmen cannot be relied on for anything except unpredictability. So we're left with little choice.'

'Another attack?' Masgava said. 'At first light, so we can maybe take them before the reinforcements arrive. Maybe at the far side this time?'

Fronto gave the big Numidian a hard smile. 'You're supposed to be more cunning and inventive than that, my friend. No. Here's what we now know about our friend over there. He thinks like a Roman. He set anti-horse lilia pits down in the lowlands, set up artillery ambushes. He uses terrain and all his available auxiliaries in order to preserve his own force. And here, right at the end, he used hot sand. *Hot sand!* Can you imagine how hard sand must be to obtain in the mountain passes in that quantity? He'd planned this for months. Long enough to ferry two or three cartloads of sand up from the coast or a lowland river. He's cunning, and he's planning. But there's one advantage. He thinks like a good old Roman general. And that means he's limited by the same thinking.'

'You think you can outmanoeuvre him?' Galronus said.

'I'm sure of it. Like any normal commander, he's resting on his laurels right now, happy that he's won. He's almost certainly thinking that I'll lead some last ditch attempt in the morning, and that's what he wants: me – *Caesar* – desperate enough to join in the fight. So we have to do the unexpected. He knows we've retreated to lick our wounds. But that's not what we're going to do. It's almost dark now, and we're going to try again tonight.'

'Attack in the dark?'

'Yes. Do you realise that since my days in Hispania I have never yet lost a battle I commanded. I've been in a couple of debacles led by other people, including Caesar, but I've never led a lost cause. And I don't intend to start now. I refuse to blemish my record because of that smiling bastard behind those walls.'

'But how do you hope to win in the dark when we couldn't win in the light?' Galronus frowned.

'Simple,' Fronto grinned. 'We'll cheat.'

'What?'

'I shall take a unit of the best, sneakiest sons of motherless whores in the whole army. We'll head east, hidden by the ridge, then move into the trees. Then we'll head up into the hills and come down the other side sometime around midnight, hopefully taking them entirely by surprise. With grapples, we might be able to get inside. And once we're inside, we'll try and move round to secure the south wall and the gate above the bridge. You lot will have every last man ready to move into a fight. A melee. That includes the wounded, the archers, the cavalry, the teamsters and the lot. Every man in this army who can lift a sword will be in position just at the camp edge, ready to move. When we secure the gate, I'll send up a signal and you get there as fast as you can. Once we start the men pouring through the gate, we've won. It's that simple.'

'Oh?' Carbo raised an eyebrow. '*That* simple?'

Fronto laughed. 'I'll take the best men I can, including Arcadios. No one can launch a fire arrow like him. That'll be your signal.'

'Why do *you* have to lead this?' Masgava frowned.

'Because this is all about me. Well, it's all about *Caesar*, but you know what I mean. There are answers in that place waiting to be discovered. I intend to find them tonight.'

'It's mad.'

'But it'll work,' Fronto grinned nastily. 'Get everything ready. I leave in an hour.'

Late Maius

THE king stood atop the walls of the fortress, his cloak billowing in the night winds that rushed down the valley from the snowy peaks above. His keen eyes picked out the tiny shapes moving in the distance, despite the near-darkness. Shapes that believed themselves hidden, unaware that nothing in this valley was hidden from the king of the Arenosio. Eyes blinked in every tree and hollow, reporting back to the fortress by lesser paths.

'What could they hope to achieve?'

The king turned to find Ategnio standing beside him, watching the enemy sneaking away. He smiled. The great, deadly Arenosio warrior who had been by his side since the early days was a clever man for his upbringing, and strong – gods, but he was strong – but his intellect still only stretched so far. The Gauls were weak and the Belgae were arrogant, but the Aquitanii were simple. That was not to say they were stupid – they were far from that – but more that they were straightforward and not given to deceit, and it had taken some work for the king to find men who thought in curves rather than straight lines. Ategnio was one of the most innovative and intuitive of his tribe, but next to the Romans he might as well have his features painted on and strings attached to his limbs to dance for the laughing crowds. But then, they were all puppets of a sort – the Arenosio to him, and all of mankind to the laughing, wicked Fates.

'You have so little experience of Rome, my friend. I told you Caesar would manage to find his way in. That is what he is doing.'

'You should pay more attention to the warriors beneath your own banner than beneath Caesar's bull, sire.'

'Oh?'

'The men are concerned that you play dangerous games. First you let the Romans get too close, then you ruin them and then, instead of finishing them off, you sit back and let them try again.'

'You know my reasons, Ategnio.'

The warrior nodded. 'I know. You want Caesar to come to you. And you will gradually cripple him until the need to avenge himself on you sends him personally into the fight.'

'It is called hubris, Ategnio. And Caesar is a martyr to hubris. He *cannot* lose, and he will make sure he stands triumphant in my hut as his soldiers rampage around the fortress. And that is exactly where *I* want him, but this is all an enormous balancing act. I need Caesar kneeling before my sword, but that means I cannot simply obliterate his army. Caesar has a habit of fighting last struggles alongside his men, and he is no use to me dead. But also I cannot let him simply walk in with his army, for then it would be *I* at *his* mercy. No, this all requires care.'

'I saw him today, sire. White horse, red cloak, white tunic, red plume. He stood and watched, nothing more.'

'I saw him too, Ategnio, committing his men but not himself. But he *is* coming.'

'Sire?'

'He comes now. It is too dark and distant to confirm it, but somehow I know that old bastard is among those men heading north, believing themselves to be hidden. They come against us now somehow, but the darkness is dangerous to them as to us. If Caesar is with those men coming in a circle to the east to take us by surprise, then I want him. He endangers himself unnecessarily. While I am willing to sacrifice anyone – Taranis himself, if need be,' Ategnio made a sign against bad luck and flicked his eyes up to the sky at those words, but the king was going on. '… I would still prefer to save our people. Now, perhaps we have that chance. If Caesar is out there with a small group, we could take him and finish the battle before it truly begins. Send out patrols. Tell them that any man with a red plume needs to be captured healthy and intact and any man who wounds the general will add to the *fascina* hanging from my banner before he is slowly roasted..'

'And if Caesar reaches the walls and attacks us?'

'Then I will let him in if I must, and he will be mine.'

'Sir,' Ategnio replied and scurried off to give the orders.

The king remained on the rampart. He had seen Caesar today for the first time since all this had started, and had not felt what he'd expected. Somehow he'd thought gods would sing dirges of vengeance in his mind and sparks would fly in the aether. Yet while he felt an unsettling nothingness in relation to the general, there was still *something* about that figure in red and white that had sent a shiver endlessly up and down his spine for half a day now.

Chapter Nine

FRONTO puffed out his cheeks and pushed on with weary feet, the sound of dozens of breathless soldiers climbing behind. Fronto and Centurion Pulcher had hand-picked the quietest, strongest, most agile men in the army and formed a single century of them. They had armed lightly, with no mail and no apron of jangling straps. They wore only leather vests – the subarmalis that protected a man from the pinching of metal armour – over their tunics, and bore only a sword, tightly positioned so that it did not swing. They had not taken their shields, for they would be inconvenient in thick woodland to say the least, and crossing the ramparts with them would be extremely difficult. Then the century had moved off east through the scrappy sections of woodland in the valley bottom, following the river to make use of its sloping banks.

Once they had moved almost a mile up the valley and the Arenosio fortress was little more than a constellation of tiny, twinkling lights in the distance, they had turned and begun to climb the bare slope. Here and there small copses and areas of scrub marred the hillside, though much was open heath, yet despite the freedom of open ground the gradient was steep and the men laboured up it with difficulty. Horses here would have struggled with the slope long before they ran into trouble in the trees, so like shields and armour they had been left behind.

The slope rose to become a high spur – the foot of the mountains that divided the two valleys at the confluence of which the fortress stood. The view from the top was impressive even under a dark, fleecy sky. With bright moonlight, Fronto considered the very real possibility he would be able to see Gaul if he squinted hard enough. With some relief all round, the slope began to level out as they reached the crest, and the legate called a brief rest.

As the men paused and recovered from the climb, Fronto found himself with Pulcher at one shoulder and Aurelius at the other, and took in their surroundings

They could not quite make out the fortress that sat at the far end of the spur, though the legion's large, rectangular camp across the valley was clear enough in the distance. They could, however, see the wooded slope which sat at the northwest side of the enemy location. It was thickly-forested with bare patches of sheer rock higher up, and Fronto could imagine how troublesome it was going to be shortly, though perhaps not so bad as what was to come next. The slope down the far side of the narrow spur, into that secondary valley, was twice as steep as the one they'd just ascended. Definitely a good job they'd not been on horses, really. A dozen or so of the legionaries, resting their weary legs, strode to the crest to look down, some whistling quietly under their breath at the steep, shadowed descent.

'Lovely night for a stroll,' Aurelius said, his voice heavy with sarcasm.

Fronto opened his mouth to reply, but was cut off as one of the legionaries standing to his left was suddenly plucked from the ground and hurled backwards, his face gone, replaced with bloody pulp.

'Slings,' barked Pulcher, shoving Fronto back away from the edge. The unit pulled back from the slope, whence the shot had clearly come from the damage done to the soldier. No more stones appeared and Fronto paused, content that they had moved out of view. Slingers would not come further up the slope to pursue, but perhaps if the slingers were not alone, that crest of the hill might soon bristle with armed warriors.

'Do we pull back?' Aurelius asked quietly.

'Shit, no. The Convenae are on their way and we'll be trapped against the fortress walls if we delay. We have one opportunity here to take the place, and we've got to persevere. We *have* to succeed. That bastard in the fort has manoeuvred us so bloody convincingly that we have to either give up or press on. And I refuse to give up.'

'So what do we do, sir?' Pulcher asked. 'What's the plan?'

Fronto shrugged. 'A little something I learned from Arruntius.' He turned to the gathered legionaries. 'There's thickets and small stands of trees on the slope down there, but it's not heavily wooded. The slingers were hidden, else I'd have seen them, so that means they're hiding in those trees. And that means there's not too many of them, there's no cavalry, and probably no armoured warriors, just fast moving pickets. On my signal, we're going to run over that ridge and down the slope, charging the bastards head on.'

'Sir, we'll break our necks,' argued one of the legionaries.

'It's a risk, but we need to take them down and fast. If you run and fall, you'll just have to roll and hope. Let's show these bastards the sort of men they're up against. Are you with me?'

The men nodded and muttered their affirmative, aware that even with enemy pickets close by the fortress probably were not aware of their location yet, and therefore mindful of the need to keep disturbance to a minimum.

The century shuffled forward and Pulcher took the fore, moving his hideous face – all the more disconcerting in the darkness – to the ridge, marking the point of visibility for the enemy. As if to provide confirmation of his judgement, a slingshot whipped across the ground close by his feet, tearing up blades of grass.

'Hurry now, lads,' Pulcher said, waving them into position. 'I make a big mean target while I wait for you lot to unknot your underwear.'

The legionaries, grinning, moved into position, and Fronto stepped up with them.

'Sir,' admonished Aurelius, tugging at his sleeve.

'No. This is too important. Every man's needed, you and me included.'

The bodyguard, his expression black with concern and disapproval, nonetheless stepped up next to Fronto.

'Everyone in position?' Pulcher asked, glancing over both shoulders at the double line of legionaries as a stone clonged off the very tip of his helmet, pulling his head backwards for a moment. 'Good. Come on, you beauties.'

The unit broke into a run and crested the hill in odd silence, the pounding of feet and unsheathing of swords the only noise. More slingshots dinged and whizzed up from the small knot of trees ahead. Fronto cast his eyes this way and that, paying little attention to the terrain. After all, by the time he saw trouble he'd already have hit it at this pace. The slingers appeared to be based in only one small corpse, which made things easier, and the century converged upon it..

The century charged at the treeline some fifty paces away and twenty lower. The first casualty of the terrain came almost simultaneously with the first victim of the slingers. A legionary squawked in shock as something on the slope tripped him. Rather than the usual fate of falling back and being trampled by his mates in the attack, though, the combination of slope and momentum just sent him on further ahead, the painful rolling and bumping bringing other yelps as he fell. Another legionary disappeared with a shout as a sling stone hit him in the centre of the chest, knocking him back and down.

Twenty five paces were eaten up in mere heartbeats, bringing them halfway to the copse as another man fell with a shout, taking down his neighbour in the process. The slingshots were becoming more accurate at the closer range, too, and men were crying out as missiles struck them here and there. Again, a man disappeared with a cry and a broken cheek, then another fell and tumbled on down the slope. Maybe Arruntius' rather blunt tactics only worked for him, Fronto mused as he ran on. The trees were close and now he could see vague shapes flitting between the trunks among the undergrowth. He was about to slow and dive into the copse with the rest, when movement caught his eye and he turned.

Two men had broken cover and were running down the slope away from the fight, heading west.

'Aurelius!' he barked, pointing with his sword. His bodyguard spotted the two men fleeing, likely heading for the fortress to carry word of the Romans' location, and the two men peeled off, leaving the rest to wade into the woodland and take on the slingers. Fronto and Aurelius pounded on down the slope and the two fleeing men turned, catching sight of their pursuers. One, unable to maintain the dangerous run while looking the wrong way, fell foul of a dip and lost his footing, tumbling into a roll that carried him off at a tangent. Without needing to be told, Aurelius veered off and ran for the rolling man.

Fronto concentrated on the other one, who was running full pelt down the turf, heading for another small stand of trees.

'Oh no you bloody don't,' Fronto snarled. The man was faster than him, considerably younger and probably bred climbing slopes like this all his life. He would outrun Fronto, and the legate knew it, so before he could consider the idiocy of his plan he sheathed his sword and leapt.

The legate had meant to tackle the man, his arms around the warrior's hips, bringing him down swiftly and easily. The result of his leap was less spectacular than it had been in his head. He took a running foot to the eyebrow that made his head spin and hit the man awkwardly, sideways. His shoulders struck the man's calves and the warrior hit the ground with a shout, tumbling on, tangled with Fronto.

The momentum on this slope was impressive, and the pair had rolled another twenty paces, locked in a struggle, legs and arms grasping and flailing, before they slid to a halt. Through sheer chance, Fronto finished the tumble on top of the warrior, but the man was quick. Two hands reached up, one grasping Fronto's reaching fingers, the other his opposing elbow, fighting the legate off, trying to unpin himself.

Fronto struggled and pushed, but his left arm seemed to have been wrenched somehow during the fall and was extremely painful, and he found that the warrior was managing to push him away with surprising ease. Gritting his teeth, Fronto smashed his head forward and down with all the strength he could muster.

Despite the lack of armour, the century had kept their helmets, which made little noise without the other armour to scrape and clatter against. Fronto's decorative brow plate smashed into the bare head of the hirsute native with an audible crack of bone, and moments later the arms holding him off went limp. Wheezing, Fronto straightened and looked down. A huge red welt adorned the warrior's forehead – an imprint of the decoration on Fronto's helmet. The legate paused and examined the man beneath him. His chest was still. A hand across the mouth and nose confirmed lack of breath. The warrior was dead. Hauling him to one side, Fronto spotted the stone jutting from the turf. When the legate had head-butted the man, his skull had jerked back against the ground and the projecting stone had broken his neck. Satisfied that they had prevented the runners taking news to the fortress, Fronto stood painfully and looked for Aurelius. His bodyguard was stomping toward him with a fierce expression and a splash of blood gleaming in the darkness across his leather subarmalis.

Fronto tested his left arm. It ached badly when he moved it backwards or out, but nothing appeared to be broken and he could still grip his fingers.

'Come on.'

The two men jogged back along the hillside to the copse, where already Pulcher was marshalling his men.

'All done here, centurion?'

'No survivors, sir. You got the runners?'

'We did. Casualties?'

'Seven men dead or unable to go on. Not bad, considering.'

Fronto nodded. 'Get the dead back to the top and leave the badly wounded up there with them for now. Where we're going everyone needs to be strong and ready.'

Moments later they were gathered once more and, at the nod from Pulcher, they moved off, leaving their unfortunate companions on the hilltop. Seventy seven of them remained. If any loss of men could be considered acceptable, then Fronto was forced to admit such of this. It could have been so much worse.

'Question is,' he muttered to the centurion as they descended slowly, 'was that a random set of pickets – an enemy patrol maybe? Or was it set there specifically for us? The more I think on the nature of the man in that fortress, the more I wonder whether he's running this show in its entirety. Certainly he's trying to. He wants me to attack him personally, I think. But I intend to make his wish come true anyway.'

The century descended the slope carefully, with only one wrong-footed fall and no injuries, and by the time they reached the valley and the terrain levelled, Fronto's legs were shaking uncontrollably with the effort, his calves tight. Aware that everyone was in much the same state, he called another rest by the same narrow watercourse which further down, where the valley met its larger sibling, the legion had attempted to cross that afternoon in their abortive attack.

The stream was lined on both sides with trees and the vegetation of the valley in general was thick enough that there was no sign of the enemy fortress at the end of the slope. Once every man's breathing had returned to normal, the soldiers had massaged the knots and aches from their legs, and most had taken a welcome drink from the cold, refreshing waters of that stream, Fronto gave the signal to Pulcher, and they were on their way once more.

The clouds were beginning to separate now, the fleecy grey lining of the sky stretching and pulling apart to leave sparkling stars against infinite black in their place. Fronto frowned as he peered up and after a few moments spotted the moon, momentarily sliding between clouds.

'Almost an hour before midnight. We're doing well.'

Pulcher nodded. 'Best stop the talking now, though, sir. Every step takes us closer to the enemy.'

The legate nodded as they ascended the far side of the narrow valley. This slope, which led all the way down the valley past the Arenosio fortress, was more forbidding than the ones they had already traversed. The lowest areas of the slope were fairly thickly wooded, but the higher one climbed the more rocky it became until there was nothing but scree slopes and sheer cliff. That, Fronto was gambling, was why the enemy would not think to look for trouble coming from that direction. Fronto and Pulcher scoured the woods until they located a game trail that headed the right way, west along the foot of the slope, toward the fortress. Then the century moved into single file with Pulcher at the lead and slipped into the woods, cracking and rustling their way along the track.

The journey was only half a mile, but due to the difficulty of branches and undergrowth it took them as long to traverse the woods as it had to cross the hill at the beginning. Finally, Pulcher held up a hand to stop the column and moved into a small clearing. Fronto scurried forward to join him.

Through waving foliage and occasional tree boles, the two men could see the northern walls of the enemy fortress. They were now almost diametrically opposite the legion camp, with the Arenosio's stone fort in the middle. They were maybe two hundred paces from the walls. This side was not protected by ditch or river, just by the general inability to get an army there in numbers. But Fronto was not going to rely on numbers. After all, he didn't *have* huge numbers in the first place. No. His century would attempt to make their way through the fortress and open the gate for the rest of the legion. But to do that they needed to get inside, and that in itself required another distraction.

Fronto tapped Pulcher on the wrist, recoiling automatically as that remarkably ugly face turned to him, and then pointed at the fortress. He gestured to the centurion and then sought out with his finger the north-east gate that faced the small valley they had just crossed. He held up both hands and flashed his fingers four times, to indicate forty men. Pulcher nodded. Fronto now moved his finger west until he came to a projecting section of wall, almost like a bastion in the defences, atop which stood a brazier and a small knot of men. He then flashed his fingers three times and pointed to himself.

It was agreed. Pulcher would take forty men against the gate and make a lot of noise. With luck, the distraction would draw enough attention that Fronto would have less difficulty getting over the wall further along. That bastion was a strong point in the defences by day, well-manned and heavily walled. The enemy would be unlikely to expect an attack there. But better still, what was strong during the day provided a useful weakness by night. The heavy projecting bastion formed an area of deep shadow where it met the wall, and that gloomy corner was Fronto's goal.

'Alright you cunning bastard,' Fronto whispered under his breath, 'let's see just how clever you are.'

* * *

'Aurelius,' Fronto hissed in the quietest whisper, 'if you get any closer to me I'll be more or less wearing you, now back off.'

The bodyguard, who had been doing his utmost to cover Fronto from all angles, stepped slightly away, his face disapproving, though the expression changed moments later at a shrill squeaking above the trees as the small local bats flittered and swooped. With every tiny noise, Aurelius ducked as though they were diving at him and not somewhere high up, largely oblivious to his presence. Four years on from that harrowing time in the Forest of Arduenna the strapping, solid legionary still shat himself when something squeaked in the dark.

Thirty men came along behind Fronto, four of them carrying coiled ropes and four more bearing heavy, four-pronged grapples, all of which had been strapped tightly to their belts as they travelled. As Fronto edged just that tiniest bit closer his men closed on him, and Aurelius once more almost clung to him, forcing the legate to shrug and heave his guard slightly further away. Honestly, it was like launching an attack with your mother at your shoulder.

Crouching, he peered out from the last line of trees, across thirty paces of ground to the walls. Guards were spaced periodically along the ramparts along with blazing torches, which rose behind them rather than in front so as not to ruin their night vision. Consequently, the grass below was lit well, with the wall shadow stretching out from its foot, intermittently broken up with the shadow of men on the parapet. As yet there was no sign of movement off to the left, where the north gate sat silent and quiet.

As the legionaries dropped into position in the undergrowth, they attached the grapples to the ropes and tied the ends tight, testing them by pulling them apart between two men. In a matter of heartbeats the whole forest edge was silent, pensive, as the men waited for the off.

Everything changed suddenly as Pulcher burst from the forest with his men, running at the gate and bellowing invocations to Mars, Minerva, Jupiter and half a dozen lesser gods. Fronto held his hand up to steady the men and keep them in place. They watched as Pulcher's legionaries reached the walls, the enemy surprised enough that they managed to loose only two or three arrows before the Romans were below them and climbing the rough stone walls, hand and foot grips made easy by the gaps where the stones had been stacked rather than mortared. Legionaries were surging up, but Arenosio warriors were also flocking to the gate and jabbing down with their weapons, trying to hold off the onslaught. For a moment, Fronto considered the very real possibility that Pulcher and his men might actually *take* the gate in the process of creating a diversion, and that Fronto's own assault would be entirely unnecessary. He could only imagine, thinking of Pulcher, what the baffled defenders must be thinking when they looked down and saw that hideous, ruined visage glaring back up at them calling them filthy names and snarling as it climbed. Shit, an assault from Pulcher would frighten Fronto out of his wits, and he *knew* the man.

But more and more warriors were appearing at the wall top near the gate, rapidly answering the urgent 'sick bovine' calls of the carnyx warning the fortress of an attack to the north. Fronto clenched his teeth and watched the bastion. There were four men on the top and other guards every ten paces or so along the wall to either side, and not one of them seemed to be moving in reaction to the threat at the gate. So, the king was clever enough, then, to have drilled into his men the necessity of holding their positions. Many

Gallic-type armies would by now have run to help their comrades, abandoning their posts. It was irritating but at least the reinforcements pouring onto the gate top were all men who wouldn't be at the bastion to meet Fronto and his legionaries.

Clucking his tongue irritably, Fronto held his men in position, aware that every two or three heartbeats there was a scream of agony from the gate. Yes, some of those cries would be Arenosio, but at least one in three would be Roman. He couldn't wait too long. Every few heartbeats the centurion's force diminished slightly, yet still Fronto waited.

His prayers were answered when there came another shout, and the men on the wall near the gate ran off to bolster their friends, taking one of the warriors from the bastion with them. As they moved away and momentarily every eye on the wall swivelled to watch their comrades move, Fronto gave the signal and started to run.

Thirty paces might sound a lot, but in action it passes in the blink of an eye. There is no time to worry, nor to form *any* sort of coherent thought. Fronto's mind was simply filled with a jumble of violent images and possibilities as he crossed the open ground and dropped into the shadow formed by that bastion. He had hoped that Pulcher's distraction would be enough to momentarily draw away all defending manpower, leaving him with the opportunity to move his entire unit into the shadows unobserved. Clearly the enemy were too well commanded for that to happen, but at least the shadow also served a secondary purpose.

Even as Fronto and the lead men of his unit dropped into the darkness at the foot of the wall where the bastion joined it, the enemy above had recognised a second threat, spotting the legionaries hurtling from the treeline into the shadows. The few men up there with slings and bows moved to the parapet and began to load and loose their missiles into the shadow, but with the torches atop the wall and a deep shadow below, they were releasing blind. Nine in every ten missiles thudded harmlessly into turf as Fronto and his men pressed against the wall, hidden in the pitch black. While the stragglers were still crossing the open ground, one of them picked off and hurled aside with a well-placed arrow through the neck, the men in the shadows nodded to one another and stepped back from the wall, swinging their ropes twice each before releasing the grapples upwards.

One of the four was unlucky, a sling stone striking him hard on the helmet, denting the bronze and sending him falling away, his brains fogged and his ears ringing, the cable he'd been holding flapping loose. Fronto leapt for the rope, but with no pressure on it the Arenosio above merely detached it from the wall top and the whole thing came back down, almost braining Fronto in the process. The other three men with grapples had immediately tugged on the rope, throwing all their weight into it to prevent the same thing happening, and swung back to the wall, their feet thudding into the stone as they began to climb.

The enemy above were shouting now and the pointless missiles stopped while the defenders concentrated on trying to dislodge the grapples. The legionaries, old though they might be, ascended like lizards on a warm sunny wall, speedy and effortless. Only moments after the assault had first started, a man reached the parapet and tried to pull himself over, receiving an axe to the shoulder for his effort. With a scream he fell away, plunging back down into the shadows, landing close to Fronto with a crunch and a squelch. The defenders had given up trying to dislodge the grapples themselves now, having discovered that with a man's weight hanging on the rope they were simply immovable. Instead, four warriors were now at the occupied grapples, using their blades to hack at the ropes.

The third rope was loose due to its fallen climber and a man went to shift the grapple, but already another legionary had grabbed the bottom and was climbing. Good. All three ropes were being dealt with by the defenders, and it seemed they didn't even need the fourth. The enemy had fallen for yet another distraction.

Once, long ago, when discussing tactics and the value of diversions and surprise attacks, Verginius had expressed his opinion to Fronto that the very best plans were made like an onion, with layer upon layer protecting the heart. And so here they were. The legion was the outer layer, sitting threateningly across the valley, blinding the enemy to the threat from the north, where a single century would make the vital push. That second level, a century of tired men, was split in two, with half the legionaries under Pulcher distracting the enemy from the third layer of the

211

onion: Fronto's force. And finally, Fronto had sent up a few brave lads with grapples, their brutal straightforward attack and the distinct danger posed by the ropes blinding the enemy to the fourth and final layer of the onion.

A wave of legionaries tipped over the parapet, taking the defenders utterly by surprise, a second wave right behind them where they climbed the wall using the gaps in the stones as grips. After all, who needed to climb a rope when the very walls were made with handholds? The enemy had been so busy hacking at the ropes they had not noticed the main threat until it fell upon them with gleaming blades. The onion was unwrapped.

Some of the legionaries had climbed with free hands and drew their swords as they emerged onto the wall top. Others had ascended with their pugio in their teeth and fell straight into the nearest enemy, bellowing and stabbing in a frenzy. Chaos reigned on the wall top, and Fronto smiled and swung the last, fourth, rope twice, releasing the grapple. It hit the wall top with a satisfying clunk and he dragged it toward him until the prongs bit into stone and the rope went tight. Aurelius was there in a moment, trying to take his place, but Fronto launched himself upwards before his bodyguard could get in front of him, and Aurelius, his expression irritated, ran across to the wall close by and started to climb, gasping and wincing with every stretch of the arm he had hurt earlier in his fall. He would pay for the ongoing strain later. Tomorrow he'd hardly be able to move it, but at the moment there were more important things to concentrate on.

By now, more and more men were flooding to the wall top, but the extra pressure put on the defenders here at the bastion had drawn away some of the men facing Pulcher, and now legionaries were starting to cross the wall top there too.

Fronto emerged onto a rampart in the midst of a battle. The century had suffered rather a lot of casualties, and Fronto estimated their current numbers at less than forty, but they were in. The legate took stock of the situation on the wall and turned back, gesturing down into the shadow, where Arcadios, who had been given strict instructions to stay at the back and out of danger, nodded and began to climb.

So far, so good. Now they just had to get to the other end of the fortress and open that gate. Two Arenosio warriors came barrelling along the bank, making for Fronto, marked out by his officer's plume and white tunic, and a legionary leapt forward to head them off, his sword jabbing and whirling as he kept them both busy. Fronto turned his attention to the interior of the fortress as Aurelius clambered over the parapet beside him and grunting sounds announced the arrival of Arcadios at the top of the rope. Aurelius immediately joined the troubled legionary, evening the odds quickly while Fronto fretted.

The wall was backed by a grassy embankment and the whole place was not particularly large, with perhaps thirty structures, mostly small and tightly-packed in a rather random, haphazard fashion, as though a settlement had sprouted on the hill like a cluster of mushrooms and then someone had walled it in. Which was, of course, very likely what had actually happened. One symptom of this odd shambling nucleus and formation, however, was a total lack of recognisable thoroughfares. Getting to the south gate was already a tricky proposition. Following the walls would be the simplest solution, but the 'L' shape of the place would make that journey a long way round, and would put them very much in the open and make them clear targets for the defending Arenosio. Running between the houses was a safer plan in many respects, but finding their way to the gate would be more difficult, and it would be very easy to become turned around down there.

His decision was made for him by a gruff shout of alarm that drew his attention along the wall. A small flood of warriors had emerged perhaps twenty paces away and were rushing up to the parapet, scaling the bank as they shouted native imprecations at the Romans. Among them, a standard was wavering, some sort of metallic decorations clonking around beneath. That meant a chieftain – maybe even this king? And *that* meant that the knot of warriors there would be the best in the fortress. Given that they also seriously outnumbered Fronto's small force, running into that lot would end this fight long before it truly began. Whoever it was seemed to be making for the most direct open space – the wall top – to cut off Fronto and his insurgents.

'That must be their bastard king,' Aurelius shouted over at him as he used his foot to push a dead warrior off the end of his blade.

'Yes, but we can't fight him now. We have to open the gate for the rest.'

The legionary beside Aurelius, overhearing, shouted across his shoulder 'Avianus? Fonteius? Over here!' He then turned to Fronto. 'Go, sir. We'll occupy them.'

Fronto blinked in disbelief as the two named men ran across to join their friend and at a nod the three of them set off, pounding along the wall top toward the knot of wealthy and dangerous warriors beneath the enemy banner. Mad. Fronto wouldn't risk his diminished century against that core of strong warriors, and yet three legionaries were happily whooping as they ran to certain death. They were as bad as Arruntius. In fact this whole legion was clearly barking mad. Shaking his head at the three men running at an enemy ten times their number, Fronto gestured to Aurelius and Arcadios. 'Come on.'

Half a dozen legionaries managed to detach themselves from the fighting on the wall and the ever-increasing number of enemies there and joined Fronto and his companions as they half ran, half slid down the embankment and toward the gap between two looming, dark timber buildings. There, the meagre moon and starlight that had granted so much clarity of vision in the night-time attack would be nullified by the narrow passage between houses, and Fronto felt his nerves rising with each footstep.

More shouts were coming from that group of nobles and warriors along the walls now, and Fronto risked a sidelong glance as he ran. The Romans' departure from the walls had been noted and the mob had split, a few of them running to take on the three legionaries on the walls, while the rest veered off with their banner, once more descending the bank and making straight for Fronto and his men. It *had* to be the king.

It's me, Fronto thought. *I knew he wanted me – wanted the Caesar they thought me to be. I should have been prepared to attract the fury of every warrior in the place.* Another shout drew his attention and turning he saw Pulcher, one arm hanging limp, a gore-coated sword in the other as the centurion ran toward him with another four legionaries.

'The king!' Fronto yelled, pointing at the approaching warriors.

Pulcher rolled his working shoulder. 'Open the gate, sir. Leave this lot to me.'

Fronto simply nodded, clasped a comradely hand on the centurion's shoulder and squeezed for a moment. It still made his eyes water to leave his gaze on that hideously ugly visage for too long, and he flicked his sight back to the dark alleyway. 'Come on, lads.'

Before he could run into the darkness Aurelius barrelled past him, taking his place at the front, sword in hand and expression of impending violence on his face. Arcadios fell in behind the legate, and the other legionaries followed on at the rear. As they moved into the gloom, Pulcher and his men sealed off the alley, preparing to hold it against the king's warriors, and Fronto could hear the angry shouts of the Arenosio as they closed. Leaving the capable Pulcher to buy him time, Fronto concentrated on the way ahead. He would have to keep heading south as best he could, attempting to maintain his sense of direction in the warren of native buildings.

The small group of insurgents passed those first two houses and looked around. To the right, someone had parked a small wagon that still held several barrels. It effectively sealed the alley, which could only be a good thing, since that was the direction the king's men had come from and it would provide almost as good a delay as Pulcher, should some of the warriors try to come round that way. Left, the alley went a short distance then turned to the right as it reached another building, and a third narrow way doglegged ahead.

In that moment, Fronto realised three things. Firstly, that he had seriously underestimated the number of buildings in the fortress. There was only room for thirty structures placed sensibly as a Roman would, but the way they had been crammed in close together in a higgledy-piggledy fashion would allow for perhaps even twice that number of houses, which might support a population of over a thousand if they were all given over as barrack space, which seemed likely in this austere and militaristic place. Secondly, that holding on to his sense of direction in this maze would be a matter of pure chance and nothing more. Thirdly, with the exception of just a few structures, almost every building in the fortress was more or less identical to its neighbours. Simple dark timber structures with daub filling the gaps and a roof of thatch that overhung so that the eaves almost met above the narrow alleys, adding to the air of gloomy oppression. The similarity of almost all the fortress' buildings would just add to the confusion of the place. All in all, the nine-man force would be damned lucky to do more than wander round in circles in the place until the enemy finally trapped them.

'Left,' Fronto said as decisively as he could manage, though even he noted a tremor of uncertainty in his tone.

'Lovely place,' Arcadios noted sourly. 'How do you know where you're going?'

'Luck and guesswork,' Fronto replied honestly. 'Any time now I won't even know what's up and down, let alone what's north or south.' With the others behind him, Fronto pushed past Aurelius and ran to the left even as the sounds of fighting reached them from Pulcher and his men holding off the locals. The centurion was one of the toughest Fronto had yet encountered, and his men were all grizzled veterans, but against a superior force of the best the king could raise, even he would not hold them off for long.

'Come on.'

At the end of the alley he turned right – south, he believed – and was foxed a moment later as he hit a T-junction, both branches of which angled slightly back to the north again, in more of a 'Y' shape. 'Oh, for the love of Dis, what next?'

The squeaking of a passing bat sent Aurelius scurrying to the side of the alley, where he pressed against the timber wall, wild eyes rolling upwards to the narrow strip of night sky visible between the projecting thatch eaves.

'I can't even see enough of the sky to make a guess,' Fronto grumbled, increasingly aware that he was running out of time.

As he was contemplating how lucky they were not to have encountered a small force in the alleys, and assuming that most of the population would now be close to the north walls in the open, a door opened a few paces away and several men ran out with swords brandished, proving him at least partially wrong. Aurelius, his bat issues taking second place to immediate deadly danger, launched himself at them, and two of the legionaries managed to pass Fronto and ran over to join him. There was a short, brutal struggle in the narrow confines of the alley, with the legate fretting

216

about the delay all the while, glancing this way and that and wondering where best to move next. As if reading his commander's thoughts, Arcadios ended the last struggles of the fight swiftly by nocking an arrow to his bow and pinning one of the last two enemy warriors to the house wall by the neck. The three soldiers dealt with the other man quickly and efficiently, and Arcadios hurried over to retrieve his arrow. As he examined it and gave up, unable to save the missile as it had buried itself too deep in the timber, he gave a slow smile.

'You don't need the sky, Fronto.'

'What?'

Arcadios was examining the wall, and then scurried to the next building. 'They look different. *That* building is untouched timber, I reckon, but look at the weathering on *this* timber? It faces east, up the valley. I reckon the winds blow mostly east to west down from the peaks. Look. Every timber facing that way is weathered.'

Fronto joined the grin. 'Gods, you're right. Well done, that man. Alright, we go left again for now and try to peel back round to the right, keeping our eye on the weathered boards.'

Armed with this new information, Aurelius and Arcadios rushed ahead with the two legionaries, and Fronto followed them, four more legionaries bringing up the rear. A cry in the distance announced the heroic end of Pulcher – a hoarse shout: 'Legate… they come!'

'Hurry,' Fronto said, and the small group picked up their pace as they twisted this way and that through the narrow ways of the fortress. At one point they passed a heavy grey structure of stone and timber, twice the size of the surrounding buildings, with a raised granary beside it, and what looked like it might be a temple on the other side. Almost certainly the king's house, Fronto thought to himself, considering attempting to commit the location to memory and then chiding himself for the ridiculousness of the notion, given that in this maze he'd be lucky to find his own backside twice. Still, they had to be relatively close to the south gate now.

By his estimate they had been in the maze of alleys for less than a quarter of an hour before they suddenly emerged into an open stretch of ground that lay between the south wall and the houses. Despite the fact that the sky was still largely covered with scudding clouds and it was around midnight, the area before the south rampart felt like the brightest, most spacious and clear piece of ground Fronto had ever encountered after the narrow gloominess of the streets. The south gate was a little way off to their left, but they had been almost spot on, and Fronto made a mental note to thank Arcadios properly when this was over. The archer had almost certainly saved them from blundering around aimlessly in that warren for at least another quarter hour.

The situation was still dire, though. A moment's quiet confirmed that there was no longer fighting back across the fortress, which told him in no uncertain terms that the attacking century had been obliterated back at their point of entry and that Fronto's small nine-man party was now the entire Roman presence in the fortress. A small group of half a dozen enemy warriors stood beside and above the south gate, with a single man atop the walls at each corner nearby. Almost one on one, then, but the sounds of approaching horns back across the settlement suggested that the entire population of the fortress were now descending on the south rampart, having removed the threat at the north. Fronto and his friends had been inordinately fortunate in having moved through empty alleys due to all the warriors having rushed to the walls at the initial warning. Now, however, hundreds – maybe even thousands – would be moving to stop any further trouble here.

'Loose your arrow,' he said to Arcadios as the small party started to jog across the open space toward the small knot of warriors.

'The gate's still shut.'

'Loose the bloody arrow. I'm not holding that gate open for half an hour while Atenos brings the men closer. They need to be moving now.'

With a nod, the Cretan archer dropped out of the running cluster, drawing the special arrow from his belt, where it had been sheathed separately from the others in his quiver, and jammed it in the ground temporarily. With practised efficiency, he pulled a small fire-fungus from his belt pouch and unwrapped it. He could feel the heat of the glowing ember deep within, which had been a warm and comfortable thing to carry this high in the mountains. Discarding the wrapper, he carefully pulled the two halves of the fungus apart and blew on the core. Immediately, a slender coil of smoke rose from it. A few more puffs with his hands wrapped around it, and tiny orange sparks came to life. Bending, he collected the arrow and removed the protective binding just behind the steel head. The acrid smell of pitch bloomed in the night air and Arcadios gently touched the tinder fungus to the stinking wad. It took moments only for the flammable missile to take, and the soaked flax burst into orange life. Casting aside the fungus half, the Cretan retrieved his bow, nocked the arrow, hissing at the warmth of the flame so close to his knuckles, then tilted the weapon high and released. The blazing arrow shot high into the air, leaving a bright gold trail across the inky night followed by a long winding tail of black smoke.

Fronto and his small force ran at the gate, their pace picking up as they left the archer behind until they were running full pelt. Shouts of alarm had gone up in the moments they had burst from the houses and the two men on the walls and those above the gate were converging on the portal itself. The shouts from back across the fortress were getting worryingly close.

'It's going to be tight,' puffed Aurelius as they ran.

'Mark your man,' Fronto shouted, 'it's one on one.'

The pounding feet of the Roman force took them full tilt into the braced defenders gathered before the gate. The warriors were big, bearded bears of men, roughly half of them armed with swords, the rest with spears, yet their eyes widened at the age, ferocity and sheer mettle of the soldiers running at them, snarling. After all, to have emerged from *within* the fortress had to add something to the shock. Two of the Arenosio had the wit and reactions to turn their spears and lower them at the charging Romans, and one took a legionary in the gut, the other knocked contemptuously aside with a sword. Fronto caught a glance of the stricken legionary and what he saw brought a lump to his throat. There was pain in the man's face, and shock, but no fear... just determination. The legionary pushed on, heaving himself along the pole that transfixed his middle, his guts leaving dark, wet smears along the wood behind him. The warrior gripping the spear stared in disbelief and let go of the spear with one hand, reaching down to draw his sword, but the dying legionary reached him first and slammed his gladius into the Arenosio, killing him. The soldier then fell, agonised, on top of his victim and started to try and heave the spear out of himself. He would be dead in moments, but his resolve humbled Fronto.

Similar unsought and simple heroism was being played out across the fight. Aurelius was battling a huge man, at least a head higher than him and much wider in the chest, and was slowly wearing the man down. Other legionaries were killing men with brutal efficiency. Then the legate was at the man he had marked – a tall, narrow warrior with a long sword and a helmet that gleamed bronze in the dim light. The warrior shouted something unintelligible and thrust with his sword. It was a clumsy blow and Fronto simply twisted aside from the lunge, then struck back with his gladius lancing out twice like a viper's tongue, once into the V of his collarbones, the other into his extended arm. The man's sword fell, forgotten as both his hands clutched his throat and the jet of crimson that bubbled out of the hole. Neither strike had carried much strength, but that had been Fronto's intent. Some killing strokes required a great deal of weight, driven in deep, but with tendons and the soft matter of the throat sometimes the tip of a blade would do enough. Such had been the case, allowing him the speed to strike twice before the warrior could fight back, and simultaneously negating the possibility of the blade sticking in the wound.

Aurelius' voice called for Fronto to duck and the legate did so, trusting the judgement of his friend without question. He felt a blade sweep through the air just above his head, and twisted to face that direction. A warrior with a slow-bleeding wound had dispatched the legionary facing him and had turned to Fronto. Still crouched, Fronto found that he was level with the surprised warrior's waist. The native wore a mail shirt that hung to his thighs, and his lower legs were criss-crossed with wraps down to his boots, but his knees were protected only by wool trousers.

In a trice, Fronto was on him, his sword sweeping round behind the man. Even as he dragged the sharp edge of the blade across the back of the knees, he used his free hand to push at the man's waist. The warrior shrieked and fell backwards, his hamstrings snapped by the wicked edge of Fronto's blade. His father had always maintained that a keen edge to a gladius was unnecessary, as they were to be used for thrusts around a shield. But then his father had never fought in close combat, and Fronto knew the value of flexibility. Rising once more, he realised the enemy were all down, and so were four soldiers, though one of those was still alive, trying to rise on a crippled leg.

'Get the gate open,' he bellowed to Aurelius, who grabbed another legionary and ran to the heavy locking bar.

'Fronto!'

The legate turned at the shout to see Arcadios running toward him and repeatedly drawing arrows from his quiver, turning and loosing behind him as skilfully as any Parthian archer in the world. Enemy warriors were flooding out of the heart of the fortress and along both ramparts. In truth there would be less than a thousand, he was sure, but it felt like millions of them from the point of view of the six remaining Romans.

Come on, Atenos.

* * *

Another legionary hurried to help Aurelius with the bar and between the three of them the gate was quickly unfastened and pulled inwards. Fronto, readying himself for what looked like certain death running at them from the heart of the fortress, spared a moment's glance through the aperture.

Atenos and the legion had crested the rise on the far side of the gulley, the wooden bridges between giving them ample access to the fortress as long as the gate stayed open. But even at a run, they were further from the gate than were the Arenosio. The six Romans would have been cut down long before the first legionaries burst through the gate, and there was every chance the gate would be shut again by then too. Once again, Fronto cursed the influence Arruntius' blunt approach to war had gained on the legate's strategic mind. He'd never have come up with such a rash scheme in the old days. Then again, it had been the Arenosio king who had forced this action. It was rather saddening to realise he could have perhaps met that king on the ramparts to the north and killed him there. The fortress would have remained secure and the legion would have been crushed by the reserve force of Convenae, of course, but at least maybe the king would be dead.

'What do we do?' Arcadios gasped between breaths as he fell in alongside them, still fumbling for his last three arrows and loosing one into the crowd running at them.

'We hold the gate as long as we can and pray that Atenos and his men's' feet have grown wings!'

Regretting the fact that they had left their shields in the camp, the six man unit braced themselves, swords out and ready, most men with their daggers also drawn and gripped in their left hands. Arcadios loosed another arrow, then dropped his bow behind him and drew a Greek-style *xiphos* sword, joining the others. Fronto frowned at the single arrow still clattering around in the archer's quiver.

'Saving that?'

'Never use *every* arrow, sir. You just can't know what the Fates might throw at you.'

'Nigh-on a thousand howling Aquitanii not enough for you?'

'Ha,' Arcadios snorted without humour and flexed his arm a little.

'Would you mind stepping aside, Legate,' a voice grunted. 'You're blocking the gate for my lads.'

Turning in surprise, Fronto could see a figure in a centurion's transverse crest silhouetted in the gate, a century or so of armoured men approaching behind him.

'Arruntius?'

'Seemed prudent to have some men in place, sir,' the old centurion grinned. 'I've been slowly sneaking men across the bridge and up to the walls all night, ever since you left.'

'You cunning old bastard,' Fronto laughed as the fresh, fully-equipped legionaries rushed past him and braced into a shield wall in the space in front of the gate. More legionaries poured in behind them, bracing to form second and third rows. The howling of the barbarians turned from hunger to frustration at the sight of the new arrivals, but quickly bled back into violent lust as they realised that there were no more than a hundred Romans there, and they might still defeat them and secure the gate before the rest of the legion arrived.

Fronto, now protected by the rows of men, turned to see Atenos' century approaching the bridge at the bottom of the gulley, more ranks of legionaries crossing the ridge behind him. The

Arenosio were mistaken. The gate would hold now, and Fronto felt himself sag with relief at that realisation. Arruntius was peering intently at him with narrowed eyes.

'You have an odd look, Legate. Reassure me that you're not about to run through my men screaming curses and launch yourself at the natives?'

Fronto chuckled. 'Frankly, right now, I'm happy having a rest. The past hour's been quite exciting enough, thanks.'

Arruntius nodded and said something, though his words were completely lost in the din as near a thousand howling tribesmen hit the shields of a hundred steadfast and angry legionaries. The din of battle began instantly. The centurion took a few steps closer and shouted in Fronto's ear.

'Would you and your men care to step up to the walkway and command the fight?'

Fronto smiled at the old centurion. It was an order phrased as a question in the same manner as Fronto had often used in his time to send senior officers out of his way.

'Alright, Arruntius, I'm going. But I'll warn you, once they break I'm heading into the middle of the place. I've seen the king's house and I want to meet this man personally.'

'I can have him dragged before you, sir.'

'Honestly, Arruntius, I don't think you can. He's planned and played us every step of the way, and I doubt that if the bastard had really wanted us kept out, we'd ever have got over the walls into the fortress in the first place. He *wants* me inside, though probably not accompanied by the rest of you, so that's something of a win for us. He must be rather frustrated that he missed me at the north walls. He was so clearly coming for me personally, but Pulcher held him at bay and bought me the time we needed. Be assured that this king is expecting Caesar, and he won't let himself get caught until that happens, so I intend to go and meet him and find out what it is that's driving him.'

The centurion looked for a moment as though he might argue, but he was clearly getting used to Fronto, and he simply shook his head in exasperation and turned to join his men. Fronto called after him 'There's a big house in the middle – the king's house. *No one* goes in there until I'm on the scene.'

There was no acknowledgement from the centurion that he'd heard, which was quite possible given the din. Fronto and his companions who'd taken the gate staggered up the embankment to the walkway on the parapet and wandered along above the gate. The fight was in full swing now, and the legionaries were taking heavy casualties, slowly being pushed back into the gate, but Atenos' men were mere heartbeats away now, closing on the walls. Even as Fronto watched them arrive, units of legionaries peeled off the main force, hurrying up the bank and along the ramparts, securing the walls, while the bulk hurled themselves into the hard-pressed century of Arruntius, slowly pushing back against the enemy, gaining ground one booted step at a time.

Fronto's gaze rose above the struggle and spotted the king's house, as it must be, rising slightly above the surrounding roofs. That had to be Fronto's goal, and as if to confirm it his gaze caught sight of that tall standard with the swaying pendants bobbing through the crowd toward the back of the Arenosio army. A small band of warriors emerged into the open space and paused. Fronto peered at the royal party, and could see that the king was looking back across the fight at the small group of Romans above the gate. There was too much distance between them for Fronto to make out the king's features, and couldn't tell what made him the 'smiling king' of whom he'd heard. Presumably he wasn't smiling so much now, anyway. He wondered for a moment whether the king could see that the officer on the parapet wasn't actually Caesar, but he doubted it. If Fronto couldn't make out the king's details, then the same presumably held the other way round. One of the warriors in the small party said something to the king and the group turned and strode off toward the houses.

There was a creak next to Fronto and he turned to see Arcadios with his bow string stretched, that last arrow nocked and ready. The legate opened his mouth to tell the archer to lower his bow, but he was too late and the arrow hissed off into the night.

It was a spectacular shot, arcing up into the darkness, where it fell perfectly on target. And as if laughing at fate, or chance, or both, the king simply took a step to his left without looking. The arrow slammed into the back of the man who'd been walking in front of him, and that warrior cried out and fell to the dirt. The king never looked back.

'There's a god protecting that one,' Aurelius said quietly. 'There's a legate's going to jam a foot so far up his arse before dawn that he'll be able to bite my toenails from the inside.'

* * *

The Arenosio fought hard, and Fronto had to grant them more than grudging respect, but as the first quarter of the hour passed and more and more legionaries flooded into the fortress, constantly pushing the natives back across the open ground toward the buildings, so the heart drained from the enemy. Then, with a collective sigh, the enemy front finally broke and the Arenosio turned and fled.

Fronto watched from above the gate as the first groups of warriors broke off and ran for the illusionary safety of the narrow streets. Then more, and more, and then the whole force was on the run, the yelling legionaries released into centuries by their commanders and pursuing with purpose and organisation. At the command of Arruntius, each centurion took a street and led his men there, others moving around the ramparts and encircling the place, rushing to cut off any route of escape at the far end. They would ring the town and then squeeze until every last one of the Arenosio was dead or captured.

Fronto watched the legion swamp the fortress, then smiled at those with him.

'What are your names?' he asked the three men with them.

'Egilius, sir.'

Lecanius, sir.'

'Ulpius, Legate.'

'Right,' he said, gesturing to the man with the lame leg. 'Egilius, get yourself back to camp. Lecanius, you help him. When you find the medici, tell them to send for the legate's wine, and the pair of you get as royally drunk as you like. You've done more than your bit.' He then gestured to the third man. 'Same will go for you later, Ulpius, but I could do with a hand for now. We're all very weary, but Arcadios, Aurelius and I are going to go have a quiet word with this king before we can rest again, and I'd like to have you along.'

'It'd be my pleasure, Legate,' the man grinned.

225

Fronto smiled and took a deep lungful of air, then almost fell over. Surprised, he straightened and put the weight on his good knee. He was exhausted, despite the brief rest atop the gate, and only now that he'd stopped running was he realising it, as the adrenaline of battle finally drained away. Still, he flexed his knuckles, it was almost over now. And he would find extra reserves of energy to see him through this last leg. For he was about to meet the smiling king of the mountains, and nothing was going to stop that.

The noises of battle were now oddly muted. What fighting there now was had become a sporadic thing in pockets around the fortress, the sound muffled by the buildings and the projecting thatched roofs.

'Come on. It's time.'

Leaving the legionary with the wounded leg and his mate to head back to camp slowly, Fronto and his three weary companions carefully slid down the embankment and picked their way between the stinking torn bodies of Roman and Arenosio alike, ignoring the desperate pleas of the wounded and dying and avoiding those enemies who still looked capable of lashing out. Sickening moments of treading in filth and gore later, staggering through an all-encompassing cloud of metallic-tinged stench, they emerged into the open space where only a few corpses lay widely scattered, cut down as they ran. The legate paused at the body of the royal bodyguard – for this was all Fronto could assume he was – and bent down. Arcadios' arrow was still lodged in the spine and the shaft broke as the legate turned the body over. He was not a young man, and clearly of noble rank. Fronto removed two silver arm rings from the body, each beautifully crafted with images of leaping stags, and passed them to Ulpius. 'A prize for making it through the place with us.'

The legionary smiled and nodded gratefully, taking the precious rings and slipping them into his belt pouch as they walked on toward the nearest street. Oddly, as they passed into the alley from which they'd emerged half an hour ago, Fronto found he could picture the various turns and directions, and they swiftly moved through the fortress toward the king's house. The signs of battle were evident wherever they went, bodies and parts of bodies scattered through the streets, legionaries left in doorways with spears through them, unidentifiable wobbly, squishy things underfoot, a miasma of gullet-clotting stench, and blood – so much blood.

Around one particular corner, they came across two legionaries busily hacking at a desperate, dying warrior. Around another, a panicked looking native came running at them, an axe above his head, his eyes rolling and wild. Fronto ducked to the side, meaning to stab at the running man, but his knee gave way at the last moment and he fell to one side. The warrior died a heartbeat later as Ulpius drove his sword into the chest, while Aurelius reached out a hand for Fronto. The legate bit down on an angry retort that he wasn't a helpless old cripple. It was blindingly clear that all four of them were so wearied they were near the point of collapse. It had been a long campaign and a long journey into the mountains, punctuated with hard fights. Then there had been the failed attack yesterday, the hike over the mountains after dark, and finally the fight through the fortress. No wonder they were shattered. With a smile, he took Aurelius' hand and hauled himself up, rubbing his knee.

'Almost there.'

Another two corners, and Fronto spotted the king's house, just past the raised granary. The door was shut and half a dozen bodies lay in the street, four natives and two legionaries. This fight had been costly. Fronto found himself beginning to feel the edge of tension, a touch of nerves. He was going to kill this king. No slavery. No parading through Rome or languishing in a cell like Vercingetorix. This piece of shit was going to meet his gods tonight. And yet the very thought of facing the man who had done all this seemingly to bring Caesar to his threshold sent a shiver of fear through him. The sense that the gods were rolling dice again and that even the Fates were looking elsewhere was strong in him.

A moment later, Fronto's fingers were reaching for the handle of the door – a section of a stag's antler cunningly driven into the timber. He frowned as his hand gripped the smooth bone, and twisted. The handle tilted on some drum set into the door and he heard the latch come up on the inside. Lovely workmanship. He pushed, and the door swung open to reveal a dim room with a mezzanine level reached by a ladder. Braziers heated the place and a fire burned in a central pit, its smoke rising toward a small central hole in the thatch and gathering in the rafters around it.

A small knot of warriors stood in the centre of the hut, well lit by the fire and the braziers despite the gloom, and Fronto took in the scene in the single moment he had. Eight men, each big and burly, one holding aloft that standard beneath which, Fronto now realised, the metal things that had clonked against one another were fascina – replica phalluses for luck – which was a curiously Roman thing for a barbarian. All had swords drawn. But at the centre, standing in front, was the king of the Arenosio. The reason for his name was suddenly clear as Fronto shuddered at the dreadful smiling wound. The king was dressed better than those around him, not armoured but armed, for he had a bow raised and an arrow nocked ready, and as Fronto had stepped through the door, that gleaming tip had turned fractionally to centre on Fronto's chest.

It all happened in a heartbeat and Fronto stood no chance. He'd not even the time to drop to the floor. In that single blink when he took in the locals and the manner of his death, he realised there was nothing he could do. And in that curious slow-motion that occurs at such times, Fronto saw the triumphant glee on that savage, savaged, ever-smiling face turn to disbelief.

And the arm moved even as the arrow was released. The missile whispered across the room, glittering in red firelight, tearing through Fronto's sleeve and scoring the tiniest line across his arm before it struck, with a thud, wedged in Ulpius' chest. The legionary peered down in surprise at the feathered shaft jutting from his torso, then gave a short gasp and folded to the ground.

Fronto was aware of shouting, but his eyes were on the smiling king. A look of utter shock was about the man. There was something odd about him beyond the smile that nagged at Fronto. He was clean shaven, which was almost unique among these mountain men. His hair was long, but clean and neat and not wild like the others. His dress was austere but wealthy. In short, he was not the sort of chieftain Fronto was used to meeting. And the frayed edges of Fronto's mind were trying to tell him something. Then Arcadios and Aurelius were pushing past Fronto with swords raised, and the king's warriors were running forward to meet them. More legionaries seemed to be arriving through the door from the street, shouting and running to help, but Fronto could not take his eyes from that face.

And the king was gone.

Fronto blinked, then blinked again, as if a spell had been broken. The king had disappeared behind his warriors. Fronto frowned, and then started to run, even as the door behind him opened once more to Latin shouts. The legate skirted the edge of the room, moving around the growing fight now filling its centre. When he reached the far side, there was no sign of the king. How had he disappeared so easily? Snarling, the legate found the ladder and began to climb. Four heartbeats passed and he cautiously poked his head over the lip. The mezzanine was empty. Only a low bed and a simple desk stood there. Just in case, Fronto clambered up and searched the place. The king was not there, hiding behind or beneath the bed as he'd momentarily fancied would be the case. Thwarted, he returned to the ladder and, placing his feet either side of the uprights, slid down to the ground again. The king had *gone*. More legionaries had clearly come from somewhere and the fight was ending as he crossed to the centre of the room. On a whim, he counted the Arenosio bodies. Six. That figured. Not only had the king escaped somehow, but one of his men had done so with him.

'Where is he?' Aurelius shouted, puzzled.

'No idea,' Arcadios replied.

'He somehow got out before the fight started,' Fronto snapped. 'This lot bought him enough distraction to make an escape somehow, though I can't see how. Bollocks!'

'He won't get far,' Galronus said, limping into the room, one leg trailing blood. 'We've secured the whole place. The fighting's almost over and even a mouse fart wouldn't get past the ramparts with our lads on watch.'

But Fronto knew better as he picked up a stool and flung it at a wall in anger.

'He's gone, Galronus. The clever little prick's gone. Somehow he'll get out of the fortress, too. We won't find him. And until we can track him down, he'll remain a threat. This won't be over. But I don't know what he'll do now. He was ready with a bow. He was going to kill Caesar as he walked in, but when he saw it wasn't Caesar, he mis-shot on purpose and killed Ulpius. But I don't understand that. Why not kill me anyway? I've still got so many

229

questions. Round up any survivors you can find and have them confined in a house. We can't deal with them yet, but as soon as we have the chance, I want to hear from every tongue in the place until we know what this king wants and where he's gone.'

And then I'm going to find him, Fronto added silently, *and I'm going to kill the bastard very slowly.*

Late Maius

THE king was grateful for Ategnio's presence, though the other three warriors were less helpful and more of a hindrance. Slipping through the hidden exit in the wall had been easy enough, though – the wattle and timbers had been hinged and the whole thing painted with daub to look like the rest. One thing he had learned in his time was that even kings were never truly safe and that a means of secret egress was more or less a requirement of the position. And Ategnio had done an excellent job of directing his guards' attention at the Romans while he slipped quickly out the back, followed by his most loyal warrior. They had made their way swiftly to the east, picking up three Arenosio warriors on the way. None were of his loyal guards, but with a legion of Romans in the fortress and scant time to make an escape, beggars could not be choosers.

Even then, he was starting to become irritated with the three as they neared the rampart. One kept asking in a panicked voice what they were going to do now, another had a limp from a foot wound that was slowing them down, and the third? Well he was just irritating for no clear reason. The king just disliked him. Perhaps he smelled.

'That's the one,' the king said, pointing to a house near the ramparts. Ahead, at the end of the alley, the grassy embankment rose to a walkway now patrolled by legionaries, and the three warriors huffed nervously.

'How do we get past them?' asked the nagging one, while the limping one slowly caught up and the third stood there being dislikeable.

'For a start,' the king hissed in reply, 'we silence the ones who make too much noise.' The warrior's frown of incomprehension turned to a gasp of shock as Ategnio's hand flattened against his mouth and the tip of a knife drove into his brain through the ear.

'Then we make sure we are uninhibited,' he added, turning and raising his sword just as the surprised one with the limp arrived. The heavy blade slid into his chest and the king's hand flattened across his mouth to stifle another gasp.

As the two men fell dead, the third warrior stared in horror.

'Anything to say?' hissed the king.

'No, lord.'

'Good. I'm feeling irritable, but you might yet prove useful.'

Ategnio pulled open the door to the house the king had indicated and the three men entered, the trusted second closing the door behind them. It took the king only moments even in the dark to find the trapdoor.

'Always have adequate precautions in place,' he advised his two remaining men, swinging the trapdoor open. 'You go first,' he added, indicating the dislikeable warrior.

'Me, lord?'

'Yes. There are no guarantees the Romans have not found it, and I am tired.'

Nervously, the warrior dropped down into the underground hollow. He paused to let his eyes adjust to the gloom, but the darkness was near absolute, and so the pause was no help. Taking a nervous breath, the warrior used his free hand to feel his way slowly forward, his sword out ready. Behind him, the king dropped into the tunnel, then Ategnio, who pulled the trapdoor shut.

Over a thousand paces the narrow passage extended, partially carved from rock, with some sections dug through earth and shored up with rough timbers. The three men were filthy and scratched by the time they saw the feeble starlight marking the end. Slowly, carefully, they emerged with relief into the night air and took a deep breath, turning. They were in the river gulley below the walls, the exit well concealed by a shrub next to a tree whose roots formed part of the tunnel roof.

'Where are the horses?' the king whispered to Ategnio, peering up at the distant shape of legionaries on his fortress walls.

'With the outmost pickets two miles upstream. The Romans won't have gone near there, else we'd have seen a signal.

'Good.' He turned to the warrior with them. 'Sadly, there are only two horses.' The warrior blinked as the king lashed out with a foot, breaking his leg just above the ankle. As the man made to scream, the king's hand clamped itself across the mouth.

'Your friends are dead. You might yet live. But you must be silent until we are gone. Then you will crawl slowly back to the fortress with a message for the Roman officer.' He held his hand there, staring quizzically at the warrior until he nodded, his eyes watering in pain. Slowly, the king removed his hand, replacing it as the warrior inhaled.

'Ah, ah, ah. No shouting, or I gouge out your eyes too.'

Again, he removed his hand, and this time the warrior stared, baffled and terrified, into his eyes.

'Tell the Roman commander that you wish to barter healthcare and your freedom in return for information. He will agree. He is not like normal Romans. He will have a surgeon and field medics with him who can set your leg. The information you can use to barter your freedom and your life is this…'

The king bent and whispered into his warrior's ear. The man's eyes widened for a moment, but finally he nodded as the king rose.

'Come on, Ategnio.' The two men left the whimpering warrior, descending to the stream's bank, and began to pick their way up the valley until they were away from the fortress and relatively safe from Roman attentions.

Finally, comfortable that they were alone and out of all earshot, Ategnio stopped and grabbed the king by the shoulders.

'What happened?'

'Plans changed, Ategnio. They have a habit of doing so.'

'But why didn't you kill Caesar while you had the chance?'

'That wasn't Caesar, Ategnio. Serves me right for relying on the word of ill-informed tribesmen. All this time I've been planning what I'd do to the old goat when I had him in my hands, and all this time it wasn't him. He was clever enough to send someone to do his dirty work after all.'

'But sire, the Convenae will be here today. We can still win, even if it is not Caesar, so why run?'

The king fixed Ategnio with a look that made him shiver. 'Because, my friend, that's not just Caesar. That's someone much, *much* more dangerous than Caesar.'

Urging Ategnio on along the stream valley, the king shook his head in disbelief once more.

'Marcus Falerius Fronto, where in Hades did *you* spring from?'

Chapter Ten

SPRING seemed to mean little in the lands of the Arenosio. A cold wind howled through the narrow alleys of the fortress as Fronto marched grumpily, kicking a stone so that it skittered along the dark lane and bounced to rest against a timber wall. All around him the fortress was coming to life as the first streaks of gold laced the high streamers of cloud above the mountains. The night had seen the thick, low fleece that covered the sky pull apart and with that the temperature had fallen, though mercifully it remained dry. Four hours had passed since the legion had taken full control of the place Terpulo had affectionately named Rectum – an appellation the legionaries had quickly taken to.

Despite everyone's exhaustion there had been no time to rest. The ever-present threat of Convenae attack remained in the minds of all the men, and the need to be ready overrode all else. For four hours the centuries had been hard at work, burying the Roman dead and dealing with the fallen of the Arenosio. There had been no pyres and no burnings, though. Quite apart from the effort and time involved in obtaining the timber, Fronto had decided that they could hardly afford to send up a smoke signal that might spur the Convenae on to greater speed. So in the end, the fallen legionaries had been given appropriate rites as best they could and were then piled in a natural hollow a few hundred yards from Rectum, where sickened, tired legionaries had hastily covered them with a thin layer of earth and turf. The Arenosio, on the other hand...

That image was one that wouldn't leave Fronto's tired mind. He was no great lover of displays of gruesome power, though he recognised that in war they sometimes had their place, and he'd left Arruntius and Terpulo to deal with the dead. Outside the north and on the ridge across the gulley, stretched in two concentric rings around the place, were the six-pointed temporary camp defences formed by sudis stakes, and each of those jagged fence sections was home to the corpse of one of the Arenosio on bloodthirsty display. The enemy dead had numbered just over five hundred and there were around three thousand men left in the legion, each with a stake. Thus the numbers had worked out almost precisely, with the few dozen spare corpses thrown onto the stakes in random places for good measure.

It was an extra level of defence, and hopefully its décor would pick away at the enemy's resolve too. Fronto didn't have to like it, though.

He made his way through the fortress to the king's house where the officers were gathered, with the exception of Arruntius and Terpulo who remained in place overseeing the work. The legate could feel the fingers of exhaustion pulling at his eyelids and creeping across his muscles, but he could do nothing about it. He had laid down for almost an hour when his legs seemed to fail, but even then he'd been unable to sleep and had simply risen once more in the end and fortified himself with wine. Now, as he peered around the faces of the others, he could see his exhaustion echoed in every expression.

'Morning everyone.'

There was a chorus of polite greetings, and Fronto staggered over to the king's throne and sank into it, waving his hand at the various campaign stools and wooden seats that had been assembled. 'For the love of Juno, don't stand on ceremony. Sit down and rest as best you can.'

Once everyone was seated and silent, Fronto cleared his throat and yawned.

'Alright. Let's have a think. The signal fires the Arenosio lit burned out some time ago, but the scouts we sent up to the peaks have seen answering fires all too close. Galronus, what's the estimate?'

The Remi noble stretched and leaned forward in his seat. 'Judging by the position of their fires they'll be here by noon at the latest. I've sent men out to try and spot the enemy themselves to ascertain numbers and makeup, but they won't be back for at least an hour. Also, we found a few sites where Arenosio pickets had been based anywhere up to a mile from here. They've all been abandoned, but many of them had stabling facilities, so we can only assume that they fled on horseback. Likely they joined up with the Convenae and will be back here soon enough.'

Fronto nodded. 'The prisoners are all contained, I gather, but we'll leave them be for now.. We have too much to do and we're all tired, so interrogation can wait. Very likely that smiling bastard of a king has joined up with his Convenae allies and is marching back toward us, so there'll be little to learn from the prisoners anyway. Atenos, what're our own numbers now?'

'Two thousand, one hundred and nineteen active men and fighting wounded. A little over three hundred sick and injured. We're looking short on the centurion front. We lost quite a few in the attack.' The legion's most senior centurion cast a look around his peers in the room, rolling his eyes. 'We always have a high body count, of course, but these veterans are one link short of a mail shirt. I think they left their sense of self-preservation back in Lapurda.' Far from taking the comment as an insult, this appraisal raised smiles from the older centurions around the room.

'Then you'll have to make some field promotions, Atenos. Reform the legion into fresh centuries at full strength and see how many officers short we are. You can grant the crest to the best men then. Carbo…'

'Legate?'

'What's the latest with the fortifications?'

'We've completely dismantled the camp across the valley and brought all the baggage into Rectum.' He smiled as he used the fort's nickname, as did most of the others in the room.

'Perhaps we can speak to the prisoners after all and try to find out what they call this place so we can squash this puerile notion,' Fronto said disapprovingly, though he was finding it rather hard to suppress a smirk himself, and he knew full well that now the name was with the soldiers it would stick permanently.

'The animals are stabled in three of the larger houses,' Carbo went on, ignoring the comment. 'The goods are packed away in three more, and the carts themselves have been used to block the outmost alleyways, turning the settlement itself into a last redoubt should the rampart fall. We've completely sealed the south gate now, blocking it with stones, and the lads have extended the earth rampart across the rear of it. You have to look hard to see that there ever was a gate there. The north one we've left open for the scouts when they return, but all the materials are there to do the same thing there. By the time the Convenae get here Rectum will just be a solid ring of wall with no holes. Rectum will be sealed shut, you might say.'

This time there was open sniggering from among the officers. Fronto rolled his eyes as Carbo went on, grinning. 'We tried to dig a trench across the north, but it's solid rock a foot or so down, so there's no hope in the time we have. We'll just have to rely on what's there. The walls can't be heightened themselves, though we've put a flimsy timber palisade above them, and there's not time to mortar the stones together, so that's all we can do.'

'We found one interesting thing, Legate,' added one of the more senior centurions. 'We pulled down the outermost houses to reuse their timber on the parapet, and one house to the east contained a trapdoor. Underneath was a tunnel that ran out all the way to the gulley. It had been opened recently, so we can only assume that was the way the king escaped. We've filled the tunnel in now with rocks and earth and covered over the inner entrance with a floor of heavy timbers, so it can't be used to break back in. We also found a native with a broken leg in the gulley nearby. He was jabbering away in his own language at us, but all the scouts are out east, so we've no idea what he was saying.'

Fronto nodded. 'Good. Have some men go through every square foot of this place and check for similar tunnels. If there was one there could be another, and if the king has met up with the Convenae, he'll know any secret ways. Sounds like this survivor of yours has something to say. Where is he?'

'With the medical staff at the moment, sir.'

'Galronus? When we're finished here, can you come and help me with the man?'

The Remi noble nodded.

'Right. What's the food situation?'

'We've plenty,' Carbo replied. 'We had rations with us for another week or more, and we've taken control of the Arenosio granaries and stores. We could hold out for two months if need be.'

'If it goes on for more than a *day*, it'll be too long. I want this fight won and quickly. If the king is with them, he'll be at liberty to escape and flee when things turn sour, and if he isn't then every hour wasted he gets further away.'

'On the bright side,' Decius smiled, 'we've commandeered several thousand arrows and slingshots from the Rectum – *rectal?* – stores, so we're well supplied. I've got Arcadios and a couple of my lads going through the legions, checking out the soldiers. A few of them are showing natural ability with a bow or sling, and a few have used one before.'

'Legionaries with bows?' Carbo asked, surprised. 'I bet they don't like that. Smacks of being treated like the auxilia. No offence, Decius.'

'None taken,' the auxiliary prefect replied, though with a stony face. 'I know your men like to think themselves superior, but they also know the value of arrows in a siege, and you'd be surprised how many are interested. With Atenos' permission, I'll pass out the bows and slings and ammunition we've impounded among them. If we can double our arrow clouds, it has to make a difference.'

Fronto nodded, and Atenos smiled. 'It'll do them good.'

'Excellent,' Fronto said, leaning back in the seat. 'We need to talk a little more about specific unit placement and tactics, but I'd like to know the enemy strength first, so let's call an end to this for now. Despite the urgency of everything, we all need a little rest before we face the enemy again. Pass the word out. Every other man is to be given two hours of shut-eye, then they can swap over, officers included. We'll be no good to anyone if our eyes keep closing while we fight. Alright, people. Dismissed.'

The officers piled out of the door, leaving Masgava, Aurelius and Galronus with the legate.

'You need rest more than anyone,' Masgava said bluntly. 'I can run things while you have a nap.'

Fronto smiled. 'I'll take you up on that once I've seen to this prisoner. Then in two hours it's your turn and I'll take over again. When the enemy do attack, by the way, you've got the south side. I'm giving Carbo the east, Atenos the west, and I'm taking the north. Decius can be mobile throughout the whole place, and the centurions will each have their sector. More than that I can't say until we know what we're up against.'

Galronus stretched again. 'As soon as the scouts return, I'm going to bring all the cavalry inside. There are still two hundred and four men, including the natives. We'll stable the horses in a few of the houses along with Bucephalus and the other officers' mounts, then those men can be added to the defenders. They're all good with a spear, which could be useful at the walls.'

'Alright. Masgava you have command of Rectum. Gods, but you've even got *me* doing it, now. You two can come with me and see this captive.'

With the pair at his heel, Fronto exited the king's house and made his way through the maze of alleys that was slowly becoming more familiar, to the east rampart. The ground there was scarred in a wide swathe where the outer buildings had been torn down to give the legion more room to work around the walls, and the three of them passed a wagon that could easily be wheeled across to block the alley in moments. Men bustled around the wall, and here a makeshift hospital had been set up using two large tents. Legionaries sat around waiting to have minor wounds seen to, while there were cries of pain and sobs of hopelessness from inside. A small pile of limbs sat by one entrance, threatening to turn Fronto's stomach. For a moment it seemed they were all Romans here, but finally Fronto spotted a capsarius crouched by a native, busy fishing around in his leather medical bag while two legionaries stood guard, pila pointed at the man's neck..

'I presume, then, that you speak no Latin,' Fronto said to the filthy, drawn-looking native with the matted hair and tangled beard as he came to a halt in front of him.

The man shrugged in incomprehension.

'Galronus, can you ask the man what he wants,' the Legate asked quietly.

The native issued a stream of words in his strange, harsh tongue. Galronus listened hard, trying to translate the unfamiliar dialect into his own, let alone into Latin. There was a long pause after the man stopped, a hopeful, challenging look to his face, and Galronus coughed.

'I believe he thinks he has critical information for you regarding the king, and he wishes to bargain for medical attention and his freedom with it.'

Fronto pursed his lips and folded his arms. 'A bargain. His life and his leg for information about the king.'

Galronus nodded. '*Important* information, he thinks.'

'Gods know we need every bit of information we can get,' Fronto said, '*especially* on the king. If his information is useful, then I swear by Fortuna and Nemesis that he will have all the medical attention he requires and his freedom too. But only if it is of interest.'

There was another pause as Galronus passed on the agreement to the man, having to try several times to get some of the words right. Finally, the native smiled a smile that was more sneer than anything and rattled out more of his speech. Fronto listened and waited, watching with impatience and a little uneasiness as the Remi's expression passed through confusion to bemusement and then disbelief.

'What is it?'

The Remi turned and fidgeted. 'He says the king has crossed the mountains. He's going through the lands of the Ilergetes to the Roman town of Acco. It stretches credibility, though. Why would he go to a Roman town? The man is lying to buy his life.'

Fronto's frown deepened. 'Acco? There's no such place.' A suspicion passed through his mind, and he leaned toward the warrior. 'Do you mean *Tarraco*?'

'Tracco,' the captive nodded his agreement.

'It's rubbish,' Aurelius said in agreement with Galronus. 'He'll tell you anything.'

Fronto was still frowning, though, as he stepped back and straightened. 'I'm not so sure. I…'

Flashes of inspiration were shooting off in his brain, connections forming like dreadful bridges to the truth. 'He's going to a Roman city. What if he *is* a Roman?'

'What?' demanded Galronus and Aurelius at the same time.

'Think about it. He's been crucifying people. That's a Roman punishment. They dug lilia pits for our cavalry like a Roman. He's been mimicking the birth of Rome with his federation of tribes overwhelmed by force. He was clean shaven and much more plainly dressed than your average native chief. Everything points to him being Roman. And he knows Caesar. He thought he was luring Caesar to battle. And he's gone to the Roman provincial capital now. The man's a Roman. I'm damn sure of it.'

Galronus and Aurelius, eyes wide, were nodding at the logic of Fronto's words.

'But what would a Roman be doing *here*?'

'Someone who knows Caesar,' Fronto repeated as a connection formed and smacked him in the face like a brick. He felt his skin grow cold and prickle with goose bumps.

'Someone familiar with Tarraco…'

Wham!

'Someone with knowledge of Roman military tactics.'

240

Wham!

As he actually staggered back a step from this imaginary blow, his mind furnished him with a picture of the man standing in the king's house, his eyes widening in shock even as the arrow left the bow, nudged from its intended path at the last moment.

'Someone…. Someone who knows *me.*'

Wham!

'Shit.'

'What is it,' Galronus asked in a worried tone. Aurelius had closed on him, clearly concerned for his legate.

'Shitting shit. Tarraco. He's gone back. He's gone home. And he wants me to follow.'

His legs suddenly felt useless, weak and wobbly. He'd not realised he'd fallen until Aurelius caught him and lowered him gently to the ground.

'Who?' Galronus hissed.

Fronto could hardly see, the panic whipping his brain into a mess. It *couldn't* be. How *could* it? But it *was*, and he knew it. His subconscious had known it too, even in the hut at the moment the arrow had left the bow. It had tried to alert him then. With a shiver, Fronto felt the exhaustion claiming him as the shock removed the last of his resolve.

'Fronto… *who?*'

'Verginius,' Fronto whispered as he shivered. 'Gnaeus Verginius.'

* * *

Fronto blinked awake, startled and confused. The room stank of brazier coals and old, well-used furs. A face was peering down at him, and in his bewilderment, his mind woolly but suffused with vague feelings of betrayal and loss, he lashed out at the figure.

'Calm,' Galronus urged, dipping to the side to avoid the flailing hand.

'What?'

'You collapsed at the ramparts. The hospital.'

Vague recollections came flooding back to Fronto, slowly resolving to the memory of his horrifying realisation.

'Verginius…'

'Yes. I know. But there is not time. The Convenae are here.'

Startled, Fronto swung his legs over the edge of the bed and sat up, almost returning to blissful unconsciousness with the sudden movement. His arm had stiffened from the fall and the fight on the hillside, and his legs screamed as he straightened them.

'Already?'

Galronus snorted. 'It's been hours, Fronto.'

'What? You knew we had much to do, Galronus. Two hours per man... that was the order.'

'Tough shit, Marcus. You needed it. You collapsed, man. Masgava and Carbo have kept things going between them. All is well, barring the sea of Aquitanii pouring down the pass. But now you need to stretch your legs and get yourself armed up.'

'Verginius...' Fronto said again, the unbelievable truth still hammering at him.

'Yes, Verginius. I have many questions, but now is not the time. If we're alive at sunset you can answer them over wine. Now we need to fight.'

The Remi reached down and helped Fronto to his feet. A few moments of hobbling around the room loosened up the muscles and tendons enough for Fronto to consider arming himself, though no amount of gentle waggling was going to solve the arm. Lifting it up or outwards was clearly going to be a no, as even trying brought tears of pain to his eyes. Adrenaline had carried him through the fight last night, but now, with rest, his arm had become more or less useless.

'I'll get dressed. Find me a capsarius who can strap my arm up. I'll fight better if it can't be knocked or wrenched around.'

Galronus nodded and as he left Fronto crossed to the low table where someone had helpfully laid out a fresh tunic and underwear, socks and scarf for him. His armour had been polished and sat close by. He had at least struggled into the underwear and tunic by the time Galronus returned with the medic, who probed the arm and moved it enough to elicit yelps from the legate.

'It could be a frozen shoulder, which is problematic, or it could just have been temporarily dislocated and then knocked back into the socket in one move. I've seen that happen and it causes similar symptoms. The legion medicus will be able to examine it later and give you a full diagnosis, but you're looking at anywhere between a couple of days of pain and months of rehabilitation. Sadly, I can't tell you any more.'

Fronto nodded. 'Just strap the bastard up so I can fight.'

'I heartily recommend staying out of the fighting, sir.'

'I'll bet, but we need every man, now strap it up.'

Some quarter hour from his first bleary awakening, Fronto emerged from the house, one of those close to the hospital from whence his friends had carried him, with Galronus at his shoulder. 'They came down the pass, you said?'

'Generalising,' Galronus shrugged. 'They appeared in the northern valley that you crossed when you broke into the place. We had warning from the scouts, but they should be in sight now.'

'Strength?'

The Remi warrior flexed his fingers and reached down to his sword hilt. 'Fewer than we worried about, but more than I'm comfortable with. Maybe six thousand, including archers, but no cavalry.'

'And we have a little over two thousand. That's three to one odds and given our position, the defences negate their edge, I reckon. I thought we'd be facing twice that or more. The gods are in a favourable mood today, Galronus.'

'The scouts reported signs that more forces were converging but have turned back. We interrogated the prisoners, and it seems likely from what they say that the Convenae alliance is faltering. If the scouts are to be believed, more than six thousand tribesmen changed their mind and turned back when the news reached them that Rectum had fallen and that we had it now. They were coming to the king's summons, but since he's gone south and left them hanging out to dry, only the Arenosio are still coming. After all, we're in their land, in their fortress. But they seem to be the only ones who still care.'

Fronto grinned unpleasantly. 'And that all means that the enemy spirit must be pretty low. We have the walls and the weapons even if they have the numbers. We've won every engagement since leaving Lapurda and they know it, and now their allies and their king have abandoned them. If I'm any judge of these things, it won't take much to break them. Come on, let's go have a look.'

The two men ran around the edge of the fortress toward the north rampart. All along the green turf bank legionaries had been hard at work. Stacks of pila and shields were abundantly evident, small medical stations set up with well-equipped capsarii, periodic fires with cookpots and barrels of water ready to feed and water the men. All had been as well prepared as time could possibly have allowed. As he passed, Fronto kept finding minor faults in the organisation, but only with much searching. He would hate to have to admit that Carbo and Masgava could prepare as well as him.

The walls were packed with men, mostly legionaries with sword and shield, but interspersed among them small knots of archers and slingers, cavalrymen with their distinctive helmets and spears, and oddest of all – legionaries testing the pull of a bow or lining up arrows.

The north rampart seemed to be slightly more densely-packed than the others, in response to the threat posed by the approaching enemy. They were numerous enough to peel off and surround the place, but if they did that they would stretch their own attacking numbers as much as those of the defenders.

There *might* be six thousand Arenosio – Fronto would have to trust the word of the scouts on that. From the viewpoint of the north rampart they were just a carpet of moving figures filling the narrow valley from side to side and as far back as the eye could make out. There was, as Galronus had noted, no cavalry, but then horses would be of little value in war up in these peaks, so that was no surprise. Other than that, they moved in a massed mob, as had those tribes the Romans had encountered in their early days of campaigning in Gaul, before they had come up against the more organised tribes. That, at least, boded well from their point of view. And the Arenosio would clearly be bringing no siege engines or suchlike across mountain passes, either, so this would come down to a straight fight across the ramparts which, as Fronto had noted initially, would help negate the inequality of numbers.

They were coming at speed, he realised as he watched that sea of humanity wash down the valley like a flash flood. It took long moments for Fronto to recognise the distant rumble of thunder that was almost hidden beneath the din of thousands of thudding footsteps.

'Sounds like there's a storm coming,' he noted.

'For sure,' Galronus said with feeling, gripping the pommel of his sword.

'I meant thunder. It's distant yet, but unless this is finished really quickly, we'll probably be fighting them off in a storm, and that's a bad thing for us. Makes attacking more treacherous, but will play havoc with our archers.' Chewing his lip he scanned the rampart. Sure enough, he caught sight of Decius some distance away. He grabbed the nearest archer and pointed at the prefect.

'Go tell your commander to spare nothing in the assault. Don't hold back ammunition. Give it absolutely everything as soon as you have range. There's rain coming, so we might as well do our damage while we can.'

The man ran off and Fronto watched for long moments as the Arenosio reached the flat ground opposite the gate, emerging from the sparse trees. Fronto had half expected them to stop and send out a parley group. They didn't. There was a visible pause and a wave of rumbling across the mass as they spotted the external stake defences strewn with battered, stinking Arenosio corpses, but just as quickly the pause passed and they began to spread out in an arc around the north, east and west sides. As Fronto watched them moving into position, that same archer ran up to him with a sheepish look and cleared his throat.

'Prefect Decius said "Yes", and that he's "not an idiot", Legate.'

Fronto chuckled and sent the relieved archer back to his post.

'This will be over in an hour,' he said quietly. 'Look at them. They're all-but straining at the leash. But it's a brittle thing, this bravado, and once it breaks so will they. This is going to be short and brutal. And they're concentrating their strength at the north, where they're emerging. Unless they start to shift their strength, once they're committed, we need to pull whatever manpower we can from the quiet sections.'

There was a howl, which cut through the general tumult, and Fronto's eyes were drawn to a small group of warriors who seemed to have taken it upon themselves to launch an attack. Perhaps a dozen of them suddenly broke from the crowd and surged forward, whooping and brandishing their weapons as they ran. Fronto glanced at Decius, who was counting under his breath. Even as Fronto turned back, he heard the prefect give the order, and the missile troops on the rampart launched, each one aiming a missile at the small knot of warriors.

The front one, a giant with a mail shirt and an axe and shield, held his board up as he heard the initial call, but the shield did little to save him. Even as he reached the sudis defences with their grisly décor, he was pulverised by sling stones and punctured by three arrows, falling dead and gasping to join his tribesmen on the spikes. The others with him fared no better, two more falling on the stakes and the rest to the grass before them. One, who by pure chance had taken just one arrow in the arm during the flurry, had turned and was fleeing back toward the enemy mass that was still arriving from the valley. Without being given the order, three archers picked off the man, who fell to the turf sprouting shafts as he collapsed.

'Good. Let's keep this up.'

But it seemed that such small forays would not last long. Even as a second attack occurred further off to the west with similar results, Fronto could hear angry shouts among the tribe – leaders telling their men to stop such suicidal assaults, clearly. But there was a growing sense of urgency among them that the Romans could feel on the wall. Fronto saw knuckles paling as men gripped weapons ready, and archers kept arrows nocked and ready, slingers slowly rotating their slings with the stone in.

The attack came with little warning. A carnyx sounded somewhere back among the warriors, gave rise to a dozen commanding voices, then a dozen more carnyx blaring out with a noise like a man suffering terminal flatulence in a tunnel. And the tribe attacked.

There was no plan – no organisation or strategy. The tribe simply surged forward at the defences with a will and a lust for Roman blood. Despite his comfort with the defences, Fronto felt a moment of doubt. Such numbers might just manage to overwhelm the ramparts, and if they did, falling back to the redoubt formed by the houses would probably signal the beginning of the end. No, the enemy had to be held at the walls and broken there.

The Roman missile troops let fly at a call from Decius when the front-runners were some ten paces from the sudis fence. Arrows flew in thick clouds and stones whizzed among them, falling into the ranks of the Arenosio like a flensing knife, peeling away the front layer of the army. Fronto watched in gruesome satisfaction as the tribesmen died in their hundreds before even reaching the outer defences, the warriors behind them inconvenienced by having to climb over their companions. More arrows. More stones. Decius was making the most of the dry, and another crack of thunder – slightly louder – confirmed they were doing the right thing. More and more enemies fell to the barrage. The Arenosio had their own archers among the crowd, but they were little more than an annoyance to the defenders. The numbers of the tribesmen, though, were beginning to make their presence felt. Despite the constant hail of missiles striking the front ranks, there were simply so many that they were beginning to clamber over the stake defences faster than the Roman troops could reload their bows and slings.

Still, they were taking horrendous casualties. Fronto was pleased and impressed to note that the legionaries, who had had no formal training of missile weapons, were glorying in their ability to do such damage. They were considerably less effective than Decius' men, of course, but even then they were causing havoc, for they didn't have to be marksmen to hit the mob running at them, and many of their shafts struck home. Those legionaries waiting with sword and shield cheered on their mates with every hit.

But the Arenosio were still flooding forward. Fronto turned to one of the runners Masgava had placed strategically. 'Do a quick circuit, looking at the enemy numbers. If you find somewhere that's not in any real danger, have their commander thin their ranks and send them here.' The man saluted and ran off, and Fronto peered left and right. The legion's few bolt throwers had been set up spaced around the ramparts, each attended by their two man team. There were twenty two of them – the army had brought fewer than was standard, for they had been travelling as fast as they could and had needed to give over wagon space to the gold. Additionally, there was limited ammunition for them, unlike the archers and slingers who were loaded down with spare ammunition taken from the stores of the fortress. Even as he willed them to begin, the first weapon released its heavy bolt with a twang that was almost lost in another crack of thunder. The missile sailed down into the crowd, as well aimed as only Roman artillerists could hope to manage, and plunged through the chest of a man about to blow into a carnyx. His torso exploded in crimson and gleaming iron as the rings of his chain shirt flew in all directions, the bolt passing through him and thudding into a warrior behind. The groan that swept through the enemy ranks confirmed Fronto's suspicion: these men would break soon. They were desperate and terrified.

Again and again the archers and slingers on the walls launched into the attacking force, and the pile of dead Arenosio grew and grew, forming a bank where there had earlier been a spiked fence. Now, tribesmen were scurrying up the bodies of their fellows, coming ever closer to the ramparts, despite the terrible losses they were taking.

There was yet another crack of thunder and Fronto caught something out of the corner of his eye, turning to examine what had happened. One of the bolt throwers had fallen still, both its artillerists gone. One Fronto found lying on the embankment behind the ramparts, am arrow jutting from his face. The other was draped over the parapet fence with a single shaft rising from his neck. This was not the work of random arrows from the crowd below. To take out both artillerists with such precision required care and time. Even as he wondered, Fronto saw another arrow fall square into the face of an archer. His head rose, extrapolating from the hit to locate the source. The missile had to have originated on the hillside.

He watched, tense, as another arrow launched from that hillside and plunged down among the defenders on the walls. The enemy had sent archers to the high places where they could pick off men on the walls. The distance was frankly astonishing, and he realised then that these men were not warriors, but hunters. The archers on the slopes were men used to bringing down birds in flight in howling gales. They were loosing few shots and slowly, but each one was a masterpiece of the bowman's art, removing one more defender.

'Protect the archers,' Fronto shouted. 'Marksmen on the hillsides.'

Men turned to look and another single arrow took a slinger in the chest, knocking him back from the walls. The bolt thrower at the far corner had now fallen silent too, unmanned. Legionaries who were idle, awaiting the strength of the assault, shifted position to hold up their heavy shields protecting themselves and the archers and slingers from these pinpoint-accurate arrows. Still, the hunters managed to cause their damage, selecting their targets carefully as the missile troops on the walls concentrated once more on removing the threat below them. Still the Arenosio came on, ever closer to the walls, and Fronto was beginning to wonder whether the scouts had seriously underestimated the enemy numbers, or whether perhaps one of those other forces had not turned back after all.

'Here they come,' shouted a centurion along the rampart, and Fronto turned to see Terpulo pointing his sword down over the wall. Even as the lead elements were still picked off with arrows and stones, so the flood of warriors flowed over the last stretch of grass and reached the walls.

'Positions,' bellowed the centurions, and those men who had been protecting the archers now turned and fell back into place to defend the rampart. As the hunters on the hills began their deadly work once more, Galronus grasped Fronto's arm and pointed at the hillside.

'Look.'

Fronto did so and it took a while to pick out what Galronus was indicating. Figures were moving across the scrubby slopes and, even as he watched, one of the marksmen fell to them, the threat he posed negated.

'Who are they?' Fronto breathed.

'My scouts. I left a few units out there to warn us if any other forces might be coming to aid the Arenosio. Looks like they saw the archers and moved to deal with them.'

Fronto nodded, watching another source of deadly shafts fall silent.

'When this is over, give those men a bag of coins and a jug of wine each.'

Galronus grinned, but there was no more time to pay attention to such distant troubles, for now the main problem was at their doorstep. The endless cries and shouts of consternation in the hard native tongue had been joined by occasional Latin cries. The enemy had no plan, nor ram, nor siege ladders, but what they had in abundance was numbers, and they flooded up the walls like a plague of locusts, clambering upwards using the gaps between stones for handholds, some climbing with just one hand while clutching a weapon, others using both hands, their weapons still sheathed.

All across the defences, legionaries began their work, hacking down at the rising force. Among them, the dismounted cavalry jabbed down with their spears, proving themselves oddly more effective in this position than Rome's heavy infantry with their pila and short swords. Every other legionary used a pilum to lance down, almost as well as the spears, though more prone to bending and breaking. Others retained their gladius to deal with those who actually reached the parapet.

Fronto watched for a moment, impassive. There was still a sea of the enemy coming at the walls. The fight was going to be a tough one. The figure of Masgava appeared around the corner from the east, several centuries of men at his heel. He spotted Fronto and ran toward the legate, gesturing for his men to filter up onto the ramparts.

'South wall is being ignored, sir. I've left enough men to hold it until reinforcements arrive, but it seems stupid to man it strongly. I've brought five centuries here as a reserve.'

'Good man,' Fronto acknowledged. Where's Aurelius, by the way? He's always hovering around me like a protective gnat, but I've not seen him since I regained consciousness.'

Masgava's midnight face split into a wide, toothy grin.

'I've got a little surprise brewing and Aurelius is in charge of it. He'll be here shortly. In the meantime, just keep the rampart clear.'

Fronto frowned at the Numidian, but Masgava had already turned his attention away and had joined the men on the wall, a gladius in one hand and his old gladiator's sica in the other. Shrugging, far too used to his odd, secretive friends, Fronto stepped toward the parapet and sought a place to join in. As he approached, a legionary staggered backwards hissing, clutching his sword arm, which was bathed in blood, a long gash in the forearm. The man's sword fell from numb fingers and Fronto gestured to him. 'Get to the medicus.' As the soldier ran off, clutching his arm, Fronto neatly stepped into his place on the rampart and peeked over the edge of the wooden defences atop the wall. His curiosity was answered with steel as a sword point swept past his nose, almost taking it off. Instinctively, he lashed out downwards with his beautiful, ornate gladius and caught the man a blow on the side of the head, carving off a piece of his scalp. It was little more than a flesh wound, but enough to cause agony and send the man falling away into the mass below him.

Thus began the butcher's work to which the Roman military was bred. Fronto's entire world became a short stretch of wall and the man to each side. He managed to parry a blow between strikes that was meant for the man on his left, but failed to similarly save the man on his right, who fell back with a cry, a neat red chasm cut across his face below his eyes. The injured man was replaced a moment later by a regular cavalryman, who began to jab down sharply and expertly with his spear, skewering man after man, spinning the pole and yanking it back out only to slam it down again. The sheer butchery was staggering.

Fronto lashed out again and again with his sword, ducking back and using the parapet for cover as the enemy blades swept through the air atop the walls. What kind of people developed walls of dry stone that could be climbed? Fronto gritted his teeth as he fought on, slamming his sword down into the unprotected shoulder of a climbing warrior and clucking his irritation as his sword drew sparks from the man's helmet as he fell away. That blade would need careful attention now.

An axe hissed past the legate, narrowly missing him, but continued on to lop off the hand of the cavalryman, who screamed and fell back. A legionary took his place and still Fronto fought on, jabbing down. A spear lanced upwards suddenly in the press, caught on the brow of Fronto's helmet and very nearly went through his face. The tip scored an agonising line up Fronto's forehead, jamming between bone and bronze for a moment before the man withdrew it. Fronto felt white hot pain splash across his head yet knew even through the blinding agony that it was just a cut to the bone and he had narrowly avoided death with that blow.

He fell back away from the wall, breathing heavily, blinded by the torrents of blood pouring from his scalp and down across his eyes. He reached up with his sword arm and cuffed away the flow of blood from his eyes, warm and thick, only for it to be replaced with so much more as the deep cut bled. He realised that every move of his head was jerking the cut as his helmet shifted and he

251

stepped back carefully until he knew he was on the sloping turf of the rampart. There he cast away his sword and reached up, taking off his helmet and dropping it next to the blade. A fresh torrent of blood sluiced down across his face and he almost lashed out as someone grasped him.

'Capsarius, sir. Stand still.'

He did as he was told and hissed as the medic pressed a honeyed wad of linen to his scalp. Then, a moment later, the blood was wiped from his eyes with a damp cloth. A medical orderly was sponging his face from a bucket full of water that had already been used so much it looked more like blood to begin with. Mercifully, on the third mop, he found he could see, though he quickly blinked as more blood swam down.

'This is a bastard of a head-cut, sir,' muttered the capsarius.

'I...' began Fronto, and then stopped in surprise as something was jammed into his mouth. It tasted of leather and bad breath and old wine.

'Bite down, sir.'

Fronto frowned, which produced unutterable agony.

'And stop doing that. Bite. Now, sir.'

The legate did as he was told and tried not to whimper as the medic hauled the two pieces of flesh together across his skull and stitched them with brutal, simple efficiency. Within fifty heartbeats, the man had tied off the thread and his orderly was wadding once more, then mopping his face. Once his vision was clear once more, Fronto opened his mouth to thank the capsarius, but the man was already gone, crouching over a legionary and probing his chest, shaking his head as he did so.

'Sorry, sir,' the orderly said. 'Busy morning.' And then, shoving a damp cloth into Fronto's hand, he too was gone.

A faint trickle of blood dripped into his eye again and he wiped it with the pink, soggy cloth.

'Stand back, sir,' called a voice and Fronto had to spin to identify the source. He blinked in surprise to see carts emerging from the houses and streets of the fortress, heaved toward the slope by several dozen legionaries each. He stepped out of the way of one such cart, blood loss, confusion and pain adding to his fascination as he gawped.

Aurelius gave him a hard look as the bodyguard escorted one such cart to the walls. 'See what happens when I'm not there,' he admonished, shaking his head. Fronto peered in woolly interest at the cart as it passed. It was loaded with sacks.

'What in the name of Minerva?'

The soldiers were heaving the carts up the slope and gradually they closed on the rampart top, six carts in all, spaced out along the wall. Fronto watched in fascination as the carts were stopped, wedges hammered under the wheels to keep them in place, and then at a call from Aurelius legionaries began to work the carts.

He stared as a soldier slammed his blade down into a sack and a puff of white billowed up. Flour? Aurelius and his men had been pillaging the granary, but what for? To throw sacks of flour down on the enemy? Weird.

Yet he watched in silence as all along the wall, the legionaries hacked at sacks of flour and then carried them to the edge and threw them over. Trails of white and fragmentary grains criss-crossed the rampart, but a cloud of dust began to billow beyond the walls, and curled up like a cloud beneath them. Fronto felt a heavy drop of rain pound the cut on his forehead and realised the storm had arrived even as the thunder rolled.

'Quickly,' Masgava yelled. 'Before the rain starts.'

The soldiers sped up their efforts, that white cloud rising into the air, but the rain was beginning now, and Fronto felt it spattering his abused scalp.

'Stop,' Masgava bellowed. 'We're out of time. Arcadios?'

Fronto stared in bewilderment as the Cretan archer ran up the grassy slope, an arrow nocked to his bow.

'Back,' Aurelius yelled, and the centurions blew their whistles, ordering disengagement. The soldiers pulled back, a few taking parting wounds as they stepped away from the edge.

Arcadios nodded back to the town and a legionary with his arm strapped up to his side just like Fronto's ran forward with a blazing torch in his other hand.

'Surely...' Fronto began, but Masgava was there a moment later, none-too-gently manhandling him down the slope. The legate watched as he descended. Arcadios moved into the clearest air he could find, tested the wind, drew back the string and tilted backwards, aiming up into the air. At a call from him, the legionary set light to the arrow and the archer released instantly, sending the missile high into the air. The world seemed to hold its breath as that flaming bolt flew up high. Now, the Arenosio were beginning to cross the parapet, but they were slow, their gaze turned upwards in fascination, following the falling star.

The arrow plunged into the white cloud outside the walls, just where the north gate had once been. The resulting explosion shook the fortress to its foundations. Sections of the wooden parapet simply disappeared, and Fronto went blind for the second time in a short span, this time with a white-green blur superimposed on everything he looked at.

The screaming began outside the fortress.

Fronto rubbed at his eyes. He could only make out shapes around the periphery of his sight. Panicking, he blinked again and again, and gradually, the flash resolved into mere green-yellow blobs at the centre of wherever he looked.

Legionaries were approaching the parapet once more, swords in hand, but there were no Arenosio clambering over it now. In fact, all Fronto could hear was screaming and moaning. Slowly, carefully, recognising that he was not in the best of health, the legate clambered up the slope. Aurelius was next to him a moment later, helping him and, in his current state, Fronto felt disinclined to argue.

The land beyond the rampart was a vision to make Hades himself shudder. The world had gone black and small fires still burned here and there. There were so many corpses it was impossible to make out the burned grass.

'Sacred flame of Vesta,' was all Fronto could find to say.

'The idea of one of the legionaries, sir,' Aurelius said. 'He came from Ostia and he once saw this happen in a bakery. Flour in the air goes up real easy, he said. He was right, too, I reckon.'

Fronto stared, trying to ignore the bright pinpoints superimposed over his sight. More than half the Arenosio out there must have perished or been horribly injured in the blast. Even as another crack of thunder split the air and the rain began in earnest, Fronto saw the surviving tribesmen halted back along the valley, arguing.

'That's that,' he said. 'They'll either run or humble themselves and retake their oath. The Convenae are no longer a threat. Now find me a comfy chair and a drink.'

* * *

Rectum was a cemetery. As the sun slid slowly from the sky, Fronto watched the endless lines of dead waiting to be burned or buried. Surprisingly few were Roman. Had it not been for Aurelius ending the fight as he had, likely there would have been very few Roman survivors. But in the end, the Arenosio had felt the last of their resistance drain away with the blast that had killed more than a thousand men and burned another thousand to a living crisp. Most of them had fled, and a few – the ones whose true home was in this valley – had abased themselves and begged for Fronto's mercy. Arruntius had advocated the execution of all the nobles and leaders, but Fronto had been too tired. He'd listened to them retake their oath and let them run away and bury their dead. After what had happened in these mountains it would be a very long time before any chief contemplated rousing Rome's ire again. Besides, the true enemy had left. Verginius had gone, and he had so clearly been the *real* threat – the catalyst that had turned angry tribes into a rebellious army. Without Verginius, there would be no further trouble in these mountains.

Fronto sighed as he leaned his good elbow on the southern parapet and watched the funeral pyres blazing as the Romans were committed to ashes, the natives being buried in another convenient pit half a mile away.

'We'll be ready to move at first light,' Carbo said, arriving quietly and leaning with a sigh on the parapet close by.

'Not a hope,' Fronto replied. 'The legion needs several days to recover from all of this. And really, the fight's over now. Aquitania is quelled as per Caesar's instructions. Time to finish the job of settling the place.'

'The king's not dead, Fronto.'

'No,' the legate agreed, 'but he's no longer the same threat. Not to Caesar or to Rome. The legion's done its job. We need to take out a sizeable group and settle a new town here, or maybe across at the camp site. Then all remaining manpower and supplies can be split between every colony from here to Lapurda. The last ones can send word from there to Caesar, to tell him what we've done. You'll have responsibility for all that, of course.'

'And you, sir?'

'I?' Fronto sighed and slumped onto his elbow again. 'I have to go find Verginius. I have to… I don't really know. Kill him? Bring him home? Kick seven shades of shit out of him? I just don't know. It's beyond me. But I do need to find him. If I don't, some day *he'll* find *me*, and I feel that might be a bad way for things to work out. No, you need to settle the legion, then take whatever force remains that's not retiring and return to Caesar. I'll see you there soon enough.'

Carbo was shaking his head. 'I don't usually agree with that idiot Aurelius, but he's quite right about how dangerously impulsive you can be. You can't go running off across the mountains and into Hispania on your own.'

'I won't be on my own. I'll have Masgava and Aurelius. I'll take Galronus and Arcadios and Biorix, too. We'll take spare horses and enough food and gold to see us through several weeks. And I know Hispania, too. Once I get down to the foothills on the other side of these peaks, it's like home to me. And Tarraco really *is* home, in a way. For Verginius too. This will end there, one way or another, and then we'll come back to meet up with Caesar's army. If anything important happens before then, send word to the governor's office in Narbo. I'll hear it as we pass through.'

'*If* you pass through. Fronto, this Verginius friend of yours is way too clever. You might be underestimating him again.'

'No. If he wanted to kill me, he'd have done it yesterday.'

Still, Carbo was shaking his head. 'You're sure?'

'I am. This is personal. It's not a job for an army. Besides, the governor of Hispania Citerior might be a touch unimpressed if I march half an ageing crippled legion into his territory. Don't forget that Caesar has enemies everywhere. No, we'll be better off just the six of us.'

'Then be careful,' Carbo warned.

'I'm always careful,' Fronto said in an offended tone.

Carbo's snort echoed across the valley.

Late Maius

Gnaeus Verginius sat beside the camp fire and stared into the dancing flames, seeing in their depths echoes of what had been and what he'd lost. The future, he felt, lay somewhere beneath in white hot ashes. The wind howled like the loudest and loneliest of wolves, swooping down the pass toward Hispania, through their makeshift campsite on a narrow bluff with straggly trees. At least they were below the snowline now after days of travel. The pass had been difficult, but to a man who had spent ten years in these lands, the freezing, treacherous ways held little fear.

Now, his eyes drifted up from the flames at angry sounding words. He had to force himself back into his role as Arenosio to pick them up. Oddly, since seeing Fronto's face in that hut, he'd had sudden bursts of recollection and had miraculously begun to automatically think in Latin again – something he'd not done for many years. Switching back to the native dialect took considerable effort.

As well as Ategnio, he had picked up seven more warriors at the picket stations in the valley once they had fled the fortress. In fact he had picked up nine, but two had been so instantly fearful and annoying that he'd caused them to accidentally slip from the treacherous mountain paths, plummeting to their doom. The eight remaining warriors were arguing as if he weren't there listening. Of course, he might as well *not* be to some extent. He'd done little to inspire confidence since leaving the fortress, he knew, and most of these men were beginning to falter.

'So why *should* I follow him?' one warrior was saying to another. He then turned to Verginius. 'Why *should* I follow you now?'

'Monturos…' warned Ategnio, his eyes catching those of his master.

'No. screw you,' snapped the warrior, pulling away from Ategnio and crossing to Verginius, drawing his knife and waving it threateningly. 'Why should we follow you now? Once you were powerful, but what are you now? You've lost everything…'

The man stopped waving his knife as Verginius uncoiled like a serpent and his hand snapped out, grabbing the warrior's wrist. Monturos tried to fight the grip, but his eyes widened at the sheer strength the smiling king exhibited even now. He drew a shocked breath as Verginius twisted his hand and broke the wrist like a bundle of brittle canes. 'Why should you follow me?'

As the man's hand flopped useless, Verginius caught the falling blade and dropped to a crouch, hamstringing the man on the way down. The gasping, shocked Monturos hit the ground like a sack of grain. There, he flopped, his ruined wrist flapping this way and that, his legs spasming, largely out of his control. Verginius was suddenly on the man with the lithe moves of an acrobat, sitting astride the man's chest. With a sweep of the knife, he pinned the remaining good limb to the ground, eliciting a shriek from the man.

'That you should even have to *ask*, Monturos, shows how little you understand honour. Why *should* you follow me? Because I ask you to. Because I am your king even without my throne, and you vowed to follow me, whatever the cost. A vow is a sacred thing, Monturos. My vows drive me and will do so 'til I cross the final river. I have vowed vengeance on a man I once called brother and similar upon a man who is the closest thing to a king in Rome, and I will not deviate from my course until that vengeance is complete. All I asked from you was that you honour a vow to follow me. How paltry is that by comparison? Yet you cannot even do that. You are a sad, pointless excuse for a warrior. The world will be stronger with your loss.'

The blade was torn from the pinned arm and, as Verginius shuffled backwards, plunged into the gut, tearing this way and that, like a man trying to draw a seven pointed star in the flesh. The hopeless, helpless warrior shrieked and moaned, begging for an end, but the smiling king merely lowered the bloody knife and fished in his tunic.

'See this? I have worn this since the day I came to Hispania. The goddess you see is Nemesis – the lady of righteous vengeance. Fronto wears its twin – we bought them from the same stall on the same day. He knows the value of an oath as well as I but he, like you, broke his, and so now he has to pay for what he did. And you have to pay for your lack of strength and wit.'

Monturos stared in horror as Verginius removed the figurine hanging from a thong on his neck, then held it close for the warrior to see. His eyes almost crossed as he tried to focus on the goddess hanging before him, and then he screamed again as Verginius plunged the figurine into his eye, ripped it out covered in jelly and blood, then slammed it into the other orb. Rising slowly, Verginius used his foot to nudge the dying, oozing, screaming warrior far from the fire and into the scrub, where he rolled, shrieking, down a slope and out of sight. He then returned to the fire, staring at his hands in distaste.

'Do you know that in all the years gone by, the one thing I really miss about my old life is the baths. Who's got a flask of water?'

Chapter Eleven

'TELL me,' Galronus said quietly, leaning across in his saddle toward Fronto. The legate – *former* legate once more, he supposed – glanced around at the others. Aurelius had taken it upon himself to act as scout, riding slightly ahead, and Fronto could see him waiting patiently for them at the next rise. Masgava, Biorix and Arcadios were plodding along some distance behind with the spare horses and the baggage, arguing about something menial. They were as alone as they were going to get at the moment.

Sooner or later, given what he was leading his friends into, he would have to tell everyone everything, but some things were so personal and so long-buried that it was difficult enough to speak of them to Galronus, who they directly affected, let alone any of the others.

'What have I told you before? Of Verginius.'

The Remi nobleman shrugged. 'Bits and pieces. Tell me it all. I need to know, in case I have to face him myself.'

Fronto nodded. With Galronus all-but betrothed to Faleria, he deserved to know their shared history. 'Gnaeus Verginius Tricostus Caelimontanus, he was – is – in full. His family are one of the oldest in Rome, and some of the most noble patrician blood, too. Back over a dozen or more years ago, not long after Caesar and I had first returned from Hispania, my father, who spent much of his life in the bottom of an amphora, betrothed Faleria to Gnaeus' brother Aulus. Aulus was a haughty, priggish, supercilious fathead. In fact, in truth *most* of his family were. But my father thought their status would enhance our own. The Falerii are barely patrician, you see. We're a weird mix of Roman noble blood and Samnite from Puteoli, the Roman being an offshoot of the extremely proud Valerii lineage.' He noticed Galronus' eyes starting to glaze. 'Anyway, the fact is that father thought he could raise our family profile through connection to the Verginii. Problem was, Faleria hated Aulus. So did I, really. But at the betrothal, we met his brother Gnaeus and we immediately liked him, all of us. He was different to the rest of his family. More like me, in many ways. Anyway, over two years, mother managed to persuade father in one of his more wine-sodden nights that Gnaeus would make a better match, and he agreed. With a little apology and some shuffling round, Faleria was betrothed to Gnaeus, and all was good. For a year we lived like princes in Rome, me and Gnaeus, with Faleria never far from us.'

Fronto's gaze played around the snow-capped peaks surrounding them and he pulled his cloak tighter against the mountain winds. 'That year Caesar was in trouble. His creditors had called in his debts and he hadn't enough money to pay them. He managed to secure himself the post of Pontifex Maximus, but he needed cash badly. He knew the Verginii and approached them, but Gnaeus' father would have nothing to do with him. He thought Caesar a brash young nothing. Gnaeus had such an argument with his father, as he liked Caesar, but the old man was adamant. My own father was dying that spring, though, and he was gone by summer. I officially had control of the family finances and I helped Caesar pay his way out of trouble. From that moment I think, Gnaeus, Caesar and myself were bound together. When Caesar went back to Hispania, Gnaeus and I went with him.'

Fronto fell silent for a moment. His shivers were only partially born from the cold winds of the mountain pass. Much more of it had to do with speaking aloud things he had always kept so tightly locked away. Things that hurt.

'Verginius and I led an army via Tarraco and up into the foothills of these mountains, then across Hispania Citerior and into tribal lands. Caesar was bolstering his waning funds with spoils from the Hispanic tribes. Don't forget he still owed a lot of money, just to other people now, including me. It was the oddest situation, really. I wasn't his client or his patron in any way. I was younger than him and junior, serving under him, yet in truth he owed much of his success and position to me. Anyway, once the campaign was over, Caesar's army prepared to head back south to Italica loaded down with loot. But before we left we got a message from the governor in Tarraco asking for the Seventh to be returned. There had been trouble with the Ilergetes in the north of Roman lands, but Governor Caepio couldn't deal with it because he'd sent the Seventh with us to help Caesar, and so he was undermanned. Caesar refused to send the Seventh back. He was worried about his spoils, you see. Taking a caravan of silver, loot and slaves through hundreds of miles of tribal and then bandit-infested territory was dangerous work, so he decided to keep the Seventh along with the

Ninth and all his other forces to protect his money. But to mollify Governor Caepio, he sent a cohort with a few turma of cavalry to put down the Ilergetes. That, of course, was myself and Verginius. We rode east with five hundred men in all. Verginius fell out with the general over it all. He considered Caesar to be thoroughly un-Roman for that – putting his own wealth above the good of the state. He spat at Caesar's name all the way to Ilergetes land. To be honest, I was still a little hero-struck with Caesar in those days, and I overlooked a lot of his faults for the glory that surrounded him, but in retrospect, Verginius was right in every way. We should have refused to go, or insisted on taking the Seventh entire.'

He sighed. Aurelius was waving them on from the saddle ahead, confirming that the way was clear.

'We rode in as all young commanders who are full of themselves do, as though we were gods walking the earth. I seriously don't think we considered it possible for Rome to lose. We'd never seen it, you see. We'd been victorious in everything we did. But we learned a hard lesson at the hands of the Ilergetes. They weren't the walkover we expected. They fought us hard. They kept hitting us swiftly and running away, drawing off our cavalry, then butchering them in the hills. By the time we were deep in their territory and starting to think we'd made a mistake, there were less than four hundred of us and we were all tired. Verginius and I had joint command and when the scouts reported a small force of natives in a village not far ahead I decided to attempt the classic pincer movement as Hannibal had at Cannae. We split the remaining men and moved off to the sides of the road, sweeping round wide to come at them from two sides. It was entirely my tactic. Verginius argued against it, worried about splitting such a small force, but I was arrogant and sure of myself. We fell on the small force of Ilergetes like wolves, and only at the last moment did we realise our mistake.'

'It was a trap,' Galronus said.

'It was. Four hundred Romans fell on fifty natives, and then suddenly found themselves surrounded by more than a thousand more Ilergetes. It was dreadful. Some of the worst carnage I have ever seen on the battlefield. I saw Verginius occasionally, but we were all fighting for our lives, so I couldn't help him. I was wounded twice, but one of the centurions who had a better grasp of

262

military matters than me decided to take command out of my hands and called for a withdrawal. Just over a hundred men made it out of the fight and drew into a defensive square.'

This was where it hurt most. This was what he'd never told. What had led to him almost following his father down the same dark path of the Amphora.

'I was one of the last to pull back. I was ashamed beyond words to have led my men into such deep shit. And I was determined then to save as many as I could. There were nine of us pulling back as the Ilergetes regrouped ready to charge. We slowly made our way across the field of bodies, helping up those who could still walk, aiding them back to the Roman square. We managed to get four more men out. *Four.* And half way back across that field with the Ilergetes pumping their arms in the air and howling at us as they prepared for another attack, I found Verginius. He was dead. I simply couldn't believe it. And to my shame, the thing upmost in my mind was how I would tell Faleria about it. And this is what I cannot understand: Verginius was dead. Quite dead. I checked him myself. There was a sword still standing out of his ribs, right through into the ground below. His eyes were unblinking and when I put my hand down I couldn't find a pulse or feel breath.'

Fronto realised with no surprise that there were tears trickling down his cheek.

'I picked him up. I tried to, anyway. I was wounded and exhausted, and I couldn't carry him. I ended up half dragging him, but then the Ilergetes started their charge and the others ran for safety. There I was dragging a dead man across a battlefield while hundreds of angry tribesmen ran at me. I nearly stayed. If I had, I would probably have died there. But I heard someone back in the Roman square shout my name and I panicked. I dropped Verginius back to the ground and ran. I left him. He was dead. Really: dead. I got back to the Roman square just before the enemy and they bundled me into the middle. The enemy fell on us and we fought for our lives in that defensive formation. We were almost wiped out, but the formation worked. We did so much damage to the Ilergetes that they finally broke off and left, preserving what was left of their numbers. Less than forty of us made it to Tarraco.'

Fronto heaved in a breath.

'He was dead. That's all there was to it. It was eight months before I went back. The Seventh had been returned to Hispania Citerior once Caesar was safely back in his capital, and they marched into Ilergetes land and brought them to heel. I went and found the battlefield afterwards. The Romans had been left unburied. The natives had taken away their own dead and looted the Roman corpses, but the carrion beasts had been at work and the men of the Seventh I'd led there were just bones. You couldn't tell boy from man or officer from recruit. Their armour had all been taken away, as well as their weapons and the rest, as loot. I never identified which body was Verginius. But I had seen him dead on that field and I, with half a dozen volunteers who'd survived the same fight, buried all the bones and put up an altar on the site. Then I got drunk for a few months. I think I've told you the rest.'

Galronus stretched. 'So somehow Verginius survived, even without a pulse or breath. Is he a ghost, you think? Some sort of shade?'

Fronto frowned. 'I've been beset by shades before, Galronus. They haunt my dreams. They don't raise rebellions in the mountains. No, this is a real man. Verginius is alive somehow. And for the love of Juno, don't suggest anything like ghosts around Aurelius. The man's half-mad with superstition as it is. The fact is that Verginius survived somehow. And he still harbours a grudge against Caesar for sending us to battle with too few men to survive. What does he want with me? It has to be revenge. For leading him into the battle against his advice, perhaps? For leaving him on that field and running for my life? Whatever it is, he wants revenge on me, but not, apparently, to just kill me. He had that chance in Rectum. But he's drawing me back to Tarraco, and there I daresay I'll find out.'

'And what will you do with him?'

Fronto pursed his lips, staring off at the mountains ahead. 'I just don't know. Is he still Verginius, or has he gone mad? Is he now just this smiling king. Is there anything left of my old friend? To be honest, until I stand face to face with him, I won't know what needs to be done.'

* * *

'What, might I ask, possessed you to come this way again?'

Fronto turned to Masgava, trying to ignore the fine white snow whipping into his face, stinging the skin and making him blink repeatedly. Like the rest of them, the big Numidian was wrapped in whatever furs and cloaks and blankets they had dragged from the pack animals. The sky was a perfect azure blue, as befitted the end of spring as it slid into summer, but for all the blue sky and sunshine, it might as well have been midwinter in the pass, for the winds were strong, multidirectional and incessant, and they carried stinging snow with every icy blast.

'Because that's our best bet.'

'The locals said there were two much easier crossings,' the big, dark-skinned man grumbled argumentatively.

'They also said that a small band of Arenosio warriors went this way, therefore so do we.'

'Stupid. We could go round the easy way and maybe catch up with them.'

'And what,' Fronto countered, 'if they are still in the pass and we miss them altogether? No. Wherever I can find confirmation Verginius has passed, we will follow.'

'And what if he's leading us into a trap? An ambush?'

'Then be ready to draw a sword. You can always go back.'

Fronto glanced past the big man in the whipping snow. The view was breath-taking, in a somewhat nerve-wracking way. The valley lay well below and behind them now, shadowed and deep, the grassy central area almost invisible. The world up here was white and grey and freezing. Part way back down, Fronto could see the small black lake nestled in a ring of jagged white stone. They had refilled the water flasks from the icy pool, but had not lingered. The day was less than halfway through and they were all determined to reach the other side of the peaks before dark.

'Another lake,' shouted Aurelius up ahead, and Fronto could see him pointing into the flurry. They were all on foot now, leading their horses for safety. Another two or three miles at most, Fronto reckoned, and they would begin the descent to the valley. What had prompted Verginius to take such a high route, he could not guess, unless it were just to put Fronto and his men through the mill. After all, Verginius would be used to this territory now, while it was all new horror for the Roman party.

Slowly, huffing and puffing and feeling the burn in his muscles, Fronto hurried to catch up with Aurelius. The other four behind picked up the pace as best they could, leading the pack animals. A few moments later, Fronto struggled up the rocky incline to the crest and stopped next to Aurelius, his jaw dropping.

The view was something from a dream, something Fronto couldn't imagine placing in the real world. It was a place one could picture the gods walking, where Vulcan hammered his anvil and Minerva's owl flew. If there was anywhere in the world Nemesis lived, this had to be it. In the heart of the mountains, a valley opened up, surrounded by fangs of grey rock. Here the snow had not settled so much, sheltered from the wind by the encircling rocks. And in the centre was the bluest lake Fronto had ever seen. Jupiter chose that auspicious moment to restrain the winds, and the flurries stopped, leaving them standing in a perfect calm world that battered the senses with sheer beauty. Half a dozen birds were visible, wheeling in the air against the grey majestic rocky backdrop. Ahead, at the far end of this almost hidden valley, the last stretch of the pass climbed before descending to the deep valley that would take them to Hispania, but they would now have a stunning mile to walk along the edge of that amazing lake. Fronto felt his spirits lift with the sight and he smiled for the first time in days.

'Maybe this Verginius does know how to pick a route, eh?' Aurelius said, whistling through his teeth. 'We could camp in this valley you know? Make the last climb tomorrow?'

'No,' Fronto shook his head. 'We push on as long as daylight allows. I don't want to allow Verginius too much of a lead. Whatever he plans, I don't want to give him the opportunity to carry it out.'

The others reached the saddle a moment later and Fronto smiled at the sound of collective breaths being drawn. Then, suddenly, there was a dreadful wail, and Fronto's head snapped round, his hand to the pommel of his sword.

At the back of the group, Arcadios was swearing and struggling. While Biorix and Galronus had most of the pack horses up on the flat now, the one the Greek archer had been leading had somehow slipped on the rocky, scree-strewn path and was skittering on the edge, its weight already pulling it out over a horrible drop. Arcadios had hold of its reins as well as those of his own horse, and was the only thing keeping the poor beast up. But Arcadios was just a man, and was crying out in pain as his shoulders separated, the weight of a horse pulling at him.

'For gods' sake, let go!' Fronto yelled, running back toward him, but the advice was unnecessary, for the small-framed Greek could no longer hold it without his arm ripping from its socket. Shrieking in agony, Arcadios let go of the rope and the unfortunate horse disappeared over the edge, crying out in terror and shock. Fronto heard the sickening thuds and cries as the poor beast bounced off the rocks and finally landed somewhere with a crunch. He was running so fast that he almost followed the horse over the edge and he barely stopped in time by Arcadios. Somewhere down below in the shadowed area, he could almost make out a darker shape.

'What was it carrying?' Masgava asked quietly as he joined them.

'The gold,' Arcadios grunted.

'All of it?'

'Most of it. And my bow. Other stuff too. Some of the food. Part of the tent.'

'Things we can't leave,' Fronto said, voicing everyone's thoughts. 'Even if we could leave the rest, we'll need the money to survive longer than a day or two down in the flatlands once the supplies have run out.'

'I'll go down,' Arcadios said, irritably. 'I lost it.'

'And look at you,' Fronto said, rather more sharply than he'd intended. 'You've wrenched all your muscles. Not much hope there. You stay here and keep the other beasts steady. And don't feel guilty,' he added, experiencing a touch of remorse himself over the tone he'd just used. 'It was bound to happen somewhere up here. Galronus and I will go. Biorix, Aurelius and Masgava are the strongest, so you three can lower us on ropes.'

'Er.... Your arm?' Aurelius noted, pointing at the limb strapped to Fronto's side.

'It's getting better. I can feel it. And I only need one arm to go down the rope. My other arm's fine.'

'It's not clever,' Aurelius said, disapprovingly.

'I'm going,' Fronto said flatly. 'Live with it.'

He turned to the Remi noble as the others tied the horses safely and took out the ropes, looking for a good place to anchor them and then throwing them out over the edge of the path. The ropes were thin but strong, legionary manufacture, and each covered almost forty feet. Two tied together should just about reach the unfortunate beast. The two men donned leather gloves from the pack on one of the surviving horses.

'This might cost us the time we need to get over the high section. If so we'll have to camp near the far end of the lake tonight.'

Galronus nodded. 'Speed is important, but not at the cost of lives.'

'Precisely.'

'Done,' shouted Masgava, and Fronto and Galronus wandered across, peering over the edge into the gloom, where two long strands of rope descended. Masgava held one, braced, and Biorix the other. Aurelius hovered where the two ropes were tied to projecting rocks, ready to grab them if they slipped.

'Into Hades,' Fronto said in a dark tone as he dropped to the rocky ground and slowly climbed out over the edge, gripping the rope with his good gloved hand. Galronus followed suit on the other cable and a moment later the two of them were slowly rappelling down the ropes toward the darkness below. After a descent of maybe ten feet, Fronto found the rocky slope and pushed his feet against it, bouncing down in bursts of zipping rope. Galronus was close behind him.

Then suddenly Fronto's world ended and his heart leapt into his throat as he reached the tip of the rope and fell. The legate almost laughed out loud as his shriek of panic was driven from him along with his breath when he hit the ground just a few feet below. Nursing a bruise or two, he rose stiffly to his feet as Galronus landed lithely on his toes a few paces away.

'Exhilarating,' the Remi smiled in the shadow. 'You descend a rope, Fronto, with all the grace of a pregnant cow.'

'Thanks.'

Slowly, their eyes adjusted to the dim light and Fronto spotted the poor horse. At least it had died quickly, its neck snapped and its head at an unpleasant angle. It had not hit the ground and then suffered. The pack had exploded on impact and the goods were strewn around the gravel, mottled here and there with small patches of extant snow. Fortunately, a lack of glinting metal suggested that the coin bag had not split, which was a mercy. Hunting individual coins across the ground would be painstaking slow work.

'I can see the tent section,' Galronus said, gesturing off to the left. Fronto nodded and bent to the horse, gathering up whatever he could find and then concentrating on trying to remove the saddle bags from the poor beast so they could use them to lift everything back up on the ropes. Galronus carried the leather tent section over and dropped it, then scanned the ground.

'Think that's the coin bag,' he murmured, gesturing toward a slope down toward the water. Leaving Fronto to his work, the Remi noble stalked toward the lip of the slope, and bent to pick up the bag.

Fronto grunted as he heaved the saddle bags out with his good arm, bracing his feet against the horse. The leather bags came free suddenly and Fronto tumbled backwards, upsetting his bad arm and causing him to yelp. He'd planned to return to the path by gripping the rope and letting the muscly trio at the top lift him, but was forced to recognise that he'd been rather reckless coming down here anyway in his state, just as Aurelius had said, and that the return journey might just see him follow the horse to Elysium. Still, they would all be skirting the lake. Once the goods were back up top, he and Galronus could descend to the water from here and meet up with the others further along.

Moments later the pair had all the goods worth preserving gathered, and together they stuffed what they could in the saddle bags, discarding various bits and pieces that would be unimportant in the grand scheme. Quickly they attached the bags to one rope and Galronus tied the tent flap to the other. Fronto leaned back and cupped his good hand to his mouth.

'Haul away.'

The pair then stood and watched as the bag and the tent section were slowly pulled up the side of the steep slope to the top. There was a pause, and then the ropes came down again, with the empty saddle bag attached to one. With careful organisation, they packed the rest of the fallen gear and sent it back up.

'Haul away and that's the lot,' Fronto shouted. 'The way down to the lake is easy here. We'll meet up with you further along.' At a shouted acknowledgement from above, the two of them waited until the ropes were hauled to the top and then turned, leaving the dead horse for the crows and strolling down the gentle incline toward the lake.

They scrambled here and there over rocky shelves and skittered down patches of scree, and finally came to the side of the lake. The path the rest were following kept pace with them above, gradually descending to meet them, and Fronto was starting to recover from the shock and the exertions and once more enjoy the breath-stealing scene when Galronus grabbed him and stopped him, mid-pace.

'What?'

'Look.'

The Remi noble took a few steps toward the slope and gestured into the shadow. Fronto followed him with a quizzical frown, and spotted the bodies a moment later.

'Two?'

'Two. Seems odd, don't you think? I would reckon they're Arenosio. Neither's the king we're looking for, but they're warriors and they're recently dead.' Galronus crouched by the corpses, both of which were dressed in thick furs, armed and sporting impressive beards and wild, shaggy hair. 'Got to be Arenosio, and surely they have to have been with the king?'

'How long dead, do you reckon?'

'They look fresh. Could have been half a day, maybe a day, but it's hard to tell up here. It's so cold that things are preserved easily. For all I know they could have been here three days.'

'Looks likely we're still on his trail, though,' Fronto noted. 'I wonder why they're down here. It's a weird accident that sends two people together over the edge of a cliff. Unless maybe they were fighting and they both fell in a grapple?'

'You don't suppose Verginius is leaving you a trail of breadcrumbs to follow?' Galronus mused. 'Like the trail of crucifixions and the like he left all the way up into the mountains when he thought you were Caesar? I mean, he could surely have slipped past up here without the locals down in the valley seeing where he went?'

Fronto shook his head. 'He wouldn't know we'd be below the usual path. I just don't think he's bothered about hiding his tracks. He undoubtedly has his reasons for everything he's done, and I wouldn't be surprised if these two are his doing. Ah, shit, Galronus, we're just stabbing in the dark. We can't even guess what goes through his mind. Come on. Let's see if we can make that last climb before dark.'

* * *

For the first time in days, Fronto felt relief looking ahead instead of nerves. Four more days had passed, crossing that high saddle beyond the lake, camping here and there wherever the terrain and flora best allowed. Once past that high point, the deep valley high in the peaks had led them out to a wider valley that more resembled the one where they'd fought the Convenae. Speaking to the occupants of a small mountain village there, they had noticed a distinct change in the accent, which Fronto had confirmed was more of a Hispanic twang. Those natives had explained that the river running down the valley was the Nucario, which would eventually join the great Iberus down near the coast. The valley would take them all the way down through the foothills. Fronto had heaved a sigh of relief. The Nucario was a name he knew, for it flowed through the Roman colony of Ilerda, where Fronto had spent the night once or twice during his time in Hispania.

Once in that valley, their pace had picked up, following the meandering deep valley southwards into Roman territory, for the land became easier. The snowline now lay far behind and the terrain was soft and grassy, with scree slopes around and stands of scrubby trees.

'What's that?' asked Galronus, gesturing up to a spur to one side of the valley. Here, in the foothills, the river was wide and fast, and the peaks to either side often high, but more hill than mountain. Fronto's gaze followed his friend's pointing finger, and he picked out a single turret on the spur.

'Roman watchtower. It'll be long since abandoned. There's a whole scattering of them around the hills on the periphery of Hispania Citerior. They go back a hundred years, to when the lands had only just been added to the republic. Aemilius Lepidus, Scipio Aemilianus, Brutus Callaicus – half the great names of Rome in that era fought wars around Numantia and against Carthage and as a result much of this area became Roman. The watchtowers were built early on to maintain control over the virgin territory. But despite their age, many are still standing. I spent the night in one not unlike this after the battle where Verginius fell.'

On a whim, Fronto smiled and beckoned. 'Come on.'

Urging Bucephalus into a faster pace, Fronto made for what was clearly a local shepherd's trail up the spur's side, Galronus coming on close behind. Aurelius, complaining about his reckless master once more, peeled off to follow, while the other three led the horses on down the valley below at a steady pace.

The three riders crested the spur, which was somewhat overgrown at the edge with low twisted trees and scrubby brown undergrowth. They approached the tower and Fronto dismounted lightly, flexing the fingers of his bad arm as he tied his mount's reins to a tree branch. His arm was improving all the time now, and he felt certain that he would be able to remove the sling in a few days, though he also felt sure a medicus would tell him not to.

As the others similarly tied their horses, Fronto approached the doorway of the tower. It smelled of animal dung, and the door had long since gone, but the squat, square tower was otherwise still in good condition, a staircase of timber climbing inside to a roof-cum-walkway.

Crossing the dark interior, wary of stepping in either animals or what animals might have left behind, he gingerly climbed onto the bottom step and tested his weight. It groaned like an old man rising from a chair, but otherwise seemed solid enough, so he slowly, warily, climbed the staircase to the top. Emerging onto the roof, he looked around. The timber floor had weathered well, and there were no holes or missing boards. Once more, carefully, Fronto stepped out and slowly put his weight on the floor. It held well, and, gaining confidence, he strolled across it to the southern parapet. One or two stone blocks had fallen, but otherwise it was in sound condition.

His gaze fell upon a grand scene and he smiled. A moment later, Galronus and Aurelius were by his side, and he could feel the awe emanating from them in a silence broken only by the twittering of birds.

The river widened out here and there ahead to a series of small lakes as it meandered along the valley into Hispania. The spurs and hills to each side as the flow marched south gradually lowered, so that from this tower, Fronto could see at least thirty or forty miles, by his estimation. And the morning dew was now burning off under a hot sun, so that each side valley and hollow was filled with a gentle blanket of mist. And far away, far in the distance, Fronto fancied he could see flat land.

'This is Hispania?' Aurelius murmured. 'It knocks the shit out of Gaul for scenery.'

Galronus simply nodded, his gaze scouring that stunning landscape.

'There's more to it,' Fronto said. 'I've crossed most of it in my time, though maybe not as often as Gaul. Further south it's drier and browner, more like southern Italia. And down near Tarraco, it's so similar to the villa lands at Puteoli in places that it makes me homesick. It's a great land. I always loved Hispania. More than Italia really. One day, when the boys are grown, I think we might move here for a while.'

'Where's Tarraco, then?' asked Aurelius.

Fronto gestured vaguely ahead. 'Somewhere over there. Out of sight yet. The first big place will be the colony of Ilerda, about thirty miles downriver. Ilerda's in a wide basin of flat land, then there's another lower range of valleys and peaks between there and the sea. We'll be there soon enough, but I want to stop a night in Ilerda and see if we can pick up word of their passing. If he's been leaving bodies in his wake, I wonder how many men he still has with him.'

The two men nodded at his words and all three stood silent, looking out over the scene ahead. Whatever the future held, they were in a new world now. Left behind were Gaul and Aquitania, the legions and battle. Now they were simply six Romans in their own lands, moving through Hispania Citerior, chasing down a dead man who beckoned them on at every turn.

'Come on,' said Fronto, straightening. 'Time to go.'

Early Junius

Verginius stood and peered at the monument.

'I honestly believe he thought he had made things right. A simple altar in a sea of bones.'

'This is where you fell?' Ategnio asked, peering around.

'It is. Something of a detour, but I felt the need to come here. Fronto will, too, when he realises how close he is. This,' the king said, pointing at the simple stone altar with its lichen and weathered Latin, 'is a monument not to the fallen. It is a monument to arrogance. To stupidity. To cowardice. To betrayal. This is nothing more than a salved conscience for the tribune Fronto who left men to die while he fled with his skin intact to drink himself to death like his wastrel father.'

'You are so filled with hate for this man Fronto? I had never heard of him until the fight in the mountains. I thought it was *Caesar* you hated.'

'Oh you Aquitanii are so literal and straightforward, Ategnio,' Verginius shook his head and leaned over, both palms on the surface of the altar. 'Yes, I hate what Fronto has done to me, but I never hated *him*. How could I? He's my brother. More so even than you, Ategnio. Fronto is half my soul and has been since the first day I drew a gladius for Rome. That is what makes his betrayal cut so deep. Caesar? That's different. I was under his spell for a while like Fronto. But while Fronto still is, I started to see Caesar for what he was: vain, callous, selfish and corrupt. With Fronto in my grasp, I wouldn't know whether to wring his neck or embrace him. Caesar I would just humiliate and execute. That's why I slipped with the arrow and missed him. I simply, in that blink of an eye, couldn't decide how I felt about it all. But now things are different. I've had time to think and I have a route planned out for him. Fronto will live through everything that was done to me. I knew a Jew in my youth back in Rome and his people had a very straightforward view of vengeance. *Lose an eye – take an eye.* Simple. Fronto will suffer as I did, and it will be catharsis for both of us, for the Fronto I know will have spent a decade torturing himself over his mistakes.'

He turned and gestured to the gathered warriors.

'Have you full bones yet?'

274

The others approached the altar and began to lay out a vague skeleton from the ossified remains they had gathered, scrabbling in the dirt of the battlefield. When they were done, Verginius peered critically down at their efforts.

'There are plenty of bits missing, but the main parts are there. You can tell it's human. It has a head, ribs, pelvis and all the limbs. It'll do. Who has my sword?'

One of the warriors approached respectfully, cradling a gladius in a black leather sheath, decorated with silver filigree, its bone handle intricately worked.

'Took me a year to get this back. Now I'm just throwing it away. Oh well.'

Fishing in his pouch, Verginius dropped an officer's torc on the broken skeletal neck and then, lifting his arms and bracing himself, drove the blade down through the ribs into the stone. It was soft red sandstone, local to the region, and there was already a crack there. The tip slammed into the crack and sank into the altar. Verginius let go and stepped back.

'That's it. One more surprise for Fronto, then it's off to Tarraco. Come on.'

Chapter Twelve

THE field was just how Fronto remembered it, though perhaps a little smaller. His memory had gifted the site of the battle with a grander scale than it had in truth. But when he closed his eyes – and he'd quickly learned not to do that – he could see the Ilergetes charging. He could see the grizzled centurion who had saved the unit bellowing his orders and the desperate survivors running for their lives as the tribesmen whooped and jeered beyond. And worst of all, he could see himself, staggering, crouched, blood pouring down his arm and his leg, clutching the body of Verginius and dragging the lifeless limp form toward the Roman square, hope fleeing him with every step.

Galronus stood at the altar Fronto had paid twice the normal price for from a local mason. It had been a rushed job, but a good one, and money was nothing to him at the time. The body atop the altar was supposed to be a facsimile of Verginius, clearly in some twisted attempt to increase the feelings of guilt that surged through Fronto with every heartbeat. The fact that it was Verginius' own sword standing proud of the ribcage and, Fronto was pretty sure, that heroic centurion's torc around the collapsed neck, did nothing to help matters.

Galronus had the oddest look on his face. This whole dreadful drama had been picking at Fronto's nerves and making him shiver ever since the king's identity had been revealed in the mountains, but he'd given precious little thought to how it affected Galronus. And his friend was just as much a player in the tragedy of the Falerii these days. In half a dozen years the noble – a Belgae warrior of the Remi, of all things – had very much taken the place that Verginius had once held. A friend so close he was almost a brother, and who, when his wedding finally took place, would become an *actual* brother. For Galronus had also supplanted Verginius with Faleria. How was he taking the discovery that the man he'd replaced in so many ways was now proving to be very much alive. Did he worry what that meant for Faleria? Possibly. The Remi noble was often inscrutable in matters of the heart or soul. One thing Fronto felt certain of was that Galronus did not worry over Fronto's friendship. The two of them had been through too much now for their relationship to be sundered by something so uncertain. And Verginius remained something of an unknown quantity. How much of the young Roman officer remained behind that permanent chilling smile? Not much, Fronto suspected.

The other four hung around at the edge of the field. They had done a quick sweep of the surrounding countryside, but the area was clear, the nearest point of interest the local village that lay on a small hill close to the side of the wide valley.

With a sigh, Fronto peered down at the femur jutting from the turf. More than a decade and still the earth did not cover the signs of what took place here. He'd made sure every body was buried when he'd returned with the altar, but in such bare open ground, where starving carrion feeders prowled, bodies had to be buried deep to stay there. Something had scrabbled at the dirt and unearthed the bones in numerous places. Even nature herself seemed to want to compound Fronto's guilt with constant evidence. That was what Verginius was pushing for, of course, but the knowledge that his emotions were being manipulated did not make it any easier. Muttering a wish that the fallen here rest well in Elysium, Fronto stomped disconsolately over to the altar.

'It's a fine sword,' Galronus said quietly. 'It will need some work now, after hammering it into stone, but it's still one of the finest I've seen. A blade to rival your own.'

Fronto nodded. It had been given to Verginius by his wealthy father the day he set forth for Hispania. No words had been exchanged. Verginius' support of Caesar had created something of a gulf between the two of them, but still the father appreciated that his son was setting forth on a path to a great career, and had marked the occasion with a gift. Was Lucius Verginius still alive, Fronto wondered. He'd not met his friend's father since the day he had returned to Rome and visited to tell the old man how sorry he was for what had happened. Lucius had cuffed Fronto with the back of his hand and ejected him from the house, never to contact him again. What would the old man think if he knew Verginius was alive?

'Take the sword.'

Galronus shook his head. 'That would not be appropriate – not a good idea at all. He meant for you to have it.'

'I'm no *dimachaerus*, fighting in the arena with two swords. A blade in each hand is a last resort for me. Takes too much concentration. It's a good blade, and you're to be a Roman citizen now, don't forget. We've done what Caesar asked, and he always keeps his word, whatever other faults he may have. You'll be one of the equestrian order soon, able to wear the toga and vote in the senate. You should have a gladius instead of that bloody great scythe you call a sword. When we get to Tarraco we can get it repaired and sharpened and have a scabbard made.'

Galronus shook his head again. 'I don't want *anything* of his.'

Fronto grunted and reached out, ripping the blade from the altar amid the clatter of bones. 'It's not *his*. He left it for *me*, and *I'm* giving it to you. Just take it.'

Galronus did so with a curled lip of distaste, handling it as though it were coated in something unspeakable. 'You'll get used to it,' Fronto said quietly as he reached out and took the torc, knocking the skull from the altar in the process. 'This torc belonged to a man I respected. I can't wear it, as I wear this one,' he noted, pointing at the one around his neck that Galronus had given him years ago. 'Masgava? You take this. You deserve it. From slave to officer, it's time you were attired like one.'

The big Numidian, less bothered about such proprieties as Galronus, shrugged, took the torc with a nod of thanks and bent out the ends so he could fit it around his huge, muscular neck. It was perhaps a tiny bit on the small side, but not too bad.

'Do we rebury the bones?' Aurelius asked, strolling over.

'No point,' Fronto said. 'We buried them all years ago, but animals are clearly still unearthing them – not just *human* animals, either. Come on. It's three days' travel to Tarraco, but the evening's drawing in rapidly. Let's see if there's an inn at the village. Last time I was here the place was deserted in the aftermath of the revolt. It must be reoccupied now, as there's smoke rising from it.'

Collecting Biorix and Arcadios, the six men began to ride slowly from the battlefield up the slope toward the village on the hill. It was merely a small native settlement. No fortifications, just a small square and perhaps twenty houses with outlying farms, parts of the hillside terraced for agriculture. A dirt track led up the incline and passed between two lines of double-storey houses.

Galronus was frowning while he examined the buildings as they approached. The structures were each good, solid square buildings, some of mortared stone walls left bare, others then rendered with some sort of painted plaster. Windows with good wooden shutters occupied the walls, and the door was adorned with a small porch of timber on almost every house. The roofs were thatched neatly, and each building had a low wall to the rear, surrounding a garden. A narrow channel with a sluice at the edge of the village ran through each garden, allowing irrigation from some sort of huge stone tank.

'I had no idea they were so civilised here,' the Remi noble said quietly. 'We had always heard in the north that these tribes were our backwards cousins. Now I find that they are, if anything, more advanced than the Belgae.'

'Things are different up in the northwest,' Fronto replied, 'where Rome's not had any influence. But across much of the peninsula they've had a century or more of Roman stimulus and before that the Carthaginians had the place too, so *their* influence is all over the place. *Your* tribes were all pretty much free and always had been. Most of the peoples of Hispania have answered to one empire or another for hundreds of years. They're bound to have picked up a few things.'

'There's no one in the streets,' Aurelius said with a frown. 'Is that normal?'

'I don't know. It's getting toward sundown I suppose.'

The danger was upon them before they were even aware of it. The whisper of arrows in flight was so quiet it should have gone unheard, but the town was so still, and Aurelius' odd warning had heightened their alertness for that split second. Biorix dived at Galronus', whose attention was riveted on the nearby house's garden.

The two arrows that had issued from an upper window struck home, one thudding into Aurelius' right side, sending him lolling, gasping in the saddle, blood sheeting down from the wound. The other, which would have plunged straight into Galronus' neck, instead struck Biorix, while the Remi noble plummeted from his horse to the dusty ground.

'Scatter!' bellowed Masgava, leaping from his horse.

These were not skilled archers like the ones on the hillsides back at Rectum, for their first shots had been taken slowly at leisure, and neither had been deadly accurate, and the time they were taking to reload was longer than it should have been.

The Roman party dispersed instantly. Masgava grabbed the yelping Aurelius, dragging him from his saddle and pulling him into a side alley behind a house, leaving a trail of crimson. Arcadios sprang from his mount like an athlete, landing with the various steeds between him and the source of the arrows, unhooking his own bow from the saddle and fishing for an arrow. Galronus floundered on the floor for only a moment before scrabbling to his feet as the convulsing body of Biorix hit the dirt beside him, shaking violently and clawing at the arrow lodged in his spine at the base of the neck.

Fronto had reacted through sheer instinct, dropping from Bucephalus, and now helped scoop Galronus up to his feet, the two of them running at the building whence the arrows had come, swords in hand, where they flattened themselves against the plaster wall, taking advantage of the meagre cover offered by the porch.

Another pair of arrows thrummed from the building, one clattering against the corner of the structure sheltering Aurelius and Masgava, the other thudding into the horse behind which Arcadios lurked. As the injured beast screamed and bucked, the Cretan archer appeared as if from nowhere, loosed one arrow and then hurtled for better cover. Fronto heard with some satisfaction the resulting cry of pain from inside the house. The two archers may have had the advantage of surprise, but neither was in the same league as Arcadios with a bow.

'Come on,' Fronto said quietly, and ducked along the wall to the door. For a moment, he stared impotently at the latch, his good hand gripping a sword, the other bound to his side in a sling. Even as Galronus dipped past him and opened the door, plunging inside, Fronto, finally tiring of the arm, used his fine gladius to snick the bindings holding his arm in place. He winced as the limb fell loose, somewhat atrophied after so many days of being tightly bound. However, what had been a screaming pain when he moved the arm out or forward was now a dull ache and nothing more. His arm felt numb and throbbed, but he felt certain he was close once more to full usage. With a brief prayer of thanks to Aesculapius, he slipped into the gloom of the house after Galronus.

His friend was already rushing up the stairs and Fronto had enough time as he crossed the room behind him to note the bodies of a native family lying butchered in the corner. This was not done by – or with the support of – the village, then, not that he'd ever suspected anything other than Verginius.

He rushed up the stairs and took in the scene at once. Galronus was struggling with a big bearded Arenosio warrior, who had discarded his bow and drawn a blade. The other archer was dead, draped over the window sill with Arcadios' arrow shaft jutting from his eye socket.

Even as Fronto ran across to aid his friend, the Remi noble managed to get his blade into position and slammed it through the enemy's torso up to the hilt. The Arenosio warrior gasped, his eyes widening as Galronus twisted the blade this way and that and then ripped it back out, stepping back to find enough room. The archer coughed and moaned, then collapsed to his knees for a moment before falling face first to the dusty floorboards.

While his friend cleaned off and re-sheathed his blade, Fronto checked the Arenosio were both dead, scanned the interior for further threats, then peered out of the window. Nothing else was happening.

'This is why you need that gladius: more manoeuvrable in closed spaces. You nearly came unstuck with your bloody monster sword there.'

'*He* seems to think it worked well enough.' Galronus noted, gesturing to the body on the floor, and Fronto rolled his eyes. 'Nine men were heading south, the last few places confirmed, and that includes Verginius. He left two here, so he's got six left with him. We need to be on the alert for more trouble like this over the next few days, then. I don't think he values his men. He seems to leave them to die for him.'

'There could be more in *this* village yet. Maybe even Verginius himself,' Galronus pointed out.

'I don't think so. If he was going to commit more men, he'd have put them here with these two. He's setting traps and ambushes. It's what he knows – we've seen that all the way from Lapurda. This was just a little trap to damage us, but it's taught me one thing.'

'What's that?'

'That none of you are indispensable.'

Galronus frowned as he followed Fronto back down the stairs, across the ground floor and out into the street.

'The danger's over lads, for now,' Fronto said loudly, as he looked down with sadness at the still form of Biorix. Arcadios appeared from a wall, still with an arrow nocked to his bow, his gaze zipping from window to window around the street as he moved. Masgava emerged from across the street, helping the gasping, limping Aurelius.

'How is he?'

'Bad. Not fatal, but he needs proper medical help,' Masgava noted. 'The faster we get to Tarraco, the better.'

'No,' Fronto answered. 'You're not going to Tarraco,'

'What?'

The legate looked around at his four friends. In addition to the body on the floor, Aurelius was also clearly in danger, and the others were very much on edge.

'This isn't your fight, and I'm not leading you into it.'

'Try and stop us,' gasped Aurelius.

'No,' Fronto repeated. 'It ends here for you. Aurelius, you can hardly move, let alone defend yourself now. This little ambush wasn't meant to hurt me, else one of those arrows would have been aimed *at* me. That was set to remove *you lot*. To kill or wound my companions. He's picking you off. Well I'm not playing that game. I'm not going to play Verginius' games any more. Masgava? You and Arcadios and Galronus take Aurelius and head on up the valley, keeping southeast. Eventually you'll reach the coast, and any locals can point you the right way. Sooner or later you'll get to Barcino. There are medici there who can help Aurelius. It's maybe a day further than Tarraco, so it won't make much difference. From there you can take ship to Massilia or head up the coast to Narbo. Whatever you choose, I will eventually find you at Massilia, so wait there.'

'We're not going,' Masgava said.

'Yes you are. Don't make me do this militarily and order you. As long as I'm worrying about you lot I can't concentrate on what I need to do myself. Get Aurelius to safety and have him tended. Take Biorix too, so he can have a proper send off. I will take one pack horse and move fast. Moreover, I'm not going straight to

282

Tarraco. I reckon Verginius will be waiting for me there, so I have a mind to go somewhere else first while I investigate the lay of the land.'

'You can't go on your own,' Masgava said defiantly. 'What if you come across bandits? Fall off your horse? Or down a cliff?'

'He won't be alone,' Galronus said, quietly, undoing a belt. His sword fell away as it was unbuckled, and he swung that big Gallic blade in its scabbard, belt and all, across the back of a pack beast. As he held up Verginius' fine, if chipped, gladius, gleaming in the light, he fixed Fronto with a hard expression. 'You can send *them* away, but not *me*, Marcus. This is my fight, too.'

Fronto drew breath to argue, but the combination of the steel in his friend's eyes and the naked truth of his words robbed the legate of refusal.

'Very well. Galronus comes with me. We're going to visit an old friend and see what we can learn of Verginius. You three – Masgava, Arcadios and Aurelius – get to Barcino and then to Massilia. Take plenty of supplies and money. We want to travel light and fast, anyway.' His gaze slipped to the glinting blade in Galronus' hand.

'Time to finish this.'

* * *

Galronus peered this way and that through the gently sloping fields, striated with row upon row of vines. The ban upon native wines that held sway in Gaul was unknown in Hispania, and while the noble blood of Rome raised their haughty chins and sniffed at Hispanic wine, Fronto had better experience than most as both purveyor and consumer, and knew that the better wines of Hispania Citerior were every bit the match for most of the vintages found in Italia.

The long, slow road from the Pyrenaei had led them across a low plain dotted with small native settlements and around the periphery of a range of hills that rose wooded and impressive from the dry brown and green land, finally crossing a low set of ridges and dips before approaching the coast. Less than a mile back they had passed a five-way junction in the dirt road, with the main east-west thoroughfare properly metalled. A milestone had proclaimed somewhere called Bera to be six miles east, and Tarraco eight miles west.

Galronus had been surprised.

'Are we not bound for Tarraco?'

'Not quite,' had been Fronto's answer. 'At least, not yet.'

And so they had ridden south to the coast, ignoring the great provincial capital off to their right beyond the cacti, scrub bushes, pine trees and plants that were, to Galronus, unbelievably alien. And finally, now, as they approached the sea, Galronus could hide his curiosity no longer.

'Fronto?'

'Mmm?

'We are riding uphill toward the sea, some miles from our supposed destination and through someone's vineyard.'

'We are. I told you we weren't going straight to Tarraco, but to visit an old friend. I said I wasn't going to play Verginius' game any more. Come on.'

The two men crested the rise and Galronus blinked. On the summit of a lonely hill on the coast, far from signs of civilisation, was a series of well-appointed structures. A rural villa, Galronus realised, not unlike Fronto's family land at Puteoli, the heart of this huge, extended vineyard. A simple, small villa of four solid wings in a square stood on the crest of the hill with a cistern nearby, narrow gulleys and pipes running from it to feed both house and fields. A servants' block stood close by, a little more dishevelled, and a stable sat beside a fenced enclosure containing some of the largest, most stunningly bred horses the Remi noble had ever laid eyes on.

'You know the owner?'

'You could say that,' Fronto smiled. 'Be prepared for perhaps some anti-Gallic sentiment, though. When I first came here, the owner was a cavalry commander called Longinus. A former Legatus of the Ninth, who I'd butted heads with in Hispania. He was probably the most arrogant, supercilious and irritating man I've known, but he was also a good cavalry officer, a noble soul in the end, and simply the best breeder of horses I've known. Bucephalus was his own steed, and I've always said that when he gets too old for campaign, which will be soon, the old boy will come here to pasture. Longinus died the year before I met you, but you knew Crispus? I brought him here after the year we fought the Belgae. We delivered Longinus' ashes to his widow. I'd known her since my time in Hispania, and I thought it was my duty to deliver the tidings. I also knew she was a little… err… indiscriminate in her affections, let's say. She once went after me, but she took a fancy to Crispus. Anyway, I swore I'd stay in touch with Longina but sadly the world got in the way. I never did. But I have no doubt she will help us. She also knew Verginius, you see.'

'Joy. Let's stay in the place briefly then, Fronto. A man-eating widow can do little good for a new father and a husband to be!'

Fronto grinned, and rode up to the top of the rise, frowning a little at the state of the garden.

'I see no smoke,' Galronus noted.

'Smoke would be mostly from the bath house, and that complex is down on the beach. Longina liked to… lie naked in the sand. I think she… the baths were there to… I don't know. I suspect they were rarely a solo visit, let's just put it that way.'

'Fronto, I don't like this.'

'All will be fine,' Fronto replied, sliding from his saddle and tying Bucephalus to the wooden bar near the entrance. But the Remi was correct. Something *was* wrong. There had been no workers in the fields, the plants were growing out of control and the gardens were poorly tended. No servant had rushed out for their reins. Something was definitely wrong, but not something that had triggered Fronto's preternatural senses. What then? Verginius knew of the villa and Longina, but he shouldn't even know that Longinus was dead, let alone that Fronto had been here since then, albeit seven years earlier.

'Hello?' he called as Galronus dismounted behind him and tied up his horse, his fingers dancing around the hilt of Verginius' sword, which was strapped to his belt.

There was a long silence and Fronto's own hand had gone to his sword hilt as he moved toward the door when faint footsteps echoed from within.

'Master Fronto, legate of the Tenth,' a voice called in a friendly tone from within, 'and an unknown friend. Come in, Domine. Be welcome.' The figure appeared at the door and Fronto started in recollection. 'Arius?'

'It has been too long, master Fronto. Good to hear you again.'

Galronus stared at the well-dressed slave with the milky white eyes and the ivory topped cane.

'How did you know it was me?' Fronto murmured.

'Ha. Slight lean on the left instep, sir. Slight limp with outward turn on the right foot – legacy of the bite you were still nursing last time I saw you, sir.'

'Holy Vesta, Arius. That was almost a decade ago!'

'You'd be surprised, sir, how much sight is just a conglomerate of things your other senses can tell you if you just pay attention. Like how you have ridden long and fast from the mountains and how hungry you are.'

'Explain.'

Arius grinned. 'You smell of hill-tribe sausages and sweat. No salt. You've not been near the sea but have moved hard for days. And both your stomachs are rumbling. Cenna still runs a tight kitchen. I will tell her to prepare a meal.'

Fronto frowned. 'That's Longina's prerogative, Arius.'

'Did you not know, sir? I thought that must be why you were here? The Domina died some months back. Come to the peristyle. I will have wine brought and tell you whatever you wish to know.'

Fronto and Galronus followed the blind slave through the atrium of the small villa to a tidy garden with a beautiful pool at the centre. As another slave appeared and Arius began to issue commands as though he ran the villa – which it quickly became apparent was currently the case – Fronto and Galronus exchanged curious looks.

'Tell us, then,' Fronto urged once the second slave was gone.

'The Domina died peacefully in her sleep some months back. There was… it was… rumours circulated…'

'Tell us, Arius. We are friends and nothing less. You know I will not judge.'

The slave's white-eyed face took on a beet hue of embarrassment. 'The Domina was free with her affection, Legate Fronto. Not in a bad way,' he added hurriedly. 'She had never been unfaithful to her husband, but after the death of the Domine, she was… some would say profligate.'

Galronus grinned and Fronto glared at him, willing him to wipe away the smile.

'Well, one particular evening of jollity seemed to be too much. I saw the gentleman back into his carriage for the city, and when I returned to attend upon the Domina, she had crossed the river. I found a coin for her mouth and said the prayers, then organised everything in the absence of someone proper to do it.'

'What of her will?' Fronto said, after a moment's thought. 'They never had children, right?'

'None that were hers and survived, Legate. There are some who have reasonable claim to the legacy of Longinus, but the Dominus and the Domina left clear wills. Everything went to their nephews, Gaius and Tertius Dolabella.'

'And why are they not here?' Fronto frowned.

'There is some legal wrangling over ownership. Neither is willing to share ownership due to nuances in the text of the wills, both brothers claim the entire inheritance. Neither seems to be able to outwit the other.' Arius screwed up his face into a conspiratorial expression. 'To be honest, neither seems to have much wit at all.'

Fronto laughed. 'I remember the pair from a few nights while I stayed here and you're far from wrong. Neither could outwit a melon without help. They must have clever lawyers, I presume. Why is the villa not being worked?'

'I do not believe either of them truly wish to own the villa, Legate. Just to inherit it and sell it for profit.'

'Ah, the loving nephews of Longinus. If they'd seen him in his charge against Ariovistus' men… ah, well. Arius, I have business in Tarraco, and I need a safe place to stay. I hate to put such a burden on you…'

'Oh you must stay, of course,' the slave smiled. 'You and your Gallic friend. I will make up two rooms for you.'

'How did you know I was a Gaul,' Galronus asked, ignoring the fact that that, as Belgae, he was in truth not Gallic at all. The Romans found it hard to tell the difference.

'You smell of wild garlic, Dominus. All those who came back from the Gallic campaign smelled of it.'

As the slave wandered away, chuckling, Galronus closed on Fronto.

'This bothers you.'

'It does.'

'Why? It's just a villa. And not even your family.'

Fronto found he was unexpectedly angry over the matter, and he turned hard eyes on Galronus 'Because two ignorant boys who should know better see it as just money to be made. This is a *family* estate. As a man who's currently losing everything that this represents, I cannot stress how important it is to keep these things. Longinus is buried here, in a small mausoleum on the edge of the estate. Imagine what he would think if he knew his family had sold his tomb to a stranger? The villa should stay in the family, not be used for profit. History is everything to us, Galronus – to Romans. It makes us what we are. I shall not forget why I am here, but while I deal with Verginius, this cannot be left unresolved. I will see Longinus' legacy preserved. Don't forget, one day soon I will need to put Bucephalus to pasture here.'

* * *

'This is a Roman city?' Galronus murmured as they rode into Tarraco. Neither man wore their customary gear, having stowed it at the villa. Both wore the tunics of freedmen and no clear indicator of their true status, though they were bathed and well fed. Both had swords in the bed rolls attached to their horses, though.

The capital of Hispania Citerior stood on a rocky bluff overlooking the blue sea and a stretch of golden beach. At the far end of Tarraco they could see fishing boats and larger trade vessels issuing from a port, but much of the coast was unusable by sailors due to the cliffs and steep slopes leading up to the walls. The defences were tall and powerful, but enclosed a relatively small area. Their lower courses were formed of the same huge, shapeless stones that fashioned the defensive circuits of the native villages they had seen in the region. Above those boulders, regular shaped golden stones formed a huge wall system that Galronus had to admit rivalled those ancient ones of Rome itself. There were the signs of former gates in the walls, but they had all been blocked up.

'This is the old fortress,' Fronto replied, gesturing to the walls. 'This was built by Scipio a century and a half ago on the base of a native fortification when he made war against Carthage. It has the distinction of being the first city wall Rome built outside Italia. Once it was a simple fort like all of them, with four gates.

Now it's sealed apart from on the western side, and it contains the palace of the governor and all the official buildings.'

They rode past a dusty park below the walls where two young men with mock gladiator kit fought, laughing. Galronus' furrowed brow deepened as they rounded the wall's corner with its high tower. The insulae of the city rolled on down the hill below the walls of the governor's private city toward the port at the bottom. A wide space stood between the walls with their central gate and the city proper, dividing the two. It was dusty and churned and barren.

'They use it for horse races,' Fronto smiled. 'Never bet on Green. That's what I learned in my years here. Can you see a colonnade down in the lower city. Stands out a bit above the roofs. Yellow stone.'

'I see it.'

'That's the forum. In the old days there was a space nearby they put up wooden seating and turned into a theatre... yes, it's still there, I can see it. I had some of the best sleeps of my life in there. They've always talked about rebuilding the theatre in stone, but no nobleman's ever wanted to stump up the cash. Good thing if you ask me. There's enough boredom in the world without fostering more. But if I ever have any influence here, I'll build them a stone amphitheatre or maybe put up some permanent stands for the races.'

He laughed, the spectre of Verginius momentarily forgotten amid the reverie of his youth, but then the reason for their arrival reasserted itself.

'There are three places where Verginius might have turned up. I want to be back at the villa before sundown, but let's check them out first.'

The first, a tavern near the forum, revealed little. The two men paused there for an evening meal, despite having been well fed by Arius, and Fronto waited until he saw a familiar face. Even a decade had not marred the lascivious beauty of Parella. She was the landlady for the establishment and had been ever since Fronto first knew her. Her husband had died young and left her the bar. She had resisted a decade of suitors – including Fronto more than once – and had held a tight rein on the establishment. It still thrived in her care, and she still apparently fought off the suitors, noting the way some of the patrons regarded her. Fronto grabbed her backside with a grin as she walked past, yelling at a slave to collect more pots, and Parella delivered him a ringing slap that made his ears jangle without even looking.

'Keep your hands to yourself, old man. Some might fall for that silvered fox thing…'

She turned and noted the ring on Fronto's finger. 'Someone *did*. You should be ashamed of yourself, y'old whore!'

Fronto laughed. 'Ten years and nothing changes. I bet if I touch you here…' Fronto reached out two fingers to the rear side of her upper thigh and she backed sharply away as though the fingers burned.

'Marcus Falerius Fronto, you horny goat. Married too! Keep your fingers to yourself, Tribune.'

'Tribune no longer, Parella. Nice to be remembered though. This is Galronus. He's also spoken for, so he won't bother you much.' The Remi prince looked rather embarrassed by the introduction. 'Listen, Parella… you remember my brother Verginius?'

'Do I ever?' she laughed. 'One of few men who never tried to bed me.'

'Heard anything of him?'

Parella stared at Fronto. 'He died. Last time I heard his name was when you wailed it into the bottom of an amphora in the corner over there about a month afterwards. Why?'

'Listen, Parella, I know this sounds weird, but if you hear anything about him, or about the tribe of the Arenosio from the mountains to the north, could you send me a message? It's very delicate, so it has to be secret. You know the Villa Longina toward Bera and Barcino? I'll be there.'

While the owner regarded Fronto sceptically, the Roman nodded to Galronus, who tipped several silver coins out onto the table. 'Saved enough to buy the villa and retire yet, Parella?'

'Ha. Not quite, Fronto. Even if I sold the bar.'

'Well if your bring me useful news of Verginius or the Arenosio, I'll make it happen for you. But it has to remain a secret.'

The second establishment, a similar bar but with less savoury clientele and a miserable, ugly owner, yielded as much information but with little grace, and Fronto decided not to place his trust in the barman who was unknown to him, his friend of a decade ago now long gone.

The third place, however, fascinated Galronus. No matter how long he'd spent in the city of Rome, he'd never grown tired of two things: gambling and the baths. The dirt track here might be nothing compared to the Circus Maximus of Rome, but the baths were just as comfortable. As the Remi nobleman relaxed back in the D-shaped warm bath with Fronto on his left and some fat local councillor on his right, he sighed with pleasure. There were downsides to the Remi's simple capitulation to Rome, and the hardliners in the tribe still fought their corner, but to Galronus a warm bath, a strigil and a trained masseuse from Nicomedia could balance an awful lot of lost tribal honour.

'Can we talk?'

Fronto glanced across at the councillor, who was paying them scant attention.

'Maybe later. I heard they were having a wagered wrestle in the Palaestra shortly, and a big Gaul is challenging all comers.'

The official cast Fronto a surreptitious look and scurried out of the bath, waddling naked toward his wooden clogs and towel, hoping to place a bet. Once he was gone and the room was devoid of other bathers, Fronto pressed a finger against his lips and reached up, grabbing the towel boy as he hurried past.

'Domine?'

'You hear half what happens in Tarraco, lad, at a guess.' Fronto's hand dipped down into the water and retuned with three silver coins. Galronus stared silently, unwilling to query where his friend had kept them while naked in the bath.

'These coins are for you...'

'Rutius, sir.'

'Rutius, good. One sestertius each for three things. You will listen out for the name Verginius. Or for Arenosio. Got it?'

The slave nodded.

'And thirdly, for a man with a smile carved into his face. If you can bring me useful information about any of those, I will reward you like this tenfold, and if it leads to me finding the man I'm looking for I'll buy you your freedom. Got it?'

The lad stared for a moment, dumbfounded, then nodded vigorously.

'Good. I'll be by daily for my late afternoon bathe.'

The slave smiled, scurried off and pocketed his ill-gotten gains.

'Can you trust him?' Galronus asked quietly once they were alone.

'Him? Beyond words. People with nothing when, faced with success, have too much to lose. My main worry is that Verginius might well be cleverer than me, and I can't be sure what he's done. He might have people asking for me. In fact I'm sure he has. Come on. Let's get back to the villa before we're noticed.'

Early Junius

The pain was utterly unbelievable – so intense Verginius couldn't quite believe it was possible. From the first sharp flash as the point drove through his mail and tunic and punctured the flesh, to the agonising, ongoing grating pain as the nicked yet sharp edges scraped past his ribs, plunging through gore and organs until it burst the mail at his back and drove into the dirt... all was indescribable.

Verginius screamed. In fact, it felt as though he screamed for a lifetime as that blade, the width of three fingers and the breadth of one, tore through his living being and robbed him of life, delivering him torment in return. He screamed until his throat was parched and silent, a husky rattle all that was left of a voice that had once impressed his rhetoric tutor with its timbre and pitch.

The Ilergete warrior did not grin or whoop or howl his triumph. He did not sing or shout or even whisper. All he did was peer into the agonised eyes of Verginius with a transitory curiosity as though trying to read his victim's history through the medium of his eyes. Despite what was happening to him, Verginius found he was drawn to those cold eyes in return. The Hispanic tribes, he'd noted, generally had warm brown eyes, This man's were pale blue, icy and frosty.

Darkness closed from the periphery, gradually encroaching on the edges of his vision until they obscured the warrior's torso, then the sky around him, and finally everything but his face, his eye, his iris.

Blackness.

Verginius actually felt his heart stop.

Then there was a sudden pain, and the blackness receded. There was light. Blinding white light. His body ached, but there was no pulsing throb of pain, for his heart had stopped, his blood slowing, pooling. Tepid. Sluggish.

Fronto's face. Desperate. Pained. Terrified. He was shouting in Verginius' face, the spittle spraying insensate flesh. Then Fronto was dragging him, still bellowing. There was no feeling in Verginius' lower half, and the rocks and bumps meant nothing to him. Only that Fronto had come for him. Fronto was saving him. After everything, even though he was dead and knew it, Fronto was still going to save him. How he would come back from that last dark river, he knew not. But he would, because Fronto was there.

And then something changed. There was a look of shock and confusion on Fronto's face. He didn't know what to do. He was deciding something terrible. Those eyes, the eyes of a brother, of a friend, came down to meet Verginius'.

No!

He wanted to scream it, but his body was dead. It would not work. His head, his mouth, his throat, would not obey even the simplest of commands. He felt the final, bleak, dreadful reality of death settle upon him as Fronto suddenly let go and stepped back, a stupid apology in his eyes as he gazed down at Verginius. Then he turned, and he ran.

No. No. No!

But Fronto was gone. The vague shapes of a few other legionaries flitted on the edge of his vision, then they too were gone. Though he could feel nothing, Verginius could imagine the dusty thud as he hit the ground once more. Then the darkness began to insist itself upon him once more. He felt the cold grasp of Hades about his stilled heart.

He was dead. Fronto had left him to die and saved his own worthless hide. No one had put a coin under his tongue. Were the old tales true? Would the boatman leave him to haunt the world? If he did, Verginius would haunt Fronto. And Caesar, for Fronto and he wouldn't even be here but for Caesar's arrogance and greed and lack of care. He would haunt them both. And if he could grip something as a spirit, he would hunt them too.

White light and pain once more. Fronto? Had he come back? A shape gradually coalesced into the white, and if Verginius could move anything, he'd have reached up to grasp his old friend, to tell him how grateful he was that he'd come back. To tell him how sorry he was to have been so impulsive and harsh in his judgement. Fronto smiled...

...and Verginius realised it wasn't Fronto. If he'd still had muscle control he'd have screamed in panic. A figure was leaning over him and peering intently at him. For a moment he feared that Hades had come for him anyway, for the figure was thin and pale, almost cadaverous with sunken deep-set eyes, teeth set in withered gums and spindly arms with thin, skeletal fingers. If he could,

Verginius would have shivered at the man's touch. The walking corpse jolted as someone spoke to him, and turned, rattling off an answer. Verginius' ears, of course, could hear nothing, but he could almost imagine the harsh guttural language of the Hispanic tribes with their elongated vowels, of which they seemed to have far too many. The cadaver answered angrily, a point proved, an argument won. He sneered at his opponent in this unknown debate and then leaned down so that the heavy, spicy breath of blood sausage engulfed Verginius' numbed head and said something. What it was, Verginius could never know, of course, but from the expression on the walking corpse's face it was clearly meant to be reassuring. The thing pulled out a pack of something waxy and runny and cupped a handful, pushing it down to where the wound was. Then there was a strange increasing emptiness in Verginius' body as he felt the blade drawn out. Verginius' eyes stared blankly at the man's grin as he produced another hand, this one full of powder, and blew it into the Roman's face.

The world went red and stayed that way until the true agony began…

Verginius woke in a cold sweat. He thought that set of nightmares long since put to rest. The closer he came to the end, the more it brought him back to the start. He realised that Ategnio was watching him with… sympathy? That was new.

'Get some sleep,' he whispered hoarsely. 'The next few days will be busy.'

Chapter Thirteen

TARRACO looked different in the morning. The previous afternoon, during their short visit, the sun had already been decaying to the west, its golden light blasting the city from the port up to the gubernatorial walled enclosure on the hilltop, filling many of the streets and illuminating the upper storeys of the buildings. In the morning, though, the eastern light was caught largely by the steep hillside and the high, old walls, the bulk of the city resting in its shadows until the sun had climbed sufficiently to fill the capital with warmth.

Still, Galronus was clearly filled with fascination for this place that was an odd hybrid – an ancient tribal settlement that could so easily have been a Remi oppidum, yet now adorned with all the grand edifices of a Roman city. Fronto smiled. His friend was seeing the future of his own lands, and probably knew that. One day Galronus' home city would be crossed by streets and aqueducts, centred around a forum and with a capitol of its own. The world moved on and the future was Roman.

'What's the plan, then?' the Remi noble asked quietly.

Fronto pursed his lips. 'I want to find the lawyer who's dealing with the villa. I need to find out exactly what's going on. Then we can hit the tavern and the baths and check in to see if last night turned up anything useful.'

Their horses already sweating in the mid-morning heat, the two men rode up the slope and along beneath the high, powerful walls of the Governor's fortress. Men in gleaming helms and mail stood atop the wall, watching the two drably-dressed men below with suspicion. Soon, they rounded the corner and entered the cool shadow of the chariot-track. Races had been held here recently, as the dusty ground still held the many hoof prints and the lines carved by chariot wheels, though a day of civic activity had seen countless footprints criss-crossing the site across the top of the markings.

Two men stood on guard at the fortress' west gate, bored yet at attention. The soldiers joined their comrades in expressions of suspicious curiosity as the two riders, dressed in the tunics and cloaks of freedmen approached.

'The upper city is not open to the public,' one of the men said in a tone so bored that it was clearly a line he trotted out repeatedly. Then, after some thought, he repeated the words in the local dialect, his expression making it apparent he had learned the phrase rather than being able to speak the language.

'We are not the public,' Fronto smiled at him, trying his best to carry centuries of patrician breeding in his tone. The soldier looked at him in surprise.

'I need to find out who is dealing with a matter of inheritance in the city, and this is noble Roman lands, not some fishmonger or native farmer. I presume such records will be dealt with in the governor's city and not the provincial forum? They certainly were in *my* day.'

The two soldiers shared uncertain expressions, and Fronto smiled again. 'May I approach?'

'Dismounted,' confirmed the soldier, and Fronto slid from his saddle, handing the reins to Galronus and strolling over to the gate holding up his hands to prove he was unarmed and attempting nothing untoward.

'My name is Marcus Falerius Fronto, and this is Galronus, a prince of the Remi from northern Gaul. I once served and worked in this place as a tribune and am lately a legate of Caesar's legions in Gaul. Here is my signet ring. I presume you will find this all in order and admit me to find the tabularium inside?'

Overwhelmed by the rush of important titles and the mention of Caesar, clearly backed up with the ring of a Roman patriarch, the two men swiftly came to an agreement and hammered on the gate, demanding it be opened. The great wooden doors swung inwards and Fronto nodded his thanks at the two men as he entered, Galronus trotting along behind, leading Bucephalus.

The interior had changed a little in the decade since Fronto had passed beneath the walls. The huge imperial forum square was still the same, barring a little re-paving, and the colonnade surrounding it was still there, but now it had been adorned with statues of men in togas or cuirasses, each atop a podium with an inscription. A great red banner emblazoned with a golden eagle hung from the pediment of the staircase opposite, displaying the glory of Rome against the white stone carved from the quarry some miles to the east along the main coastal road. As the two men passed into the forum and Galronus dismounted, they examined the inscriptions. Governors and generals from near two centuries of Roman Hispania, adding to the glory of Tarraco.

Few people brought horses into the upper city other than the governor and his cronies and personal guard, but there was still a small stable off in one corner beneath a high square tower, and the two men delivered their beasts to the equisio there, receiving a chit in return.

'Where do we go?' Galronus asked as they re-emerged. 'This place isn't what I expected. It's so... bare.'

'This is where the business is done. The governor holds court in the north tower, the military are based in the south, the portico surrounding the forum is filled with offices that run the province. Up those steps beneath the banner is another square where you'll find all the temples and the governor's buildings, which spread out to cover the rest of the walled area. But few people get past that staircase unless they're with the governor's office. Everything is done in this forum. We need to find the record office and unless much has changed, it's in that corner.'

The two men strode between the statues of the great and the perceived-good and entered the shadowy portico at the far corner, locating a door and then passing inside. Rooms led off from a small office and even from here the two could see the seemingly-endless scroll racks marching off into the darkness. Three scribes sat at small desks myopically scribbling as a man in a tunic with a narrow red stripe distributed documents among them.

'I need to find a lawyer who will be dealing with a probate case in the city.'

'Name?' the clerk said without looking up from his work.

'Gaius Papirius Longinus. Well, actually, his wife, though I can't tell you which of them would currently still be on the records for the villa.'

'Papirius Longinus... ah yes, the villa out toward Bera. I'm aware of the case. You need Rubrius Callo. His office is along the far side, but you'll not find him there today. He was at the races yesterday morning and was set upon by thugs in the crowd. If it's urgent he'll either be drowning his sorrows in the *Twins' Folly* or recovering at the Tuclian Baths. Beyond that, you'll have to wait until at least tomorrow.'

'Thank you,' Fronto smiled. 'I know the places. We'll seek him out now.'

A quarter of an hour later the two men emerged from the fortress gate once more, leading their beasts. 'The Twins' Folly,' Fronto pointed off to the west, 'is near the town's northern edge. One of the better quality places. Come on.'

They passed gently downhill along the slope of the city, between the high buildings, past shops of all descriptions and through a throng of people who represented provincial life at every level, market stalls crowding the thoroughfares and making riding troublesome enough that both men continued to lead their horses dismounted. When they finally arrived at the inn, Galronus whistled through his teeth. He'd seen the odd establishment like this in Rome, catering to the rich and the powerful, selling wine by the cup at a price that would far supersede a legionary's meagre funds.

'This place was too expensive for me in the old days. I drank far too much. To drink here would have bankrupted the family, so I preferred the dives down toward the port.'

They handed the reins of the two horses over to the lad at the side door, then strode into the inn. The interior was beautifully painted with rural scenes and images of gods and creatures cavorting in gardens. Galronus was surprised at the graphic nature of some of the scenes, which would have been more at home in a brothel than a tavern, in his opinion. The few men in here were wearing either heavy togas, sweating over their wine, or the finest of linen tunics as they laughed and chatted. Fronto strode to the bar, purchased two cups of wine at a price that made Galronus' eyes bulge, and leaned close.

'I'm looking for Rubrius Callo. Is he here?'

The barman, who had already been looking at the pair of them with disdain, given their poor dress, was now thoroughly aloof. 'And who might I ask is looking for him?'

'Marcus Falerius Fronto, legate of the Tenth Legion and former attaché to the governor of Hispania Ulterior, Gaius Julius Caesar. Galronus smiled at the man's expression as he fought between being thoroughly impressed and not entirely believing what he was hearing.

'Wait here,' the man said, and left the bar, strolling out through a rear door. Fronto held up a hand to Galronus and wandered across to the door. The barman had passed outside to a terrace beneath a vine-covered arbour where two or three other men sat in the shade and the cool breeze at the very edge of the city. The view from here marched out across the plains to the north toward that distant ring of hazy blue mountains that encircled Tarraco's region. The barman approached a man sitting at the furthest table and there was a brief exchange during which the patron shook his head.

'Come on, Galronus.'

With the Remi noble at his heel, Fronto strode down onto the terrace and approached the table. The barman, irritated to see Fronto approaching, held up his hands and shook his head. 'Master Rubrius does not wish to be disturbed.'

Fronto smiled sweetly. 'I have recently fought my way across the rebellious Pyrenaei with a diminished legion and am being hunted by a man I thought dead a decade ago. I am trying to prevent a travesty of justice, and I have little patience right now for etiquette. Back to your bar before I start to lose my temper.'

The barman flashed red with indignation, but something in Fronto's expression led him to decide upon discretion rather than defiance, and with an apologetic glance at the patron, he scurried back inside.

'I thought this place would turn away ruffians,' Rubrius Callo muttered sourly, watching the two new arrivals approach his table. As he looked up, Fronto could see the bruising around his left eye and jaw where he had been attacked.

'Nasty beating. Still, it's just bruises and lumps. It'll go away shortly. You are handling the inheritance of Longina?'

'Oh for the love of Juno, will that case not leave me alone even in my bruised misery?'

Fronto frowned. 'I take it there are problems?'

'Oh, the two inheritors have a roughly even claim and they dislike each other enough to fight every foot of the way. It's a nightmare. It should be held up as an example to all families who might consider leaving wills that are not absolutely water-tight and clear. Longina was a lovely lady and her husband a clever man, but neither of them were truly focused in matters of law.'

'I understand,' Fronto said quietly, 'that both of the potential inheritors intend to sell the villa when they secure its ownership?'

'Yes. They are truly ungrateful, insensitive, spiteful little oiks, but they pay well, and those of us who rely upon the benefice of others for our livelihood cannot afford to be over-choosy.'

'Yet you can afford to drink here?'

'Pah! I drink here when I want to be unreachable by clients.' He shot a sour glance at Fronto. 'It doesn't *always* work, though.'

'How driven are they by finance?'

'Almost totally, I would say,' Rubrius sighed. 'In fact, if the matter cannot be settled soon, they will probably drop my services and hunt out someone cheaper. Good luck to the poor bastards. I'm sure something easier will come my way.'

'Would you say,' Fronto went on, a calculating look crossing his face, 'that they could be bought off?'

'What are you proposing?' Rubrius murmured, intrigued.

'What is the villa's worth at this time, over which the pair are wrangling?'

'It was valued at four hundred thousand sestertii about a month ago. Each week of non-occupancy and argument usually drops a percent or two from the value in cases like this. A new valuation would find it unworked and starting to become dilapidated, I suspect. One of the things I need to bring up with the clients tomorrow morning is the fact that it probably stands at only three hundred and fifty now, and if they do not soon come to some arrangement, it will continue to drop.'

Fronto straightened. 'Offer them six hundred thousand to split between them equally, and *I* will take the deeds.'

The lawyer's eyes widened in surprise. 'You?'

Galronus grasped Fronto's sleeve. 'Marcus...'

'I do not have that amount in coin on my person, of course,' Fronto said, 'but I can have it delivered here within the month. Two to three weeks at most.'

'Fronto, the senate impounded your funds in Rome.'

'Oh, Galronus, don't you think mother has plenty hidden away in other places. And Caesar owes me *ten times* that amount.'

The lawyer's eyes bulged at this revelation, and he was starting to sweat as Fronto turned back to him. 'They will get little more than that individually if they sell now. This way they both get a reasonable inheritance and the villa stays in respectful hands. I've considered purchasing property in Tarraco for years. Now might be the time.'

Rubrius Callo broke into a slow smile. 'I might just be able to persuade them, thick though they are. You just made my day, master Falerius.'

'You'll take them my proposition, then?'

'First thing in the morning, sir.'

'Good. You can find me at the villa if you wish to discuss matters.'

Leaving the smiling lawyer, Fronto drained his cup and gestured for Galronus to follow him.

'Is this wise,' the Remi asked as they left. 'What will your family think about it? It's so far from your home and you already have the Massilia villa. You don't know how the family funds stand right now, and whatever Caesar may owe you, squeezing it out of him in his current situation might be difficult.'

Fronto stepped out into the street and stretched. 'I'll manage. I'm not seeing Longinus' villa ruined. And I meant what I said: I've often thought about having somewhere here. The climate agrees with me. Faleria will understand, and Lucilia will love the villa. And it would be a better place to bring up the kids while we're banned from Rome and Italia. Rural, with a beach and plenty of land. Not like the villa above Massilia, which is a little more suburban. Come on.'

Retrieving their horses from the side door, the pair walked them down through stall-lined streets to the bar Fronto had frequented yesterday. Leaving Galronus with the horses in the street, he strode inside. Parella was busily sweeping detritus in one corner while half a dozen early drunks made the most of the cool interior to forget their woes.

'Heard anything?' Fronto asked quietly, wandering up to her.

'My, you're swift, aren't you. Second time this morning I've had a shock from the past. Verginius was here less than an hour ago.'

Fronto rolled his eyes. 'Should have known he'd be moving fast too. Was he looking for me?'

'Looking? Hardly. He seemed to be quite sure you were already here. He asked all about you. I asked him if he'd like me to pass a message, and he told me that lips twisted messages. He didn't trust me, I think. Told me only lifeless lips held true words. No idea what that meant, but that's what he said.'

'Parella, you're a treasure.'

'You said something about coin. Rather a *lot* of coin, if I remember.'

Fronto smiled. 'And I'm good for it. I'm waiting on word of something tomorrow morning, and I'll be sending for substantial funds. I believe the governor here might even be persuaded to advance me some. I shall drop by later tomorrow and make good. You trust me?'

'Trust you?' snorted Parella. '*Wandering hands* Fronto? Hardly. But I know you're good for the money. Alright. Tomorrow.'

With a smile, Fronto left the inn and strode over to Galronus, grabbing the reins of his horse.

'Verginius knows I'm here. I'd put a wager on him having been watching us yesterday. So much for not playing his game. He told Parella only lifeless lips could carry his message. Cryptic, eh?'

'He's left a message in a mausoleum?'

'Not that sort of lifeless,' Fronto said. 'In the old days, when we wanted to pass messages to each other and didn't want to leave a verbal trail, we'd use a messenger of marble or bronze.'

'What?'

'Statues, Galronus. And there's only two or three in the city that would work. Come on.'

Leading their horses again, the two men strolled through the streets of Tarraco until they reached the port at the bottom end. Now the sun was starting to rise properly and the heat of the day was beginning to insist itself upon the city. Where the road emerged opposite the docks, a great statue of some reclining river god lorded it over a wide marble basin full of clear, clean looking water.

'Tuclius – god of the river that runs down here from the hills. He's a hit and miss god. Half the year the Tuclius has no water in it, just a dry dusty bed. Luckily, the aqueduct brings water from higher up in the hills to supplement it. Ah, turds.'

'What is it?'

'The engineers have been at old Tuclius.' He gestured to the god's face, where a lead pipe emerged from the mouth, spewing

303

the clean water into the basin. The pipe was surrounded by a concrete fill. 'In the old days his mouth was open and water just jetted from a hole inside. We used to push folded vellum into the back of the mouth behind the spout. Tuclius is no use now. Come on.'

In the increasing heat of the day, they struggled back up the sloping streets of the city toward the local forum. At the entrance, where a grand arch invited them into the thriving heart of Tarraco, a statue of the great Scipio, founder of the Roman city, stood proud and armoured. Attracting disapproving looks from the citizens, Fronto clambered up onto the podium and stretched up to the mouth, just at the top of his reach. Where most statues would be tight-lipped, Scipio's teeth were just slightly parted.

'Never seen a Roman statue with his mouth open,' Galronus muttered from below.

'It's rare. The Greeks occasionally did it, so some of the older statues are like that, but it is rare. Maybe they don't like to carve teeth. Gah, nothing here,' Fronto grumbled, dropping back down. 'Well, of the statues we used to use there's only the Dioscuri left. Come on.'

'I'm sure you could have planned this better,' Galronus grumbled. 'We seem to be zigging and zagging all over the city, and the whole place is one big slope.'

'Stop moaning,' Fronto said, starting uphill once more toward the southern edge of the city. 'You could ride your horse, but you'd forever be dismounting to get round market stalls.' After some slogging through the streets, each of which was already lined with stalls selling food, cookware and all manner of local produce, the two men reached the end of their current thoroughfare, where it became a series of hairpin bend steps leading down to the sea. At the edge of the steep hill, two statues stood guard, each a heroic naked male gripping the reins of a noble-looking steed. As they came to a halt, Fronto and Galronus looked up at the divine pair with their horses, and then at each other, gripping their reins, and burst out laughing. Once the hilarity over the humorous comparison had died away, Fronto handed his reins to Galronus and examined the open mouths of the horses, each forced apart by their bit. On the second one he gave a bark of triumph and returned with a folded piece of vellum.

'What does it say?' Galronus asked as Fronto unfolded the missive and began to scan the contents.

'I'm afraid you have to leave me for this.'

'Not going to happen, Marcus.'

'Listen, he's telling me to go to the theatre, but he warns me to come alone. I tell you, he's been watching us. He probably is right now. If he wants me alone, he has to get that. I need to face him, and I think he's unwilling to do that with you present. Take the horses and go back to the villa. I'll find you there this afternoon.'

'No.'

'Galronus, this is not an optional thing. I need you to go, or Verginius will just go to ground once more and I'll have to start looking all over again. Take Bucephalus. I'll get back somehow. Go.'

The Remi noble stood by the statue, almost a mirror image of the Pollux in marble above him, his disapproving glare following Fronto as the Roman turned and began to march off down the street toward the wooden theatre that occupied a hollow between two high rows of insulae.

Fronto felt the past coming forward to meet the future in a heart-stopping collision. He was getting closer to Verginius with every footstep, and who knew what the result would be? Only after he'd made the first two turns did he remember that his sword was wrapped up in a roll on Bucephalus' saddle. Damn it. That was short-sighted, but he could hardly go back and retrieve it now.

As he rounded another corner and the theatre came into sight at the far end, he entirely missed the figure of Galronus following on, one street behind, both horses clopping along the stones, their hooves drowned out by the sound of Tarraco's lively populace.

* * *

Tarraco's theatre was much like the wooden affairs that were raised in Rome for important occasions and then taken down afterwards – the senate had placed a blanket ban on permanent theatres long ago as being far too Greek and inappropriate, or some such rubbish. Except, of course, that Tarraco was not Rome, and so the theatre stayed and would do so until the day some wealthy benefactor rebuilt it in stone like the one in Fronto's home town of

Puteoli. In the meantime, the wooden structure stood, hemmed in by tall insulae and sturdy warehouses, creaking and faintly dilapidated, spars, boards and seats replaced on a monthly basis.

Fronto had fallen asleep in those seats more times than he could count on his hands. After being ejected from some dive or other, one of his various companions in liquor – not *friends*, since all his friends had gone by then, while fellow drunks were plentiful – would get a hankering for a ribald comedy, or maybe it would be raining and they just had to find somewhere with a roof to wait out the downpour. Either way they would end up at a play and Fronto would often then be ejected from that establishment in turn for snoring loudly during the performance.

Little of the theatre itself had changed since those days. The great canvas roof sagged a bit and would need tightening by the deck hands from the port before the next performance which, signs outside said, would be *The Eunuch* by Terentius. Fronto's eyes rolled as he stepped into the auditorium. Terentius was far from the worst of the comedians, yet like all playwrights he seemed to think a clever play on rude words was the height of humour. For Fronto's coin, Plautus was funnier any day, with his tendency toward slapstick, but none of it was really funny. It was all yawn-worthy crap when put against the excitement of a chariot race or a fight between two master gladiators.

The theatre could accommodate maybe a thousand people at a push, in row upon row of wooden benches all facing the orchestra and the stage, which was backed by a high wooden *scenae* decorated with colourful paint and slightly faded hangings. Despite the sun of the day, the surrounding blocks of warehouses and insulae, combined with the heavy canvas roof that kept both sun and rain off the audience's heads, led to the interior being surprisingly gloomy, deep shadows filling the corners. Fronto waited for a moment to allow his eyes to adjust to the light.

'Sit down,' said a voice from somewhere toward the stage. Fronto squinted into the gloom, but there was no sign of a figure. 'Anywhere will do,' the voice came again. 'For a simple wooden theatre it has surprisingly good acoustics. I am not required to raise my voice.'

Fronto felt his heart flutter at the sound of that voice. There was something in it of the patrician tone he remembered, though this was not *quite* the Verginius of old. A barbaric edge inflected his Latin, reminiscent of the sharp tongue spoken in the mountains.

'There is no need for all this drama,' Fronto said quietly, then realised that the acoustics only worked the other way round, from the stage outwards. He opened his mouth to repeat himself louder, but Verginius had clearly heard him anyway.

'Drama. Very droll, Fronto. Your humour is as blunt as ever. Ategnio told me not to come. Not to find you. He advocates a simple arrow in the neck from a distance. He is Arenosio to the core, though loyal to me beyond reason. I have had to stop him killing you several times already. I am less concerned about your companion, though. I might let Ategnio put an arrow through him, especially if he doesn't stop lurking around up there at the back.'

Fronto blinked and turned sharply. The figure of Galronus, a blade in each hand and a strange unreadable expression on his face, stepped out from the doorway at the back.

'And armed for the fight too. You Gauls are every bit as belligerent as the Aquitanii, you know?'

'Belgae,' Fronto said almost automatically. 'Galronus is Belgae, of the Remi.'

'Beware, Galronus of the Remi,' Verginius said quietly. 'Those who cleave too close to Fronto have a very limited life expectancy. And when the furies are closing and the light grows dim, he will choose his own skin over yours.'

'Verginius…' Fronto began.

'*Be quiet,* Marcus. I have waited long years to see you. And through all that time I was never sure what I would think or do when it happened. I heard you had become a drunk like your father. Then I heard you went and re-joined that arrogant self-serving prick Caesar. I thought perhaps that your heart still ached for what you'd done, but it seems that I am easily replaced. And with a native, no less. How interesting.'

'Listen…'

'No, Marcus. You'll get your chance in due course, but this is *my* time.'

'Why did you not come back. Come find me?' Fronto forged on, regardless.

There was a prolonged silence and Fronto wondered for a moment whether his old friend had gone. Then with a throaty rasp, the voice started up once more.

'Let me tell you a story, Marcus. This one's not a comedy though. Definitely a tragedy I'd say.'

'Verginius…'

'Verginius is *dead*, Marcus. He died on a battlefield against the Ilergetes. His men deserted him and his friend left him to die. I *did* die, Marcus. I felt it happen. I knew it all, and felt everything, but I never reached the river and the boatman. I was too valuable to the Ilergetes, you see. They had a magic man with them. Sort of a druid, I suppose, but they have different approaches up in the hills here. He took a look at me and decided he could save me. Why should he, you ask? Because I was dressed like a Roman officer. They value their slaves, especially if they're noble. Capturing Roman nobles brings prestige among the tribes. My equipment and a dead Roman noble were worth taking, but if they could have me alive…?'

There was an uncomfortable silence and Fronto was about to fill it when Verginius started again somewhere in the dark.

'I lost an organ. There's a thing shaped like a wine-sack in your side that's important, but it seems you have two of them. I don't know medicine, so I cannot explain, but somehow that cadaverous bastard who had me carried from the field managed to start my heart up again. Then, while I was aware but too weak to fight back, they opened up my body like a kit bag and cut out the wine-sack organ, burning the ends of the bits that bled with sizzling pitch. I saw the damn organ as it was removed. The sword had gone straight through it. It was the most painful, horrifying thing you can imagine. But removing it saved me. *He* saved me, that evil old bastard.'

Another awkward pause.

'*Betatun*, he called his goddess. She is a healer. And you know what, Fronto? Unlike the petty, untouchable gods of Rome, I think Betatun exists. I am the proof. It was months before I could stand and walk and move properly. Even then my muscles had all wasted away and I was a ragged, reedy thing, moving like a child's string puppet. The old magic man smiled the first day I walked out of my cell. He was still smiling as I cut his throat with the stick I'd been sharpening for a week. I cared not, you see. I was a dead man and a slave, and I had nothing to lose. I killed the old man that saved me, and when the Ilergetes found me bathed in his blood, laying his heart at the base of the statue of Betatun, they didn't know what to do. They couldn't kill me, you see. In some odd way I had become sacred, blessed of Betatun. But I had killed their magic man, and they couldn't let that pass. One of their warriors, a big bastard, looked down at the gutted old man – at the wide smile still on his face from seeing me walk – and he took his knife and gave me a smile to match. I took my ruination stoically, silent through the agony. I could manage agony – I'd done it so many times by then. But although they'd defaced me, they couldn't kill me. There was a big argument and in the end they sold me on to another tribe to be rid of me.'

Fronto waited patiently for the next words, trying not to imagine Verginius' torment.

'The Bergistanii were related to the Ilergetes,' the voice picked up again, 'but were also closely linked to the mountain people of Aquitania. The Bergistanii weren't sure what to do with me either. When they discovered that I had been marked by a goddess, I was fought over by the nobles of the tribe, and the king's cousin won me. I killed him a week later with a dagger I'd fashioned from a goat's bone I took from a feast table and sharpened. I took out his heart and gave it to Betatun. When they found me, they beat me near to death, but stopped sensibly just short. They shut me in a wooden cage to keep me out of trouble. I spent a year in that cage, barely big enough to sit up in, fed on scraps and slops, sitting in my own filth. But for all my confinement, I constantly shifted and moved and tensed my muscles to prevent the atrophy happening again.'

Another pause with a strange sigh.

'One night, the king had a feast. When it was over they were all drunk, most of the nobles draped snoring around his hall. A little boy came to my cage, curious. I noticed that he was wearing my old *fascines* pendent – the one Faleria had given me for luck. He came too close and I managed to grab it through the bars of my cage. The boy tried to scream for help, but I twisted the pendant on the thong, throttling him, cutting off all sound. I killed the boy there and then with my own pendant. Pulling the body over to the bars I found a small eating knife on him and with half an hour's hard work I cut the bindings on my cage so that some of the timber could be forced apart. For the first time in a year I was free.'

'What I did that night in that hall would shock Hades himself. I *swam* in blood. I killed them all, individually, personally, slowly, and silently. While their brethren slept, drunk, I removed them one by one. And each one's heart I cut out and piled up in the fire as an offering to Betatun so that the whole hall began to smell like roasting meat, choking and thick. And then, because I knew that with my fascines back my luck had returned, I began to cut off their manhood. I hung them from a standard I found near the throne for luck. And you know what, Marcus? It worked.'

There was silence again for a moment, and Fronto and Galronus exchanged sour looks.

'When I emerged, drenched in blood and carrying a standard covered in noble's cocks, I happened to come face to face with the king of the Arenosio, who was half a day late for the feast, held up by snow in the passes but determined to attend. I'm not sure whether they thought I was some kind of god or some kind of demon, but they were clearly in awe of me. My luck was holding, too. There had been something of a schism among the ruling families of the Arenosio. Two or three of their chiefs who were related to the king thought their master weak and coveted his throne. There had been fights and while the little war was over there were many nobles dissatisfied with the result. The Arenosio king had the hall checked and, when it had become clear what I had done, he ordered me killed. No one would do it. Then Ategnio stepped forward. He was a cousin of the king, too, and he looked me up and down and told the king I could not be killed. When the king demanded that Ategnio be slain too, it erupted into a fight. Half an hour later the king and his followers lay dead and Ategnio and his companions were the surviving power in the tribe. Ategnio had me hailed as the new leader. He saw something in me and he has been my loyal second ever since.'

'So you've been living as king of the Arenosio for what? Eight or nine years? Why not contact the authorities in that time, tell them you were alive?'

There was a snort in the darkness. 'I told you: Verginius was *dead*. He died on that field. But more than once in the horror that followed I vowed vengeance on both Caesar and you for what you had done. Caesar for sending us, unprepared, to our doom, and you for leaving me there and saving your own skin. I think Betatun heard my vows. It is why she saved me time and again and why even now, when the Arenosio are beaten, I am still here facing you.'

'So are you going to kill me, Verginius?'

'Kill you? Gods, no. It's not that simple. What revenge would there be in your death? No. Death is paltry. What happened to me goes way beyond death. And my revenge will come, but I felt it important that you knew the tale first – that you know what happened to me, all because you dropped me in a panic and ran. I'd have died if you took me back, and that would have been so much better than what I endured. No. Not kill you.'

'Verginius, there can still be a good end to this.'

Now there was a bark of laughter from the shadows. 'In what way, Marcus? You'll take me back to Rome? To Faleria where we can have children and live out a happy patrician life? Hardly.'

Next to Fronto, Galronus tensed and rose, his knuckles whitening on the grip of both swords as he started to step down the stairs until Fronto reached out and grabbed his arm. The silence this time was leaden with import.

'I see. This Belgian is Faleria's now? Fascinating. I imagine she mourned for some time, though.'

'Every day for most of a decade,' Fronto said bitterly. 'She never married.'

'But now this man wants her? Is he a citizen? Has Caesar made him Roman. I hear he does that. Fear not for Faleria, Fronto. I could never be hers now. I have been the smiling king of the Arenosio too long. But this is between Fronto and me, Belgian. Run home to Faleria and comfort her. She'll need it soon enough.'

Galronus snarled something in his own language and Fronto frowned in surprise and incomprehension.

'Ha. Your language is rather odd, Remi,' Verginius said, 'to a man weaned on the tongue of the mountain men. I see you carry my sword. You have no idea what I went through to retrieve that. It had been kept by the Ilergetes along with my armour and it took me two years and a lot of threats and favours to retrieve it. I had planned to use it on Caesar when he came, but of course it wasn't

Caesar in the end. It was Fronto, and death by the blade would be too simple for Marcus. But you have to leave that sword here when you run home to Faleria, though, Belgian. If she sees it she will know it for mine, and that will cause her unnecessary pain.'

Galronus took another step forward down the stairs toward the stage, and Fronto rose and grabbed his arm again.

'No, Galronus. It won't help. He has his men with him. This Ategnio at the least.' He turned back to the stage and raised his voice.

'So what happens now, Verginius?'

Silence stretched across the theatre. 'He's gone,' Galronus said quietly, and as Fronto let go of his arm the two men jogged down toward the stage. As they went, Galronus passed Fronto his sword, and the two of them crossed the orchestra and bounded up onto the stage, searching the place. Three curtained doorways led through the scene building and into the rooms at the rear where the actors would assemble. In the middle one they found the exterior door open. Dipping through it, they glanced this way and that along the narrow alley below the brick wall of a tall warehouse. The alley was empty.

'What do we do now?' Galronus muttered, angrily.

'We move about carefully. Whatever I said and however I intended things to go, it seems I am still, inevitably, playing Verginius' game. I don't know what the goal is, but it seems not to be death, and he's not after you. We stay alert for his next move and we try and get every eye and ear in the city on our side so that we can hope to anticipate it. What did you say to him in your own language?'

'I called him a... I don't think I can say it in Latin. It's something you need to be pretty agile to do, and you need a very pliable goat.'

And despite everything, Fronto couldn't help laughing.

Early Junius

Verginius peered down at the wooden lump he had been whittling. It had formed into a rudimentary human shape now. He'd not decided entirely who it would be, though, since he was whittling largely to keep his mind from wandering to subjects with which he was ill prepared to deal. It felt somehow disrespectful to make it the goddess who had preserved him, and he had little care or veneration for the other deities of the local tribes. And the Roman gods had clearly turned their backs on him when Fronto did. He still had the Nemesis figure around his neck, though. It was the twin of Fronto's and that was important. It had taken him longer to retrieve that than his sword, for the cold lady of vengeance alone of all Rome's pantheon still came to him and soothed his heart. Perhaps he would make a Nemesis figurine for Ategnio.

'I am done with this,' said a nervous voice by the window.

Verginius turned slowly. As his eyes scoured the room in passing, they took in the body of the man hanging dead from the wall. A rather fat, sweaty Roman by the long-winded name of Gaius Domitius Gemellus Nascae Priscianus – one of the *ordo*, the ruling council, of Tarraco. In Verginius' experience it was those who felt the need to prove a lineage who pushed for every name they could achieve, his own father and family being a case in point. Priscianus was one of those men who had been tasked with the resettlement of the Ilergetes and the recovery of Roman resources after the revolt over a decade ago. Specifically, he was given the region of the battle itself and the local settlements. He had spent as little time as possible on the task, though, and even *less* effort or finance. It had been Priscianus who had not devoted any resources to retrieving the dead from the site of the battle or setting up a monument to the lost. Instead, he had siphoned off the money meant for such things to help pay for this spacious place on the edge of Tarraco and in the end it had been Fronto, oddly, who had commemorated the event. Still, Priscianus had now paid the price for his greed and laziness and in the process had provided Verginius and his people with a place to hole up that would never occur to Fronto.

Finally, his roving eyes fell upon the speaker.

'Gerexo? You have something to share with us?'

The warrior had the good sense to look thoroughly edgy. The last man who had denied Verginius had paid for it badly.

'I made no vow to a god. I promised you, my king, when you *were* my king. But the Arenosio are beaten. They are gone, and you are no longer king. My vow is done. It is void. So are those of the others. You are dragging us along on some personal revenge against a man we don't even know. And we are dying for it. And what will we get out of it in the end? Nothing. *Because* you are no longer the king. Come on, you lot... join me. Why should we die for this man now?'

'Because a vow is a vow, and vows are all sacred,' Verginius said in little more than a whisper. '*All* of them.'

'And when Fronto has paid we shall rise again,' Ategnio said in a flat tone. 'The Arenosio were nothing. A small mountain tribe who fought each other so much we were not powerful enough to worry anyone else. Then the gods brought us the smiling king. And we became the lords of the mountains, rulers of a score of tribes. So what if we lost that? Verginius rose from slavery to rule us all. You think he cannot do it again?'

There were nods of agreement from others in the room, though Verginius kept his mouth shut, his hard eyes on Gerexo. There would be no coming back. He knew it. This was the end of the game, and there was no return. But let Ategnio think it, and let him tell the others what their bruised egos needed to hear if it made them follow. What did Verginius care? But what he *did* care about was oath-breakers. It was why he would see his long-standing vows regarding Fronto and Caesar through to the end whatever his personal feelings. He *had* to. Otherwise what was he? Little more than walking meat.

'Gerexo, you took an oath. You made a vow. Such things are not lightly done, and they can only be released, not broken. A broken oath is a sacrilege to god and to man. It would make you worthless. *Less* than human. Only animals cannot understand why a vow must be kept, and so only animals can be excused from one. Are you an animal, Gerexo, to be free of conscience? Or are you a man, who is bound by his word?'

'Piss off,' the warrior said, false bravado rising in him, though his eyes still held that nervous taint.

'I see,' Verginius said quietly, rising to his feet. Gerexo took a step back, and the rest of the warriors moved away from him. In a show of disarming himself, Verginius put his whittling knife down on the table and held up the half-formed wooden figurine.

'This, Gerexo, is going to be Nemesis, the Roman goddess of vengeance. The only goddess or god of Rome who still watches over me. I am making her for Ategnio.' He strolled across the room, one hand held out peaceably, the other cradling the half-formed figurine. Gerexo peered intently at the wooden shape even as Verginius swung it up, changing his grip as he did so, forming it into a shapeless ligneous dagger, which he drove into the stunned warrior's temple. Gerexo started to shake, still on his feet, as Verginius turned and strode back across the room.

'A vow is a vow. An oath is an oath. You live by them like a human or you die breaking them like an animal. Now, someone take him down to the *cucina* and prepare him for the evening meal.'

'You want to… *eat* him?' asked one of the other warriors, shocked, even as Gerexo finally toppled forward to the floor, shaking and bucking in his terrible death.

'You heard: he is not a human. He is an animal. And we eat animals, don't we? And then also there will be no suspicious Arenosio body to bring Fronto to our doorstep. Now hurry, my man. You are oath-bound to me. Wouldn't want to break your oath to me, would you?'

Shocked, but suddenly driven to action by the appalling inference they might be next, two of the men approached the body and one leaned over and pommel-bashed the shaking warrior on the head with his sword, putting Gerexo out of his misery.

'Off to the kitchens now, swiftly. And I presume the rest of us are all good, vow-keeping humans, yes?'

Nods are silent, and the room was quiet as the tomb.

Chapter Fourteen

FRONTO strode across to the colonnade, then into the shadows beneath and through the open door with Galronus close behind. He was finally attired in his normal clothes – a striped tunic denoting his rank, a military belt, though without the weapons, fine boots and a white linen cloak. Galronus wore similar garments, and few who didn't know him would be able to tell his Gallic origins.

'Ah good, you got my message,' murmured Rubrius Callo, waving them in. His voice dropped to little more than a whisper. 'My clients are in the next room. No amount of common sense seems to seep through the bone of their heads into their brains. Neither of them is willing to settle for anything less than the total, and neither trusts a man who turns up out of the blue offering them a lot of money. On that point, at least I feel they are onto something, and sadly I do not know anything about you myself to reassure them. I thought that if perhaps you were to speak to them directly, we could move this whole matter toward a swift conclusion.'

'Nothing would please me more,' Fronto replied, keeping his own tone low.

'I am glad you have decided to dress appropriately. Our last encounter did little to promote your good breeding, if I may be frank.'

Fronto smiled. 'Yesterday we were deliberately keeping our identities hidden from someone in the city. That issue has partially resolved itself and we now have no reason to hide ourselves. Your bruising is healing well, Rubrius Callo.'

'Thank you,' smiled the lawyer. 'Regular visits to the baths, poultices of raw meat and a regular suffusion of herbs steeped in very expensive wine seem to be doing the trick. One day we will have a proper circus in Tarraco, with seating, and no one will have to stand in a sweaty crowd, jostled by the lowlifes of the town.'

'I look forward to the day,' replied Fronto as the lawyer strolled across and opened the next door. Fronto and Galronus followed him in.

Two well-dressed, coiffured and manicured young men sat behind the desk in the next room, sipping wine as they sampled pastries from a fine plate. Fronto took an instant dislike to them on sight. Though both men looked up and neither was dressed quite as well as Fronto, neither rose in deference to a man clearly their social superior. In fact, they made no attempt at greeting at all, merely launching into more of Callo's pastries and washing it down with wine.

'Gaius and Tertius Dolabella, may I present Marcus Falerius Fronto and his companion the Remi prince Galronus.'

'What's a Remi?' snorted one of the boys through a mouthful of pastry.

'*I* am,' barked Galronus taking a step forward and leaning on the table with both hands. The lad recoiled, though there was more distaste in his expression than fear. Fronto's hatred of the pair increased to dangerous levels.

'Gentlemen, please let's keep this civil,' said Rubrius Callo with an ingratiating smile, gesturing to the two seats opposite the nephews.

''The domini Dolabella wish firstly to know with whom they are speaking. Names only carry weight if they are familiar, you see.'

Fronto nodded and took a seat, Galronus sinking into the chair beside him, his eyes carrying daggers into those of the boy who'd annoyed him.

'I am Marcus Falerius Fronto, former tribune in the service of the Quaestor of Hispania Ulterior, son of one of the ordo of Puteoli in Campania, veteran of Gaul and former legate of Caesar's Tenth Legion Equestris, vanquisher of Vercingetorix and conqueror of Aquitania,' – that bit might be stretching things, but these boys would only be impressed by titles – 'son-in-law of the former legate of the Eighth legion, Quintus Lucilius Balbus, descendant of the gens Valerius, and former colleague and friend of your uncle Longinus, with whom I served against the Helvetii and Ariovistus. This is my associate Galronus, a prince of Rome's greatest ally north of the Alps, the Remi, a Roman landholder and shortly to be a member of the equestrian order.'

Galronus didn't *look* like a member of the equestrian order right now. He looked like a murderer eyeing up his next target, and Fronto had to bite his cheek to stop himself from smiling at the sight of the young lad opposite who had started to sweat uncontrollably under the Remi's glare. His friend was apparently made of sterner stuff and was unimpressed at the long lineage and list of titles. Or possibly just too thick to register the value of it.

'So you knew our uncle, who could have increased the family's position and holdings in Hispania and Rome, but instead went flouncing off into Gaul with that big-nosed would-be dictator, fighting hairy barbarians no one cares about a thousand miles from civilisation. I'm not impressed.'

'Then you fucking well *should* be,' snapped Fronto, rising to his feet, eyes blazing. The boy leaned back from the force of Fronto's anger, almost falling off his chair, his face blanching.

'Your uncle,' Fronto went on in little more than a growl, 'died like a true Roman on the field of battle, for the glory of his legion and of the republic. You aunt was a good woman, and looked after myself and a young man called Crispus for the winter after that campaign. We were good friends. How she could have been so short-sighted as to leave their precious estate to the pair of you is beyond me. I can only assume she was blinded to the truth by your ties as family. I am less blind.'

'Your offer,' prompted the other one, trying not to meet the gaze of Galronus, who had yet to look anywhere but straight at him.

'My offer stands. The villa was worth four hundred thousand sestertii at the passing of your aunt, with all land and property and slaves. The value, while the pair of you have argued and dithered, has declined to around three hundred and fifty thousand, or so Rubrius Callo informs me. Thus at the moment, if you agreed to split the proceeds, you would receive at most one hundred and seventy five apiece. If you could agree on one owner, even he would be lucky to make three hundred and fifty. Property takes some time to sell, usually, and the value will steadily fall throughout the process.'

The other boy reached out and shook his brother's arm, pointing at Galronus, who had started to growl under his breath.

'I,' Fronto went on, 'wish to see your uncle and aunt's mausoleum continually tended and maintained. I wish to see the villa thrive and be respected and valued. And because of my ties to your sadly-depleted family, I am willing to pay over the odds to see that happen. I can free six hundred thousand within a month and am willing to sign any deal Rubrius Callo comes up with to that effect as soon as you both agree. That is three hundred thousand sestertii each. More than you will get any other way.'

'Make it four hundred thousand each and I'll sign,' the stronger of the two said. His brother, wide-eyed, shook his head urgently. Galronus' growling was getting louder. The young man began to edge his chair away.

'That would be twice the villa's worth. I am not that inclined to support your future dissolute and self-indulgent lives by that amount. I am quite serious about my offer. You now know who I am. There will be no increase in the offer and there will be no other offer. I doubt any other resident in the area can come close to the asking price. Six hundred thousand is my only offer and I give you one day until I withdraw it, following which I will refer your disrespect over the tomb of a Roman veteran and hero to the former governor and ex-consul Metellus Nepos, who is a friend of both Caesar and your deceased uncle and will be most distressed to hear of the situation.'

He smiled sweetly at the two boys. 'I know you're of noble Roman blood and that is an important thing to remember, but only if you back it with a noble soul. You think you're big fish in the small pond of Tarraco, but think on this: I am a big fish in a much bigger pond and I'm about to open the sluice gate between them. Is that what you want? Think about three hundred thousand sestertii apiece. Within a year you could have caught every venereal disease going and drunk yourselves to death, which will go a long way to appeasing me. And perhaps then Galronus will not be inclined to peel you and turn you inside out for offending him and his people, which I suspect is his intention right now.'

The more outspoken of the two looked across at Galronus and his face paled. The other boy was almost back at the office's rear wall now.

'One day,' Fronto said, slapping both hands on the table and making the pair jump in their chairs. 'Speak to Rubrius Callo with your answer. Good day, both of you.'

And with that he rose and walked out of the office, through the outer room and into the light of the square. Galronus followed him and the pair crossed the square, collected their horses, and then moved through the gate and out of the upper city. Only as that gate closed behind them did Fronto explode with laughter.

'I honestly thought the smaller one was going to shit himself. When did you get so scary?' he said, wiping his eyes.

Galronus grinned evilly. 'He was annoying me. If the lawyer hadn't been there, he'd have left with a bruised face to match Rubrius Callo's. Do you think they'll accept?'

Fronto shrugged. 'I'd like to think so. They'd be stupid not to, but then we know that they *are* stupid, so who can tell?'

Galronus' brow furrowed. 'Do you need me for a while?'

'Nothing specific planned. Why?'

'I thought I might follow them around a bit. Pop up here and there as a gentle reminder. The older one might be brave enough, but I reckon the little one would sign his own head over to me if it would make me go away.'

Fronto laughed. 'You might be right. Be careful, though. Don't get into any trouble. I'll see you back at the villa by sunset.'

Galronus nodded and turned, wandering up toward the upper city's gate, where he leaned on a post and waited. Fronto smiled and wandered off down to the town. Time to make some more enquiries and prepare. Perhaps with a drink…

* * *

The *Empty Jar* was another of Fronto's old haunts, though only at the worst of his morose habits. Every city has a bar for the drunk and the miserable, and the Jar was Tarraco's. Sandwiched between a fishmongers and a leather shop, somehow the Jar managed to achieve a smell that outdid both. It exuded an odour reminiscent of one of those alleys where dysenterious creatures went to die of deflation. It looked drab, from its peeling paint that had been graffiti'd repeatedly to its cracked flagstones, and held the air of the lowest quality tavern imaginable. More than this, it served no wine a respectable citizen would drink – just the piss-poor seconds from the lower end of the Hispanic vineyards, and sour posca even legionaries might shun.

It was, on the other hand, *the* place to visit if you had a shady deal to carry out, wanted to hire a member of a dubious profession, were looking for stolen items or fancied a fight with no legal consequences. It was also a hub for rumour and talk, and it was this for which Fronto had chosen it.

At the bar, the woman looked at him suspiciously – or at least one of her eyes looked at him suspiciously, while the other swivelled downwards to peer at her foot. She poured something from a jar into an earthenware cup and Fronto peeked into it, swallowed nervously and paid the pittance for the drink. The liquid sloshed around inside with an oily consistency. Jars sat on each table containing water for the wine, but it was all stagnant, Fronto knew from old visits. It was rarely changed, and none of the inn's clientele bothered to cut their wine with water. If they were *that* sort of drinker, they wouldn't be in the Jar in the first place.

He picked up the cup and turned, sauntering across from the bar, his gaze searching out the occupants. There were the usual collection of drunken lowlifes, ex-legionaries discharged on medical grounds, missing appendages and without a pension, minor criminals or the lackeys of more major ones, and dubious merchants. His eyes fell upon a lad of perhaps twelve years with a scar across his nose, stacking coins on the table. That was the one he was looking for. A lad that age and that poor, clearly with no caring family or home, should not have that kind of money unless he had a good thing going. And that thing was not combat or trade, for he was too thin and reedy for one and two poorly-dressed for the other. So he was a runner or facilitator for the less reputable. Just what Fronto was looking for.

'I've a well-paying task, if you've time on your hands and can keep your lips from flapping,' he said quietly as he sank into a chair opposite the lad. The look the boy gave him weighed him up in one easy move, and Fronto appreciated instantly that the brain whirring behind those eyes was a thousand times faster than those well-dressed cousins up in the lawyer's office.

'I don't do nothing sexy, nor dangerous.'

'Do I look like I would…' Fronto tailed off, realising what he must seem like dressed as a wealthy Roman in this dive. He smiled. 'I'm not interested in that. I want to find a man, and he will already be keeping tabs on me. Have you met a man with a smile carved into his face or mountain tribesmen with big beards in the city these past few days?'

'Now, that strikes me as the sort of information a man might pay for,' the boy said, levelly.

Fronto chuckled. 'You might be right. I have two sestertii here for a basic answer.'

He slid the coins across the table and the lad pursed his lips. 'Well now, I've neither seen nor heard about a man with a carved smile, but I can tell you there's a right hairy warrior with a mountain accent and real poor Latin in the city and he has fingers in every jar of garum in the place now. No one likes him, coz no one likes the mountain folk here, but he pays well enough that he gets away with it. I reckon near every pair of eyes and ears in the city are his. You'll be lucky to get your sights on him without him knowing about it. He's paid me a sizeable amount for news of you, and I've had you pegged in three different inns so far as well as at the upper city and in the baths, but hadn't thought to see you here. Lucky for you, he didn't ask that I not tell anyone about him. Not subtle enough for this game, I reckon.'

Fronto raised an eyebrow. 'So you report on me to him, but for coin you'll also tell me about him. Dangerous game. I thought you didn't do dangerous?'

The boy grinned. 'What's your proposal?'

'Tell me where to find the warrior – where he's staying – and I'll match what's on the table right now. I reckon you've forty sestertii or so stacked there?'

The boy's eyes widened for a moment in surprise. 'That's a tidy sum. Worth considering, but if I betray him, he'll want me dead, and my life's worth more than that. Double, I'd say.'

Fronto nodded. 'Alright, I'm in no mood to haggle. Eighty. Not a coin more. Get me an address and the money's yours.'

With a sly smile, the lad slid his coins from the table into a pouch and nodded. Rising, he crossed to the bar and passed his pouch to the innkeeper, who took it to a back room. The lad then moved out into the street. Fronto nodded approvingly. The boy was bright enough not to carry large amounts of coin around the city on his own.

Leaning back, he took a sip of the wine and winced. If Catháin were here to try it, he'd be appalled. He'd probably only use the stuff to protect boot leather. In fact, it tasted a little like boot leather. Fronto sipped slowly at the cup, waiting for more than half an hour. He'd not arranged anything with the lad, but he'd also not said he'd be back at the villa until sunset, so he was free to mess around. Finally tiring of the dreadful wine, he left the dregs and sauntered out, down through the streets until he found the Tuclian Baths, where he spent an hour relaxing, then had a massage, checking in with the towel boy who seemed very nervous and defensive and claimed to have nothing to report.

Leaving the baths just before noon, he popped into the other tavern on his list and checked in with Parella for news. Like the towel boy she had nothing to report, but the way she was rather lacking in her usual playful banter set Fronto on edge. What the boy had said seemed very likely to be the case. Both the contacts he'd set up when he first arrived in Tarraco were delivering nothing, and both were nervous of something. This bearded warrior. Ategnio, Fronto guessed – Verginius' right hand man – had got to both of them. He was going to have to start being very careful. His enemies seemed to be on the increase, while his ring of friends was shrinking.

Within the hour, fortified with bread and meat from the inn, washed down with a much nicer wine, Fronto strolled back uphill to the Empty Jug. The clientele had changed little during his absence, and he settled back into the same table once he'd ordered a jug of the best wine they did – almost a match for the worst wine Parella sold.

He had lounged, pensive, in the corner of the bar for less than an hour when the door suddenly slammed open, crashing back against a chair, every cup and jug in the bar jumping and shaking with the force of it. Half the occupants of the place lurched back defensively, each with something to hide or something to fear. One even disappeared beneath the table at which he sat. The rest were either innocent of wrongdoings and with nothing to fear, or were simply to drunk, slow and numb to react.

Fronto was immediately alert, wishing he had his sword with him.

It took him a moment to recognise the figure that staggered into the bar. The lad he'd retained at this very table a few hours earlier had been beaten badly, his face bruised black and purple and one eye puffed up and crusted shut. His arm hung limp at his side, and he lurched as though his left leg was about to give way. Fronto rose from the table, his heart in his mouth, but the lad turned and staggered over to him collapsing to lean on the table top.

'Seems they were watching you come here too. Keep your coins.'

Fronto shook his head. 'This is because you spoke to me?'

'Maybe,' the boy admitted, probing a missing tooth with a bloody tongue. 'But they were more interested in your place, I think. They were asking where you were staying.'

Fronto's mind did somersaults as his stomach did back-flips. What did they want to know that for? And surely this lad couldn't answer their question, could he?

'What did you tell them?'

'Everything I know. Sorry.'

'And what *do* you know?' Fronto asked, the panic rising.

'About the boys you saw this morning in the upper city. The lawyer.'

Fronto's stomach curled up and puckered in shock. He had no idea what Verginius had planned for him, but he hadn't considered they might go after the villa. Why? To make Fronto suffer? Was Verginius planning to make Fronto go through what he had? Send him running to a fight where he'd die? He couldn't figure it out, but one thing was certain: Verginius had found out about Longinus' villa, or at least would do any time now, as soon as he talked to the lawyer or one of the cousins, and that would put the occupants of the villa in danger. And Galronus, too. Galronus would be there, waiting for him, unsuspecting, unprepared for an attack. Even Galronus might not be able to fight off Verginius and his men. Shit.

Fronto was up a moment later, his jar of wine forgotten and knocked aside as it fell, spilling its contents across the table. The urgent need to get back to the villa and warn Galronus drove him with such force that he even left his change – a small fortune to the boy – sitting on the table.

Fronto burst through the front door and into the odd light of the street. The wide alley was aligned just so that the lower reaches of it were in deep shadow, while the upper edges of the insulae around them glowed golden in the sun. It was at once dazzling and gloomy, and Fronto's eyes failed to adjust until it was too late. Something connected with the back of his head hard enough to send his wits rolling around the inside of his skull and he fell, smacking his forehead on a cobble for good measure. His mind reeled and whirled in a confused panic. He was surrounded by Arenosio warriors. Three of them. Or four. For some reason his brain couldn't quite work it out and his eyes were unreliable, jumping and misidentifying. Each had a weapon, though, he was sure of that. He rolled onto his back, his mind still jumbled, eyes rolling, unable to send the commands to his legs to stand.

The wounded boy was standing in the door.

'Sorry, mister. Didn't like doin' it, but business is business, and I can only take one good hiding from a customer.'

With that, the lad re-entered the inn, closing the door behind him, and Fronto was alone on the ground in a side street with three mountain warriors.

'I...' he couldn't speak properly, and realised he'd bitten into his tongue when he hit the cobbles, his mouth full of blood. He spat the coppery life onto the stones and tried again. 'Where... Verginius.'

He was rewarded with another crack around the head from a hard leather boot, and as his mind spun once more, another heavy foot trod on his left wrist, grinding this way and that agonisingly. He was lost. There was simply no hope of fighting back. On a good day, he'd think of taking on three barbarians, but not with his brain rolling around in his head like a pea in a pot. He couldn't even remember how to stand. Fortunately, it appeared that he didn't need to. Heavy, calloused hands grasped him by the wrists and dragged him across the street and into the open door of an abandoned shop. The building was clearly having some sort of renovation work done, and Fronto's eyes swivelled this way and that, trying to find some hope somewhere. He spotted things – hammers, planks, picks, sheets and chains. Many things that, had he been of sound mind, might be of use. As it was, there was simply no help in anything. Most urgently, he was fighting the urge to throw up. With his wounded tongue and a mouthful of blood, throwing up could be fatal. He could drown. Concentrating on that somehow helped soothe the spinning of his brain, but before he could hope to claim any quantity of true sense, the door slammed behind him, and another figure appeared, silhouetted against a white light.

'Ver... Verginius?'

Somehow, from this angle, the permanent smile on his old friend's face looked a great deal more sinister.

'Do you know what the Jews believe about revenge, Marcus?'

Fronto's brain was still cloudy and confused, and he could do little more than stare, befuddled.

'My personal beliefs in vengeance are founded on two things, Marcus: the patronage of the lady Nemesis which we shared since we both left Rome, and the fairly straightforward notions of the Jews, who believe that vengeance is best enacted on a one-for-one basis. And that is what I have in mind for you.'

'Verginius…'

'Oddly, Marcus, there is a large part of my soul that is begging me to turn aside from this path. Unbelievable that even after a decade and all that has been done to me, part of me still considers you enough of a brother that I should protect you. And I would, Marcus. For Faleria if nothing else. She lost me and she doesn't deserve to lose you too. But a vow is a sacred thing. It cannot be broken and I vowed vengeance on both you and Caesar in the names of two goddesses. That sort of thing cannot be simply ignored. I must carry through my vow, or I am nothing, though it pains me to do it more than anything you can imagine… thus far, at least. But then the pain is only just beginning.'

Suddenly, hands were grasping Fronto's ankles and wrists. Even through the fog of his brain, he fought and struggled, aware that something awful was about to happen.

'It took me a long time to find my sword and my Nemesis pendant,' Verginius said quietly, drawing the figurine from his tunic and displaying it openly. 'But it took me even longer to find the sword that had killed me. It's owner didn't want to part with it, you see, but I had no compunction about killing that one. He deserved it. And now I want to introduce you to that same blade on a very personal basis.'

Fronto struggled, shouting, only vaguely aware of what he was actually saying, but the warriors' grip on him was solid, and he was still weak and confused from the blows. Verginius looked sad, despite his smile, as he lifted the heavy sword – straight and wide, reminiscent of an old Punic blade – and brought it down, slowly and deliberately. Fronto cried out as he felt it puncture his flesh and then sink into his body until it touched the floor. How long he lay there, screaming at the sword standing proud from his body, he couldn't tell. By the time he was merely whimpering and gasping, the warriors were all together again behind Verginius, who was shaking his head sadly.

'I was run through with that sword. And now so have you been. Painful, isn't it. But in your case I was careful not to hit a vital organ. I don't know anyone with the medical skill of the old man who saved me, and I couldn't risk you just dying there. I know it feels like you are, but that's just a big flesh wound. Blood loss and a bit of pain. And if you'd died, you'd not be privy to what came next, would you?'

Fronto gasped as he grasped the blade and tried in vain to remove it. 'Verginius…'

'Do you remember my tale, Marcus? Do you remember what comes next?'

What? Fronto tried to think, no easy thing when every breath brought sharp blinding pain and his brain was still floundering in the mush of chaotic confusion. 'I…'

'Yes, Marcus. The slavers came for me.' Verginius turned to someone Fronto couldn't quite see. 'He's all yours. I apologise for the condition, but then you are getting him free, so I don't think we have a problem, do we?'

A local accent, Latin with a Hispanic drawl, confirmed there was no problem, and a hairy arm reached down and none-too-gently yanked out the sword, leaving Fronto gasping, weeping and bleeding on the ground. Verginius took the blade gingerly, as though he had no real wish to touch it further. Then arms were pulling Fronto up from the floor. He could feel the blood soaking his tunic thoroughly, even as hands pushed wadding against it and a wrapping was bound round him again and again. His strength seemed to have deserted him utterly.

All was pain. Pain and sadness.

Briefly, he wondered where he was being taken, as those arms pulled him up and dragged him back out of the door, but before his fuddled mind could fathom anything of use, the pain became simply too much and he succumbed to the welcome darkness where the pain faded.

* * *

327

Galronus had started to become concerned as the afternoon sun sank toward the horizon over the distant bulk of the city of Tarraco. He knew Fronto to be anything but prompt by nature but given the current situation he couldn't believe his friend would be so lax without getting word back to the villa. As soon as that yellow-gold globe touched the land, Galronus was off, leaving a list of where he was going with Arius in case he was being overly-worried and Fronto returned in the half-light of dusk. He wouldn't, though, and Galronus knew it. Something was wrong. And all for the sake of those two morons he'd followed around the city, putting the frights up them every time they looked back and saw him standing at a corner. If he'd not frivolously gone after them, he'd have been with Fronto.

Still, he had his plan.

Somehow, Verginius had clearly managed to get to Fronto. It even crossed his mind that somehow the twisted ex-Roman had managed to engineer Galronus' absence, but that was a dead end idea. He had merely taken advantage of the Remi's absence. To find Fronto now, he would have to locate the last place he was and the last person he spoke to. He would find Rubrius Callo first, just in case, but after that it would be Parella in her inn, then the baths and the towel boy. But Fronto had talked about making new contacts, and had probably been in new places. Low, disreputable places. So that would be next.

An hour later, as the evening set in and lamps were lit across the city and having learned from Callo only that the two boys had rather urgently accepted Fronto's offer, the Remi tied up his horse outside the *Leaning Slab*, Parella's bar, adorned with a painted image of a native tomb with a slipped doorway. For a moment he wondered about the wisdom of leaving on the horse the bag of coin he'd brought from the villa as potential bribes, but it was hardly something he could carry if he needed to fight anyone. And he felt sure someone was going to die this evening.

The room fell silent as the door swung open. Galronus had been in here three times now with Fronto, always dressed and equipped as a common nobody. The occupants were startled by his new appearance. He had removed his Roman tunic – though he loved the linen and the quality of the manufacture, and replaced it with a rough woollen one of Gallic origin. He had donned trousers, which he never wore south of the Gallic central mountain range, and he was armed and armoured like a mercenary, his Remi torc around his neck, arm rings in place and an expression of murder on his face. He had borrowed Fronto's fine mail shirt rather than his own, and had his own long Gallic sword holstered awkwardly on his back to leave him room for Verginius' sword on one hip and Fronto's on the other. The pugio he now often wore was uncomfortably hanging next to the sword.

To top it all, he had taken some charcoal dust from the villa's furnace and drawn patterns on his face and arms with it. Not a Remi thing at all, but he knew how such things worried the superstitious Romans.

It was not the sort of look to engender cooperation from the authorities, but then it was not the *authorities* he wanted to cooperate.

The occupants of Parella's bar variously shied away, vanished under tables, or looked on in fascinated readiness to flee. Galronus knew his personality had been rather altered by his exposure to Rome, but he had held proud to his Remi stance on women. Despite the examples of his friends, Galronus knew Romans often treated their women harshly. He, however, respected the more delicate sex, and would usually shy away from harming a woman. But there were some times when such niceties had to be brushed aside. Parella was smiling as she polished the bar, though the grin slipped as Galronus stomped across the room, jingling, his armour shushing and the sword clunking, and smacked one calloused fist on the timber.

'Fronto has vanished. If *you* know nothing about it, you know *someone* who does. Tell me.'

Parella had the grace to look embarrassed, even apologetic, then looked around conspiratorially as the pair were being listened in on.

'There's a big Arenosio warrior has the city stitched up tight. No one knows where to find him, but everyone's frightened of him.'

'Who might know where to find him?'

The woman shivered. 'I don't know,' and as Galronus started to rise to an impressive, threatening height, she blurted out 'but if anyone does ,they'll be at the Empty Jug.'

'Where is this Empty Jug?'

Moments later, he was outside, stomping off through the city with his hand on his steed's reins, and it seemed like only moments of seething and worrying before he turned a corner and smelled the bar before he even saw it. It smelled like an old sock into which someone had ejected from both ends.

He was tying his horse to an iron ring on the wall, about to march into the place, when something caught his eye. In the poor light cast by the torch beside the tavern's door, he spotted marks on the floor. Blood, some hours old and now dried, but definitely today's. Of course, blood outside a place such as this would hardly be unusual, but when combined with the potential that Fronto could have been here, casting his net wider, Galronus was convinced that the dried blood marked Fronto's meeting with a cobble. His eyes played around the narrow street and fell upon the deserted shop opposite, its original name whitewashed out, its windows shuttered. There was a fine spatter mark on the door. At the tavern, he wrenched their pitch-dipped sizzling torch from its bracket, crossed the road and tried the door. The shop opened easily, and he found himself in a deserted building site... a building site with a tale to tell. More dried blood, and now something new. A small pool that had not yet dried. Perhaps three hours old, he thought, maybe four. This was not blood from a beating, but from a true wounding.

Galronus' grip tightened on the handle of Verginius' gladius. Fronto was wounded. They had beaten him, dragged him out of sight and then hurt him badly. Not killed. There wasn't enough blood for that, and it wasn't Verginius' style. Besides, the body would have to be dragged, and from the drips and spatters, it looked like the wounded Roman had walked out, probably only with a lot of help, though. But to where?

Galronus was angry. Angrier than he had ever been. Fronto was his *brother*, damn it. No... Fronto was closer than a brother. Galronus had *actual* brothers, and yet they were less in his eyes. Fronto was his friend, too. A true friend. And the Remi would rip Hispania apart and tear pieces off Verginius to find him.

By the time he emerged into the street again, he had one gladius in each hand. He burst through the door of the Empty Jug like the wrath of the Furies, bristling with weapons and belligerence. The population managed a fascinating array of reactions. Some ran, others backed away. Some hid. A young man in the corner with bad facial bruising almost leapt out of his skin, and one particularly large Roman thug with a club bumbled toward him, growling.

'Who in Hades do you think you are?' the Roman roared, raising his club threateningly.

Galronus cut his hand off with Fronto's sword and swung Verginius' upwards from the waist, arresting its deadly arc as the tip touched the thug's throat apple from below.

'I am Galronus of the Remi, and if you want to see the dawn back... the fuck... away.'

The huge man wilted like a daisy in the parched sun, shrinking back, tossing away his club and raising his remaining hand even as blood sluiced from the severed stump. Galronus, instantly losing interest in the damaged thug, turned. The wounded boy. Blood on the street... blood in the shop... blood on the boy. Coincidence?

'Where is Marcus Falerius Fronto?'

The lad shrank back against the wall, an expression of terror crossing his face, but Galronus' eyes narrowed. He knew intelligence when he saw it. The lad was putting on a show. Already his eyes – one of which was a barely-open slit – were shielding a mind calculating his best way out of this situation.

Galronus loomed over the table and raised his sword. The boy stared at him, seemingly unable to ascertain whether this was merely threat or true danger. Well, he'd learn soon enough.

Galronus' sword slammed down into the table, driving through the old, worm-eaten wood, and driving through the boy's thigh beneath. The lad screamed, and Galronus heard the scrape of several chairs behind him as other patrons rose. Still with a sword through a table and a human leg, he turned his fiery gaze on the bar. 'Anyone comes within sword range of me and I'll send you to Charon in so many pieces he'll need an abacus to make sure you're across the river entire.'

The various unpleasant figures faltered for a moment, then backed away once more. Galronus turned to the boy and was pleased to see that all guile and façade seemed to have melted away. The lad was now genuinely terrified.

'One question: where is Marcus Falerius Fronto? And don't try to deny anything, coz I saw the recognition of the name in your eyes then. Tell me where he is and I might not use another blade.'

He let go of Verginius' sword, leaving the leg pinned and the boy weeping.

'I don't know.'

'Wrong answer,' Galronus barked as he lifted the other blade.

'I really don't. I *really* don't know!' the lad shouted desperately. 'But I can tell you who will.'

The tip of Fronto's blade hovered a finger-width from the boy's eye and he swallowed nervously. 'If he finds out I sent you…'

'He'll not be in a position to cause trouble, lad. And if you *don't* send me, then whatever he might do to you will seem like an afternoon with a pink girlie from Narbo compared with what *I'll* do to you.'

The boy weighed up his chances for only a moment.

'There are three of them – big mountain warriors, led by someone who never comes out in public. I don't know where they're staying, but I have an arrangement. I hang a red scarf on the statue of Marius at the end of the port, and they come and find me. They're your men. They'll know where he is.'

Galronus nodded and leaned back, removing the sword point from near the boy's watering eye. He then wrenched the blade from the leg, out through the splintered table and wiped it on the rag at his belt.

'I strongly advise you all forget this happened and stay here for at least another two drinks. If I find any of you have followed me I shall not be pleased.'

A moment later, he was outside the bar, untying his steed, mounting and trotting off for the docks. It was a long chance, but the best he had. What if Verginius and his men had left the city? What if, now that they had Fronto, they didn't need the boy any more?

No. This was Verginius, the smiling demon king. This was the man who had set traps and planned a whole rebellion just to draw Caesar into Aquitania. He would not be finished yet. He still had Caesar to revenge himself upon, and somehow Galronus doubted he himself would be free of the lunatic's attentions entirely. At the very least there would be a man left in touch.

The darkness had truly set in by the time he had hung a red soldier's scarf on the statue and then ridden hurriedly away and backed his steed into a dark alleyway.

He waited. The sound of the sea slapping the dock and the groan and creak of a dozen moored vessels mesmerised him as he watched ceaselessly, occasional citizens wandering back and forth about their own business, even though the port was quiet, business shut down for the day. The better part of an hour had gone by when the first character took notice of the scarf. He was no Arenosio warrior, but he was the first person wandering past who was not drunk, busy, or tired and hurrying home. The figure was a lad of maybe seven summers, and Galronus would have paid him no attention had he not crossed the open space and climbed the statue, clearly making for the scarf. It was just a ragged soldier's scarf and of no value, even to a beggar. Galronus watched with narrowed eyes. The boy fondled the scarf for a moment, and then ran off.

Damn it. Galronus was faced with a choice. Follow the boy or watch the scarf? Either might be the right choice, but for some reason the sheer purpose with which the boy had gone to the statue suggested his involvement, while loitering here was uncertain in its efficacy at best.

Chewing irritably over the decision, Galronus slid from the horse, tying it to a shutter hinge on a warehouse, then quickly jogged out of the dark alley and across to the end of the street up which the boy had run. Over the shushing of his own chain shirt and the jangle and clatter of his weapons – sneaking was clearly not an option – he lost the sound of the boy, and as he turned the corner he faced a street devoid of urchins. A few folk with purpose or a skinful of wine wandered the street and a disfigured legionary sat by a dilapidated door with a bowl containing a pitiful few coins, displaying his half a leg in hope. Galronus ran up to the soldier and fished two sestertii from his belt pouch, holding them up in front of the man's face.

'A boy, running. Where did he go?'

The legionary looked hungrily at the coins and pointed to a side street up away from the docks, heading north toward the city's edge. Galronus nodded his thanks and dropped the coins into the bowl. A few moments later he was at that street. Houses and shops led off from each side, but they petered out halfway along. The latter half of the street was sided by bare walls, then an expensive looking house frontage. Galronus frowned. Something was out of place, and he couldn't quite work out what it was. Quickly, he looked back up and down the main street then back at the house, and it struck him. The city was dark, and every house had lamps or torches to light their doors, unless they were too poor to do so. This house was both wealthy and dark. There could, of course, be any number of explanations, but somehow Galronus couldn't put it down to abandonment or absence. The rich had slaves and kept everything running even when they were not there. This house should not be dark.

There were some times when Roman civility and subtlety just had to be pushed aside and replaced with brute force and directness. Building up pace into a run, Galronus hit the front door of the house with all his weight, the interior latch splintering and bending, the whole leaf of wood slamming inwards against the wall. The interior was lit with only a single oil lamp in a delicate atrium just ahead past the house's altars, and it illuminated two figures. The boy was already turning to leave again, but the warrior was busy shouting at him, his tirade cut short by the explosion of the door. Galronus didn't stop, though his shoulder ached terribly from the timbers, and he ran into the atrium, hitting the warrior square-on even as the man drew his sword. The pair of them plunged into the small, square pool at the room's centre, Galronus atop his target. The warrior tried to bring his sword to bear, but he simply couldn't find the room in the small pool with this maniac on top of him. Galronus, however, had given himself to the rage of Taranis, thunder drumming in his veins, lightning flashing in his eyes. He knelt up, his knees on the warrior's chest.

'Where is Fronto?'

Without waiting for a reply he stabbed down with both swords, each raking along the man's scalp, narrowly missing a killing blow, but both agonisingly cutting a deep furrow along his head, blood and hair washing out into the water of the pool. The warrior screamed. The blades still standing in his flesh, Galronus yanked them downwards, cutting off both ears, then flung the swords across the room and grabbed the warrior by his oozing, ruined scalp.

'Fronto! Where is he?'

The warrior burbled something, but defiance was creeping back into his expression.

'Not good enough. Where is he?' Galronus turned the head until the face dipped into the water, and held it there, the man's face panicked and wide-eyed in the increasingly opaque pink water. Galronus saw the sign of desperation in the face and realised he was about to draw a drowning breath, then pulled the head back out. The warrior gasped and coughed.

'Fronto!'

'Slave… trader…' the man coughed.

'Where?'

'Carthago… Nova.'

Galronus frowned. The name was not familiar, though it had something to do with Carthage, obviously. It mattered not – *someone* would tell him. He looked into the warrior's eyes and the rage resurfaced for a moment. This was one of the men who had caused all this trouble, who had taken Fronto and wounded him. Slowly, deliberately, he lowered the face into the water again as the warrior panicked and thrashed. He was bigger than Galronus, stronger too, but Taranis was in the Remi's veins now, filling him with god-like power. Perhaps Nemesis was there too, after all his time with Fronto. There was no mercy in him, and he held the man there until he stopped moving. Nemesis had been served, but Taranis was still in his veins and would be until Fronto was by his side once more.

He turned. The boy was standing near the door. He'd not run, which surprised Galronus, though he did look utterly terrified.

'Carthago Nova. Where is it?'

'Hundreds o' miles, master. South. Along the coast.'

'Go home. Find safer work.'

Leaving the boy to his own devices, Galronus ran out into the street once more and jogged back toward the port and his horse, hoping the very presence of a small sack of coins had not drawn thieves to it. The slavers would have only a few hours' head start, and they would move slow. They couldn't have gone more than ten miles, he reckoned, and they would be following the main coast road, for there was nothing illegal in their trade.

And that was an obstacle he was going to have to overcome: slave traders were legal and protected with the same rights as any other business under Roman law. Admittedly, Fronto should not be among their cargo, but that was not *their* doing. It would be unworthy to load upon the traders the guilt that should lie solely with Verginius and his men. But law or no law, Fronto was coming home tonight.

* * *

Galronus peered at the encampment. The slaves were still locked up in their wagons, purpose-built affairs like strong wooden cages on wheels, with a latrine hole the width of a man's palm allowing the cargo to defecate on the move and keep their cage relatively clean. Now, they had been encamped for several hours and already the smell from beneath the three wagons was strong enough to waft on the night breeze across the outskirts of Oleastrum.

The slavers had camped close to the shore, between the beach and a farmstead with a small two-winged villa, perhaps a quarter of a mile from the town itself. No one liked slave caravans to camp on their doorstep, but the beach was clearly not owned by the farm, and the slavers had made use of the tree-spotted open land.

The three wagons were in a rough arc around a fire where the merchant and his men sat, their tents making up a matching arc on the far side. These traders were taking no chances. The three wagons each held between twelve and twenty slaves, crammed in, but despite their secure cages there was also a guard of fifteen men that Galronus had counted, with two thirds of their number alert and on duty at any given time. His heart had sunk when he realised this would not be a simple retrieval carried out by violence, or by the threat of it. Two or three men he could deal with, or a whole room of men who would react well to threat. But these were professionals, several of them ex-legionaries, no doubt, and they would not be cowed easily. And they would fight well and die hard.

But need they die at all? the Remi thought as he loitered by a tree, close to the beach, and listened to the laughter of the merchants and the keening of their cargo in the wagons. Romans were usually willing to listen to reason, and merchants doubly so, especially if money was involved, and Galronus had enough money on his horse to buy a full wagon from that caravan, by his reckoning. The question was: did these merchants have a hand in Fronto's downfall and therefore everything to lose by his freedom, or were they simply merchants who would always consider the best business opportunity?

He settled his swords in place, a gladius at each side, though he had left his Gallic sword on the horse. It was not easy riding with it on his back, as he'd quickly found out. Stepping out from behind the tree, he led his horse by the reins with his other hand resting on a sword pommel. He might be trying to do this peaceably, but he had to be prepared for trouble. He'd not crossed half the tree-spotted sward before a shout of warning went up from a guard and three men converged on him.

'I wish to speak to your master,' he said evenly, looking past them at the men by the fire. They were swarthy men, he noticed, not locals. Probably from Africa across the water. One of them nodded at the guard and rose. The three ex-soldiers escorted Galronus to the camp, and moments later he was face to face with the lead slaver, their features lit orange by the firelight.

'I believe you have a slave that belongs to someone else, and I wish to purchase them.'

The slaver frowned. 'This is not a market. Find us at Dertosa or Saguntum and we'll happily sell to you at market. This is just the overnight camp of a caravan, and we do not trade now.'

'Come now,' Galronus smiled, 'surely business is business and a price could be agreed?'

'What do you want with a slave in the night anyway?' asked a second, younger man coming to stand next to the merchant. 'This is all very suspicious.'

'I want a *particular* slave, as I said,' Galronus replied, his eyes flicking to the wagons. He'd not yet spotted Fronto in the crowded cages, but was sure he was there, nonetheless.

'I don't like this, uncle,' the second man said, but the merchant waved him into silence. 'Specific needs can be expensive.'

'I have money. And no slave is *too* expensive these days, since Caesar flooded the markets with Gauls.'

The merchant laughed. 'I don't know what you've heard, stranger, and that may be true in Rome or Gaul, but precious few of the proconsul's captives come to Hispania. There's no glut here, and prices are good as ever. This slave... she's a looker?'

'She's a *he*,' Galronus said flatly.

'A gladiator? I have a few. One musician, two who can read and scribe and know their histories, if you're after a tutor.'

'How much are your gladiators?' Galronus probed.

'Varies,' shrugged the merchant.

'Four thousand for our Thracian retiarius,' blurted the younger one. 'And he's a champion.'

The merchant flashed his nephew an irritated look. 'Varies,' he repeated.

'Let me look for the one I'm after, and we'll talk money.'

The merchant paused for a moment, then nodded. The small party wandered across to the wagons, where desperate, thin, grubby arms reached between the bars imploringly. Galronus wandered along the sides, peering in. It was hard to see in the gloom. The nephew obligingly lifted a torch to illuminate the stock, and the party moved to the second wagon. They were about to pass to the third when Galronus felt his heart lurch. There was a patch of blood next to the bars of the wagon, a few drips running down the side to the wheel. He stopped and peered carefully inside. Fronto was lying on the wagon floor, dressed only in an unbelted tunic of grey that looked to be made from a sack. He was wrapped with bandages, but already the blood blossomed on the dirty wrappings.

'That one. He's wounded.'

The merchant shrugged. 'My medicus, who used to be a Roman capsarius, tells me he's in no danger. Unless he succumbs to the wound rot, his wound will have crusted over and be healing by the time we get to Carthago Nova.' He frowned. '*This* one is yours?'

Galronus nodded, wondering if his gambit would work. How aware were these people of whom they were carrying? 'He was my boss' personal slave, but he ran away. The boss wants him back badly. There are *fugitivarii* looking for him. But he's not worth what he was. Not in this state.'

The merchant's eyes narrowed. 'He's fine. A flesh wound is all.'

'He's wounded. He wasn't when he left. My boss' property has been damaged. You wouldn't want a legal row over it, would you? I'm willing to take him off your hands for five hundred, though, just so I can have the kudos of being the one to bring him back.'

'Five hundred?' snorted the nephew, earning another acidic look from his uncle.

'A thousand,' the merchant said. 'And that's cost price. I *bought* him for a thousand, and he's had medical care and one meal since then, so even that puts me out of pocket.'

Galronus felt relief flood through him. It was better than he'd hoped for. 'I'm in a generous mood,' the Remi said. 'It'll be good for my career. I'll give you eleven hundred to cover all your costs, then we don't have to bother the courts or the fugitivarii.'

The merchant peered into his eyes for a moment, as if trying to peel away layers of deception, then finally shrugged and nodded. 'I have documents of purchase. Danel... go fetch the records for this one, and my seal.'

* * *

Fronto staggered for a moment and righted himself only with difficulty, refusing the help of the guards and only managing as Galronus put out a hand.

'I'll... I will... when you find out who I am...'

'I've told him how angry your master is,' Galronus said sharply, glaring at Fronto and trying to carry the weight of the situation in his gaze. If the traders suspected for a moment that they were holding someone as important as Fronto, they would be left with little choice. If they wanted to avoid unpleasant questions, neither Fronto nor Galronus could ever afford to be found alive. Fronto seemed to catch his meaning after several waggles of Remi eyebrows, and sagged.

'I can't ride.'

'You can be draped over a horse's rump like the runaway you are,' Galronus grunted, potentially overdoing it, 'and be sure not to fall off. You've one wound already. A second would just pass unnoticed.'

The slaver's nephew nodded approvingly, and Galronus none-too-gently slung Fronto over the back of his horse, turning his face from the stink. Fronto had been forced to use the cart latrine twice and there had been no water, no spongia and no vinegar to cleanse.

'Urk,' grunted Fronto in pain.

'Be quiet and be damned grateful it was me who found you and not the fugitivarii. They would scourge and brand you straight away.'

Ignoring Fronto's whimpers, he threw a long-suffering look at the slavers. 'I am profoundly grateful. May my gods and yours smile on your endeavours for the rest of your journey.'

The slaver bowed and he and his nephew retreated to the fire while the guards watched intently until the two men on the horse had vanished into Oleastrum and out of sight. As soon as he was sure they were out of view of the camp, Galronus heaved a sigh of relief and glanced round at Fronto. 'I'm stopping here. Partially to check your wound and change your dressing and partially because you smell like a terminally-ill sphincter and I'm not relishing riding the horse in front of you. You can dip in the sea and wash yourself down. The salt will do the wound good.'

As he helped Fronto down off the horse, tethered the beast and aided his friend across the soft sand of the beach toward the wine-dark slapping waves, Fronto made an odd noise. Galronus turned to remove the bandage and was surprise to see tears running through the grime down Fronto's face. He stopped, stunned. In all the years he'd fought alongside the legate, with everything they'd been through, he'd never seen Fronto cry. Not like this. When the children were born, yes. Tears of relief or exhaustion, yes. But this was different.

'You don't know,' Fronto said quietly. 'It's... it was... there's no describing it.'

'Nasty, I'm sure.'

'No,' Fronto said quietly, turning a look of bleak horror on Galronus. 'It's the end of all humanity. Not because of *them*, though. I think, for slavers, they were probably quite humane. But still, when you're stripped of everything and turned into cattle, it changes everything. And with it comes the realisation that it's all over. Not only everything you had, but everything you dreamed of, or might *ever* have. It's a total ruination of the soul. Because I knew I was done for. There was no way you'd find me, and I would end up in some mine in Africa or something like it. I had lost everything. The boys. Lucilia. You. Mother. Faleria. Everyone. It is a chilling, chilling thing, my friend. I just… I don't understand how you found me. Verginius is too clever to have left a trail.'

As Galronus reached the bandage's end and revealed the wound, Fronto hissed, the wrapping pulling the glistening, puckered red flesh out from the damage. 'Looks nasty,' the Remi noted, 'but the slaver was right. A few weeks and this will be on the mend. A couple of months and you'll be more or less your old self.' He pointed to the sea, dropping the filthy bandage on the sand. 'Wash. It'll hurt, but it'll help too. As for Verginius,' he added as Fronto winced and began to step slowly into the sweeping waves, 'he can't be as clever as you think. There *was* a trail.'

'Tell me,' said Fronto, as he began to wash and scrub, hissing with pain every time he bent or the water came near his midriff.

'I talked to Parella. She wasn't happy, but she pointed me to a bar where all the shitsters hang about.'

'The Jug?'

'The Jug. I found where you'd been beaten, then the room where you were stabbed. I found the lad who knew about it and poked him a bit 'til he told me how to get in touch with his Arenosio friend.'

'Poked with a *sword*, I presume. Good. Little shit sold me out. Deserved it. But Verginius didn't *need* his network now. He'd not have left a man out for you to find. That makes no sense.'

'But he was there. I found the house where they'd been staying. Verginius and the others had gone, but he'd left one man.'

Fronto yelped suddenly and disappeared beneath the waves, scrabbling back up swiftly and whimpering in pain before Galronus could wade in after him. 'The sea pulls hard on these beaches, and I'm short on strength right now. No, Galronus, none of it makes sense. Verginius is far too clever to leave a man… unless…' Fronto fell silent and turned to his friend.

'Unless?' prompted the Remi.

'Unless he *meant* for you to find me. He *did*. He wanted you to save me. The game isn't over, it's just moved on a stage. He wants me to live through what he lived through. He wants to make the revenge fit his suffering, like those Jews he was talking about. So now what? I can't imagine. He's going to remove my *Romanitas*? Make me like he was? Or make me suffer the ministrations of a vicious medic? I don't know, but I know I have no intention of letting him hurt anyone any more. This has to end now. I have to find him, and…'

'Kill him,' finished Galronus.

'Yes. No. Perhaps. I don't know. There is still my old friend in there. He's working through some warped vow he made when he was at his lowest ebb, but I really don't think he wants to. He's fighting *himself* far more than he's fighting *me*. And for all the evils he's heaping on me, it would appear he's never yet put me truly in permanent, lethal danger. If… if there's no chance of saving him, then yes, he needs to be killed, else he'll go after others. Caesar if no one else, and Caesar holds the future wellbeing of our family in his hands. I can't allow that, even though I tend to agree with him in some ways. No. I don't know what I'll do until the decision has to be made. But I'm not dragging this out. As soon as we get back to Tarraco, we find him. Tonight if need be, in the morning if not.'

'Two problems with that, Fronto. One: you can hardly bend, let alone help me take on Verginius and his remaining men. Hades, a bouncy horse ride could still kill you. Secondly: we have no new leads. I killed the warrior at the house, so there's no one left to tell us where he's gone.'

Fronto sloshed and staggered from the water, naked and soaked, his skin glistening as he came to a halt on the beach, curling his toes in the sand. Galronus looked him up and down. 'You look like a you've been eaten and shat out by a whale, but at least you're clean.'

Fronto smiled. 'Bandage me up, man, then we head back to the city. Verginius will have left us a message.'

'The statues?'

'The statues,' Fronto smiled.

Chapter Fifteen

FRONTO unfolded the vellum for the tenth time since they had left the city.

LAUTUMIA MEDELLAE

Galronus glanced across and tutted irritably and fiddled with his reins. 'I don't understand why. A quarry, of all things?' He harrumphed at Fronto, who once more folded the scrap and tucked it back into his pouch, noting as he did so the fresh bloom of blood on his bandages, glistening black in the pre-dawn light.

'And whatever you say,' the Remi went on, 'we should have stayed in Tarraco for a while and had your wound looked at by a professional. It might not be life-threatening in principle, but *any* wound can kill if it leaks enough blood. You should not be on a horse, either. It's pumping blood out of you like a bellows.'

'Maybe you're missing the joke,' Fronto said without a trace of humour. 'Lautumia Medellae means "quarry of healing". I wouldn't put it past Verginius to have chosen it purely for that playful little name. But there are other reasons too, I'm sure. The quarry's way out of town and only used sporadically when there's a big building project, so for whole chunks of the year it lies empty and silent. It's not one of the big private affairs with permanent manpower, so the governor drafts slaves in when he needs stone for something – otherwise they use the smaller quarries closer to Tarraco – which means we'll likely have the place to ourselves. It's on the road east and north, back toward Roman and Gallic lands and suspiciously not far from Longina's villa. Perhaps most important of all, Verginius and I both know the place. During the short time we were both based here, while we were gathering the forces for our campaign with Caesar, we used it for exercise and training. We had the men – and ourselves, of course – running the circumference of the place, racing along the quarry bottom and even climbing the walls. Horribly dangerous, but kept everyone in shape.'

'Is that it?' Galronus muttered, pointing ahead.

Fronto peered along the road and could see the opening to the place leading off to the left, into the hillside. A dip like a saddle, at the entrance of which stood two large buildings where the various ropes, tools and vehicles were stored between uses. 'That's it.'

'I still don't understand.'

'You could go mad yourself trying to ascribe meaning to the actions of the insane,' Fronto grunted. 'And no matter how focused he is, it's hard to draw any other conclusion about Verginius' state of mind. He's crazed. Driven by vows that even he doesn't want to carry out. I still don't think he means to kill me, and if that's the case what else is there in his eye-for-an-eye vengeance plan? To make me a king of a tribe? He should have been done with me once the slavers took me. He knew I'd get out and he told me where to go next so there's something else, but I won't know what it is until we're there.'

'There is an alternative,' Galronus said quietly. 'Walk away. He's all-but powerless now. Just leave him to his empty revenge. How much harm can he do?'

Fronto turned a hard look on his friend. 'He had even *less* power after that battle with the Ilergetes, yet he became a king and threatened Roman peace in a whole region. He's not an ordinary man, Galronus. He's capable of almost anything, and left to his own devices he will *always* be a threat. Besides, I have to know what he wants.'

Galronus nodded his understanding. 'If we must, then. So how do we handle this?'

'The whole place is like a 'U' cut into the hillside, with a narrow mouth. It gets deeper as you move into the hill, of course. There's a needle of stone in the middle where the overseers dish out water and so on when the quarry's in use. The two buildings at the entrance are sealed up tight when not in use, but there's only tools and ropes and planks and so on in them. A cart or two, maybe. There used to be a watchman on duty to look after them, but I remember the councillors in the city putting a stop to that, as it was costing the city more to pay the watchman than the value of the occasional theft of a cart or the like. Good old fashioned military sense tells me not to walk into the middle of the place. Being trapped in a 'U' is not a good way to start. So I suggest we climb the hill this side and work our way around at the top, keeping an eye out down into the quarry. Check out the lay of the land.'

'I think we should leave the horses,' Galronus noted. 'Being on horseback near a cliff on stony ground sounds like an invitation to a grim death to me.'

'Agreed. We'll tied them up over there.'

Shortly after, having left the two steeds on a patch of greenery not far from the flat entrance where they could graze while they waited, the two men hefted their swords ready and stalked up the long slope toward the upper lip of the quarry. The night had worn on throughout the pair's return journey from Oleastrum, their scouring of the city's statues and then their five mile journey to the quarry. Their pace had been somewhat restricted by Fronto's need to move as slowly and carefully as possible, along with periodic pauses to rebind his midriff using four tunics Galronus had torn into strips and stuffed into a saddle bag. Now the earliest strains of gold were beginning to creep into the eastern skies, telling of a bright morning to come. Yet for now the scrubby, stony ground was treacherous in the dim light and the pair made their way up to the quarry carefully, the Remi halting periodically to support Fronto when he felt especially weak from his wound.

Clambering up the slope, the two men reached the edge and Galronus peered down into the quarry with wide eyes, letting an impressed breath whisper between his lips.

The floor of the quarry was some sixty feet below, light grey and dusty with gravel. A number of shaped or part-shaped blocks had been left in situ, seemingly surplus to requirements on previous excavations. The walls of the wide horseshoe shape were of a faintly yellowy-white and were eerily unnatural, stepped in rigid, geometric patterns where huge sections had been taken away. It looked to Galronus as though nothing less than a god's chisel had been at work on the stone. Down at the bottom a couple of basins had collected water, and a tall, slender spire rose at the centre, its tip on a level with the two viewers marking where the original ground level had been. The whole was one of the most impressive sights Galronus had ever laid eyes upon.

'It's grown since I was last here,' Fronto murmured in quiet tones 'Must have been building like mad in Tarraco, though I'd not noticed much change there. The rear of the quarry has extended some way and there's a whole new curve in the cliff opposite.'

Galronus nodded, dumbly, looking off toward the rear, which was still mostly occluded, sunk in shadows.

'One of the benefits of this place,' called a voice from down in the depths, 'is that at night and unworked, sound carries very well. Hello Marcus. I see your friend rode gallant and loyal to the rescue. What it must be like to experience that kind of loyalty, eh?'

Fronto peered down into the quarry. The irregular cliffs and the depth, combined with the pre-dawn gloom, made it impossible to locate the source of the voice.

'Are you intending to lead me around *all* our old haunts, Verginius? Because Italica is a long way away and it you want me on the south coast at some point I'd best set off straight away.'

'Very funny, Marcus. Your sense of humour is as impenetrable as your sense of loyalty.'

'Blah, blah, blah,' grunted Fronto. 'Why are we here?'

'To talk, Marcus. I know you like to negotiate by iron and muscle, but sometimes words are the best way. Come down. No harm will come to you. We're done with all that. Nemesis is sated, and my vow fulfilled.'

'Then why not just come to me openly? Why all this performance?'

'*Come down* and talk, Marcus. One of the long-term effects of the things they did to me early on is a rather scratchy, quiet voice. It takes a great deal of effort shouting up to you. Why do you think I used the acoustics of the theatre before?'

'Because this was all a farce, I'd presumed. Alright, Verginius, we're coming down.'

Galronus gave him a serious look and lowered his voice to little more than a whisper. 'This is not a good idea. Whatever he says, he might try and kill you. He's mad. You said it yourself.'

'I believe him on this,' Fronto replied. 'Come on. I'll certainly need your help.'

'Well, we're not going in there without swords out, for certain,' the Remi muttered. 'What I wouldn't give to have Arcadios sitting up here with his bow right now.'

'If I'd brought anyone else to Tarraco, they'd be dead,' Fronto countered. 'I think he figured you for something unusual, else you'd have been picked off before now too.'

With Galronus' supporting arm Fronto grunted and winced his way slowly back down the slope, past the unconcerned horses once more and toward the entrance, where the pair turned and peered along the quarry floor. It was still impossible to spot Verginius, though the light was now beginning to increase, the sun perhaps half an hour from the horizon.

'A new day is dawning,' called a voice from ahead, as though plucking thoughts direct from Fronto's mind.

'Tends to happen after dark. And it goes on doing it, if you keep watching.'

'I'd like to say I've missed your humour, Marcus,' said a shape, stepping out from behind that thin pillar of rock, 'but I think we all know that would be a lie.'

Two more men stepped out, one on each side of Verginius. Fronto's old friend was seemingly unarmed, his hands open by his sides, but the other two were very much equipped for war, chain shirts hissing as they moved, one with a large axe over his shoulder, the other with one of those long, broad Gallic blades in hand.

'So much for talking,' Fronto noted. 'Your friends seem to prefer blades to words, after all.'

'The axeman is Cison, son of Baigorixo – one of the strongest, most feared of the Arenosio. He doesn't speak any Latin. He hardly speaks at all, really. The one with the sword is Ategnio. He is my...' Verginius paused. '*Galronus*, your friend is called, yes? He is my Galronus. My second in every way. My right hand and my courage or conscience if I find either lacking.'

'I'd not noted a hint of conscience about you,' said Fronto in barbed tones.

'That's not worthy, Marcus. Everyone I have killed has deserved it. Or, if not, then they have been a sacrifice to the greater goal. Sacrifices are acceptable, Marcus. They're sacred. Part of the Roman way. And that's why we're here, old friend. Because of sacrifices and vows.'

'You never used to talk in riddles, Verginius. Your time among the Aquitanii has made you confused, I think.'

There was a bark of laughter. 'Oh, Marcus, I am thinking clearly. I have a clarity that I lacked as a child of the republic. It took death and a view from *outside* that republic to see so clearly. And, as I say, that is why we're here.'

'Alright,' Fronto said. 'Talk, then.'

'I am done with you, Marcus. My debt is paid, as is yours. My vow is fulfilled and I am at peace with that. I was so angry at you for such a long time after the battle that it rather defined who I was for years. But since seeing you again, I found oddly that I felt more companionship again than hate. My bile had all run away, my anger faded over the years, leaving only an empty vow that I had to fulfil. I am even at peace with your Remi friend comforting Faleria. She deserves happiness. I had rather hoped he would save you from the slavers. Faleria would have hated to hear *that* news. But now all is good for you. The Remi can go back to Faleria, and you, Marcus, need no longer fear my wrath. So yes, I am done with the pair of you. This is your exit, but like Rome's glorious *Porta Triumphalis*, it has two doorways. Have you ever felt the presence of Janus, Marcus? The god of doorways and choices?'

'I know who Janus is.'

'But your friend might not. Janus is the god of change and choice, Remi. Of beginnings and endings. And he is here with us now. Something has ended, and something is beginning. Janus fills the quarry with portent and possibility. This place, Marcus... can you remember what it's called? If not, I left you a handy note you can refer to, remember.'

'Lautumia Medellae,' Fronto said.

'Yes. The "quarry of healing". Poignant for this meeting. Not because of your wound, though – oh, Marcus, you should have seen a medicus on the way. You must be close to bleeding out. I would have waited for you. You know that. I've waited eleven years already, after all.'

'Get on with it. I might die of boredom long before I run out of blood.'

Verginius laughed. 'That's more the Fronto I remember. Well this place can be the start, under Janus' watchful eye. The beginning of the healing of the republic.'

'You're talking crap, Verginius.'

'You know I'm not. I'll wager you don't know the reason for the place's name, though? This hill used to be a sacred site for the Cessetani, Marcus. Ever heard of them? Of course you haven't. I

348

hadn't when we were here as Romans either, because the Romans of Hispania Citerior don't like to mention peoples they have more or less exterminated for their own petty gain. The Cessetani were the tribe who originally built Tarraco. And here, on this hill, right where I am standing but sixty feet or so higher, was one of their greatest sacred sites. A temple. The quarry of healing, Marcus. But their god is forgotten, the sacred waters gone. The temple gone. The priest gone. The whole damn hill gone. And why? So the great Scipio could build high walls for his fortress. So that great men of Rome can build their palaces and their villas on the bones of the locals. Greed leading the way as always.'

'You're starting to sound like one of the rabble rousers among the plebs in Rome, Verginius.'

'Good. Because they might have the right idea. Listen, Marcus... I know you for a good man at heart. You're a solid republican, through and through. You support democracy in the form we've always known it. You used to be full of spite and disgust for men like Marius and Sulla, who almost brought us back to the days of monarchy. You don't like that any more than I do.'

'This is getting boring again, Verginius.'

'*Listen* to me, Fronto. I have yet to fulfil my other vow. I have to bring down Caesar, and while I regretted carrying out my vow against you, I hunger to bring justice to that selfish rat. But I know you've taken no such vow, and turning on your commander will sit badly with you, so I cannot hope to appeal to you on the grounds that he is a monster and a betrayer and a selfish user of others. So I *do* appeal to you on the grounds that he is a criminal and a danger to the republic you love. I will see Caesar fall in battle, Fronto, to the sword. I *will* do it, for I have sworn as much both to Nemesis and to Betatun. But I do not wish to do it alone... *you* owe him this as much as me, Marcus. He sent us *both* to our death on that battlefield, not just me. Our quarrel is done, Marcus. Join me and we'll make Caesar pay for his crimes.'

There was a long pause, and Fronto took a deep breath, clutching his painful side as he heaved in cold early morning air. How often had men appealed to him to turn on Caesar. Paetus. Pompey. Even Balbus in his time...

'I can't do that, Verginius. He's not what you think, as I realised once I knew Pompey and the alternatives. And even if he was, my horse is irrevocably hitched to his cart anyway. My family has been exiled by the senate, you know? Faleria and mother are in Massilia...'

'Don't tell him that,' hissed Galronus, but Fronto waved him quiet.

'They are in Massilia,' he went on, 'with my wife and my boys and my father- and sister-in-law. We cannot pass onto Italian soil for ten years without being hunted as enemies of the state. Our property impounded, our name blackened. Exiled from Rome for a decade. You know how that feels better than anyone. And now the senate seeks to take Caesar through the courts and prosecute him, so he's currently trapped in Gaul, unable to cross into Italia without pitting himself against the Roman authorities, so we share a common foe. But the general can *win* this thing. He believes he can, and I believe him. And with his hopes of success rides the fate of the family. Don't you see? Only Caesar can bring the Falerii back into Rome. Without him, we fade and become distant provincials at best. Fugitives at worst. What kind of future would that be for my boys? I *cannot* turn on Caesar.'

'Janus is watching you closely, Marcus.'

'I'm sure he is, but so are Venus and Fortuna. Caesar is Venus' son, and Fortuna has given me the general as a last straw at which to clutch for my family. Janus understands. Do you?'

'Marcus, Caesar will *destroy* Rome. He will use it and rape it and corrupt it as he does with everything, and in the end he will leave the republic in ruins. It will be like this sacred place of healing – shattered, broken and quarried away. Morally bankrupt. He will leave Roma to die on a dusty battlefield with a sword through its ribs. Caesar *has* to die. And it's the only way to fulfil my vow.'

Fronto sighed. 'I cannot let you do it, Verginius. I can see and appreciate the truth in some of your words, but it changes nothing. I am Caesar's man and he carries the future of the Falerii in the palm of his hand now. Go home. Either back to your father in Rome or back to your mountains, whichever is your home now. But I can't let you hunt Caesar.'

Galronus huffed. 'They are three men. Caesar has legions and bodyguards. Let him try.'

'No,' Fronto murmured. 'A determined man can often do what an army cannot. Look at what he achieved in the mountains. I can't let him do this, because there is a chance he might succeed.'

'My voice is damaged, Marcus, but my hearing is excellent,' Verginius called. 'I *will* see Caesar dead. I had hoped you would see sense and come with me, but if not then be assured that I will do it alone. Stay here in this healing place and try not to bleed to death.'

And with that the figure over by the tall pillar of rock turned toward the rear of the quarry and began to stride away. Fronto shared a sidelong glance with Galronus, and the two men started to pace slowly after him.

'I can't let you do this, Verginius.'

'You can't stop me, Marcus,' Verginius called over his shoulder. 'Look at you. You've lost so much blood you're almost white. You can't walk without clutching your middle. You couldn't wrestle with a tough decision at the moment. And your Remi friend is strong and brave, I'm sure, but so are Ategnio and Cison, and there are two of them.'

As the smiling king slowly plodded off, Fronto and Galronus picked up their pace, crunching across the gravelled surface as the sky began to lighten visibly high above the white cliffs.

'Slow them,' Verginius said to his men. 'Try not to kill them.'

And as he walked on toward the rear of the quarry, where Fronto could now see in the rising light there was a series of wooden gantries, walkways and ladders rising the full height of the cliff, the two Arenosio warriors turned and Fronto peered into their eyes.

Verginius was clearly troubled – he was somewhat torn between what he perceived needed to be done, and what he would prefer, in his heart, to do. These two warriors suffered no such conflict. The eyes of both were hard and sure. This was a sign of Verginius' power. This was why he was still dangerous. At this last sad juncture, with seemingly nothing to offer them, he still had such a hold on these two that they would die for him. A man like that might just get to Caesar in the end.

The bulkier warrior made for Galronus, heaving the axe from his shoulder and swinging it in wide, terrifying arcs. Ategnio moved toward Fronto, his sword in his hand. His eyes held murder.

Whatever his master had said, this man wanted to kill Fronto, and might just do it regardless of his orders. Fronto raised his glorious blade and prepared to meet the first blow.

* * *

Fronto had the unpleasant leisure to watch Galronus take the first strike. The big warrior Cison was like a bull in a chain shirt, charging his quarry with that anger that seemed to lie just beneath the Celtic skin and which had fuelled four centuries of belligerence toward Rome. While Fronto remained ready to parry a blow, his sword wavering with the effort of holding it up above his painful, aching wounded torso, Ategnio advanced slowly, cautiously and with a glare of pure malice.

Cison, however, swung his axe in a continuous seemingly-random sequences of circles, loops and figure eights and, coming on implacably, Galronus was faced with a disastrous set of options: stand and attempt to weather that first strike, or give ground and back away. The latter would leave Fronto open, though, and the Roman was relieved beyond belief to see his friend hold his position, even though it put him in mortal danger.

The axe swept in from the right and would have bitten deep into Galronus' leg had the Remi not thrust Verginius' blade in the way and turned it slightly aside. Even then, the immense momentum the axe carried could not be entirely shifted, and the tip of the blade bit into Galronus' waist, shearing through his belt, exploding his chain shirt in a shower of links, and drawing blood in a deep line that could so easily have done for him entirely.

Try not to kill them indeed!

Galronus yelped and staggered to the side. He tried to take advantage of the man's extended arms to strike at him, but Cison was quick for a big man and the axe haft came back in time to knock the blow aside. Fronto's attention was lost to his friend at that moment, for Ategnio was there, jabbing with his sword.

Fronto knew he was doomed from the very first exchange. Ategnio was as fast as Cison, but while Galronus could claim to be a match for either of them Fronto was wounded and slow, and every sharp move sent torrents of pain flowing through him. More than that, he could feel his strength ebbing. The blood loss had reached dangerous levels. He could feel weakness creeping over him.

He turned Ategnio's blade with enough effort that it left him staggering back two paces, clutching his middle and burbling in agony. His sword wavered and floundered out to the side as he concentrated on not blacking out.

Ategnio was there again, right before him, sword swiping. Another parry that almost did for Fronto as he used every ounce of his strength not to collapse to his knees.

'I could kill you with a breath,' the Arenosio warrior sneered in surprisingly good, if heavily-accented, Latin.

'I don't doubt it. You smell like a cow's arse even on the outside.'

A look of fiery hatred passed through the warrior's eyes and his upper lip acquired a twitch.

'I *would* kill you. I would not bother making it slow and painful. Only idiots drag out the kill for their own joy.'

'I might argue that that is exactly what you're doing with all this chatter,' murmured Fronto, heaving in more breaths and slowly bringing himself to a fighting stance again, the tip of his blade coming up, wavering.

'If I were going to kill you, I'd have done it,' Ategnio growled. 'But the king wishes you to live, so you shall live. Never follow, though, for I do not wish my loyalty tested like this again.'

With a contemptuous flick, Ategnio knocked aside Fronto's blade and, reversing his sword in a masterful sweep, jabbed the rounded pommel straight into Fronto's wound.

The former legate screamed and fell to his knees, his sword clattering to the ground, forgotten. The soaked bandage started to pulsate with extra torrents of blood, and he clutched the wound, whimpering, his eyes streaming at the pain. Unable to do anything to prevent it, he watched the Arenosio warrior back away and sheath his unsullied blade, wiping the blood from the pommel with his sleeve. The man turned with a sneer and walked away after Verginius, paying no further heed to the Roman on the ground.

Galronus almost died on the spot. His attention distracted by Fronto's howl he turned, expecting to see the Roman cleaved in two and as, with relief, he found Fronto alive, the great axe smashed into his left arm. A misjudged angle, miraculously, saved the Remi's limb from severance. By chance, the axe blade slipped on the iron links of the chain sleeve and turned sideways, but there was an audible crack as the weight of the axe head, side on, broke the arm. Verginius' beautiful sword fell to the floor and Galronus stumbled back, shocked, in pain and unarmed.

They were doomed. Cison, it seemed, was not loyal enough to his king to hold anything back in the fight. Instead, he took a step forward, growling, preparing to kill the Remi facing him. Fronto looked desperately off after the retreating shapes of Verginius and Ategnio, then at his endangered friend. Hissing in pain, he scrabbled around until his fingers closed on his fallen sword. Gripping it by the upper end of the blade, he turned and flung it toward Galronus with all his pitiful strength.

The Remi failed to catch the badly-thrown sword, but it skittered along the gravel near his feet and he managed to stoop and sweep it up in his left hand. Cison said something in his gravelly dialect, and Galronus barked something back at him in a similar tongue.

'Fronto?'

'What?'

'This animal doesn't speak Latin. He doesn't know what we're saying.'

'Oh, well everything's fine then.'

'Fronto, I'm going to circle backwards. My left arm's not so strong with a sword, but I might be able to manage a few parries.'

'Just bring him close,' Fronto said.

Galronus gave ground one pace at a time, staying out of the way of the swinging axe, using Fronto's sword to turn blows whenever he could. Fronto was impressed. He himself could barely peel fruit with his left hand, let alone swing a sword. Galronus was doing pretty well by his estimation. Now: a weapon...

He couldn't reach Galronus' fallen sword without scrabbling across the ground, and that would draw attention to himself. Currently, Cison seemed to have forgotten the downed Roman was even there. Slowly, quietly, Fronto drew the pugio dagger from his belt and waited.

Galronus was bringing the big man closer, carefully leading him. Fronto took a deep breath, knowing he was running out of strength with every passing moment, and then the fighting pair were beside him, Galronus backing past first, then Fronto saw the leg-wrappings of the mountain man and his big fur and leather boots.

He swung the dagger over-hand, slamming it into the unprotected calf muscle, where only woollen trousers covered the flesh. The blade sank in deep, grated between the tibia and fibula and lodged there, ripped from Fronto's hands as the big man passed. It took a moment for the message to reach the warrior's brain from his leg, and then all at once he howled and fell to the side, his axe swinging wildly and almost taking off Fronto's head by pure chance before it struck the ground and bit deep.

With a roar, Cison turned to rise as best he could and met Fronto's sword in Galronus' hand coming the other way. The blade slammed into the big warrior's mouth, sending teeth and chips of jaw flying in a shrapnel cloud, some of which drew blood from Galronus' face. The blade grated as it slid into the mouth, punched through gristle and bone and emerged from the back of the neck, spraying Fronto in warm blood where he half-kneeled, half-lay beneath.

The legate barely managed to slide out of the way before Cison hit the ground, convulsing and gurgling, a rasping scream cleft by the blade on its way out of his bifurcated mouth. Fronto stared.

'You've ruined my sword,' he grumbled.

'You're welcome,' snapped Galronus irritably, his right arm hanging useless by his side as he reached down with his left and with some difficulty yanked the sword from the mouth. It was quite clearly nicked and chipped along the blade, and the burnished orichalcum of the hilt had been scraped dull where it had slid along the gravel.

'Verginius…'

'He's away,' Galronus muttered, tucking his broken arm into his belt with a hiss of breath. 'Somewhere back there.'

'We have to catch him. Stop him.'

'Are you mad? Can you see yourself? You look like a ghost in a bloodied shroud. And I have one arm. Hard words and the odd kick are not going to put those two down.'

Fronto rose to his feet with some difficulty, swaying this way and that. His tunic was soaked, and mostly with his own blood. 'The horses. They're close, at the bottom of the slope. We can get to the top of the gantries before them if we ride fast. They've lots of ladders to climb.'

'Marcus, a horse ride will kill you. Besides, how are you going to get to the horse? Crawl?'

Galronus peered down into Fronto's face and sighed with a roll of his eyes at what he saw there. 'You're a lunatic, you know that? Men like you are the reason Rome has an empire.'

'Just help me up.'

Galronus staggered across to Verginius' fallen blade, collected it, then passed Fronto's sword back to its owner. 'Hold on tight and keep that point away from me.' With that, he sheathed his own sword, grasped Fronto's arm, bent in front of him and heaved the weak legate up onto his shoulder. He could sense the sudden extra gush of blood from the wound flooding down over his shoulder and felt a panic that he might just kill Fronto by carrying him.

'Marcus...'

'Just...' hissed Fronto breathlessly, 'go!'

With a deep breath, Galronus trotted off across the ground, his good arm holding Fronto in place as the blood slicked over his chain shirt. The gash in his side from the weak axe strike was beginning to fill his trousers with his own blood and he wondered now if any part of him was not crimson and gleaming with the blood of Roman, Remi or Aquitani. Their horses were close to the entrance and, huffing and puffing, the Remi staggered out of the quarry, past the locked sheds and round to the patch of greenery where the beasts grazed.

'It's going to be a close run thing,' he gasped as he heaved Fronto up to the saddle. His eyes held a brief moment of panic when he thought Fronto might fall off again, but soon the bone-white legate was in his seat and, using arms that flopped with weakness, untying his reins.

'Then we'd better hurry.'

Wincing, using his good arm, Galronus pulled himself up onto the horse and similarly untied his reins. 'What are we going to do even if we're in time to stop them? Neither of us is much use.'

Fronto heeled Bucephalus and began to walk, then trot, then canter up the slope along the side of the quarry, Galronus was beside him a moment later, his natural Gallic horsemanship more than a match for Fronto's.

'Can you take Ategnio?' Fronto breathed painfully, wincing.

Galronus blinked at his friend. 'No. No I can't. With my right hand, maybe. With my left? No.'

'Can you keep him busy?'

'I could let him spend a happy half hour carving small pieces off me, if that's any help!'

'It might. I need to stop Verginius, but that means keeping Ategnio out of it.'

'Fronto, you'd lose a fight with a moth right now.'

'I have a sword. Verginius is unarmed.'

'But healthy. Marcus, this is madness.'

'It has to be done,' Fronto said, then broke into a satisfied smile and pointed as they crested the top of the hill and came rather perilously close to the edge, in his opinion. Galronus followed his gesture. Two figures were just visible in the growing light, only four ladders below the top. Their horses were tethered to trees not far back from the edge. Fronto and Galronus would be in time, if they hurried.

'Come on,' said the Remi, sudden determination flooding his tone.

'You sound full of yourself.'

'Fortuna favours you, Marcus. Always has. And I think Taranis has me in his grip now, too. I think we're *meant* to do this.' Almost as if bestowing her blessing on their endeavour, Aurora chose that moment to put in an appearance, a blinding flash of golden light rising over the horizon at the far side of the quarry.

The Remi put his heels to his horse's side and broke into a gallop, racing around the edge of the quarry. Fronto tried to do the same, but almost passed out the with effort. Besides, while he could ride a horse as well as most Roman nobles these days, that was still with far less skill than Galronus, and they were rather too close to a sixty foot drop for Fronto's liking. With slightly more caution, he rode in his friend's wake, reaching the top of the scaffolding and sliding with pain and care from Bucephalus as Galronus, already dismounted, stepped out onto the wooden gantry.

'Here we go,' he said.

* * *

Verginius stopped two ladders from the top and a slow smile of respectful disbelief crossed his ever-smiling face. Fronto's friend was already down the first ladder and waiting on the top gantry. Even as the Remi stamped his foot and tested the safety of the whole rig, he was jabbing and swinging with his sword in his left hand, practising. That was one of a number of things Verginius had seen in his time among the Celtoi – the people who occupied all the Gauls. Romans were useless with their left hands. If they had any natural talent with that hand it was bred out of them in their youth, especially among the legions, where a shield wall could not be maintained if some men had their shield on a different arm. The Aquitanii had been different, using whatever hand felt most comfortable, and the Gauls and Belgae had clearly been much the same. So the Remi had a broken arm? His right was tucked into his belt, a clear sign it had suffered badly.

Behind Galronus, he could see Fronto starting gingerly down the top step, clinging in with both hands, his face drawn and bone-white, his skin feeble and pale even in the glorious golden light of morning. Verginius had to hand it to his old friend: he had strength – of character and will if not of body. He was determined. He had that same fire that had driven both of them in the old days. But Verginius was compelled by a different fire now. He had to accomplish his vengeance against Caesar, else he was nothing. The goddesses – that of the natives and his own precious Nemesis, had kept him alive only on his vows to revenge himself upon Fronto and Caesar. He saw now that his vow against Fronto had been misplaced, while Caesar deserved everything coming to him, but vows were vows and had to be kept no matter how unnecessary.

This Fronto – the one who was astoundingly overcoming the footsteps of Charon in his shadow just to stop Verginius – was a man of principle, as the Fronto he remembered had been. A brave man. Somehow in his dying moments on that battlefield, Verginius must have perceived something wrong. The man climbing down to meet him now would never have left a friend to die. Look at the lengths he was going to now. And the Remi? He was an echo of that same bravery and honour. He was about to let Ategnio kill him just to help Fronto. Sad. Had the three of them never met Caesar and instead come across one another in a tavern somewhere, he had a feeling he would have liked the Remi. He was an odd mix, far more Roman than many of the republic's subjugated peoples, more cultured than the Aquitanii, yet still with that Celtic drive and pride Verginius had seen in his time among the tribes.

He would find a way past Fronto and his friend, hopefully without harming them further. He must. Caesar had to die for what he'd done, and what he might yet do to a whole generation of young hopeful young echoes of Verginius and Fronto. After that? After that, Hades could come for him. He was done. The Aquitanii were no longer his people, and neither was Rome. There was nowhere left for Verginius, as Verginius was no one. A ghost. A last shadow in the dead retina of his former self – that eager young man who had died on a dusty field.

'Stop there,' he shouted, knowing that his voice carried little power, but that he was close enough anyone could hear him. 'Back up and leave. I don't want to fight you. Neither of you are my enemy now. And Faleria and your wife sit in Massilia waiting for you. Don't endanger yourself. I wish neither of them the heartache of losing you.'

'Then come with me, Verginius,' shouted Fronto as he reached the bottom of the ladder and drew his blade.

'There's nowhere for me to go, Marcus. I'm not a Roman. I'm not Aquitani. I'm not even a person. I stopped being that when I died. I am a male fury, Fronto. One of the *Dirae*, born of the blood of Cronus and sent by Nemesis to bring Caesar to the underworld. I have no other purpose. I have no future. I am vengeance incarnate, and when that vengeance is done, I am spent, and I can die again, hopefully in peace, crossing the river and seeing all those who fell in the field with us. Do you not see? I cannot stop, and I cannot be stopped. Don't pit yourself against me.'

'You never believed all that claptrap when you were young, Verginius,' Fronto shouted down from the top gantry. 'Nemesis was our goddess because she was stylish and unusual. That was all. We were boys. All the great names of Rome cleaved to Venus or Minerva or Mars or some Olympian, because it made their family lineage impressive. Not us. We chose Nemesis to be different. You know that. We broke the mould. We were different – not led by the fashion. Do it again. Break the mould. I still have Nemesis around my neck,' the legate shouted, 'but now I have Fortuna too. For almost as long as I've not had you, I've had her. Fortune is a worthy thing to put stock in too. Don't get so caught up in vengeance you can't see any further.'

Verginius smiled.

'You've become persuasive as you've matured, Marcus. Not enough, though. I'm not a child, and I know what I must do. I brought you here, Marcus, because I believe you have the same right to vengeance as me. As all those who died on that field. If I'd believed for even a moment that you might put Caesar above me, I'd never have left the note. But we are strong, Fronto, and you are weak. I don't want you to die. Last chance. Leave and let us go.'

* * *

Galronus felt the whole gantry shake as Ategnio grasped the ladder. Above, Fronto was involved in some long-winded exchange with Verginius, but it came to an end quite suddenly as the smiling king barked an order and Ategnio began to climb. Galronus struggled for a moment in indecision. Common sense told him to take advantage of the man's distraction climbing the ladder. It would be the Roman way: use whatever presented itself to your advantage. But it was not the way of the Remi and no matter how Galronus cut his hair or what type of tunic he wore, or even if he sat in the senate in support of Caesar, he was still Remi to his core. Acknowledging that it might be a suicidal decision, and very possibly the worst he could make, he backed away and allowed Ategnio the leisure to climb the ladder and step out onto the timbers.

The Arenosio warrior took two steps forward and produced his sword, twisting it this way and that, exercising his wrist. Galronus noted, with a mix of relief and trepidation, Fronto drop lightly to the gantry behind the warrior and carry on down the next ladder to Verginius. Well, it was done, then. For good or for ill, Galronus had done what Fronto had asked. He had kept Ategnio out of the way and allowed his friend the chance to get to Verginius. Now, would the barely-upright legate be able to hold his own against the smiling king?

Of course not. In the same way as Galronus stood little hope of living through the next fifty heartbeats.

Ategnio practised a little, modifying his technique to account for the timber struts of the gantry that hemmed them in. Galronus watched the Arenosio warrior closing on him, sword weaving in preparation, and took a momentary glance over his shoulder. At least fifty feet below, probably a lot more since they were at the quarry's deepest point, the dusty ground looked as hard as it was. Rock. No giving earth or sand. Acknowledging the fatal nature of that drop, he stepped forward a few paces, allowing himself room to fall backwards and still land on the wooden walkway.

Ategnio lunged without warning, but Galronus was ready. He felt the searing, burning pain in his side where Cison's axe had drawn a crimson line, but managed to get his own sword in the way, and the enemy blade skittered off with a metallic rasp, clanking against a side timber for a moment before he pulled it back and readied himself once more.

Galronus took a deep breath and jabbed low, ducking, twisting to the side and then withdrawing to stay out of too much danger and prevent over-extending. Ategnio was quick. His Gallic blade dropped and knocked Galronus' aside, though at least the speed of the manoeuver protected the Remi from an immediate counter-strike.

'You fight well for a one-armed man,' the Arenosio warrior acknowledged in his own guttural tongue. Galronus shrugged as he stepped back a single pace. 'We both know we're all better than any Roman individually, but Caesar wrote diaries about his wars. Did you know that? And in them he acknowledges the Belgae as the bravest of all the peoples. Bear that in mind, mountain man.'

Ategnio snorted. 'And yet you handle that little Roman eating knife instead of a proper sword.'

'This?' Galronus held it up. 'This was your king's sword. And one thing you will learn shortly is that it is far more manoeuvrable in tight spaces than our own traditional blades.'

With that, the Remi noble leapt several paces toward Ategnio without warning, bringing his sword up and driving it in from the side. Ategnio moved to block, but his sword thudded against a supporting timber, too cumbersome to bring up so close to his enemy. Galronus' blade bit into Ategnio's shoulder. The blow was too restricted to be truly damaging, but it cut through the layers of leather and sent chain links scattering across the boards, drawing blood and making the Arenosio a little less confident of an easy victory. Ategnio backed away a few paces, eyes narrowed as he reached up with his free hand and felt his shoulder, pulling the hand away and seeing the red smear across it.

'No man has wounded me in years.'

'Get used to it. It's about to happen a lot.'

Galronus stepped a pace back, allowing space to open between them. He needed to think and to work out a way to gain further advantage. Ategnio would not let him close ranks the same way twice, and in every other way he was at a disadvantage. Even as he listened to himself taunt the mountain warrior, the Remi shook his head at how much Roman behaviour was beginning to seep into his being. That kind of talk was not endemic of Remi warfare.

'Come on, little man. Let's end this.'

Ategnio took a step forward and lunged again, the only true manoeuver he could attempt which was in no way disadvantaged by the closeness of the chiselled cliff or the wooden posts. Galronus saw it coming and swept down and to the side with his new Roman blade, only to have his opponent change direction mid-lunge, his arm twisting like a snake in long grass, the blade, which had been coming left, now stabbing to the right. For the second time in as many flurries Galronus was grateful he bore the nifty Roman short blade and not his own comfortable Remi sword. Where his own would have been simply too unwieldy, he managed to twist the shorter Roman blade back across and catch the clever thrust, turning it just far enough aside that it tore away a piece of tunic but did no damage.

The Arenosio warrior snarled as he came on. Having recognised in an instant that his blow had failed and that in withdrawing he would leave himself open to the neater, shorter blade, he barrelled into Galronus and the two fell back against the gantry, which shook alarmingly with the force of the fall, chalky dust billowing out in clouds from where the wooden walkway touched the rock face.

Galronus gasped in pain as the big warrior landed on top of him. Struggling with his good arm, tears of pain pricking his eyes as Ategnio's weight ground against his broken bone, the Remi gradually succeeded in shifting the man enough to breathe. The Arenosio rose to his knees, towering over Galronus with sword

362

still in hand, and lifted it. There was no room while kneeling to turn the blade down to face his prey, so he slammed the pommel down at Galronus' face. The Remi, scrabbling to pull his sword closer, saw the blow coming in the blink of an eye and twisted his head desperately. The pommel smacked into the timber, raising another cloud of dust, but Ategnio was not done. Snarling, the warrior pulled back the sword and smashed the heavy bronze pommel down again and again, Galronus thrashing around beneath, desperately avoiding having his eyes burst open or his brains smeared across the wood with each blow. Finally, howling in frustration, Ategnio changed tactic and with his last strike, shifted his blow.

The pommel of the sword hit Galronus at the meeting point of his collarbones and something gave a loud crack, sending waves of pain through him. For a long moment he was blind with agony, struggling to breathe or make any sense through the cloud of pain, and then his eyes opened to impending death. While he had been incapacitated with pain, Ategnio had taken the opportunity to rise to his feet once more, cursing and growling, and had lifted his sword with both hands wrapped around the hilt, ready to plunge it down through his prey. Galronus panicked. Instinct alone made him shuffle backwards, away from the sword point, but closer and closer to the deadly drop. His whole body was in agony, his upper torso and arm afire with pain, but certain responses are born in the bone and require no conscious decision. He inched back again and again, and each tiny move brought forth an angry snarl from Ategnio as he shuffled his feet forward, trying to position his sword point over the chest of the shuffling, writhing body beneath him.

Shuffle, shuffle.

Left foot, right foot.

Angry shout.

Shuffle, shuffle.

Left foot, right foot.

Cursing in Aquitanian.

Shuffle.

Left foot…

Galronus moved with a grace and speed born of desperation, his hand snapping upwards, grasping the Arenosio warrior by the belt and heaving forward while the man's right foot was still slightly raised. Unbalanced, Ategnio gave a cry of shock and stumbled, tumbling forward. He had room to fall safely, but as his surprised gait faltered and his feet tottered, Galronus let go of the belt and kicked out at his enemy's leading knee.

Ategnio staggered and fell, wavering forward, and the agonised Remi rolled into his path, tripping him just as he almost righted himself. The big sword clattered useless against the timbers as the Arenosio warrior, shocked and recognising a disastrous end upon him, fell forward out into space above the quarry floor.

Galronus watched him go, twisting in an attempt to keep out of the way. He was damaged and weak. Too weak to stop what happened next. With a snarl of defiant disbelief, Ategnio went over the lip of the gantry, but even in death he was deadly. His hand lashed out as he fell and grasped Galronus by the belt almost in mimicry of his own downfall, dragging the Remi backwards across the timbers and out into the air.

Galronus shouted something as he fell, but he knew not what it was.

* * *

Fronto tried to ignore the fact that the wooden ladder was vibrating and jumping with every move of Galronus and Ategnio above. The whole edifice seemed alarmingly fragile from the way it moved and the regular clouds of white dust that rose into the morning air. The Roman slid the last few steps and landed on the wooden walkway lightly. He had almost no strength left. He had almost died so many times over the years. From that first close call against the Ilergetes alongside the man before him now, to the many brutal fights in Gaul and Rome, he had almost met a cruel end so many times. And yet he had never felt so close to death as now. He was near to bleeding out and losing the last of his energy. And then, unless Galronus somehow managed to beat Ategnio, which even the Remi deemed unlikely, Fronto would die anyway, unable to reach medical attention.

But he had made a deal with Caesar. Whatever happened to him or Galronus, he had succeeded on his side of the contract, settling Aquitania. And now Caesar would see Lucilia and the boys back to safety and security once he sorted out the problem with Pompey and the senate. It would be awful not to see the three of them any more, but it was far more important to stop Verginius from embarking on his next mission. Because Fronto had little doubt that if his old friend walked away from this quarry alive then Caesar would die, and consequently the Falerii would fade from history.

'Fronto, put down your sword. You can hardly lift it.'

Verginius stood at the ladder down to the next gantry. He was unarmed and unarmoured, wearing get-up that was much more Aquitanii than Roman. No matter what he wore, though, in Fronto's mind he bore a military tunic and was a decade younger, missing that disfiguring smile.

'I can't let you do it,' he said.

'You can't *stop* me, Marcus. Look at you. You're a dead man still on his feet.'

Slowly, deliberately, Fronto lifted the blade so that the point hovered in front of Verginius' eyes, wavering and dancing, barely held in place.

'I don't want to hurt you, Gnaeus. I really don't.'

'Do you know,' his old friend noted conversationally, 'that that's the first time you've used my name since all this began. Verginius this... Verginius that... You won't hurt me, Marcus. We're brothers. We always were. My own true brothers paled beside you. You won't kill me any more than I would kill you.'

'You're wrong.'

Fronto stepped forward with his sword point close to Verginius' neck. 'I loved Gnaeus Verginius Tricostus Caelimontanus like a brother, but you keep telling me that he's dead. Well I'm starting to believe you. The Gnaeus I remember wouldn't put petty revenge above his friend's wellbeing.'

'*Petty* revenge?' Verginius looked genuinely astonished.

'You know what I mean. You told me this is a place of healing and that Janus is watching. Endings and beginnings, right?'

'Correct.'

'Then I'm giving you a choice, Gnaeus. End your vengeance. I will take whatever punishment you think you're due for breaking a vow onto my own shoulders. I will stand by you. But take a *new* vow. To me. To your old friend. Give me your oath you'll not seek

365

Caesar's demise and we'll all walk out of this place alive and well.'

There were thuds and a shout of pain from the gantry above and the whole edifice shook again, dust rising in puffs from the cliff.

'Two good men, neither of them Roman, are busy killing each other up there, and they're both doing it out of loyalty to *us*. Can we not manage that level of trust with one another after all this time?'

Verginius sighed and his hand dipped to his belt, drawing a pugio from behind his back.

'I had no intention of using this. It's the one you gave me all those years ago. Do you remember?'

Fronto blinked. 'In this quarry.'

'In this quarry. I lost mine during the exercises and you knew that the quartermaster didn't like me. You gave me yours so that I wouldn't have to go begging for a new one. And you went and got a replacement yourself.'

'Actually, I bought the new one in the forum,' Fronto snorted. 'From a dubious Greek with a lisp and a gammy leg. It fell apart a year later, after the battle. I'd never even drawn blood with it.'

'My vow is immutable, Marcus. I cannot change any more than you can. I destroyed tribes and levelled towns, executed innocents and murdered Romans just to get Caesar into my lair, and I failed. You cannot imagine that I would stop now, even if it means pitting myself against you? Go home. Save yourself while you still have enough blood to walk.'

Another thud above brought shaking and clouds of dust.

'Then we're stuck,' Fronto said flatly. 'I won't let you go after Caesar and you won't abandon your plan.'

'It would seem so.'

Fronto struck, without warning, if also without power. His jabbing blade was knocked aside by the dagger in Verginius' hand, but only just, and only with effort.

Fronto staggered and recovered, trying to raise his sword. He was dying, and quickly. He had hardly the strength to grip the sword, let alone lunge with it. Finally, with much trouble, the sword point came up again.

'Marcus…'

Fronto lunged, staggering and almost collapsing to his knees. Verginius knocked the blade aside just in time once more, stepping back out of reach. 'Give it up, Marcus. You can't win. Whatever happens here, neither of us wins.'

Fronto's next lunge barely reached as high as Verginius' thigh, but as the man with the dead smile twisted to the side, using his dagger to block the blow, his foot slipped on a large stone shard and skittered from under him. Fronto watched him step back into the open air, eyes wide, disbelieving. The former legate felt unaccustomed panic thrill through him and tried to lurch forward to grab his old friend, but his strength had gone. Weak as a new-born lamb, he fell to the timbers, his face at the edge, and watched Verginius plummet through the air, landing with an unpleasant thud on the dusty rock so far below.

Fronto passed out.

He was in the blessed blackness for mere heartbeats – long enough to experience the very beginning of a dream and no more. Verginius lay dead, shattered upon the rocks of his dreamscape, but a voice was still calling from his dead mouth, reaching up into the air.

Fronto....

Fronto...

FRONTO...

For the love of Taranis, Fronto, wake up!

He woke with a frown. He was lying in a pool of his own blood and felt weaker than he believed a human could feel. Something was urgent, and he couldn't think what.

'Fronto...'

Taranis?

Fronto rolled with some pain and effort onto his back, the whole gantry shuddering with the movement. His befuddled eyes took a moment to make out the shape at the far end of the gantry. An elongated shape. No... *two* shapes...

He was up a moment later and staggering forward, sword still in hand. Galronus was hanging precariously from the gantry above at the far end, one hand gripping for dear life, scrabbling and re-gripping periodically. His broken arm was hanging limp by his side. Ategnio of the Arenosio hung from Galronus' belt, swinging in the open air, trying to grab hold of the gantry below upon which Fronto stood.

'Arsehole,' Fronto snapped, and staggered across the timbers, lifting his sword. Somehow there seemed to be a reservoir of energy in him that had not been there when fighting his old friend. But the sight of Galronus about to die purely because of Ategnio hanging from him was something different. As Fronto approached he twisted, bringing his gladius back and to the side. Some soldiers – *most* in point of fact – kept the point sharp for stabbing and the edge just enough to break a bone. Those like Fronto, who had experienced the true chaos of battle, kept a sharp edge too, since you never knew what you might be required to do in order to survive.

With every ounce of strength he could muster, Fronto swung the razor-edged blade, hacking through Ategnio's arm below the elbow. The warrior fell without a shout, plummeting and landing with a thud, almost mirroring his master at the far side.

'Help me, you pillock,' grunted Galronus, his fingers slipping.

With some difficulty, Fronto used one arm to anchor himself to the gantry and grasped Galronus around the waist with the other. There was a heart-stopping moment as the Remi let go of the timbers above and both men almost followed Ategnio out into the air, but the two men hit the timbers together and lay there, heaving in deep breaths.

'Verginius?'

'Dead,' Fronto replied quietly.

'Then we have to get you to a medicus before you follow him into the mist.'

'Soon. First I have to visit the body.' He gestured to indicate where Verginius had fallen and Galronus rolled his eyes. 'He's dead. Leave him, or you might join him.'

'Get the horses. Bring them down the slope and into the bottom of the quarry. Meet me at the bottom of the ladders. *Then* we'll go. Besides, I have the strength to slide down from here, but I'll not make it back up two ladders.'

Galronus gave him a calculating look but, apparently coming down on the side of concord, he nodded and started slowly, with barks of pain, climbing the ladders once more. Fronto waited only a moment, and then started to part-climb, part-slide, part-fall down the successive ladders, slowly closing on the ground level of the quarry. After what seemed like an age, he staggered out across the rock and to the broken form on the rock, close by one of the water tanks.

Healing water? He remembered what his friend had said about the native temple and momentarily staggered over to the tank, gulping down handfuls of the cold, clear liquid, then scrubbing his face with it before rising and approaching the body. Verginius lay broken in a pool of his own blood that had collected and hardened with the dust of the quarry. As Fronto, a tear emerging in the corner of his eye, closed on the corpse, he was astounded to see Verginius blink.

'Gnaeus?'

'Marcus? Gods but this hurts more than I expected.'

'You're not dead!'

'It's a matter of moments, Marcus. That's all.'

'If I could turn back time. Stop this…'

'I know. Me too, Marcus. But *one* of us had to fail. In a way I'm glad it's me. Caesar is a cancer, but I'd hate to sacrifice you just to remove him. I will be one of the lemures, now, you realise? I will never get to rest, for I left a vow unfulfilled.'

Fronto shook his head. 'I have coins. I'll put one in your mouth. Charon will take you across, I know. The gods are not that cruel.'

'Oh they are, Marcus. You have no idea. It has been good to see you again, though. But before I die, I charge you with something, Marcus. I want your promise, and then I want you to kill me. I could linger an hour or more in agony. Put a sword through me and make it quick, as a friend should.'

'A vow?'

'You know what it is,' Verginius said, quietly.

'What?'

'Caesar has to die. The boatman will not take me with an unfulfilled oath. Take on my vow and let me pass in peace. I've done ten years as a ghost. Don't make me go on longer.'

Fronto shook his head. 'Gnaeus, I can't.'

'You *can*. You have years ahead of you, Marcus. You can watch Caesar help your family rise again while he begins to ruin Rome. You have that luxury. But one day, when you realise I'm

369

right and your own deal with the proconsul is long forgotten, you must fulfil my vow so that we can both rest. You must. You *must!*'

* * *

Galronus walked the horses across the dusty gravel, his eyes locked on his friend ahead who was leaning over the body, as if listening. Then, sharply, the Roman rose to his knees, fiddled at his belt and then did something with the body's mouth. Then, with care, he raised his gladius, placed the point above the heart, and put all his weight on it, driving it through the body and into the stone. Galronus waited respectfully some distance away with the horses until Fronto stood, yanking out the sword. Finally the deathly-pale figure registered Galronus' presence and staggered over, grasping the horse and pulling himself up into the saddle with some difficulty.

'You know any medici in Tarraco?' Galronus said quietly.

'I'll be dead before Tarraco. It's five miles away. But the villa is only about three miles and Arius is a good man with needle and honey. He can save me if we're quick.'

Galronus nodded as the pair started to ride toward the quarry entrance and the coast beyond.

'And as soon as you sign that document, you'll own the villa outright anyway,' Galronus smiled.

'And I'll free Arius and everyone else on the estate. They can work for me, but my days as a slave owner are done, Galronus. I can't do it.'

The Remi noble frowned at Fronto. 'Before you killed him, I saw you in conversation with Verginius. He survived that entire fall, which is little less than miraculous. What did he say?'

Fronto's eyes darted this way and that nervously. 'He... he was concerned about his afterlife.' When Galronus waited in expectant silence, Fronto cleared his throat. 'He asked me to do something. He couldn't die easily without it.'

'Fronto. What did you do?'

'I just nodded to let him die well. It's nothing important.'

But Galronus could see the haunted, black look in Fronto's eyes, and knew it for anything but trivial...

Late Summer

FRONTO watched the three figures riding slowly up the dusty track from the main road as the late summer sun began its descent over the city of Tarraco to the west. The vineyards almost glowed with an unearthly, divine, Bacchic green in that golden light, dazzling and beautiful. The Roman leaned back against the warm marble of the seat on the veranda, wincing as his stomach muscles bunched and contracted around the now-healing wound while he reached out and took his glass from the table.

Smiling, he looked at the three riders, stretched and distorted through the glass and the deep red liquid within. A wine from the villa's cellar made from the very vines through which those men rode. No matter how standard the practice of watering wine, for the past two months, since that brutal fight in the quarry, Fronto had taken his wine neat. He had explained, when Arius and Galronus expressed concern, that since he would own this place – after a fashion, at least – then he should know its wine, and Catháin had always told him that the only way to truly judge the quality of an estate's produce was neat and with an unblemished palate. The fact that this gave him license to drink as much strong wine as he felt like on an empty stomach sat well with Fronto, as the heady drink eased the constant ache of his wound.

Of course, that pain had now largely faded unless he moved wrong or over-exerted himself, but he wasn't quite ready to let go of his liquid crutch just yet, despite Galronus' disapproving glower every time he came near.

They had spent two months at the villa recuperating, Galronus only now starting to move his arm once more, and far from testing it with a sword. Fronto was walking normally now and had reacquired his healthy colour, as Arius had proved to be a more than adequate medic. Fronto was alive, and improving with every passing day. Soon…

The figures were close now, close enough for him to make out the expressions on their faces: the two younger men bleak and angry, the older one smiling fit to burst. Fronto felt his own lips slip up at the corner in response.

He still did not own the villa, though since Rubrius Callo remained executor of the wills of the previous owners, only he had the legal right to eject the visitors, and he had no inclination to do so. Besides, Galronus had been quick to point out that the villa was solidly within territory controlled by the republic and the moment Fronto's name went on that deed the whole place and everything in it would be liable to seizure by the senate and their representative in Hispania Citerior – the governor. It had vexed Fronto only for a short while before he had settled upon a course of action.

The day they had returned from the quarry they had learned that, despite what had been said, the two cousins had declined to sign the contract. True to his word, Fronto – through Galronus and Rubrius Callo – had rescinded his offer. It seemed that the boys had been rather unnerved by the sight of a Belligerent Remi warrior lurking on the corner whenever they turned around, and had finally settled into a bar and drunk themselves into insensibility. There they had been persuaded by a shady individual that he would better serve their interests legally, and they had dismissed Callo without payment for services thus far rendered.

It had been a dreadful decision for the pair. Over the next few weeks they were systematically bankrupted and ruined by the shifty new lawyer. Simultaneously, Callo had levelled against them charges for non-payment of legal services. Within little more than a month, the two had been forced to sell the small estates and business interests they had controlled to pay even a portion of their debt. Rubrius Callo had seen their names blackened in mercantile and judicial circles, and the impoverished pair now shared rooms above a fishmonger's shop not far from the port.

Several further weeks of playing with them had ensued, making their already miserable lives as bad as he could. It had made his recuperation a lot more fun, and Galronus had seemingly enjoyed it too. The Roman had employed Rubrius Callo now that there was no conflict of interest and the lawyer had positively delighted in helping ruin the cousins. The time had been useful in another way, too, giving Fronto time to implement his plan for saving the villa. Now, on this last day of Sextilis as autumn began to loom, everything would come together. Fronto sighed with happiness and shouted in through the villa door.

'Arius? Galronus? Could you join me on the veranda for a moment?'

The major domo, who was the only remaining slave on the estate since Fronto had granted manumission to the rest, emerged from the door and onto the sun-lit veranda. Behind him came the Remi warrior, gingerly testing his arm, as the three riders neared the villa buildings and reined in, dismounting. Rubrius Callo took the three sets of reins and tied the beasts to the hitching posts, then he and the miserable, dejected cousins strode across to the veranda to join the three waiting men.

'Ah, good master Rubrius Callo,' Fronto said with a smile. 'I trust you have brought all the relevant documents?'

'I have, Marcus. It's going to be a matter of careful timing how I lodge them all. If I get one paper stamped in the wrong order it could throw everything out. Which means: no thank you, I will not have the seven glasses of strong wine you are bound to offer me. The last time I left here I rode clear past my home and fell off my horse on the beach.'

Fronto chuckled. 'I have full confidence in your ability to sort everything, my friend. Alright. First thing's first.'

He gestured to the two cousins who, with sneers of hate and disdain, stepped forward.

'I withdrew my offer some weeks ago after your somewhat unwise change of heart. It is my understanding, though, that your fortunes have somewhat come undone, and so I have invited you here, in my capacity as philanthropist and benefactor, to make you a new offer.'

A glimpse of hope shone through the misery and anger on the two faces, though the younger of the pair was more concerned with Galronus, who had not stopped glaring at him since he stepped forward.

'Here is my offer. There will not be another, and I advise you to take it. Rubrius Callo will confirm, I'm sure, that you now have little option. With your names black-listed around the province and beyond, you will receive no credit and find no patron to support you. You have no remaining property or business interests. In fact, unless you both soon find gainful real employment, you will end up in the gutter. For the sake of your uncle and aunt's memory I would not see that happen.'

Callo slapped a document down on the marble table next to the seat and Fronto unrolled it, perused it for only a moment, and then nodded.

'This is a contract of sale for the villa, with extra provisos. You will sell me your aunt's villa for the lavish price of one silver sestertius each.'

Looks of appalled shock crossed the faces of both boys, and they began to splutter their refusal.

'I urge you to accept and sign,' Fronto smiled. 'Because of the extra provisos. In addition to that single coin each, I will pay off your debts, effectively freeing you from future indentured servitude. Rubrius Callo will remove the black marks against your names, and you will be free men with no debts. Moreover, to prevent you ending your days begging in the gutter, you will be offered employment at the warehouse facility in Tarraco's port where the villa's wine is transported to ship.'

Realisation dawned on the two faces that there was simply no alternative that did not end in abject poverty. With a snarl of hatred, the older scribed his name on the vellum, almost carving it into the surface, then turned and spat on the land. 'I hope the vines die and your crops fail.'

'Be careful what you wish for,' Fronto grinned. 'If the wine business here fails then your new jobs might be at risk. Remember the gutters, boy.'

The younger of the two scribbled his own name, then backed away, shaking slightly under Galronus' fierce gaze.

'Very well,' Fronto smiled and rose, fishing two silver coins from the fat purse at his belt. He then tossed one to each of the boys. The older snarled and let the coin fall to the floor, turning his back on them and making for his horse. The younger scrabbled round and picked up both, then hurried to his own steed. The four men remaining on the veranda watched in silence as the pair mounted and rode swiftly back to the main road and away from the estate.

'Alright, time for the second business of the day. Arius? I am sure you have harboured feelings of bitterness these past few weeks that you alone have been maintained as a slave.'

'Domine, it is not my place to have such an opinion.' He relaxed a little. 'In truth, Domine, I have always considered myself more than fortunate with my lot. I have had the joy of serving three of the most considerate masters a man could wish for: Marcus Mettius Rustius, Gaius Papirius Longinus and now your illustrious self.'

Fronto chuckled. 'Well the time has come, Arius.' The lawyer beside him, echoing his smile, slapped two more documents on the table. 'Rubrius Callo here carries the governor's authority to grant manumission. Rubrius? I hereby free the slave Arius from my service.'

Arius gazed in happy surprise as Rubrius Callo produced a rod, touched him on the pate with it, and intoned in a deep voice *Vindicavit in libertatem.*'

Fronto smiled and grasped Arius by the upper arms. '*Hunc hominem liberum volo*,' he said, then turned the man and gave him a gentle shove forward. 'You're a free man, Arius.'

'Thank you, Domine,' smiled Arius.

'Don't call me Domine. There's more, though, I'm afraid. You see, I'm in something of a precarious position, and I need your help. I am officially under exile from Italia and Rome for the period of ten years and the senate have impounded all my property and goods. As such, I cannot afford for the deeds of this villa to remain in my name, else within the month the senate would have heard of it and will snatch the property and everything on it. You see my difficulty?'

'You wish master Galronus to take on the property?' Arius smiled.

'Not quite. Galronus will have complicated interests of his own and will be busy elsewhere. I want *you* to take it on, Arius. You need to take a new name, now you're not a slave, but I need you to break with tradition and eschew my family moniker. You cannot be Arius Falerius, else the senate will come after you too. And you cannot take on Longinus' name, or the cousins will have the opportunity once more to fight you for ownership. I would suggest you take the name of your first master and become Arius Rustius. In fact, I've already had Rubrius Callo draw up documents to that effect. If you will just put your mark here,' he said, tapping the second document, 'then Callo and I can witness it.'

The freedman simply stood, stunned.

'Arius, this is important. You might think I am being generous, and perhaps I am, but this is also for the benefit of my family. The third document Rubrius Callo brought with him is a new contract for the villa's deeds. This contract will place the villa in your ownership for the duration of your lifetime in return for no payment, though it imposes certain addenda. Upon your death, the ownership of the villa will pass to my eldest son. You will find the contract forbids you to sell the villa in the meantime, and it makes allowances for myself or my family to take up residence at any time, regardless of ownership. You will understand, I am sure, that I need to protect my family's interests.'

Arius nodded silently, wide-eyed.

'But the running of the villa will now be your responsibility, and any profits from it will be yours to deal with appropriately. Should you take a wife and have a family, I heartily recommend that you put plenty of money aside regularly against the day the villa returns to our family.'

Arius was still nodding.

'Well, Arius Rustius, will you accept this and sign?'

His jaw working with no sound issuing, the former slave confirmed his new name and then used it to accept the contract on the villa.

'Good. Now, Rubrius, be a good fellow and pop in with Arius to finalise the details.'

The lawyer, grinning, strode off inside, directing the astonished Arius with him, leaving Fronto and Galronus alone on the veranda. Fronto smiled and took a quick sip of his wine, than sank back to the marble seat, groaning at the surge of the ache in his middle. Gingerly, he prodded his midriff, recoiling with a gasp and leaking eyes.

'It's going to be a long time yet healing,' Galronus said patiently. 'Stop testing yourself. The medicus said it would be another month at the earliest before you should even try anything like riding a horse.

'Boats are easier than horses, Galronus. I need to get to Massilia. It's been too long, and now that everything here is under control and wrapped up...'

Galronus snorted derisively. 'You on a *ship?* If a horse is dangerous for you then a ship would be deadly. With your seasickness and a healing belly-wound, you'd be dead before you left port. I've seen you almost turn inside out when a big wave hits.'

'I have to get to Massilia, Galronus.'

'All in good time. Nothing will happen for a month or two. Rest. Recover. I can almost guarantee that the moment you head west you'll be at Caesar's table again being given a new, even more dangerous command.'

'Maybe one day I'll end up in there?' Fronto noted with an oddly sad/funny tone, pointing to the drum-shaped white stone mausoleum beside the main road at the edge of the estate. 'I'd be in good company.' A few days after their return to the villa, Fronto had had Verginius' body retrieved from the quarry, given full funeral rites, cremated and interred in the villa's mausoleum beside the family of Longinus.

'That's long years away, Fronto.' Galronus sighed and leaned on the balustrade, peering out at the tomb beyond the rows of vines. 'You never did tell me what you said to him in the quarry.'

'It was nothing. Easing a dying man's conscience is all.

'That's exactly what I mean. That's not an answer. Just more evasion, every time.'

'If I can't head east yet, then the time has come to write a few letters, Galronus. One to Caesar, informing him of most of what happened. A debrief as far as he's concerned. And one to Lucilia. You should send one to Faleria too.'

'My writing is too poor. It's worse than a Roman boy's.'

'You've had less practice. But Faleria deserves it anyway.'

'Perhaps you're right.'

'And then once the medicus pronounces me fit, we shall go home and reap the rewards, my friend Galronus of the Remi, member of the equestrian class and future senator of Rome.'

Autumn

GALRONUS straightened where he leaned on the bannister. In the small, gravelled, half-moon before the villa's front door Fronto danced this way and that with the agility of a dancer, albeit an elderly and wounded one. His sword lanced repeatedly and then lashed out at the three palus stakes driven into the lawn.

He missed only one.

'Well done. You're already almost back up to the standard of most legionaries.'

'That's not enough. I need to be good.'

'Why? What are you expecting to find in Massilia?'

Fronto paused and turned, breathing heavily. 'No trouble, as such, but I want to be prepared for anything, Galronus. You remember what Lucilia said in her letter. The place is nervous and tense. Something has to happen soon, and when it does, I can see a wave of violence coming with it.'

'You Romans. When there's finally peace, you just get bored and fight each other.'

'This from one of the Belgae? How many cousins have you killed in your life.'

'That's neither here nor there. Those cousins were arseholes.'

Fronto chuckled. 'Still, I feel the weight of something approaching. It's like the build-up before a big thunder storm. I wish Caesar or Labienus would reply to my letter. I'd love to know what was going on up in Gaul.'

'I feel the pressure building too, Marcus. I'm not sure any of us are going to enjoy this storm. Look,' he said, raising an arm and pointing down the access track toward the drum-shaped mausoleum and the main road. A small party was approaching in a light cart. 'Arius is back.'

'Good. I'm sick of being asked what to do by the servants. I don't know this place like Arius.'

The Roman sheathed his sword, stooped with a grunt at the effort, and swept up his towel, wiping the sweat from his head and torso. He paused to examine the puckered line in his middle where Verginius' sword had impaled him. The man really had known his anatomy. Driving a blade through a man without hitting anything

378

vital was a tougher skill to master than going for a killing blow, any day.

'Stop playing with it.'

'I'm allowed. It's my scar. One of my best, now.'

'If you're that pleased with it, I can give you another one,' snorted Galronus.

As Fronto finished towelling himself and slid into his tunic, fastening the belt, the sweat already starting to seep into the linen, Arius and his small party approached the villa. The small cart, drawn by two donkeys, bore the villa's new owner and three of the household's servants as it bumped over the stony track and came to rest not far from the pair at the entrance.

'Arius, good to see you. I wondered when you were coming back. Have you secured a ship?'

The former slave clambered down from the vehicle and directed his servants to take the cart around the side to the stables and unload it there. Once the vehicle had rattled off out of sight and the three men were alone, Arius bowed his head to Fronto and then straightened.

'The courier vessel Demeter's Pride leaves Tarraco for Massilia in two days' time as long as the weather holds. No merchants are planning to sail this next week as the reports are of violent storms all along the coasts of Hispania and Narbonensis. Only the courier ship will go, as they are required to on the governor's orders That means you'll be paying through the nose I'm afraid. It's almost three times the price of a normal commercial transport, unless you're willing to put off your journey?'

'No. We go as soon as we can, now.'

Galronus gave him a dubious look. 'Even with big storms at sea. Fronto? I've seen the smallest breakers turn you white as a toga.'

'I don't care. Even if I'm ill all the way, I want to get to Massilia.'

'We could still ride?'

Fronto shook his head. 'Apart from shaking up my wound all the way, I'm nervous about passing through Narbonensis. If the senate have finally decided to pursue my interests outside Italia, the first places they will look are around Gaul because of my connection with Caesar. Let's avoid trouble as far as we can. No one will be looking for me at sea.'

'Alright,' Galronus stretched. 'We go on the Demeter's Pride. She has room?'

Arius nodded. 'I've tentatively booked your passage. I felt sure you'd want me to.'

'Good man,' Fronto confirmed, then frowned at the look on the former slave's face. 'Something troubling you, Arius?'

'Tarraco is full of news, master Fronto. And not good news, I fear. About Caesar and Rome.'

'Oh?' Fronto and Galronus stepped forward, all attention now.

'The senate apparently ordered Caesar to stand down his armies and return to Rome. In response, the proconsul refused and demanded the consulate in absentia for the coming Januarius.'

'Same old argument,' Fronto sighed.

'Not quite, sir. A senator called Curio apparently tried to mediate and demand that both Caesar and Pompey stand down, but not only did Caesar refuse, so did Pompey, and the consuls refused to back the proposal as they're both in Pompey's purse. The senate have demanded a legion from each of them to send to Parthia, and Caesar's sent the Fifteenth and Pompey's First who've been with him in response, but the rest of the proconsul's legions...'

Fronto shrugged. 'The senate can't touch him while he's up in Gaul. He'll figure a way out.'

'But that's it, sir. He's *not* there. That's the big news. No one can confirm it for gods' truth, but the big rumour in the city is that Caesar's taken his army back to Cisalpine Gaul. He's distributed his legions around the Alps and the north of Italia. If *all* the rumour's true, Caesar's at Ravenna on the Italian coast now with the Thirteenth. They say he's taken the best men from all his armies and turned the Thirteenth into the biggest, strongest legion Rome's ever seen.'

Fronto turned a horrified expression on Galronus and the Remi shrugged, unconcerned. 'What? He's still governor of the province. He's allowed to have his legions there.'

Fronto shook his head. 'Not like this, Galronus. Ravenna's maybe twenty miles from the border. He's put together a strong veteran legion and moved it up to the Roman border. He's testing the senate. It's a deliberate threat. And Pompey's unlikely to back down. It's a dangerous provocation. It's not far off being an act of war, in fact. I think we need to get back to Massilia, Galronus. Sounds like Italia's on the brink of disaster.'

* * *

Fronto and Galronus urged their mounts on to greater speed, hurtling up the slope from the port of Massilia. Their goods were being transported slowly by cart behind them, but Fronto had been desperate to arrive as soon as possible. Massilia was alive with news. All of Arius' rumour, it seemed, had been accurate. Caesar was at Ravenna with a legion of almost double strength. Ten thousand men, each a powerful veteran of a decade of war, armed and equipped for battle. In response, it appeared that Pompey was gathering men in Italia. The two legions bound for Parthia by senatorial order had been waylaid by the consuls and remained on Italian soil under Pompey's command. It was like a game of latrunculi, with two of the most powerful players in the world, and no good could possibly come of it. Romans all over the independent city of Massilia were mobilising, either heading for Cisalpine Gaul and the general they had served in previous years, or fleeing back to Rome. Everyone seemed sure that Massilia would soon be involved, for all their nominal independence. They had signed a contract with Rome, yet their city was so close to lands under Caesar's control.

Fronto slid from Bucephalus and left Galronus to tie up the beasts, running in through the door even as the slave opened it to the new arrivals.

'Lucilia?'

'Marcus?' Fronto's wife came hurrying from a side room into the atrium, the two boys shouting in glee as they ran into the room from some hidden play place. Fronto dropped to a knee and embraced the children, kissing them both on the forehead, and then looking up at Lucilia as he held them tight. Behind his wife, Balbus and Catháin appeared in surprise.

'Pack your things.'

'What? Marcus, make sense. What is happening?'

'Lucilia, pack the most important things and be prepared to leave. There's a ship in the port called the Demeter's Pride and she leaves for Tarraco in Hispania in the morning. I want you and the boys on it. And the servants. And everyone else in the villa. You included,' he added, glancing up at Balbus.

'Marcus, you're scaring me,' Lucilia said, her tone breathless.

'Good. You *should* be scared. Everyone should be damned *terrified*. You've heard about Caesar?'

Balbus nodded.

'Well, Pompey's arming himself in Rome and he controls the consuls. Do you think for a minute they're going to acquiesce to Caesar?'

'No,' agreed the old man, 'and Caesar cannot bow to them. They're at an impasse.'

'You know what that means?' Fronto said quietly. 'Caesar has his veterans a spear's throw from the Rubicon. Pompey will push him, he'll march south, and the shit will truly rain down on us all.'

He turned back to his wife again as Galronus arrived in the room behind him. 'Lucilia, listen to me. You and the family – mother and Faleria too – you all have to go. I've secured the Demeter's Pride for you all. It's a fast courier and will be in Tarraco in three days, weather allowing. A man called Arius Rustius will meet you at the port with a wagon, and he'll take you somewhere safe – a villa near Tarraco that I sort of own.'

'*Sort* of own?'

'Long story, Lucilia, but it'll be safe. Massilia is close to Caesar's legions, but declared for the senate. This place is going to be Hades incarnate soon, and you need to be gone when that happens, all of you.'

'Then you can come with us, Marcus. You *have* to come with us.'

'No, I can't.'

'Marcus…'

Balbus reached forward and put his hand on his daughter's shoulder. 'Marcus has gambled all your futures on Caesar. He had to. Now he's bound to Caesar. If your children are to have a future in Rome, it's all dependent on Caesar's success. Marcus has to go.'

'No, Marcus. You can't. You *can't*. You cannot go running off to that man when he threatens Rome itself. Sell your sword to the senate instead. They might lift your exile.'

'It's decided, Lucilia. Go to Tarraco. I'll come there as soon as I can, I promise. You have to get the children away from here, somewhere safe. Tarraco is that place. Arius will protect you.'

'But what is going to happen?' Lucilia said, her face pale and horrified.

'Simple,' Fronto said. 'Caesar will wait until the election of the consuls in the new year, and if he is not made one of them then he will give the order and he and the Thirteenth will cross the Rubicon and march on Rome as Sulla did all those years ago.'

'And then?'

'And then Rome will be at war with her own greatest general.'

THE END.

Author's Note

Pax Gallica is the ninth book in the Marius' Mules series (which is intended to run to a final book 15). That means we are almost two thirds of the way through Fronto's saga. But it is also something of a milestone for me, being the 20th book I've released, a fact that staggers me even to consider it. That so many readers have stuck with me through this many books (9 or 20, either way) humbles me. I do appreciate you all. I really do.

Marius' Mules 9's story was inevitable. There is a hole, you see. Several holes in fact. I had intended from the early days of the series to release one book for each year of Caesar's diaries (the Gallic Wars and the Civil War). That was all well and good all the way to book 7. Last year's research was rather challenging for Sons of Taranis, for the diaries of the time were not written in great detail by Caesar himself, but sort of dashed out urgently in almost note form by his ghost writer Hirtius. And with the exception of a few bits of stomping around and shouting at Gauls, the only major event of fifty one was the siege of Uxellodunum. I didn't mind, though, as I had a story to tell that took us away from the drab lack of action in Gaul. I needed certain things to happen to Fronto in order to bring about the second half of the series. Then I came to write volume 9, and the realisation hit me that the previous year was action packed compared to 50BC. I brushed aside the temptation to write a spin off of the Asterix books (also set in Gaul in 50), and decided that I could fill the hole left by Hirtius, who more or less mentions this year only in passing.

You see, I had a hole in the geography I've put forward. We've visited Gaul repeatedly. We've done the lands of the Belgae in several books. We've done Italy on occasion and Britain once. We've even dipped across the Rhine into Germany. But Caesar divides France into three peoples. The Belgae, the Gauls and the Aquitanii (modern Aquitaine and the Pyrenees.) And yes, I had Crassus stomping around there briefly making his presence felt, but we never really explored the land or its people as we did with the Gauls and the Belgae. So I felt that gap needed to be addressed. It was time to write about them, especially as pretty much the only thing Hirtius tells us after Uxellodunum is that Caesar toured Aquitania. No more detail than that!

Moreover, I had a gap in my history. Here and there, along the way from book 1 to book 8 I have dipped momentarily into Fronto's past. I've mentioned fragments of his time in Spain and hinted at interesting things. And the history of his friend Verginius, Faleria's former suitor, had been touched on occasionally. It was a story that had to come out eventually. Hey presto. Here was Fronto with a year to kill, a stone's throw away from his old stomping ground. The plot more or less wrote itself, as I'd had portions of it in mind for years, including the history of the two Romans. The inclusion of Galronus to give it extra volume was great fun.

The most challenging part was to start with Verginius the Smiling king, as a thoroughly dislikeable villain and gradually, through the course of the revelation and beyond, to make him seem reasonable and understandable, and maybe even a little sympathetic in the end. Certainly, I felt sorry for him at the end. For all his faults, he displayed so many of those traits endemic of a true Roman of his time. Of course, another troublesome aspect was trying to trickle in appropriate information without making it blindingly obvious who the smiling king was from the get-go. Hopefully I hit the balance. Only you the readers know.

There seems to be far less known, or at least recorded in scholarly works, about the Aquitanii than their cousins across the rest of France and Belgium, so there is a little poetic license in my portrayal. I chose to make the mountain tribes slightly different from their lowland kin. It made sense to me and still does. The idea for Verginius' gathering of the tribes under one ruler comes mostly from the nature of the Convenae. As their very name suggests, they were formed from an amalgam of other tribes. Tradition puts their formation down to Pompey, but that is in no way confirmed and is mere speculation. I have chosen to make it the work of a Romano-Gallic rebel rather than Pompey, but the idea is still the same. I have a passing familiarity with lower Aquitania, and not a lot of experience with the Pyrenees except at their extreme eastern end, but when we head for Tarraco? Oh my.

Tarragona is one of my favourite places, as regular readers might have discerned. It appears time and again in my books, though this is the first time we see it directly. Tarragona is full of Roman remains, and the form of the Roman city can still be seen today, maps and models of this provincial capital not being hard to find. However, if you look at any map of Roman Tarraco, you are invariably looking at a map of the Imperial era city, and not the republic. Many of the city's great buildings were not in evidence at the time, from the amphitheatre to the theatre, the circus and the aqueduct. I have taken great pains, including stomping around the city myself, examining sunlight angles and relative heights, to reconstruct a theoretical republican city before these great structures were built, and yet to allude to their future existence where possible. Tarraco was an extremely important city throughout Rome's presence in Iberia, and was the first major settlement in Spain founded by a Roman.

The villa I use nearby is the one still visitable at Els Munts, Altafulla. If you go to Tarragona, I highly recommend hiring a car and driving out to some of the remains in the area. Els Munts is a stunning villa but, once again, mostly of a later date. In fact there is no evidence that the villa existed in republican times, but many of these villas had republican predecessors, so I have chosen to create an early history for Els Munts. It fitted my requirements in every other way, and I'd been referring to it since the end of book 1 when Fronto went there with the body of Longinus.

The quarry is still there. It is now called El Medol, and is a supremely impressive sight. Now, of course, it is overgrown and full of trees, but it is not hard to mentally strip them out and see it as it once was. The quarry is now much longer, cut into the hill, than my vague horseshoe shape, and there are areas that have been cut away all around the edge. But the quarry was used throughout Tarraco's life, and so the republican quarry had to be much smaller logically. There were several quarries in use around the city, including one close to the aqueduct, from which it was built, but El Medol remains the most impressive.

Essentially, if I have achieved what I set out to do with this volume, I have created a bridge between the two great works of Caesar, leading us from the last throes of the Gallic Wars, in my entirely fictional Aquitanian uprising, to the very first salvoes of the Civil War, with Caesar poised to cross the Rubicon. In the process I needed to bind Fronto to Caesar's cause, a task I began in the previous book with his exile. And while I looked at it, I realised just how much of Fronto's past could come to light here. From his adherence to Nemesis and Fortuna through his service in

Spain under Caesar to the mysterious death of Verginius and so much more, I've taken the best opportunity I'll ever get to fill in the blanks.

You now know most of Fronto's life and, if I'm to be brutally honest, in doing all this I've had the perfect opportunity to explain away tiny flaws that have lived throughout the series, such as why Fronto does not bear one of the great patrician names, yet claims patrician blood. It's all good, folks. I've tweaked and played and had so much fun with one of my favourite bad guys I've ever written.

And now, as you're well aware, I've left our hero once more almost intact, rushing off to Caesar with his closest friend and preparing to cross that most famous river in Roman history, for all its diminutive and unimpressive size: the Rubicon.

From here on, things are about to become extremely brutal. Fronto will be back next year in book 10. Until then, there will be other adventures to follow as I move onto book 21. More Tales of the Empire are coming, Rufinus is back next year in Praetorian 3, the kids' adventures will be abroad again in Pirate Legion, and there are other projects on the go. But never fear – Fronto will be back within the year facing off against his own people as the civil war begins in earnest.

Thank you for reading. I hope you enjoyed it.

Vale

Simon Turney

September 2016

If you liked this book, why not try other titles by S.J.A. Turney

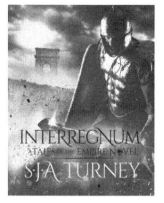

Interregnum (Tales of the Empire 1)

For twenty years civil war has torn the Empire apart; the Imperial line extinguished as the mad Emperor Quintus burned in his palace, betrayed by his greatest general. Against a background of war, decay, poverty and violence, men who once served in the proud Imperial army now fight as mercenaries, hiring themselves to the greediest lords. On a hopeless battlefield that same general, now a mercenary captain tortured by the events of his past, stumbles across hope in the form of a young man begging for help. Kiva is forced to face more than his dark past as he struggles to put his life and the very Empire back together. The last scion of the Imperial line will change Kiva forever.

The Thief's Tale

Istanbul, 1481. The once great city of Constantine that now forms the heart of the Ottoman empire is a strange mix of Christian, Turk and Jew. Despite the benevolent reign of the Sultan Bayezid II, the conquest is still a recent memory, and emotions run high among the inhabitants, with danger never far beneath the surface. Skiouros and Lykaion, the sons of a Greek country farmer, are conscripted into the ranks of the famous Janissary guards and taken to Istanbul where they will play a pivotal, if unsung, role in the history of the new regime. As Skiouros escapes into the Greek quarter and vanishes among its streets to survive on his wits alone, Lykaion remains with the slave chain to fulfill his destiny and become an Islamic convert and a guard of the Imperial palace. Brothers they remain, though standing to either side of an unimaginable divide. On a fateful day in late autumn 1490, Skiouros picks the wrong pocket and begins to unravel a plot that reaches to the very highest peaks of Imperial power. He and his brother are about to be left with the most difficult decision faced by a conquered Greek: whether the rule of the Ottoman Sultan is worth saving.

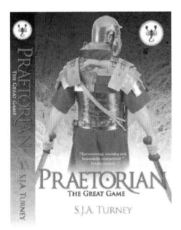

Praetorian: The Great Game

Promoted to the elite Praetorian Guard in the thick of battle, a young legionary is thrust into a seedy world of imperial politics and corruption. Tasked with uncovering a plot against the newly-crowned emperor Commodus, his mission takes him from the cold Danubian border all the way to the heart of Rome, the villa of the emperor's scheming sister, and the great Colosseum.

What seems a straightforward, if terrifying, assignment soon descends into Machiavellian treachery and peril as everything in which young Rufinus trusts and believes is called into question and he faces warring commanders, Sarmatian cannibals, vicious dogs, mercenary killers and even a clandestine Imperial agent. In a race against time to save the Emperor, Rufinus will be introduced, willing or not, to the great game.

"Entertaining, exciting and beautifully researched" - Douglas Jackson

Printed in Great Britain
by Amazon